'The authors of *Monimbo* extract the last drop of dramatic tension'
New York Times Book Review

'As authentic as a confidential briefing, but reads like the bestseller it's bound to be'
Playboy

Robert Moss is a recognised authority on espionage and terrorism, and is currently a visiting lecturer at a number of universities and NATO defence academies, including the Royal College of Defence Studies in London. For six years he was Editor of *The Economist*'s intelligence bulletin, *Foreign Report*. He is the author of a number of books including the best-selling spy novel, *Death Beam*, and, with Arnaud de Borchgrave, the celebrated *roman-à-clef*, *The Spike*.

Arnaud de Borchgrave was *Newsweek*'s Chief Foreign Correspondent from 1951 and covered most of the world's major news events from some ninety countries. He resigned from *Newsweek* in 1980 and now divides his time between writing, reporting and lecturing.

Both authors are currently editors of a new confidential newsletter, *Early Warning*.

Monimbo

ROBERT MOSS and ARNAUD DE BORCHGRAVE

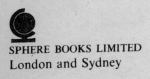

SPHERE BOOKS LIMITED
London and Sydney

First published in Great Britain by
Weidenfeld & Nicolson Ltd 1983
Copyright © 1983 by Mossgrave Partnership
Published by Sphere Books Ltd 1984
30–32 Gray's Inn Road, London WC1X 8JL
Reprinted 1984

TRADE
MARK

Printed and bound in Great Britain by
Cox & Wyman Ltd, Reading

PROLOGUE

MONIMBÓ, NICARAGUA, JULY 1980

Jesús Díaz, the boy they called Monkey, was so excited he had hardly slept. He had been up late, helping the Licenciado to finish his painting. How the old man had acquired his title of respect was a mystery; he had never gone to college. As long as anyone remembered, he had been making artifacts and little hand-colored drawings of adobe dwellings and *típico* rural scenes to sell to the tourists who drove through the dusty streets of the Indian barrio on their way through Masaya. Weeks passed when the Licenciado did no work at all, but just lazed in the shade drinking, recounting the tale of how he had fought with the great Sandino to anyone who would listen. But for several days past, the Licenciado had been working like a Michelangelo on what he had promised would be his crowning artistic achievement, ready to greet the important visitors who were coming to honor Monimbó.

Monkey Díaz got up early to look at it. He was wearing the green uniform he had had on when he slipped away from the National Guard encampment at night to join the rebels. But he

5

wore a red-and-black armband and a baseball cap in the same Sandinista colors. The Licenciado's mural sprawled across the walls of two low buildings, near the celebrated church where the Revolution had come to Monimbó two years before, when National Guardsmen had fired tear gas into a congregation of Indians celebrating Mass, and the dictatorship had learned that the legendary passivity of the Indians had its limits. The Licenciado's mural depicted a frightened Uncle Sam taking flight from heroic guerrillas as the peasants broke their chains. Sandino, in his wide Stetson and red bandana, galloped across the sky on a ghostly horse, Fidel Castro smiled approval and the ousted dictator, his pockets overflowing with stolen money, swung from a gibbet. The likenesses were not good, but the Licenciado had made up for that with the boldness of his colors. To Monkey Díaz, the painting looked better than anything by Diego Rivera.

He was still admiring it when the first soldiers from the capital drove into Monimbó. There were Cubans with them, some in civilian clothes, flint-eyed men who asked questions and went about inspecting everything. They did not pause to examine the Licenciado's mural, though one of them gave an ironical salute to the seventeen-year-old *guerrillero* standing beside it.

Monkey Díaz stood stiffly to attention and returned the salute. He was bursting with pride. It was the first anniversary of the fall of the dictator, and he had been selected for the honor of serving Fidel Castro, the first successful revolutionary in the hemisphere, in the Indian village where the Nicaraguan revolution had caught fire.

The visitors were sitting in a bare, whitewashed room hung with Cuban and Sandinista flags, around a long wooden table. The man in the *keffiyah* with a patchy beard sat at one end. Monkey Díaz could not understand him, because he spoke in English. Fidel sat in the middle, dominating the room with his physical presence and his voluble bursts of oratory as he puffed

6

on a big cigar. Next to Fidel sat a much shorter, dumpy man with pale green eyes and a bright red beard. One of the Sandinista guards had whispered to Monkey that he was Manuel Piñeiro, the most famous of the chiefs of Castro's secret services. Monkey did not recognize any of the other men. But names, and snippets of conversation, blew to him in gusts as he hurried in and out of the room, bearing plates and soft drinks and bottles of wine.

There were Cubans all around the building. There was even a Cuban in the kitchen, sampling the dishes before Monkey carried them through. Monkey had thought, to begin with, that the man was snatching a bite to eat, but one of the cooks took him aside and warned him that he was Fidel's personal foodtaster. Monkey nodded knowingly. There were still counter-revolutionaries in hiding all over the country, he had heard on the radio, as well as the ones who made cowardly raids across the border from Honduras.

At the long table, Fidel was doing most of the talking. He toasted the Nicaraguan revolution, and a Sandinista leader—Monkey thought he must be Tomás Borge, from the photos he had seen—responded by praising Cuba for the contribution it had made to the struggle. Then Fidel spoke, in long, windy sentences that swept his listeners along with him, of how, having established its foothold on the mainland, the Revolution would spread through the whole of Central America.

"The Revolution can never be secure within the frontiers of one country," Monkey heard him say. "Nicaragua will not be secure until El Salvador, Guatemala and Honduras are liberated too. It is our duty as proletarian internationalists to bring that about."

The men around the table grunted approval. The Guatemalan, Monkey noticed, had the flat features and high cheekbones of his own family; he was an *indio* too. The boy had never heard of proletarian internationalism before, but could guess what it meant as he became conscious of how many different countries were represented by the men in the room with Fidel.

7

Apart from the Palestinian and the Central Americans, there were three black men, from Jamaica, Grenada and Haiti. The Jamaican, he gathered, was Minister of National Security in his country's government. There was a lawyer from Panama, who seemed well informed about weapons. There was a Cuban who had come not from Havana, but from the United States. From the way he talked, it was obvious he was no *gusano*—Fidel's word for renegade. There were Russians, too, looking uncomfortable in their suits and ties. Two of them, heavyset men with pink, sweaty faces, had come in a black limousine from the embassy in Managua. A third, who looked as old to the boy as the Santiago volcano that overlooked the town, had come from Havana, with Fidel. It was all very confusing.

When Monkey had removed the lunch plates and returned to serve coffee, Fidel was talking about the *yanquis*.

"We do not need to live in fear of the Americans anymore," Fidel declared. "We can all see how weak the Administration in Washington has become. Look at what happened with Mariel."

Monkey did not recognize the name. Nor, it seemed, did the Palestinian, who asked a question.

"Mariel is a small seaport in Cuba," Fidel explained in English for his benefit. "We allowed more than a hundred twenty-five thousand people to leave for the United States via Mariel." Reverting to Spanish, he added, "The capitalists tried to make propaganda out of it. They tried to say the fact that these scum wanted to live in the United States proved that the Revolution no longer had the support of the people. We paid them back for those lies. We sent them the lowest dregs of our society—convicted criminals, lunatics, *maricones*. We even told them ahead of time what we were going to do unless they stopped threatening us and agreed to a genuine dialogue. When we did exactly what we had warned them we were ready to do, they didn't have the *cojones* to turn back the boats. It was more of a humiliation for the Americans than Pearl Harbor, since this time they were

8

forewarned and still did nothing. And El Gran Cacahuete—The Big Peanut—in the White House knows it. You bet he knows it."

"A wounded animal is often the most dangerous," the Salvadoran said quietly. "The Americans have suffered many humiliations these past years. The fall of their puppet in Iran. The flight of their *perrito* from Managua. The taking of their embassy in Teheran. The sealift from Mariel. All this, and more. The Americans are a people full of pride. They are used to being on top. Who is to say that they will not lash out—against my country; maybe against all our countries?"

"This is also an election year in the United States," the Costa Rican added. Monkey had heard someone describe him as the secretary-general of his country's Communist Party. "The reactionary forces in America are already beating their wings. These people are not like the British. They will never learn how to give up an empire gracefully. They were not even prepared to give up the Panama Canal. If they win the elections, they may send soldiers to fight for the corporations in Central America. Every butcher in the continent is counting on their victory, and Wall Street is spending millions to ensure it."

"*Basta.*" Fidel waved his cigar.

The sudden gesture threw Monkey off balance as he reached forward to serve Castro his *cafecito*. The cup clattered against the saucer, and a few drops spilled.

Aghast, the boy stuttered his apologies. "*Perdón, señor.*"

"*No importa,*" Fidel said curtly. "You may leave us."

But Monkey hovered at the door for an instant, long enough to hear Fidel say, "It may be Manolo is right. It may be the right will win the American presidency in November. We know that everywhere in the Americas, elections are a tool of the rich. We have no reason to fear, whatever the results. We may even benefit from a Republican victory. The present American Administration has grown used to losing all over the world, and is scared of losing any more because of its critics on the right. If the

9

rightists take power, we will teach them soon enough what it means to lose. And the men who have just lost power will be anxious not to allow them to succeed where *they* failed."

A Cuban officer in fatigues without badges of rank shooed Monkey away from the door. Fidel was still in full spate. His voice carried along the corridor as the boy walked back to the kitchen with his tray.

"We have many weapons," he heard Fidel declare. "We have agents of absolute confidence all over the United States who are ready to undertake whatever actions are necessary at the time of our choosing. The *yanquis* cannot even begin to imagine the capabilities that we have in their country. You all read about the riots in Miami this spring. We can accomplish things that would make the riots in Florida look like a sun-shower."

Chapter

1

SAN JUAN, PUERTO RICO

It was on the last leg of the cruise, between Martinique and San Juan, that Robert Hockney conceded that he had not been born a sailor.

The tail of the hurricane caught them before dawn. When the sun came up, it was lost behind massed thunderheads. Lightning pitchforked through the northern sky. For all its breadth of beam, the *Duchess* yawed and plunged like a leaky shrimper.

Hockney lay down on the bed in their cabin for a long time after waking, willing the sea to be still. Julia seemed to be impervious to the storm. She was awake in an instant, as always, quick and light as a bird. Soon she was tugging playfully at the sheet that covered him.

He groaned and burrowed his nose deeper into the pillow.

"Time for breakfast," Julia chirped. "I'm starving."

"I don't know how you can even *think* about food," he complained, uncomfortably reminded of the spareribs and rum punches he had consumed the night before.

Another yank, and she had the sheet down around his ankles.

Reluctantly, Hockney pulled on jeans and an old football jersey and followed her up the stairs toward the dining room.

Julia looked so healthy, so *alive,* he thought. A few days in the Caribbean had peeled off several years—as well as a small, lozenge-shaped patch of skin at the base of her neck. Her face glowed, the tan accentuated by her simple necklace and earrings, fashioned from white seashells. She had lost the slightly stricken, indoor look she had begun to develop in Washington. She moved with a new springiness, a pride in her body, even as the ship heaved with the waves.

People noticed her, and smiled with their eyes. Hockney had begun to notice again too. In Washington, two years into the marriage, both of them locked into their competitive, conflicting routines, he had let her become a predictable stranger, a fixed image that he inspected no more closely than the framed photograph on his desk at the *World* bureau. He had seen it happen in other people's marriages. He had watched busy, socially accomplished couples grow so remote from each other that to spend even a single week away from the safe, well-worn conventions of the office, the cocktail circuit, the dinner-party crowd was to risk the collapse of everything. It might have been because Hockney feared he had reached that stage with Julia that he had put off this trip for almost a year, on the pretext of having to field a crisis somewhere or other—in Beirut, or Warsaw, or San Salvador. Now he knew he had been foolish to wait so long. It had taken him a day or two to get over his initial sensation of guilt at not seeing his by-line in print every morning; for a reporter, withdrawal symptoms can be as severe as for an alcoholic. Since then, he had been able to give himself over to the enjoyment of discovering things with Julia—she had the words for trees and wild flowers and tropical birds that, but for her, would have passed nameless—and of rediscovering *her.* Their lovemaking, perfunctory and mechanical before, had become fresh and exciting.

Even now, halfway up the steps, as he steadied himself against the railing, Hockney marveled at the change that had come over both of them. A week ago, he had had all the premonitions of divorce. Now he suspected he was falling in love again. When they stood together, he felt as if they were enveloped by an aura of light. Was a week away from Washington all it took?

In the dining room, several passengers were lined up at the buffet table, loading their plates.

"You've all got cast-iron stomachs," Hockney commented. "I think I'll get some air."

"Are you feeling that bad?" When Julia frowned, a short vertical line appeared between her eyebrows.

"I'll live," he grinned ruefully, nuzzling her cheek. "Go ahead and have breakfast."

She joined the line at the buffet, and he lurched out toward the main deck, wishing that the rain would ease off so he could go outside. In choppy water, he always felt better on deck than cooped up inside.

To his surprise, he saw through a porthole that another passenger was out there, leaning against the railing, seemingly indifferent to the salt spray and the slanting rain. Hockney watched the man through the glass. He recognized him as one of the handful of passengers who had joined the *Duchess* at Martinique. The man was tall, with broad shoulders that tapered to a narrow waist. His thick, matted hair was the color of damp hay. He was wearing a red windbreaker, white pants and moccasins. He stared out across the violent waters toward Puerto Rico, not yet visible on the horizon, with a look of such intensity that it seemed to Hockney everything the man had left to hope or fear must be waiting for him in that place.

"Mitch! Mitch! *¡Ven acá!*"

Hockney turned toward the voice. He saw a lovely girl with an olive-round, olive-hued face, sheltering her abundant black hair under a towel as she ran out toward the man at the railing. The man swiveled around to face her, and for the first time Hockney noticed his eyes. They were an extraordinary shade of green, the green of shallow waters above a sandbar, so pale they might have been bleached. For an instant they fastened on Hockney, and he felt a curious sensation, as if there were some

13

predatory force behind the eyes that was assessing him—as victim or menace. Astonished by the irrational strength of his reaction, Hockney turned his attention to the girl.

Her sodden yellow silk blouse clung to high, firm breasts. The effect was more provocative than if she had been naked. It was enhanced by skin-tight jeans and the absurdly high-heeled sandals on which she was now teetering back inside, her arm around the man's waist.

"You're better seamen than I am," Hockney greeted them. "It's pretty rough out there."

The girl smiled, but the man merely grunted, and moved to go past Hockney to the stairwell. He seemed angry at being approached.

But Hockney felt a compelling desire to strike up a conversation. He stuck out his hand and introduced himself.

The man considered Hockney's hand as if uncertain what to do with it.

Finally he responded with the briefest possible handshake and mumbled, "Mitch Lardner."

Hockney was looking at the girl. Even her collarbone was *perfect*.

"My wife," Lardner added reluctantly. "We're on our honeymoon."

"Nice to meet you, Mrs. Lardner," Hockney said formally.

"Rosario," she corrected him. *"Encantada."*

Hockney saw that dangerous look in Lardner's eyes again. Water from their drenched clothes was forming a pool around their feet. Mascara ran, like a black tear, down one of Rosario's cheeks.

Perhaps it was the girl, at once sensual and vulnerable, who kept Hockney talking. He had forgotten that he felt seasick. He wanted to know everything about these travelers from Martinique, exotic on board the *Duchess,* whose passengers were mostly over sixty.

"I'm a journalist," Hockney volunteered. "I write for *The New York World.* How about you?"

"Appliances," Lardner said curtly. "Electrical appliances."

"Oh."

The man with pale eyes did not *look* like someone who sold vacuum cleaners or TV sets. He reminded Hockney of a man he had known in Vietnam, a former Green Beret who lived alone in the hills with his Montagnards, a man half-crazy with killing and unable to stop killing even when ordered to.

"Are you staying in San Juan?" Hockney asked.

"Just a few days," Lardner said, shuffling his big feet.

"Maybe we can get together for a drink. My wife and I are at the Caribe Hilton."

Lardner grunted tonelessly and started to walk forward.

"Where are *you* staying?" Hockney asked.

Lardner looked ready to explode, but the girl put her hand on his forearm and squeezed it gently.

"We're at the Caribe Hilton too," Rosario said.

"That's terrific. Maybe we can share a cab."

But Lardner was already marching off to the stairwell, with the girl hanging on his arm.

As he watched them go below, Hockney realized that he had probably behaved no better than the intrusive busybodies on board the *Duchess* whom he and Julia had been trying to avoid for much of the cruise—people who were forever hovering around you, looking for a place to alight, as persistent as the small black flies on the beach. But there was a mystery about Mitch Lardner and his Latin beauty. With his reporter's eye for detail, Hockney had observed that neither of them was wearing a wedding band. That seemed a curious oversight for a couple on their honeymoon. And something about the way the girl had held Lardner's temper in check made Hockney feel sure that the man was hiding more than his real occupation.

He lingered over coffee in the dining room after Julia had gone below to pack. The Lardners did not appear, and he wasted half an hour or more commiserating with a retired garment manufacturer and his wife over the crime wave in Miami. Hockney looked out for the travelers from Martinique as they disembarked at the cruise-ship terminal, inside the jaws of San Juan harbor. He made the taxi driver idle for a while after stowing their bags in the trunk, on the pretext of inspecting the splendid pink bulk of the Customs House.

"It looks like a palace in Seville!" Julia exclaimed, peering through the rain that was beating against the windows.

Hockney glanced back at the gangway. It seemed that everyone had got off the *Duchess* except the Lardners.

Skirting the narrow streets of the old town, Hockney and Julia drove to the Caribe Hilton. They passed the picturesque ruin of the Normandie Hotel, derelict except for the shiny new Burger King out front.

Hockney was not surprised when the pretty girl at the registration desk told him that the hotel had no record of a Mr. and Mrs. Lardner. The couple from Martinique could hardly have bettered their vanishing act if they had jumped overboard.

A pair of Long Island widows who had been on the *Duchess* waved to Hockney as they shuffled past the desk in the direction of the red-carpeted stairway leading up to the hotel casino. They had not even waited to see their rooms before trying their luck at the tables. If the storm did not let up, Hockney realized, he and Julia might be left with the choice of following their example or camping out at the bar.

"Is the weather going to stay like this?" he asked the bellman as they rode the elevator in the tower block.

"Very small hurricane. Gone to Florida." The bellman grinned. "Very changeable here," he went on in his staccato English. "You'll see. Even on a rainy day at the beach, you can get burned."

Hockney shook his head in disbelief.

"I swear to God," the bellman insisted. "You gonna find out."

The travelers from Martinique waited a full twenty minutes after the Hockneys disembarked before they left the *Duchess*. A man in a fawn Toyota was waiting for them near the spreading ceiba tree that dominated the open space in front of the Customs House. On sunny days, roving vendors wheeled their carts of ice cream and hot dogs into its shade. The wind had already begun to abate, and the rain fell in intermittent, though heavy, bursts, as if someone were tipping out one bucket of water after another. The rain did little to alleviate the oppressive, steamy heat of San Juan in early summer.

The Lardners did not go to the Caribe Hilton. Instead, their driver turned south on the Muñoz Rivera Expressway and drove out to a three-building apartment complex in the suburb of Hato Rey, not far from the gray cement fortress that housed the headquarters of the Federal Bureau of Investigation in Puerto Rico. Frank Parra, the head of the FBI's antiterrorist unit, could see the three apartment houses from his window. They looked like low-cost housing anywhere. But on especially frustrating days, the FBI man could sometimes be found cocking his thumb and forefinger at them, pretending to take aim and fire. The board of the condominiums had ruled that as a condition of tenancy, residents were not permitted to cooperate with any law-enforcement agency, federal or local, under any circumstances. More recently, the board had issued a circular to all residents requesting them not to dump explosives or detonators in the waste-disposal system. The FBI man regarded the complex balefully, as the biggest safe house for terrorists on the whole island. The clever lawyer who acted for the board of the condominiums countered that the aim was merely to provide a haven for people of liberated opinions.

The Cuban was waiting for the Lardners in a sparsely furnished apartment on the fourth floor of the middle building. His skin was stretched tightly over his elongated, almost hairless head, giving the impression of an ebony skull. His guayabera shirt bagged out from his flat belly, as if borrowed from a fatter man.

The Cuban folded the girl in a warm *abrazo*.

"Que linda, Rosario," he murmured to her.

Then he patted Mitch Lardner's shoulder and said, "No trouble at the docks?"

"They didn't even check our bags."

"You Americans have it easy, Beacher," the Cuban said. "The *guardia* make more trouble for Dominicans." When he grinned, he displayed his flawless teeth, all the way to the gums.

The Cuban had been searched when he had arrived, via Santo Domingo, a few days before, bearing Dominican identity papers. This was his preferred route to San Juan, and he had used it a dozen times before. Whenever possible, however, he sought to conduct business with Puerto Ricans in St. Thomas, because of the excellent duty-free stores on the island. The Cuban was especially fond of Ballantine's thirty-year-old Scotch. It could be bought in St. Thomas for less than half the going price in New York.

The Cuban made brief introductions, referring to Mitch Lardner as "Beacher" and to the other two men in the room by nicknames. "Paco," a wiry, taciturn man of middling height, was the one who rented the apartment. He too had a Dominican passport. "El Gato," the only Puerto Rican in the group, was the man who had chauffeured the Lardners from the cruise-ship terminal. One of his eyelids dipped lower than the other, so he looked as if he were always about to wink. He was built like a beer barrel, but moved with surprising agility on small, precise feet.

"Your target," the Cuban announced to the group, holding open a copy of that morning's *San Juan Star*.

One by one, they examined the photograph on page three. It showed a man with an impressively ugly, corrugated face, talking into a battery of microphones.

Using a sketch map, the Cuban ran through the plan for the operation—where the guards were posted, how they would scale the walls, where the boat would be waiting.

"Your final rendezvous will be *here*." He showed the Lardners a spot on the Cataño side of the bay, near a rum distillery. "Gato will take charge of the prisoner, and you will disperse according to your instructions. Any questions?"

There was silence for a time. They were all slightly in awe of the Cuban. His past exploits in the Middle East, Africa and Latin America were legendary. In Havana, he used his own name: Calixto Valdés. As chief of Bureau 13 of the Dirección General de Inteligencia, he was entrusted with the enormous responsibility of recruiting, training and directing terrorists for operations all over the world. Despite his exalted status in Castro's secret service, Calixto Valdés was still nostalgic for the front lines. Whenever it could be managed, he liked to be close to the scene of his operations.

It was Rosario who spoke first.

"What about the consequences?" she asked. "Where does it lead?"

Valdés studied her for a moment. A pink triangle appeared at the corner of his mouth as his tongue flicked in and out, like a lizard's.

"Our Puerto Rican comrades—Gato's organization—will claim responsibility," he said. "The Americans will overreact. That will help to polarize the situation here, and to build support for the independence movement. We will also neutralize one of our most powerful enemies in the United States.

"This is not an isolated act," he went on. "You have all heard of Monimbó. We know we are facing an Administration in Washington that is bent on the systematic oppression of every popular movement and every underprivileged community in this hemisphere. We also know that it is unnecessary to make war on the Americans, or to wait for them to make war on us. The United States is already being torn apart by its internal contradictions. Under the right conditions, it will self-destruct. As Fidel says, the United States is a colossus with feet of clay. All its missile silos and multinational corporations won't keep it from falling flat on its back if we push at the right places."

By midafternoon the storm seemed to have blown over, and the Hockneys ventured out onto the small crescent beach of the Caribe Hilton. But no sooner had the attendant spread orange towels over a pair of loungers than the rain started again. They beat a hasty retreat into the bar.

They sank into low-slung wicker chairs and ordered one of the local beers, Corona.

Hockney started leafing idly through a copy of the *Star* that had been abandoned on the chair next to them.

"Hey, look," he said to Julia, "your boss is in town."

She glanced at the photograph of Senator Joel Fairchild addressing a press conference. Fairchild, a conservative Republican from Texas, was chairman of the Senate Internal Security Committee. Julia had mixed feelings about him. The Committee had been revived by the Newgate Administration, and was regarded with dark suspicion in liberal circles as an effort to start a McCarthyite witch-hunt against the President's enemies. Fairchild had turned it into his personal platform. He never missed a chance to get the TV cameras into the Committee room. In televised hearings, he had called upon the FBI Director to explain why the Bureau was not spying on a number of foundations and progressive lobbies in Washington that had been identified by a Russian defector as Soviet-front organizations. The Director started to talk about First Amendment rights and the so-called "Levi guidelines"—restrictions imposed by the Attorney General under the Ford Administration, which forbade the FBI to carry out surveillance unless there was evidence of criminal activities.

Senator Fairchild interrupted the Director in mid-sentence. "Hell," he erupted, "Where I come from, you either shit or get off the pot."

It went down well in Texas. Before long, the fan mail was streaming in from all over the country, and the Senator was getting more publicity than he had bargained for. Article after article denounced him as "the new Joe McCarthy" and covered his lifestyle in prurient detail—his fleet of vintage sports cars, his taste for fluffy blond secretaries, his stake in a mob-related resort development. Undeterred, Fairchild returned to the attack.

He had just held hearings on Puerto Rican terrorism. The first day's show was poorly attended. But on the second morning the Committee room was cleared after somebody phoned in a bomb threat, and the TV cameras were back. The Senator told the media that the scare was proof of "a carefully laid plot by the Communist Castro regime to use its Puerto Rican dupes to destabilize the United States." No bomb was found, and Julia had a sneaking suspicion that the whole episode had been staged by Fairchild himself to reclaim the limelight.

It had got to the point where Julia and one or two other staffers were wary of giving the Senator information, for fear of what he might do with it. She had told him about the case of a drug trafficker arrested in Mexico who had confessed to having contacts with the Cuban DGI, and Fairchild had promptly invited himself onto a TV talk show to announce that "in the imminent future" the Committee would prove that the Cubans were behind the dope rackets in the United States. Since then, Julia had found that her usual sources were more tight-lipped than before.

"I wonder what Fairchild is doing in San Juan," Hockney said.

"Getting his picture in the newspapers," Julia suggested.

"Why don't you give him a call?"

Julia made a face, but Hockney said, "Go on. It might be amusing to have a drink with the old bastard. You remember what he said to me when you introduced us?"

"Yes," she recited: "'Are you still writing for *Pravda West*?'"

The rain sounded like hail as it hammered against the plate-glass windows across the bar.

"Well," she conceded, "I guess it's not much of a day for sight-seeing. But rainy days are good days to stay in bed."

He stroked her auburn hair and said, "We'll have lots of time for both."

The bartender smirked at them as he plopped long fingers of pineapple into a row of piña coladas.

"Honeymoon?" he inquired.

"Sí," Julia replied, practicing her rusty Spanish. *"Luna de miel."*

It was true enough, Hockney reflected an hour or so later as he lay across their bed, letting his hands rove over her as she straddled him, until her eyes and her mouth opened wide in pleasure and surprise as if it were her first time.

The streets of Old San Juan gleamed metallic blue under the

rain. They were paved with bricks made of slag from English ironworks, bricks that neither chipped nor corroded. The taxi nosed up Fortaleza Street, toward the main gate of the Governor's Palace. La Fortaleza, as the palace was called, was a six-teenth-century Spanish fort rising above massive seawalls that had been polished smooth to repel attackers in the days of the pirates and privateers. Down a side street to the right, Hockney could see the shabby Plaza Colón, with its bus terminal. Off to the left were imposing but deserted houses with shattered tile-work, gutted windows and ruined wrought-iron balustrades that looked as if they had been pulled apart with crowbars.

Senator Fairchild had been insistent. The Governor was holding a dinner party for him, and the Hockneys had to come along. Julia observed that the Senator was probably less inter-ested in *her* presence than in that of a well-known correspon-dent from the Mainland press.

One of the policemen at the gate of La Fortaleza checked Hockney's name against a list, and soon they were shaking hands with the Governor and his wife, a trim brunette from New Jersey who spoke faultless Spanish. They stood near a big open fireplace, under heavy oak beams. On the wall was a blue-and-white tapestry displaying the Puerto Rican coat of arms. White-coated waiters scurried about the room, bearing trays of drinks, empanadas and hors d'oeuvre.

Senator Fairchild grabbed a whiskey-and-soda from a pass-ing waiter and rushed up to Julia. Hockney was struck, as he had been before, by the man's remarkable ugliness. His brown eyes were small and close-set. His black hair was parted an inch above his left ear and plastered down over his bald pate. His mouth looked like the sear mark of a poker against old rubber. He was much smaller than he appeared on television.

The vivacious, busty blonde who was with him seemed young enough to be his daughter, even his granddaughter. Hockney guessed she must be Fairchild's new wife, the office girl he had married. She was said to have ambitions to become a country-and-Western singer. The *World* had run an article on the wed-

22

ding. It had taken place on the Senator's sixty-seventh birthday, a couple of months after he buried his third wife.

The Senator greeted Hockney like an old friend.

"I want you to meet my new Nancy," he boomed. "The prettiest li'l thing in all of Texas."

When Nancy Fairchild smiled, two perfectly symmetrical dimples showed on either side of her Cupid's-bow mouth.

"What are you doing in San Juan?" Hockney asked the Senator.

"I'm down here to show the flag," Fairchild said cheerfully. "Nobody in Washington wants to know about Puerto Rico. They think it's just some big Indian reservation where nobody works and everybody just lies around all day screwing or getting drunk, all on federal money. Now, that's mostly true, of course," the Senator confided, not minding that the Governor was within earshot. "But there's a bigger picture. This island is critical to our whole Caribbean strategy—if we've still got one. And it's the base Fidel Castro wants to use to spread terrorism all over the United States. If we want to stop people blowing up our cities, we've got to start by dealing with terrorism down here."

"How do you propose doing that?"

"By giving the FBI the men and the resources it needs. Here, you can put this in your paper. The FBI has about seventy agents to cover Puerto Rico and the whole Caribbean. There are four times as many terrorists, and God knows how many Castro agents."

"Is it really that simple?"

"You bet it's that simple," the Senator went on aggressively. "There are people who want to turn this into our Northern Ireland, and they spout all kinds of Marxist claptrap about wicked Gringo colonialism. People who swallow that are forgetting a couple of facts of life. If Puerto Rico is a colony, it's the only colony in history that managed to rape the occupying power. We're providing nearly five billion a year in subsidies."

Fairchild drew breath to seize another drink.

23

He turned back to Hockney and said, "It's the same old problem. A lot of your friends in the media want to make us believe that terrorism comes about because people are poor and downtrodden. They don't want to recognize that there are guys who are trying to stir things up, and we've got to play hardball with 'em."

Nancy Fairchild's attention had fluttered away to Julia's black chiffon dress.

"Is that an Adolfo?" she trilled.

Julia shook her head curtly, tuned into the men's conversation.

"Mine is," the Senator's wife said proudly.

"I'm giving a speech about all of this to the Rotary tomorrow," Fairchild was saying. "You should come along. I've got some facts that might interest your readers."

The Governor called them in to dinner, and it was a welcome interruption for Hockney.

"One of our more primeval statesmen," he whispered in Julia's ear as he shepherded her toward the banquet room. "I don't know how you stand it."

"Well, *you're* the one who wanted to see him perform," she reminded him.

The Governor got his second wind after midnight and, when a suitable opportunity presented itself, enjoyed sitting up talking and drinking until dawn. But his guests left early. Hockney and Julia went back to the Caribe Hilton in a government car before 1 A.M., and the Fairchilds retired to the official guesthouse shortly thereafter.

The guesthouse was a short walk from one of the side gates of La Fortaleza. It had a steel-plated door and a red-tiled roof and was known as La Rogativa. The name honored the bishop who had supposedly saved the capital from being sacked by the English in 1797. He had led the women of the town, bearing torches, to say a special Mass in supplication to Saint Ursula. Seeing the torchlit procession, the commanders of the English

24

fleet in the harbor had thought that Spanish reinforcements had arrived, and had sailed their ships away.

Tonight, there was a pervasive smell of honeysuckle around the Rogativa gate. Nancy Fairchild remarked on it as the Senator steered her through the door of the guest house—held open by Jim Tucker, one of his aides—toward the larger of the two bedrooms.

"Buenas noches," Senator Fairchild called out in an excruciating drawl to the guard who was standing stiffly at attention outside his nearby shelter. The policeman responded with a smart salute and retreated out of the rain. He was one of the garrison of forty guards assigned to the Governor's Palace. In the early hours of the morning only a handful of guards were on duty, although, in deference to the visiting Senator, a couple of policemen had been posted outside the Rogativa gate.

Nobody heard or saw the black rubber dinghy glide to the water's edge at the foot of the seawall.

A drowsy policeman, sheltering under the edge of the red-tiled roof of the Rogativa gate, stirred at the sight of the dark-colored Pontiac sloshing toward him along the rain-filled road from another of the capital's forts, the one called El Morro.

He relaxed when the driver rolled down his window and waved at him. In the light of the lamps around the walls of the Fortaleza, the guard could see that the man behind the wheel was a *norteamericano*. That was obvious from his fair hair and green eyes. No doubt a tourist who had lost his way.

The policeman was not inclined to venture out into the wet to give directions. But then he noticed the girl who was sitting in the front seat. She smiled at him invitingly. He puffed out his chest and swaggered over to the car.

"Can I help you, please?" he said in his best American accent, leaning into the window on the passenger's side.

He watched the girl smile. Then he saw the driver's hand move from between the seats and found himself looking into the barrel of a .38 revolver. With the silencer attached, it seemed monstrously long. The policeman tried to jump backward, clutching at his holster, but the bullet caught him in the center of his forehead, and he dropped without a scream.

There was no sign of a second guard outside the gate, although the green-eyed man had been told to expect one.

"Gone to the *cantina*," the passenger in the back seat suggested. He was the quiet one with the Dominican passport, the one they called Paco.

The three terrorists slid out of the Pontiac simultaneously. They wore matching blue plastic windbreakers. Rosario pulled up her hood against the rain.

Paco leaned his weight against the wall beside the Rogativa gate, locked his hands together and braced himself. The American—Beacher—set his foot into Paco's cupped palms as into a stirrup, and swung himself upward in one smooth motion until he was straddling the wall. He could make out the shape of the official guesthouse and, immediately below him, the flat roof of the sentry box.

Beacher helped the girl to clamber up beside him. She squatted awkwardly, as if trying to ride sidesaddle, with a thick coil of rope bunched up over her shoulder.

There was a sudden thunderclap, and at the same instant the American let himself drop to the cobblestones inside the wall. The storm blotted out the noise of his fall.

Holding his revolver parallel to the slope of his chest, Beacher darted his head around the side of the sentry box. He saw the guard slumped on the wooden bench inside, dozing. The policeman's head lolled forward, the features hidden by his cap.

Beacher never saw the face of the man inside the sentry box. He simply leveled the gun, the tip of the silencer an inch away from the crown of the policeman's cap, and pumped a single bullet into his skull.

It took less than a minute to prise open the heavy bolts of the Rogativa gate, and Paco ran through, cradling an Uzi automatic. His windbreaker was unzipped to expose a brace of grenades clipped to his belt. In his free hand he carried more rope and a mechanical device like a pulley.

While Paco secured the gate, Beacher and the girl ran to the guesthouse and started hammering on the door.

Several minutes later, a voice that was thick with sleep called back, "Who's there?"

"Sorry to roust you out," Beacher shouted at the closed door. "The phone lines are down. With the storm. There is an urgent message from the White House for Senator Fairchild."

"Hold on a minute."

Inside the guesthouse, Tucker, the Senator's aide, had been sleeping naked because of the heat. Bleary-eyed, he pulled on his shorts and shirt. He had begun to open the door before he realized that his shirt buttons did not match the holes. He looked like a rumpled schoolboy.

"What's the message?" Tucker asked, blinking uncertainly at the green-eyed man in the doorway, who did not resemble anyone he had seen in the Governor's entourage. Tucker made out a girl with a generous mouth and black hair tumbling from under a hood who was hovering in the background. In the sudden flash of lightning, he saw something that shone like metal.

Tucker's scream was stifled as Beacher drove his thumb and forefinger into the loose flesh of the aide's throat on either side of the windpipe. In less than seven seconds, the flow of oxygen to Tucker's brain had been choked off. His legs buckled; he fell to the floor and blacked out. Crouching over him, Beacher kept his hand clenched in an eagle's claw until he was sure that the aide was dead.

Feeble groaning noises filtered through the oak door to the master bedroom. Beacher cocked his head, momentarily puzzled. Then his face slowly molded itself into a grin. He padded to the oak door on his crepe-soled shoes and eased it open.

The Senator's head reposed on the heaped down pillows of a canopied bed. His eyelids were closed. His mussed black hair hung over his ears in spiky tendrils, exposing his bald patch.

"No, no," the Senator was murmuring. "Don't give up now. I'm almost there."

Through the crack in the door, Beacher could see, below the

27

pale folds of Senator Fairchild's belly, his wife's shapely buttocks, raised high in the air. She was going down on him, her head twisting and bobbing as she labored to bring him to a climax.

"*That's* it," the Senator groaned. "Take all of it. Oh, *yes*. Faster, faster."

Beacher pushed the door wide open.

"Yes, yes," the Senator said. "I can feel it. I'm coming."

Neither of the Fairchilds was in a position to observe the two strangers moving to flank them on both sides of the bed.

"Senator Joel Fairchild," Beacher said, in the flat tone of a man reading names from a roster. "I must apologize for our poor timing."

Nancy Fairchild never saw the faces of the terrorists who kidnapped her husband. They pulled her away from his body; thrust her face downward on the bed; trussed, gagged and blindfolded her. She noticed only that one of them had small, delicate hands.

Beacher dragged the Senator, deflated and protesting, to his feet, and Rosario tied his hands behind his back.

"You're under arrest" was all that Beacher would offer by way of explanation.

"But I'm a United States Senator!" Fairchild protested.

"*No estamos en los Estados Unidos,*" the girl snapped at him, yanking the cords tighter.

The Senator's disappearance was detected twenty minutes later, when a policeman came up from the barracks to the Rogativa gate and found one of his comrades lying dead with a bullet between the eyes. By that time, the Senator had been transferred to a motor launch which had crossed the bay to a rendezvous point near the rum distillery.

On another corner of the promontory, the Hockneys were still sitting up in bed, talking and planning. Like New Year's

Day, the end of a vacation is a time when people think about starting over, a time of resolutions.

It started when Hockney brushed his teeth and then, true to habit, poured himself a generous slug of brandy.

"Do you want something?" he called to Julia, who was propped up against the pillows with a book.

"Uh-uh."

Hockney glanced at the warm brown liquid in the glass, then dribbled it back into the bottle.

"I haven't seen you do *that* in a while," Julia commented approvingly.

He wandered over to her. "What are you reading?" he asked.

She showed him the title. It was a paperback about real estate bargains within a hundred-mile radius of New York. She had it open at the section about Columbia County.

"What are you planning to do? Join the Chatham Hunt Club?"

"Listen to this, Bob." She read out the description of an 1800 Colonial farmhouse, with a swimming pond and a trout stream, on a hundred acres of wooded hills near the Hudson River. "Doesn't it sound beautiful?"

"I bet the price tag is pretty too."

"Less than a Washington apartment. A *lot* less than a Manhattan co-op."

"What do you want me to do? Resign from the *World* and become a gentleman farmer?"

"I was just thinking—it would be lovely to have a place we could get away to. I sometimes get to feeling I just can't breathe in Washington. I'd like to be able to run away somewhere and not have to eat and drink politics all the time. Didn't you get that feeling tonight, listening to Joel Fairchild showing off? God, that man is so *gross*."

"Stop working for the Committee if you're fed up," he suggested. "There's no need for you to work at all."

"I'm not really cut out to be the passive little *Hausfrau*," she said, smiling at him. "And I still think what the Committee was set up to do is important—when Fairchild doesn't manage to take it and twist it beyond recognition. It's just—well, it's Washington. People seem to become monodimensional, monomaniacal."

"All right," he said, taking her hand. "We'll go away for part of the summer. We can go and stay with Peter and Selma in East Hampton." Peter had worked for the *World* until he had written a couple of whodunits that were sold to Hollywood.

"I wasn't just talking about holidays, darling. We've never owned the roof over our heads. Wouldn't it be nice to have a place that really belonged to us?"

Hockney thought it over. They lived in a big apartment near Dupont Circle. When his book about the defection of Viktor Barisov—a KGB spy he had helped to escape from Geneva—had made the best-seller lists, they had looked at some town houses in Georgetown, but had been scared off by the prices.

"Also, you've been talking about settling down to write another book," she pressed him. "You're never going to do that in Washington."

That much was certainly true, he thought. Like most reporters (and most other people), he had often thought of trying to write a novel. The pressures of running the Washington bureau of *The New York World* gave him an excellent excuse not to make a start. The pressures were real, but when he looked into himself, he knew he was also scared. He made his living with words, but he was scared that words would fail him when he attempted the transition from one vehicle to another. It had been hard enough to set his thoughts down in orderly form in the book on the Soviet defector, hard to work to a deadline that was further away than tomorrow. He had come to accept that he was a reporter and that was that.

But what Julia was saying touched a responsive chord. Over the past few months in Washington, he had felt no happier, no more fulfilled, than she. He had lost that sense of vocation which had guided him as a younger reporter, and worse, he had become increasingly resentful of those who had it. He was bored with his lunches at the Maison Blanche—the "MB," as other habitués, like Art Buchwald and Ben Bradlee, called it—and with having to expend the better part of his working hours overseeing a busy news bureau. Lately, he had wasted a lot of time wrangling with Jack Lancer, a young investigative reporter who had graduated to the *World* from a fringe libertarian publication on the West Coast. What irritated Hockney was that Lancer had made up his mind not only about what was wrong with the United States—he talked about the incumbent Administration as if it were the biggest threat to world peace since Hitler—but about his personal mission to bring back truth and justice.

Lancer's unblinking certainties made him gullible. Hockney had first got into a fight with him when Lancer wrote a story claiming that the CIA was running a school for torturers in El Salvador. It turned out that Lancer had been fed the story by a staffer at a radical institute who had close ties to the Cuban Mission in New York. But Lancer worked hard, and produced genuine scoops. And Hockney was not sure that his reactions to the younger man were uncontaminated by personal insecurity.

Living in a time in which the Fourth Estate in America had never been so powerful, Hockney found more to question than ever about the way that that power was exercised. It is the job of the press to keep governments honest. He had used that helpful tag on one of those TV talk shows on which media luminaries interview each other about the state of the nation. But he did not believe it was healthy for the press to arrogate the power to make or unmake the nation's policies without submitting itself to the same degree of scrutiny and inquisition to which it subjected all of America's other institutions. He even believed that there are some secrets of government that are best kept secret.

Hockney's views on such matters made him an eccentric among his peers. But in the end, he was guided by professional opportunism, like most of the others. You did not turn down a hot story. And in Washington, such a story was more likely to involve a new blunder by the Newgate Administration, or a new scandal in its ranks, than what the Soviets or the Cubans or their friends were doing. On those occasions when some new revelation about, say, the KGB came to light, its news value was likely to be challenged, sometimes ferociously. European press accounts of KGB involvement in the disarmament movement, for example, had never been reported in *The New York World*. When Hockney had suggested a follow-up piece, his editor had said airily, "Oh, I didn't see those articles." When Hockney offered him the clippings, he had said, "Don't bother. I only read the *World*. Anyway, that stuff is old hat."

"Living in Washington," Julia was saying, "is like breathing with one lung."

He finished leafing through the real estate guide and said, "Columbia County, huh? I guess we could drive up there one weekend."

She hugged him, and soon he was reaching for the bow at the throat of her nightie. She gave him a long, passionate kiss, then drew back.

"Bob," she said shyly, "is it all right if I don't use the diaphragm tonight?"

He stared at her, momentarily perplexed, before he mumbled, "Oh . . . I see."

She turned coy, peeking at him from behind her hair, curling a tress around her little finger.

"Are you sure we're ready?" he fumbled.

"I'll be thirty-two in August," she reminded him. "It mightn't be safe if we go on waiting much longer."

He leaned over and kissed her clumsily on the corner of her mouth.

"I think we're ready," he agreed. "I wasn't sure until now. Yes, I think we're ready. I suppose you'll want to milk our own cow for the baby in Columbia County, huh?"

The room was in seamless darkness when the phone began to shriek, close to Hockney's ear.

"What time is it?" he heard Julia groan.

He switched on the bedside lamp. "Not quite eight," he told her, plucking his watch from the clutter of books and glasses around the phone.

"Yes?" he said into the receiver.

"You are Mr. Robert Hockney? From *The New York World*?" The connection was terrible. The heavily accented voice sounded as if it were bubbling up from underwater.

"Who is this?"

"I speak for the Macheteros."

Hockney merely grunted at first, as if the caller had named the business corporation for which he worked. Then the meaning of the word sank in, and the reporter snapped fully awake. *Los Macheteros*—the Machete Wielders—was a name used by one of the most feared terrorist organizations on the island.

"Yes," Hockney said, grabbing for a note pad.

"I will say this one time only. You will go to Isla Verde. There is a *callejón*—an alleyway—that leads to the beach. On the other side of the road is a discotheque called the Flying Saucer. You know it?"

"No. What the hell is all this about?"

"The disco is easy to find," the caller explained patiently. "Any taxi driver will know it. Go there now. At the end of the alley, there is a trash can. You will find our communiqué there, and proof that this is a serious matter."

"Look, I still don't have the faintest idea what you're talking about."

"Senator Fairchild is the prisoner of the Macheteros. The rest will be explained to you in the communiqué."

There was a sudden click, and Hockney was left listening to a low, monotonous whine.

He climbed out of bed and pulled back the draperies in front of the sliding picture window that covered a whole wall. The sky was almost clear. He looked out through a shimmering haze, over a tiny ruined fort like a broken tooth inside the lip of the bay, toward the ragged skyline of the tourist district. The

33

haze of the tropics filmed everything, so dense, so liquid-seeming that you felt you could rub it between your hands like coconut oil.

"What's going on?" Julia called out to him.

"Someone just called to tell me that Senator Fairchild had been kidnapped," he responded calmly.

"My God!" She sat up in bed, wrapping the sheet around her body like a toga. "What are you going to do?"

"I'm going to check."

So he called the Fortaleza and asked to be put through to the guesthouse. Instead, he was transferred to one of the Governor's secretaries.

"Please put me through to Senator Fairchild," Hockney said. "He's expecting my call."

"I'm sorry, sir. You cannot speak to the Senator right now."

"I assume that is because the Senator has been kidnapped."

There was a pause before the official cleared his throat and said, "I can't comment on that." Then he asked, "How did *you* find out?"

Hockney just said, "Thank you" and hung up.

As they drove out along the wide road known as the Marginal toward Isla Verde, past yellowed, abandoned housing projects, Julia said to Hockney, "Why did they call *you*?"

"I've been trying to figure that out," he said. "Maybe the terrorists got hold of the guest list for the Governor's dinner."

"That doesn't make sense, Bob. We were invited at the last minute."

"That's right," he acknowledged. "I suppose the terrorists could have found out about us from the hotel." He had put the name and address of *The New York World* on the registration card. "Nobody else in town knew we were here."

"Except the other passengers on the *Duchess*," she observed.

"Oh, yes. A typical bunch of Puerto Rican terrorists." He grinned, thinking of the elderly golfers in plaid pants and the bouffant Long Island widows. Then he checked himself, remembering a smoldering Latin girl and a green-eyed American who did not want to talk to strangers. Was it possible that he had rubbed shoulders with the terrorists without realizing it?

They found the disco easily enough. It had been built to look like a flying saucer in a fifties comic book, an aluminum dome with portholes and a dishlike ledge all around. Although the day was just starting, there was already a crowd of Puerto Ricans gambling at an illegal roadside stand. The men were betting on mechanical horses—*caballitos*—that raced each other around a miniature course. They were as excited as if they had been at the track, egging on the favorite to win.

Hockney felt slightly feverish himself as he hurried down the alleyway toward the beach, beside a wall that had been defaced by rival gangs of pop-music lovers. They had daubed their names in red and black paint: "LOS SALSEROS," "LOS ROQUEROS," "LOS COCOLOS." The words were an incomprehensible blur to Hockney as he quickened his stride, so that Julia had to run to keep up. It was disturbing, this sensation of being singled out, of being made responsible, perhaps, for another man's life, without knowing why *he* had been chosen. He wondered whether the anonymous caller was watching him as he rummaged through the trash can at the edge of the sandy beach.

The envelope was inside a crumpled Burger King sack, along with greasy wrapping paper and the remains of a cheeseburger.

Hockney ripped it open. The message was typed on several small sheets of yellow paper. A crude stencil of a revolutionary emblem was at the top of the first page.

"It's in Spanish," he said.

"Here. Let me try," Julia said, taking the communiqué from him. She frowned over the text for a moment, then began to make a summary translation.

"'We, the EPB Macheteros, address ourselves to the people of the United States,'" she interpreted. "'We wish to explain the line of thinking behind the arrest of Senator Joel Fairchild, one of the most notorious defenders of colonialist oppression, by freedom fighters of our movement. In the present historical conjunction, the design of United States imperialism is to convert Puerto Rico, through the mask of statehood, into a secure base for aggression against the free peoples and liberation movements of Cuba and the Caribbean.'"

Hockney sighed. "Why don't they ever spit it out in ten words when a thousand will do?"

"Maybe because their press releases always seem to be written by postgraduate students."

"Let's get to the guts of it," Hockney urged. "What do they want?"

Julia skimmed the rest of the communiqué before settling on a couple of paragraphs close to the end.

"There's a list of political prisoners they want released," she said.

"Puerto Ricans?"

"Some of them. But there are some Weather Underground types too. And there are some names that look Arabic."

"Let me see."

She showed him the place, and Hockney recognized the names of two Palestinians who had been arrested after a bomb attack on the Israeli Mission in New York, as well as the *nom de guerre* of a black militant who was one of the founders of a new group that was threatening to bring "Islamic guerrilla warfare" to the United States.

"It looks as if the Macheteros are pretty eclectic when it comes to choosing their friends," he observed. All together, there were about thirty names on the list of prisoners they wanted released in exchange for Senator Fairchild. "What do they say at the end?"

Sifting through the Marxist jargon, Julia said, "They're making a threat. They say the Fairchild kidnapping is just a beginning. They say the guerrillas will launch a major attack on the symbols of U.S. capitalism in Puerto Rico and on the Mainland unless the statehood proposal is scrapped. There's a lot of stuff about how the movement in Puerto Rico is the vanguard of the liberation fighters throughout the United States. They say the blacks and Hispanics on the Mainland are also living under a

36

colonial system, and that they will all fight shoulder to shoulder."

"Hot air," Hockney said dismissively. "They'd make a better case for themselves if they weren't forever writing Ph.D. theses."

He was about to throw the Burger King sack into the trash can when he realized there was something else inside. He fished out a four-by-six snapshot. The colors were blurred, as if it had been taken with a cheap Polaroid.

He showed it to Julia.

As the flashbulb had caught him, Senator Fairchild's skin appeared chalk-white, apart from the livid purplish welt under his right eye. His eyes were as pink as a pet rabbit's. He was propped up against a bare yellow wall, holding a placard that read, "INDEPENDENCIA O MUERTE." Independence or death.

"That poor man," Julia said softly. "What's going to happen to him?"

"I don't know," Hockney replied. He took her arm and steered her back to the road.

The gamblers playing the *caballitos* were yelling and stamping their feet.

"I'm afraid our vacation is over," he said to her as they boarded the waiting taxi.

As they rode back along the Marginal, the car in front of them stopped without warning. The taxi driver swore as he slammed his foot down on the brake.

Hockney watched a couple of boys with sly old men's faces run up to the man in the car ahead. They were carrying trays of sweet corn.

"*¿Mazol con o sin?*" one of the boys hissed.

"*Con, con,*" the man said impatiently, waving some dollar bills out the window.

The taxi driver turned around and winked.

"You know what that is?"

Hockney and Julia shook their heads.

"You get it *con,* and you get a smoke as well." The taxi driver

37

made the gesture of puffing furiously on a cigarette. When he saw they were still puzzled, he burst out laughing. He obviously thought the whole thing was enormously funny.

Julia caught on first. "Reefers," she said. "They're selling pot."

One of the boys came up to the taxi, and she waved him away. But in a lightning movement, the boy reached into the back seat and grabbed her handbag. He was too fast for Julia, but Hockney, throwing himself across her, managed to grab the boy's wrist and twisted it until he let go of the bag. The boy turned on his heel and fled into the labyrinth of derelict apartment houses beyond the strip of sawgrass and naked baked earth beside the road.

"What a nerve," Julia complained.

"It happen all the time," the driver said, enjoying himself more than ever. "They try with all the *turistas*."

"We were lucky this time," Hockney remarked, patting the envelope on his lap.

The boy had already vanished into the housing project, and Hockney's attention flickered back to the road. A dark green Pontiac was trying to nose its way through the solid columns of traffic moving in the opposite direction, toward Isla Verde and the airport.

He saw a woman framed in the open window on the passenger side. Her slender arm was casually draped along the side. Her face was almost heart-shaped. Though she had tied back her rich black hair in a ponytail and was wearing a loose, nondescript checked shirt, there was no mistaking her. It was the Latin girl Hockney had met on the ship.

"Pretty girl," Julia said, following the direction of Hockney's gaze.

"I met her on the *Duchess*." He leaned forward to the driver on a sudden impulse and said, "Can we turn here? I want to follow that car."

The driver waved his splayed fingers at the bumper-to-bumper traffic streaming past them and looked at Hockney as if he were crazy.

Helplessly, Hockney stared back at the green Pontiac. He could make out only the last two digits of the license plate: 66. Not hard to remember.

"What's got into you now?" Julia was asking. "She isn't *that* pretty."

"Just a hunch," Hockney said. "I thought there might be some connection."

"With *this*?" Julia tapped the envelope they had taken from the trash can.

"I just thought—oh, it's too crazy. Coincidences like that just don't happen. Anyway"—he glanced over his shoulder again—"I've lost her now."

"We'll have to take your fingerprints. You got them all over the fucking communiqué."

"I'm sorry," Hockney said. "It didn't occur to me . . ."

"Don't fuss about it," the FBI man said. "We probably won't find anything anyway. These people know their business."

Hockney was sitting in a paneled office on the top floor of the gray cement fortress in Hato Rey—the Gray Elephant, Bureau people called it. A yellowish laminated card was clipped to his shirt pocket; the words "NON–FBI EMPLOYEE" were printed on it in bold black letters. The man behind the desk did not match Hockney's image of the typical FBI agent. He had longish dark hair that lapped over the collar of his striped cotton shirt. He had sensitive, alert brown eyes, and the profile of an Indian chief. He wore a simple gold bracelet on his right wrist. Frank Parra was one of the few Hispanics who had reached a senior position in the FBI; there were only three hundred fifty of them among the Bureau's eight thousand Agents. As chief of the antiterrorist unit in Puerto Rico, Parra—a Mexican-American from San Antonio—often felt that his task approximated the labor of Sisyphus.

"Tell me this," Parra said: "Why did the terrorists pick *you*?"

"I've been trying to figure that out. The only explanation I can come up with is that they knew I was here. This may sound crazy, but . . ." He described the mysterious couple from

Martinique, and the chance encounter with Rosario on the road from Isla Verde.

Parra seemed extremely interested in the girl. He asked for a full description, and made notes.

"What about the car?" he asked. "Did you get the license number?"

"Just the last two digits. Six-six."

"Okay. We'll run them through the computers." Parra called in an assistant and gave him the instructions. "Now," he said to Hockney, "I want you to take a look at some photographs."

He led the reporter into a large oblong room crowded with desks and filing cabinets. All four walls were covered with mug shots and Identikit pictures, grouped according to membership in the island's five major terrorist networks.

"She's not here," Hockney said after a few minutes.

"I didn't expect she would be," Parra remarked. "If she came via Martinique, it was an outside job. That's one of the favorite routes for people who come here from Havana. That and Santo Domingo."

The assistant came back with a ragged sheet of teletype.

"I think we got something," he said.

Parra glanced at the text. "You were on the right track," he informed Hockney. "The Pontiac is registered to a man who lives in an apartment building five minutes from here. It's a kind of safe house for radicals. One of our informants found a silencer behind a washing machine in the laundry room there last week. I've had my eye on this guy for some time. He came here from the Dominican Republic a year ago—with a circus troupe, if you can believe that. I think he's a Cuban. But so far, we haven't been able to touch him." He looked at Hockney warily. "I wouldn't want to read any of that in *The New York World*," he added.

"This is all off the record," Hockney agreed. "But I'd better tell you, I've already filed a piece on the kidnap. Background stuff on the Senator—the hearings he held on Puerto Rico, that kind of stuff. I guess that's why the terrorists made him a target."

"Maybe," Parra said, noncommittal.

"What's your next move?"

"We'll follow up on your lead, and see if we can pick up the guy with the green Pontiac. But I expect he's flown the coop. *If* the Senator is still alive, they've probably got him in some *bohío* up in the hills, or else they've smuggled him off the island. They used a motorboat last night."

"I suppose the dragnet is out already."

"Oh, sure. And the Bureau is flying in another hundred Agents from the mainland. *And* I'll be lucky if six of them speak Spanish," he added bitterly. "You want to know the real problem? We're coming at this cold. We used to have undercover men inside all these terrorist groups, but we were ordered to pull them out back in '73, and for eight years after that we had virtually no coverage. It hasn't been easy developing new sources. A lot of the people in the local terrorist cells have been clubbing together since they were in school. They don't take kindly to new faces. And when Havana Cubans are in the picture, forget it. That's CIA territory, and the CIA doesn't talk to a brick agent like me. I doubt that the CIA even talks to my Director."

"I'd like to take a look around that apartment building," Hockney said quietly. "I feel sort of—personally involved."

"Your wife worked for the Senator, didn't she?"

"She's with Nancy Fairchild now." The Senator's wife had refused to leave the island until her husband—or her husband's body—was found.

"I think you've done as much as you can," Parra said, not unkindly. "I know your First Amendment rights. But I don't want to catch you in the line of fire, and I don't want you blundering in there tipping people off."

"Well, let me go in with you."

"No way. Listen," the FBI man said, sounding weary now. "You can have your exclusive. You'll be the first reporter to know whatever we find out. But give us time. Okay?"

Hockney nodded.

Julia was sipping her third cup of tea in a private sitting room at La Fortaleza. Ignoring the doctor's advice, Nancy Fairchild was drinking bourbon, on top of the sedatives he had given her. Her makeup, her jewelry, her smartly cut beige suit were all perfectly in place. Only the trembling gave her away. The glass clattered against the table as she set it down.

"I keep getting a funny feeling about this," she said to Julia. "I think it had something to do with all those phone calls."

"What phone calls?" Julia asked gently.

"Joel was involved with something. He never told me what it was. He said he didn't want me to worry my head about those things. I guess he meant I wouldn't understand."

She started to cry, and Julia passed her a wad of Kleenex from her handbag.

"You have no idea what it was about?" Julia pursued.

"It had something to do with the Committee," Nancy Fairchild went on when she had recovered sufficiently. "He would get these phone calls, late at night. I think they were from Miami. He was really excited about it. Once he hung up and said, 'Goddamn, I'm going to nail those bastards now.'"

Miami. Julia thought hard, but could not work out the connection. Maybe Dick Roth, the Committee's chief investigator, would know.

"When did these calls begin?"

"About a week ago."

She thought back. The last thing she remembered, before she and Bob had left on their cruise, was the Senator's disastrous TV appearance in which he had boasted about how the Committee was going to expose the Cuban involvement in the drug traffic.

"Then there were the threats," Nancy was saying.

"What threats?"

"I took one of the calls myself. It was horrible. It was a man saying to tell Joel to drop what he was doing, or else they were going to off him."

"Off him?"

"That's what the man said. Off him."

"Did you call the police? The FBI?"

"Joel said not to. He said it was just another crank. We got calls like that when he took over the Committee." Then she started sobbing again. "What are they going to do with him?" she said. "He's not strong. He had that heart operation a couple of years ago. And he was going to buy me that little ranch near Austin."

They could not have made their intentions more obvious if they had announced them on TV, Frank Parra was thinking as he inspected the scene around the Hato Rey apartment houses. He counted five unmarked cars in which men—some in suits, none of them Puerto Rican—were sitting around with newspapers and coffee cups. A communications van was parked up the road. It was disguised with the logo of a TV-repair company, but it had been stationary for almost two hours, and the residents of Hato Rey did not rate that kind of service. A police helicopter circled overhead.

Back along the roads that led to the housing complex, blockades had been set up, and busloads of FBI Agents and police in full riot gear were waiting for the signal to move in.

Frank Parra had requested permission to move in quietly, with a handful of Puerto Rican Agents who knew the streets. He had been told firmly that the whole operation was being coordinated from Washington, and that he was not to move until the FBI reinforcements from the Mainland had arrived and the whole area around the apartment houses had been secured. Every car crossing the police lines was to be searched.

"You don't understand," Parra had objected. "It's a jungle inside those buildings. Our only hope is to take them by surprise."

But he had been made to wait nearly five hours, until Malone, a New York Irishman with a face like a side of raw beef, arrived to take charge. Malone had announced that he would lead the raid in person, using six of his best men. As a concession to the local field office, he agreed to include Frank Parra in his team.

Kids—none of them older than twelve—jeered and made faces at them as they walked through the grimy lobby to the elevator.

"The *New* FBI," someone called out, parodying a popular TV series. An angelic-looking girl, about six or seven, came up to Malone, smiled and spat a gray wad of gum onto one of his diligently polished wing-tips. Malone swallowed, stuck out his big jaw and led the way into the elevator.

It stopped just below the eighth floor, and the FBI men had to wait for the two Agents who had been detailed to take the stairs before they could prise the doors open. Malone made an undignified exit on hands and knees.

"That was no accident," Malone grouched.

Frank Parra was engaged in checking the corridor. The disabled elevator would have made the perfect scene for an ambush. But the corridor was deserted except for Malone's team and a sleek, bespectacled man in a white shirt and tie who was walking briskly toward them.

"I represent the board of these condominiums," the lawyer said to the FBI men. "I assume that you have a search warrant."

"Show him, Parra," Malone growled.

"This entitles you to enter apartment Eight-G," the lawyer observed. "It does not entitle you to enter any other apartment without the tenant's permission."

"Go screw yourself," Malone said.

Malone was wearing one of those earphones which nobody ever mistakes for a hearing aid.

"Alpha Two," he muttered into the microphones strapped to his chest. "Have we got the roof and the fire escape covered?"

"Affirmative," the voice came back over the earphone.

"You better get the hell out of here," Frank Parra said to the lawyer as he steadied his gun with both hands.

Then Malone was banging on the door of 8-G.

"What's the scumbag's name?" he hissed to Parra.

"Hernández."

"Hernández!" Malone roared. "This is the F-B-I. Come out with your hands above your head!"

44

There was no response.

"Break it down," Malone ordered the burliest of his Agents.

"Hold on just a second," Parra interjected. He reached forward and tried the handle. It turned smoothly, and the door was open.

"Stand clear," Malone commanded. "It could be a trap."

In the next instant, Malone was inside the apartment, swinging his automatic in front of him in a broad arc.

The place seemed deserted. One of the drawers from a cabinet was lying upside-down on the floor, as if someone had tipped its contents out in a hurry.

Malone followed his gun into the kitchen, then the bedroom. There was a pile of soiled clothes in the bottom of a closet, but the hangers were empty.

"The bastard's gone," Malone announced.

"I think you'd better come and look at this." Frank Parra's voice, sober and restrained, filtered through from the bathroom.

Malone slammed the door of the bedroom closet shut and hurried to join him.

Senator Joel Fairchild was propped up in the bath. His hands, frozen in rigor mortis, still clutched the placard that read, "INDEPENDENCIA O MUERTE."

"Sweet Jesus," Malone breathed. "Would you mind closing his eyes?"

"He died of a heart attack," Frank Parra told Hockney on the telephone that evening. "After they gave him the third degree. There were some burn marks on the soles of his feet, and blood under one of his nails. It's not hard to figure out what they did to him."

"What *I* can't figure out," Hockney said, "is why they held him in that apartment house, and why they left the body there. They must have known you were watching those buildings. And now the whole thing is tied to this guy you think is a Cuban."

"Hernández. Paco Hernández. Yeah. Well, they haven't lost anything so far. He's just vanished clean off the radarscope. Nobody in the building knows anything, of course. Maybe they

45

couldn't be bothered to dump the body somewhere else. But I get the feeling they *wanted* us to find Fairchild that way."

"I don't understand."

"Well, one interpretation might be, they wanted to show us up. All those cops and FBI Agents to pick up a stiff."

"What about the ransom demands? If they'd hidden the body, they could have tried to bluff for a while."

"I don't know for sure," Parra admitted; "but I'm not convinced that getting those prisoners freed was the terrorists' main objective. Why would the Cubans send in outside hit men for that?"

"What's your theory?"

"I think the guys who did this had some more important score to settle with Fairchild, and they used outside professionals to make sure the job was done right."

The FBI man sounded exhausted. Hockney heard him yawn at the other end of the line.

"Let me ask one thing more," the reporter said. "Did you find out anything more about the girl? Or Mitch Lardner?"

"We checked on all the flights that left San Juan today. One of the airline people remembers a girl who could fit that description of this Rosario. She took a plane to Miami. Whatever name she's using, it isn't Lardner. That's not for publication."

"Okay. But can I use the stuff about a possible Cuban link?"

"As long as you don't quote me. And you better remember, we've got nothing to nail it down. It's just a theory."

"Have you got anything on the guy who rented the apartment where the body was found? Hernández?"

"Check with me tomorrow," Parra said. "Maybe you'll hear something first. *You're* the one the Macheteros seem to be calling."

Hockney put the receiver back in its cradle and looked at Julia. Her face was pale and strained. Her makeup was furrowed by tears. She had finally broken down when she heard about the discovery of Fairchild's corpse, seeming to blame herself for having talked about the Senator with such bored disdain the night before his death.

46

Hockney picked up the phone again and gave the operator the *World*'s number in New York. He checked through his scribbled notes as he dictated an update on the Fairchild investigation for the morning edition.

When he had finished, Julia said, "Maybe this has nothing to do with Puerto Rico at all."

"What do you mean?"

"Nancy Fairchild told me that Joel was involved in something new, something connected with Miami. A man was calling him late at night. And Nancy said he started getting death threats over the last week. Somebody wanted to silence him."

"Has she told anyone else about this?"

"I don't know."

Hockney's mind started working fast. He remembered the last phone bill they had got from Ma Bell, the one he had complained about to Julia because it included about fifteen calls she had made to her college roommate, now living in London. Every long-distance call had been itemized.

"If there's anything to that Miami story, it's easy enough to check out," he said thoughtfully.

"I guess Nancy's going to fly back to Texas with her husband's body."

"No," Julia replied, "she said something about needing to tidy up in Washington."

Hockney held out the receiver to Julia and said, "Let's find out."

"Bob, it's awfully late."

"Let's try," he insisted. "I doubt that she'll be sleeping much tonight."

Chapter

2

WASHINGTON, D.C.

On board the 8 A.M. flight to Baltimore–Washington International, Hockney read through the story that ran under his own by-line on the front page of *The New York World*. It was accompanied by a grim photograph of Senator Fairchild's body being hustled out of an Hato Rey apartment house on a stretcher. Hockney was mildly surprised to find that the material he had phoned in late from the hotel had survived intact, including the bit about possible Cuban involvement in the Senator's kidnap and death. He guessed that Ed Finkel, the *World*'s Managing Editor, had been ending his weekend in Sag Harbor when the Monday edition was put to bed.

"Mind if I take a look?" The stocky man in the first-class seat next to Hockney's leaned across as the reporter stuffed the newspaper into the pocket in front of him. Hockney's neighbor was the Secret Service agent who had been assigned to escort Nancy Fairchild back to Washington. At the start of the flight he had been sitting next to the Senator's widow, two rows back in the smoking section, but Julia had persuaded him to swap places.

Hockney surrendered his copy of the *World* to the Secret Service man and got up to stretch his legs. He glanced back and saw Nancy Fairchild ask the stewardess for a Bloody Mary. He caught Julia's eye, and she responded with a quick little nod.

They dodged the cameramen who were waiting at the airport

and drove together in the Senator's limousine to the Fairchilds' apartment in Watergate East.

The library was hot and stuffy. The stale aroma of the Senator's cigars clung to the heavy green draperies. The household mail that had come while the Fairchilds were away was neatly stacked on the desk. One of the piles, Hockney saw, was of telegrams and hand-delivered letters of condolence.

"Millicent, at the office, used to deal with all these awful bills," Nancy sighed as she riffled through a sheaf of envelopes. "But I insisted on handling everything myself after the wedding. Lord, I don't know how I'm going to manage now."

It took her a couple of minutes to find the blue-striped envelope from the telephone company. Nancy handed it to Julia, who slit it open carefully with the gold paper knife on the Senator's desk. The Fairchilds' monthly phone bill, she noticed, totaled more than nine hundred dollars. The itemized list of long-distance calls covered about twenty slips of paper.

Julia took a pen and circled all the calls to Miami. She found that six different numbers in the 305 area were listed.

"I'm going to freshen up," Nancy announced.

"Do you mind if we use your phone?" Hockney asked.

"Use whatever you want. The booze is in that cabinet, under the bookcase."

Methodically, Hockney started dialing the Miami numbers in the order in which they were listed. On his first try, he got through to the receptionist at a real estate company in Coral Gables. Other numbers belonged to a bank, a local TV station and the Mayor's office.

On his fifth call, Hockney was answered by a woman's voice that said, "Miami Police Department."

He hung up and asked Julia, "Why would the Senator be talking to the Miami police?"

"I have no idea. I guess it could have something to do with the Committee."

Hockney tried the last number, and got an answering machine.

The recorded message was without frills. "This is Jay Maguire," it announced. "Leave your name and number and I'll get back to you." It was a not unpleasant no-nonsense kind of voice, slightly constricted, as if the speaker were chewing gum.

"Maguire," Hockney reflected aloud. "Does that sound like a cop's name to you?"

"Either that or a saloon," Julia responded.

Hockney dialed the Miami Police Department again. "Do you have a Jay Maguire?" he asked the telephonist.

"Hold on." After a short pause, the woman's voice came back and said, "Would that be Sergeant Maguire in Patrol?"

"I guess so."

"He's on duty. Would you care to leave a message?"

"Thank you. I'll call back later." It struck Hockney that if the police sergeant was the man who had been trying to protect his anonymity by phoning the Senator late in the evening at home, he might be less than overjoyed at finding a message on his blotter from a *World* reporter.

"Well?" Julia said.

"I think we found the night caller."

MIAMI

Sergeant Maguire came on duty a little before 2 P.M., and his partner, Wilson Martinez, could see at once that something was wrong. Maguire was hyped, bouncing around on the balls of his feet like a prizefighter limbering up for the big event. The Sergeant slammed the door of the white Plymouth, crouched into the wheel and gunned the car out of the lot behind Police Headquarters as if they were making a getaway. Maguire liked to do the driving himself, even if he *was* a sergeant.

"What's eating you, Jay?" the Cuban cop asked casually. "Did your girl stand you up last night?" He knew that Maguire had been chasing a pretty redhead—he always went for redheads—who worked behind the Hertz counter at the airport.

"Mind your own fucking business."

Now Martinez sensed that something was *really* wrong. Jay

Maguire—handsome in a lean, roughneck way—was usually coarsely good-humored about the ups and downs of his energetic sex life. There was no competition between the two cops on that score. Maguire, in his early thirties, was a bachelor, and planned to stay that way. Martinez, five years younger, was happily married, with two small kids.

The dispatcher's voice crackled over the radio.

"Three-fifty," she rapped out the number of their cruiser. "Proceed to Six-three-six Southwest First Street. Baby reported dead."

"QSL," Maguire acknowledged.

The patrol car screeched to a halt outside a three-story tenement with a peeling sign that read "FARM ROOMING HOUSE." As the policemen got out, half a dozen people squatting and standing around the stoop stared at them with eyes of cold hate. A pallid, unwashed girl with black grease marks on her hollow cheeks was trying to nurse a baby. She looked like a rag doll abandoned on a garbage dump. Several unshaven, shirtless black men were passing around a can of beer. One of them was puffing on a reefer that he did not trouble to conceal.

Sergeant Maguire walked over to them.

"You guys know anything about a dead baby?"

Nobody spoke.

"Shit. Wilson, you try."

Martinez repeated the question in Spanish. A man in a straw hat said something and motioned for the policemen to follow him around the back of the building and up some rickety stairs to the top floor.

"This guy says he's the manager," Martinez told Maguire.

The fetid stench of urine and excrement assailed Maguire before he reached the landing.

He appraised a blistered corridor with rotting, splintered floorboards. It was lit by a single naked bulb. Five rooms opened off either side. The man in the straw hat pointed to one of the few that had a door.

"*Aquí.*" The manager thumped on the door with the flat of his huge hand, and it came off its hinge.

51

Scores of startled cockroaches took shelter behind the strips of damp, flaking wallpaper and in the dark corners behind three bare, yellow-stained mattresses on wooden frames. There was no plumbing, no window and no other furniture in the room. Only a pile of soiled clothing on the floor. And a red plastic bucket.

From the doorway, Maguire could see the soles of two tiny feet protruding above the lip of the bucket.

He looked inside the bucket. It was half-full of urine. The baby's head and shoulders were fully submerged. Maguire guessed the dead infant was ten, maybe twelve months old. A girl.

"Like this?" he challenged the empty room. When he turned back to his partner, Martinez saw that his fists were clenched so tight the knuckles showed white.

"Call Homicide," he ordered the Cuban cop.

While Martinez went back to the cruiser to make the call, the Sergeant tried to construct a picture of what had caused the baby's death. He inspected the solitary bathroom that did service for the whole building, and needed no further explanation of why most of the rooms had urine pails.

When Martinez came back to interpret, he was able to prise a few scraps of information out of the man in the straw hat. The baby's parents were Haitians. The father had split a few months earlier. The mother had not been seen for days. But the mother's brother was in the building.

They found the uncle among the gaggle of Cuban and Haitian refugees that had gathered on the landing to see what all the fuss was about. The Haitian—a boy of sixteen or seventeen—was naked except for a pair of torn shorts, a red headband and an incongruously opulent gold pendant on a chain around his neck. The boy had the sinewy grace of an antelope, and an antelope's imploring, unmenacing eyes. He spoke only Creole, and Martinez had trouble communicating with him in pidgin French. The manager slapped the boy, as if to encourage him to speak, and he cringed in a way that suggested he was used to being abused.

Maguire grabbed the manager's shoulders and pushed him away.

"Jesus," the Sergeant swore, "what the hell is the matter with these guys?"

"Easy, Jay," his partner cautioned.

"I'm asking you, what's wrong with these people?" Maguire's angry look took in the whole crowd that had assembled at the top of the steps, idly curious and unfriendly.

"I know, I know," Martinez said softly. "Remember I got kids myself."

"Then ask this one"—the Sergeant pointed to the Haitian—"where the fuck the mother is."

The boy had only a precarious sense of time. He was unsure whether his sister had disappeared that day, or the day before, or the day before that. He had no idea where she was. He thought that the baby's father was dead.

Maguire ruled out murder. He could visualize, in uncomfortable detail, what must have happened. He could see the baby's mother, spaced out on drugs, abandoning her baby to look for her next fix. He could see the baby crawling to the edge of the bed, rolling over, drowning in the bucket of piss. He could see the mother coming back hours later, finding her child dead, panicking and running away—to one of a thousand other hellholes in Miami no better and no worse than the Farm Rooming House.

His partner, watching his anger turn into a cold, set expression of bitterness and pain, was more worried about Maguire than he had been at the start of the shift. One of the conditions for being able to carry on in their job, both policemen knew, was to be able to place a wall of indifference between yourself and what happened on the streets. When that wall cracked, so did you.

So when they were back in the cruiser, and Maguire said, "We're spitting into a sewer. You know that?" his partner just nodded and shook another cigarette out of his pack.

They were driving through Overtown, a section of Miami some twenty-five blocks long by ten wide, only a few minutes away from Police Headquarters. It was a jumble of clapboard shacks, falling tenements and corrugated-iron shanties. It had no movie houses, but plenty of shooting houses—deserted dwellings where users converged to shoot up heroin. The expression was an ominous *double entendre,* since according to the records kept in Room 512—the Crimes Against Persons unit at Police Headquarters—there had been at least one murder committed on every street corner in Overtown over the previous five years. The district had a few sleazy hotels with preposterous names, like the Imperial, mostly frequented by black and white hookers turning ten-dollar tricks. The claptrap bars had names like Honey Pot or Busy Bee.

Overtown had its fortress, at 1130 Northwest Second Avenue. Street people and cops called it simply The Hole, as in Black Hole of Calcutta. It was a vast, three-story U-shaped pile whose original color was pink. It was not defended by ramparts or battlements, but by a teeming, impenetrable wall of humanity. Impenetrable, that is, to members of the Miami Police Department. By night, people seemed to hang from every window or balcony. The gap between the two arms of the U swarmed with hundreds of pushers and users, defended by a phalanx of black youths all along the sidewalks. Rich white kids who ventured down Second Avenue to buy their dope did not have to stop their sports cars to take delivery. Rounding the corner by Annie's Grocery Store, the customer would simply flash a hand signal, showing how many packages he wanted by the number of fingers raised. By the time he reached the next corner, leaving The Hole safely behind, he had paid over his money and collected his dope.

Maguire never stopped his car when passing The Hole.

"Ro-Ro, Roll-Roller."

He heard the steady murmur growing louder, building into a warning, threatening chorus as he rounded the corner past Annie's Grocery Store.

"Roll-Roller!"

It was the expression the black street people used to signal that cops were approaching. Maguire guessed that it had probably originated in the huddles of black men you saw shooting craps on street corners. Rolling dice for money was supposedly illegal. All Maguire ever did about it was roll down a window and yell, "Pick them up!" or "I saw that!" The gesture, he knew, was probably worse than useless. It helped to underline the fact that the police were not going to take action over all sorts of minor felonies, even when they were being committed in plain view. You don't bother with KEEP OFF THE GRASS signs in the jungle.

Because of the race riots in the spring of 1980, Liberty City had been publicized all over the world as one of America's worst black ghettos. By comparison with Overtown, Maguire thought, Liberty City was a reasonably safe neighborhood. Maguire himself had been born on the fringes of Liberty City. It was a mixed neighborhood—black, Irish, Hispanic—and a rough one. Maguire had learned to fight long before the River Rats accepted him as one of their gang. He had had his first serious encounter with the cops when he was eight, when he had raided the family refrigerator and pelted a passing patrol car with eggs. His father had disappeared a few years later, leaving his mother to raise five kids on her own. He had started ripping off cars to supplement the welfare checks.

So, though he rode in the patrol car with "SERGEANT" painted on its flank, Maguire was conscious that there was still an umbilical cord between him and the street people. It helped him to recognize the "bad guys," to know if they were "dirty" or not, to intuit their next move before they made it. If fate had worked differently, he could have stayed one of them himself.

Now Maguire was scanning the crowd that was milling around outside The Hole. He spotted a youth he had picked up a few weeks before, after a liquor-store holdup. He saw Blue, one of the neighborhood enforcers, a black giant dressed all in blue, from his floppy hat to his denims and suede shoes. And he saw a small group of blacks in berets and white skullcaps. One of them, a man of slightly less than middling height with fine, smooth features and a chin beard, was wearing smartly pressed khakis.

"There's the Jamaican," Martinez said, pointing to him.

"I see him."

"What's he doing in The Hole? Those people aren't into that Islamic guerrilla shit. They're into smack."

"Maybe the Jamaican wants to change that."

Maguire decided to take a second look. He cruised around the block and drove slowly back past The Hole. The Jamaican and his friends were rigging up some kind of public-address system and handing out flyers. The Jamaican tapped the mike and said, "Brothers." A few of the youths on the street gathered round to listen.

"Brothers," he boomed, standing too close to the mike, so that the words were almost unintelligible, like a roll of thunder, "we are all the victims of economic genocide. The only answer to genocide in America is guerrilla war. We will fight it with shotguns and handguns and gasoline bombs and knives and razors and steel clubs and our bare fists. These are our only tools of defense. But we will only win if we got *discipline*. It's not cool to go out without planning and dog a cop or rip off a store. You gotta have planning. The Black Fedayeen are here to give you that planning. You gotta raise your spiritual and political consciousness, brothers. You gotta get it together. We're the ones who can help you, because we are part of a world movement and we are carrying out the laws of the Holy Koran."

"Holy shit," Martinez said. "He doesn't sound like a Jamaican."

"He was born in Kingston," Maguire said, "but he grew up in this country. Gets around, though. I heard he spent a lot of time in Cuba. Now he calls himself Commander Ali."

"What's with this Islamic bullshit he's spouting? This is Miami, not Beirut."

"That's what *you* say," Maguire commented.

"But the blacks around here have never been into this guerrilla-war stuff," Martinez protested. "I don't believe they'll buy it."

"Maybe," the Sergeant said, noncommittal. "But the Jamaican's sure doing a selling job."

As they drove on, the man who called himself Commander Ali was scything the air with his arms. The spectacle deepened Maguire's sense of unease. It seemed that everywhere you looked in the city, someone was working to create trouble, as if the dopers and the crime wave were not already enough. While the Black Fedayeen toured Liberty City and Overtown, no less violent groups—from the pro-Castro left to the near-fascist right—were trying to whip up support within the Cuban community and the other Latin American exile populations, and he sensed a vigilante mood among some of the Anglos. The city had received its warning in 1980, when Liberty City had been set ablaze. The politicians observed a polite consensus not to talk about the chance that race riots could be sparked off again. But Maguire, who had watched a white kid's brains spilled out—the color of sausage meat gone off—because he was driving in a black neighborhood at the wrong time, and had witnessed a force of impersonal hate deeper than even he, who knew the streets, could have imagined, recognized that the tinder was still there, and that it would become drier and more flammable day by day through the long, hot summer.

In a dusk that was grainy, like gunpowder, they pulled into El Pub, opposite Domino Square. Martinez ordered steak *cebollado*, while Maguire nursed a can of Iron Beer. Despite the name, and the picture of a musclebound type pumping iron on the label, the drink was nonalcoholic. Maguire drank enough off duty to compensate for his enforced temperance on the job.

"Did you hear the latest on that Senator they killed in Puerto Rico?" Martinez asked, to make conversation.

"What?"

"Some of the guys were talking about it at Headquarters. They say there were Cubans involved, and they could be here in Miami."

Maguire grunted, as if the subject bored him stiff.

"This Senator Fairchild said he had the goods on Castro and the drug business," Martinez persisted. "Maybe that's why they offed him."

"Maybe."

Maguire had no reason to distrust his partner. He liked Martinez, and he believed him when he lapsed into long harangues about the evils of the Castro regime. "If the Americans ever try a serious invasion of Cuba," Martinez had declared to him once, "I'm gonna be the first guy on the first boat." The father of the Cuban cop had been killed in the Bay of Pigs, and the family had lost all its money in the Revolution. There was no doubting Martinez' animus against Fidel. But he was naive about some things. You had to rely on your partner. That was the first rule of survival for a cop on the streets. But you didn't have to share everything with your partner, and Maguire had not shared with Martinez the knowledge that weighed heavier since he had heard the news of Senator Fairchild's death.

It was out of character for Maguire to have made up his mind to confide in the Senator. Fairchild was a politician, and the cop had no time, in general, for politicians. But he had watched Fairchild on TV, and decided that the Senator was seriously bent on getting to the bottom of the drug problem. The cop had known he was taking a risk. The least part of that risk was that if the higher-ups in the Department found out, they might take away his badge. It had never occurred to him that he was putting the Olympian Senator Fairchild in danger too.

"Hey, look," Martinez interrupted his thoughts. "There goes Mr. Big."

Maguire looked out through the window of the restaurant and saw a car progressing at a leisurely pace along Calle Ocho. At a conservative estimate, the car must have cost the equivalent of Maguire's salary for four years, including overtime. It was a Rolls-Royce Corniche, and as if to advertise its value, its owner had had it painted the color of champagne.

Maguire did not miss the undertone of respect, even admiration, in the Cuban cop's tough-guy language. The owner of the champagne-colored Rolls, Julio Parodi, was a big man in every respect in Little Havana. It was his money that paid for the paramilitary gear and training camps and bungalow headquarters of the newest and most extreme of the anti-Castro exile groups, the Brigada Azul, or Blue Brigade.

As he watched the car, Maguire could make out the mass of Parodi's chauffeur/bodyguard, "Mama" Benitez, in the front seat, and the glow of his master's burning cigar in the back. For an instant, he saw Parodi's profile: the shag of gray hair, the cruel beak of a nose, the long, wedge-shaped chin, the sagging flesh of his jowls and his gut, under the folds of his silk shirt. At that moment, he felt an insane impulse to run out into the street and stand face to face with this man who had come to embody—in his waking thoughts and even in his dreams—the sickness that was overpowering the city.

Mr. Big, as Wilson Martinez had called him, was one of the most successful cocaine lords in Miami. Parodi's network extended from street-corner pushers in Overtown and Little Havana to suppliers in Colombia and Bolivia. His profits had bought him the controlling share in a local bank, a couple of restaurants, a real estate development and an arms company— Camagüey Internacional, which was selling weapons all over the hemisphere. His take enabled him to sustain a lifestyle that included three penthouse condominiums in Key Biscayne, a yacht and a private jet, and a stable of fancy hookers.

His money and his connections had also bought Julio Parodi immunity from the law, at least until now. That was the root of Sergeant Maguire's obsession.

Maguire had once had a friend in the Intelligence Unit who had tried to zero in on Parodi. The friend found a confidential informant—CI in police jargon—who was ready to betray the doper because he had been cut out of a deal. True to procedure, the friend had filed a photograph of his CI in the Intelligence Unit's archives. The next day, the picture was gone, presumably "borrowed" by someone else at Police Headquarters. By the

59

end of the week, the CI had vanished off the face of the earth and the investigator had been transferred to Fort Lauderdale.

When he found his own CI, Maguire ran her by himself; no photographs on file, no compromising reports. Gloria was a five-hundred-a-night hooker who mostly circulated between the Omni and the new Holiday Inn, where the party rooms had appropriately been dubbed "Bogotá" and "Colombia." Maguire had first encountered Gloria before she made the big league. A year or so before, he had responded to a dispatcher's report of a sexual battery in progress at a seedy motel on Biscayne Boulevard. When he broke through the locked door, he found a naked girl sobbing on the floor, her legs and hands lashed together with a belt and torn strips of sheet. Her deranged client—a traveling salesman from Cleveland—was laboriously attempting to unravel a wire coat hanger.

Maguire knocked out the salesman with a clean blow from the butt of his revolver.

"What the fuck did he plan to do with the coat hanger?" Maguire had asked Gloria afterward.

"He said he was going to hang me."

Gloria was eighteen then—or so she claimed—a curvy redhead who had run away from a mom-and-dad grocery store near Lake Okeechobee. On her mother's side, she was three parts Seminole. The wacko had roughed her up badly, but not badly enough to spoil her looks or deter her from pursuing her trade. Since then, she had moved a long way upscale.

Gloria had an obvious way of showing gratitude, and Jay Maguire hadn't rejected it. After all, she was a redhead. She also told him that he was the only man she had known since she was fourteen who was able to make her come, and he chose to believe her.

As her circle of clients expanded to include big-time drug traffickers and the pilots who humped their consignments from airstrips in Colombia and the Bahamas, Maguire had realized Gloria's potential as a snitch. He had still not been prepared for the devastating information that she brought him on Julio Parodi.

Two months earlier, he had been sitting sipping a *cafecito* with Martinez at the Dockside Terrace when the dispatcher called through on his Motorola.

"There's a lady who wants you to call, urgent," the dispatcher reported. "You better hurry up. It could be a two."

The female dispatchers were not supposed to know about "taking a 2." In the vernacular of the Patrol Unit, that meant fucking on the City's time.

"Never heard of a two," Maguire had responded, jollying the dispatcher along. "But I might ask her to show me."

Gloria had something more pressing than a 2. She explained that she had spent the night, after a party at Parodi's private apartment on Key Biscayne, with an aging former Air America pilot. After a sufficient number of Scotches, the pilot had blabbed about how he was being paid to do something he had never attempted before—to land a 727 on a highway by night. In the course of their cavorting, Gloria had wheedled the information out of him that he meant Highway 27, near the entrance to Everglades National Park. Her companion had said he would see her before the week was out to celebrate.

Maguire had passed on the lead to a contact in the FBI, refusing to reveal his source. For three days and nights, Dade County police and FBI Agents had staked out the location. Finally, at 3 A.M., they had watched four cars position themselves on either side of the highway, at two-hundred-yard intervals, a mile from the entrance to the Park. The car headlights marked out a makeshift landing strip.

Within half an hour, a battered 727 that might have been one of the first ever built lumbered to a stop just beyond the lights of the last car. A container truck backed up to the cargo doors in the side of the plane. The cops waited until the unloading was complete before they moved in.

They met no resistance from the men around the plane, who included Mama Benitez, Parodi's chauffeur. They dragged open the doors of the truck and slit open one of the sacks inside, then several more. They contained Colombian coffee beans. Not coffee mixed up with cocaine: just coffee. All they could do

61

was book the pilot for making an unauthorized landing.

The FBI made an official complaint, which filtered down to Maguire via the Chief's office. He knew then that Parodi had been tipped off. He had no way of finding out whether the leak had come from inside the Bureau or from one of the other agencies. But he realized that Parodi's network was operating at higher levels than the street cops who were on the take—cops like the black patrolman he had met one night in the Grove who was openly flaunting a diamond-studded Rolex Presidential, retail value eighteen thousand bucks. And he was grateful that at least he had had the sense to protect Gloria's identity.

It had crossed Maguire's mind at that point that Parodi's survival capacity might be due to more than his money and the people it could buy. He had sneaked a look at the patchy file on the drug lord at Police Headquarters, and seen that the clue might lie in Parodi's early history. Born twenty years before Castro's revolution, Parodi had fled the island within months of its triumph. He had returned with the lost band that fought at the Bay of Pigs. Parodi had then spent a couple of years in a Cuban jail. After he was ransomed by the U.S. Government— which bought the freedom of Bay of Pigs veterans with food and tractors—he bobbed up in the middle of the civil war in the Congo as a contract pilot for the CIA. Home again in the late sixties, he had become a familiar presence in the bars of Key West and Marathon, leaving the impression that he was mixed up in the covert paramilitary missions that the CIA was running out of the Florida Keys.

About the same time that Maguire was graduated from the Police Academy, Parodi had set about using his specialized skills to make himself one of the richest men in South Florida. Parodi had built up his seed money, so rumor had it, by flying bales of marijuana from the Guajira peninsula in Colombia. He was soon smuggling more expensive cargo—cocaine and heroin—and earning two hundred thousand dollars for a single run.

It was the CIA connection that puzzled and fascinated Maguire. Parodi openly boasted about it to Gloria and the other girls in his stable, and with his drinking cronies at the Mutiny Room. It was impossible to tell for sure whether Parodi was still working for the Agency or trying to use the CIA for a cover. The CIA link might explain the doper's seeming invulnerability. It was as if some unseen hand were always there to shield Parodi from the consequences of his actions.

Maguire had been wrestling with all of this when Gloria had brought him something even more intriguing than the tale of the 727 flight. About ten days before, she had called him to a rendezvous at her shabby apartment—littered with pricy electronic gadgets and hot-pink love cushions—on Biscayne. The hooker told Maguire that she had been at another party at Parodi's place, and that this time she had been paid to entertain one of his Caribbean friends.

"He was black," she told the cop. "Well, almost black. He went at it like a jackhammer."

"Spare me the details. Where was he from?"

"That's the funny part. He was from Havana."

"You mean, he came out on a boat or something?"

"No, Havana Havana," Gloria insisted. "He was going back there."

"You're sure?"

"Sure I'm sure. I think he had a trip arranged for Julio, too."

"Are you saying that Parodi is going to Cuba?" Maguire had asked in stunned disbelief. The idea didn't exactly square with the doper's public involvement in the most violently anti-Castro movement in Miami.

"Yeah. The way they talked, I think he's been there before. Now," Gloria had said, "do I get a prize?"

Maguire had spent the better part of that night trying to make sense of what Gloria had told him. If Parodi was traveling to Cuba, that meant he was conning his rightist friends in Little Havana. It could mean he was working undercover for the CIA—or for Castro's people. Either way, it strongly suggested that the Cubans must know about his drug operations, and might be actively supporting them.

It was at that stage that he had happened to catch Senator

Fairchild's appearance on *Meet the Press*. The Senator talked about Castro's drug involvement with such vehemence that the Miami cop began to feel that for once, a politician might be an ally. His first, tentative phone call to the Senator had reinforced that impression. The Senator had agreed to deal with him personally, and not to bring in his staff. Maguire had been feeding him bits and pieces over the past week. Now the Senator was dead, and as he watched the taillights of Parodi's Rolls receding into the distance along Calle Ocho, Maguire could not suppress the instinct that there was a connection there too.

"I want some action," Maguire announced to his partner as he rose from the table. "It might be a good night to hit some of those Mariel bars."

"I'm still eating," Martinez protested.

"Aw, come on. You'll get fat on that rice and beans and your wife won't let you make any more babies."

He used his walkie-talkie to call up the other three cars in his squad and told the drivers to meet him at the usual rendezvous: the parking lot at the northeast gate of the Orange Bowl.

The eight cops assembled around the hood of the Sergeant's car.

"Hey, Magic," Maguire said to Andy Riggs, the senior patrolman in Car 352. "Where's your vest?"

"It's too hot, man. It slows me down."

They had had the same dialogue before. Riggs was not the only patrol officer in the squad who detested having to wear the regulation-issue bulletproof vest, which covered chest, back and groin.

"What about you, Linda?" Maguire turned to the black patrolman's partner, a rookie girl fresh out of the Academy. "Are you wearing your vest, or is all of that real?"

Linda looked about half as tall as Magic, and three times as wide. She was into weight lifting, and her biceps, when she flexed them, were as thick as Maguire's thighs. She could hit a softball three hundred yards.

"Want to feel me and see?" She spoke around a wad of gum,

her lower jaw relentlessly grinding back and forth.

"Not on the City's time, honey."

When Maguire was satisfied that everyone was wearing his flak jacket, he started the briefing.

"Okay," the Sergeant said, "we're going to hit a few bars and see how many handguns we can pick up tonight. Last week you guys were a little slow. I want to see you rookies go through those doors, front and back, in five seconds flat. Pepe"—he turned to one of the Cuban patrolmen—"tell us what's jumping tonight."

"I saw a couple of guys who looked dirty outside Brindi's. There was a shoot-out at Sugar Shack last night. And a robbery at River Inn. There's a lot of guys in Molino Rojo. Take your pick."

"We'll take them all," ruled Maguire. "Let's start with Sugar Shack. Magic'll like that. They got go-go girls."

"Lead me to them, Sarge. These night shifts have really been screwing up my sex life."

"Aw, Linda," Wilson Martinez ribbed Magic's partner. "You been givin' Magic a hard time?"

"I wouldn't want it soft."

The Cubans Maguire's team was set to visit were not the old-established residents of Little Havana. They were *marielitos*— or, as the cops had abbreviated the expression, "Mariels." In the spring and summer of 1980, Fidel Castro had flung open the tiny seaport of Mariel to a new exodus of Cuban refugees. Hundreds of boats had set off from Florida to ferry them to a new life in the United States. In Miami, the Cuban community waited to receive them with open arms. It took the Americans several weeks before they began to realize that there was something different in kind between the Mariel exodus and previous boatlifts and airlifts of refugees from Cuba.

For the most part, the earlier refugees from Castro's revolution had become hardworking, law-abiding, patriotic U.S. citizens, ready and eager to look after their own. Everyone was shocked to discover that among the one hundred twenty-five thousand *marielitos* who made it to the United States were not only several thousand probable Castro agents, but some five thousand hardened criminals and psychiatric cases who had been taken directly from their jails and asylums to the docks. Castro had hit upon a diabolically simple way of achieving the Stalinist goal of social prophylaxis: by dumping Cuba's human refuse—murderers, rapists, psychotics beyond redemption—on the United States.

In Miami, *these* Mariels had spawned a new subculture. It had driven older, respectable Cuban residents out of many side streets off Calle Ocho, and frightened Anglos—the term used in South Florida for everyone who is neither Hispanic or black—out of the city altogether. The crime rate in Miami had doubled in the year after the Mariels began to arrive, and most people believed that *they* were the reason.

Maguire's routine work on his nightly shifts had doubled too, he reflected grimly as he shepherded his little convoy into a side alley, discreetly out of the line of sight from the door of the Sugar Shack. Lights flashed on and off around its garish pink sign. "ALL-NUDE GO-GO GIRLS," it advertised. The strains of an old rock-and-roll number blared out into the street from the jukebox inside.

Maguire waited outside, sneaking a peek through the door, to allow time for the rest of the squad, led by Magic, to slip around the back. He could see two dozen male customers, their backs to the bar, watching an aging blonde with sagging bosom and heavy thighs gyrating clumsily to the music. Several wilting *putas* were sitting among the men, pressing them to order more drinks.

No one reacted at first when the police burst into the bar through both doors. When they noticed the blue uniforms, some of the men moved like automatons, swinging around slowly to face the bar, leaning against it, legs spread-eagled, waiting to be searched. Others, who had not been through the routine before, raised their hands nervously. Maguire could tell the recent arrivals among them from the new blue jeans they were wearing. Some of the customers were too drunk or too high to know what was going on and had to be ordered and prodded into place.

The boss of the Sugar Shack turned off the jukebox, and the dancer stood passively, arms crossed beneath her breasts, waiting for the music to resume. For a moment, the only sound in the room was the monotonous blip from a video game.

"Don't forget the tattoos," Maguire called out as the search began.

"I got one over here," Martinez called back.

"I got one too," Magic yelled from the end of the bar.

Maguire went to take a look. That was a common mark of hardened criminals among the latest intake from Cuba: minute tattoos, on the web of the hand between thumb and forefinger or, less frequently, on the inside of the lip or even the eyelid. The signs had been badges of rank inside Castro's jails. Some attributed an occult significance to them also—a link to the Cuban cults of *santería*.

Martinez' man looked like most of the others in the bar: unshaven, prematurely wizened, scrawny in build. His eyes were unfocused, his tongue lolling in his open mouth.

Maguire examined the marks on the man's right hand. Three small dots.

"That means drugs, doesn't it?"

"Yeah. Drug carrier," Martinez confirmed.

"Find anything on him?"

"Two Ludes in his pocket." Martinez displayed two white pills. "I think he had another in his mouth. But he swallowed it."

"Book him."

The sergeant moved on to join Magic.

"Take a look at this mama's boy," said the black cop.

Maguire examined the palm of a barrel-chested mulatto who looked younger and fitter than the other customers. His red T-shirt was also the only clean piece of clothing in the establishment. His fly was still unzipped. He was the one Maguire had seen from the door, getting a hand job from a hooker who looked twice his age. The man was belligerently drunk, and his temper had not been improved by the fact that his pleasure had been interrupted at a critical time.

67

"Let me see," said the Sergeant.

"Put it there, you dumb mother," said Magic, grabbing the Mariel's wrist and pushing his hand onto the bar.

Maguire looked at the tattoo between the man's thumb and forefinger. It showed a heart, superimposed on a ribbon, with the word *"Madre"*—Mother—inscribed on it. The heart was pierced by the pole end of a pitchfork tipped with arrows.

Maguire recognized the mark from a police Intelligence file that had been circulated to all supervisors. The sign of the executioner.

"He's clean," said Magic. "But he's givin' me a lotta lip. I think it's a B 'n A."

The Mariel spat copiously on the floor, spattering the tips of Maguire's shoes.

"Yeah," growled the Sergeant. "It's a B 'n A."

B 'n A meant "Being an Asshole." It was cop talk for giving the police a hard time. It sometimes resulted in a charge of being drunk and disorderly, or of obstruction. Magic started frog-marching the man in the red T-shirt toward the door.

Maguire stood back and studied how the rest of the search was proceeding. Linda, he saw, was frisking a man's trouser legs up to his crotch while the *marielito* screamed obscenities in Spanish.

"Maybe you should stop Linda from searching the men," Martinez whispered to Maguire. "This could be big trouble. Cubans aren't used to it, you know? It goes against *machismo*."

"I guess you're right."

He was moving to intervene when Linda called out, "I got a gun."

Linda held up a cheap Saturday Night Special. "He dropped it on the floor. Claims he's never seen it."

As she moved from her search position, the Mariel swung around and spat *"¡Puta!"* at her.

In an instant, Linda had pinioned the man with his hands behind his back.

"B 'n A?" she implored Maguire.

"Okay," he conceded wearily. When the police trawled the

bars, they normally stopped at confiscating the guns and giving their owners a warning to keep them at home.

As Maguire followed the last of his patrolmen to the exit, the jukebox came on again and the geriatric go-go girl began to wobble her awesome flanks across the dusty stage. The Sergeant's last impression of the Sugar Shack was of the bigger-than-life-size plastic Jesus that protruded from the front wall at the angle of a ship's figurehead.

"Oh, Jesus," Maguire groaned as he left the bar, "tell me what I'm doing with all this shit."

On the sidewalk, the three men arrested were lined up against the wall, handcuffed. The squad had just started discussing who would take whom in what car when Maguire heard a long beep on his walkie-talkie. He took it out of its leather holster.

"QRX, QRX," the dispatcher called. "We've got a twenty-nine at the Twelve Hundred."

"QSL," Maguire responded. "We're on our way." A 29 was a robbery in progress. The 1200 was a bar at the city end of Calle Ocho, a cut above most of the *marielito* hangouts. The girls were younger and prettier, and they charged two seventy-five for imported beer.

"What about these dudes?" Magic asked.

Maguire was already running toward his patrol car. "Let 'em go!" he yelled over his shoulder.

"It's your lucky night, bruiser," said Linda as she uncuffed her prisoner.

When they got to the 1200 minutes later, they were told the robbers had just left. The hookers and the patrons were still lying face downward on the floor, beneath the image of an out-size plastic Virgin Mary. But the owner had managed to catch a glimpse of the getaway car: a beat-up green Chevy with a twisted fender. He had also spotted the last three digits on the license plate: 558.

"There were four guys," Martinez translated. "Sounds like they came equipped for war. They had one automatic, two shot-guns and a couple of handguns."

69

"Were they Americans or Latins?"

"Black Americans."

"The bridge!" Maguire yelled. The bridge led north, over the Miami River, toward Overtown and Liberty City. And Police Headquarters. "You got the tag?" he checked with his team. They all nodded. "Okay. Fan out. Make for the bridge. If you spot the Chevy, tail it and call in. Don't move until you've got reinforcements. Just remember, guys: try to be a hero, you'll wind up a zero."

It was advice that Maguire himself occasionally forgot.

He caught up with the green Chevy not far from Police Headquarters, three blocks into Overtown.

"QRX, QRX," he said into his Motorola. "QTA is Northeast Second Avenue and Fifth. Bad guys moving north."

Maguire punched the Chevy's license number into his mobile digital terminal. The response that came back within seconds was what he expected: it was a hot car.

"I think they've spotted us," said Martinez. The two blacks in the back seat of the Chevy were staring back at the patrol car. The Chevy suddenly picked up speed and swung west down a side street in a screech of rubber.

Maguire switched on his blue-and-red lights and his siren and gave pursuit. When he glanced at his rearview mirror, he saw that Magic and Linda were riding close behind.

"Ro, Ro," chanted the street people. The chorus grew to a roar as Maguire's squad car closed on the Chevy.

He yanked his wheel hard left to follow the getaway car as it careened past Annie's Grocery Store.

When he saw what lay ahead, he slapped his forehead with his left hand. "The Hole," Maguire groaned. "The goddamn fucking Hole."

The driver of the Chevy braked so suddenly in the middle of the road, burning rubber, that Maguire plowed right into its rear bumper.

The robbers abandoned the car and raced toward the milling crowd of blacks on the sidewalk in front of The Hole.

Maguire unholstered his .38 and yelled, "Freeze!"

No one paid any attention.

Maguire and Martinez dropped into the classic half-crouch position, steadying their guns with both hands. For a fraction of a second, the barrel of Maguire's revolver was pointing straight between the shoulder blades of the last of the four robbers, who were running in single file. The man was carrying an automatic rifle, maybe a Mac-10.

In the next instant, the crowd on the pavement opened like a sponge and swallowed up the four men.

Their ranks closed again as Maguire ran forward.

"Move aside or I'll shoot!" the Sergeant yelled.

Nobody stirred. The mob's hostility formed a protective moat around The Hole and the four men who had dived into it.

"There's a lot of artillery around, Sarge," Magic murmured as he came up and took a position at Maguire's left side. In the dim light, Maguire could see guns among the crowd. And among the people hanging from the balconies.

"Hey, Magic," the street people started heckling the black cop. "Why you be workin' for the Man?"

"He ain't no chill dude."

"You be gone or you be dead."

The rest of Maguire's team had arrived on the scene. They all had their guns out.

"I guess we don't want a riot, huh, Sarge?" Magic suggested quietly.

"No, that we can live without."

Maguire ordered his team back to their cars. The crowd taunted them as they left. Someone threw a brick that made one more dent in Maguire's hood.

It was long past midnight, but Maguire was used to working overtime. He was on double duty that night. Because the Department was undermanned, he was frequently asked to supervise two sectors of the city that were twenty minutes apart. That night, he had to go and check up on the four squad cars patrolling Coconut Grove.

It was ten hours since he had come on duty, he was thinking.

And what did he have to show for it? Zilch. The tragedy of a baby in a bucket of urine, whose parents would probably never be traced. A lone handgun confiscated in a city where there was an average of seven guns per family. And a useless chase after four robbers who had been swallowed up by The Hole.

Maguire's record for arrests and convictions was one of the highest in the force. In the previous month alone, he had logged fifty-seven felonies, three homicides and eleven sexual batteries.

But even on the nights when he succeeded in bringing the bad guys in, Maguire was often overwhelmed by a sense of hopelessness, bordering despair. Night after night, he and his squad risked their lives for nickels and dimes. Most mornings, before his shift began, he had to go into court to testify against small-time hoodlums and drug peddlers from the Mariel bars and the ghettos—pruning a few bushes on the outer edge of the jungle.

The men who had vanished into The Hole had got away with eight hundred dollars—the kind of loose change that big-timers like Julio Parodi might spend on a single hooker.

Jay Maguire didn't need any Ph.D. in sociology to tell him why kids in the slums turned to dope.

If the American Government were serious about stopping the plague, he believed, it would napalm the poppy fields and spray the marijuana plantations with paraquat, and to hell with the reactions of the foreign countries where the stuff was grown. The Air Force would be ordered to shoot down any unidentified plane approaching South Florida. The Navy would be told to forget about territorial limits, hunt down the smugglers' mother ships and blow them out of the water. And the Julio Parodis would be sent to the slammer for life.

Maguire did not believe that any of this was likely to happen.

If you can't beat it, join it: that was the attitude of some of Maguire's colleagues on the force. And when he saw Parodi acting as if he owned the city, he began to wonder if they weren't right. You could double your salary by looking away at the right time. There was that cop with the diamond-studded Rolex. He had heard of a highway patrolman who had been paid off with more than two hundred Ks in cash when he flagged down a runner who was carrying a jerry can full of pure heroin. But Maguire hadn't given in yet.

Martinez whistled softly at a tall blond apparition in a leather miniskirt and fishnet tights, teetering along on six-inch heels outside the Mayfair shopping mall.

"Forget it, Wilson," said Maguire. "That's a he-she. Used to hang out around the Cactus Lounge on Biscayne."

They drove back down to South Bayshore Drive, where Maguire's attention was diverted by a big car bowling along toward them at what he guessed to be fifty or sixty, in a thirty-five-mile speed zone.

He flicked on his revolving lights, swung out into the left lane and drove straight toward the oncoming car. The Rolls managed to stop inches away from his buckled bumper. Its champagne color made the Corniche unmistakable. There were two men in the front seat, one of them Mama Benitez.

Maguire quickly reversed, then eased the patrol car forward to stop opposite the man in the back seat of the Rolls.

Julio Parodi stared straight ahead, puffing on a cigar, leaving it to his driver to deal with the cops.

Maguire motioned to the Cuban to open his window. Parodi affected not to notice.

"Hand me the light," Maguire said to his partner. He took the heavy metal-cased flashlight, which he sometimes used as a nightstick, and banged hard on Parodi's bulletproof window.

This time, Parodi took notice.

"What can I do for you, Officer?" he asked urbanely, after he had pushed the electronic window control.

"I'll tell you what you can do!" Maguire shouted at him. "You can tell that monkey up front to slow this piece of shit down!"

Maguire got back to his bachelor apartment in the Grove in the early hours. The place obviously lacked a woman's touch: the bed was unmade; there was a stack of dirty dishes in the sink, and a clutter of beer cans and half-empty bottles in the living room.

He sawed a hunk of cheese from the block of Cheddar in the

73

refrigerator and wrapped bread around it, popped open a can of beer and flung himself into the overstuffed armchair in the front room. He started fiddling with the dial of his radio, and finally found a news broadcast.

The first item was about the hurricane the meteorologists were calling Celia, which was reported hovering off the Florida coast. "Now we have a follow-up on the Fairchild murder," the newscaster's voice babbled on brightly.

So they're calling it murder now, Maguire was thinking.

"The police manhunt continues all over Puerto Rico for the kidnappers of Senator Joel Fairchild, and the search has expanded to the Miami area, where investigators believe that one or more of the terrorists may have fled. The Macheteros terrorist group has issued a new communiqué threatening to avenge what it describes as intensified repression. A sister organization of the Macheteros, the FALN, claimed responsibility today for a bomb explosion at the Citicorp Building in Manhattan in which two people were killed and more than forty injured. An FBI spokesman says that all of this confirms that the motive for the Fairchild kidnap was the strong stand the Senator had taken against Puerto Rican terrorism."

"What do those meatheads know?" Maguire muttered aloud to himself as he switched off the radio.

He finished his snack and had gone into the bathroom when the phone began to shrill. He hesitated for a moment before going into the bedroom to pick it up.

"Maguire," he rumbled into the receiver.

"Sergeant Maguire? I'm sorry to call you so late. I was trying to reach you all day."

"Yeah?"

"My name is Robert Hockney. I'm the Washington Bureau Chief of *The New York World*."

"I don't talk to reporters after midnight." Maguire's tone indicated that he didn't want to talk to reporters any time of day.

"I was a friend of Senator Fairchild's," Hockney explained carefully. "My wife is on the staff of the Internal Security Committee. We were with the Senator in San Juan the night he was killed."

".So?"

"Well, I thought you might be able to tell me something."

"You should be talking to the cops in San Juan."

"I mean about the drug investigation."

Maguire was silent for several seconds, and Hockney, listening intently on the Washington end of the line, was scared he had guessed wrong and blown it.

Then the sergeant said, "What do you know about that?" and Hockney knew he had guessed right.

"My wife works for the Committee," he repeated, sidestepping the question.

"The Senator promised not to talk to anybody at the Committee at this stage," Maguire said, with rising anger. "He promised no leaks."

"Well, I think we have to go forward now," Hockney urged, as delicately as he could.

"What are you saying?"

"I'm saying I'd like to come down to Miami and talk to you. I'm not talking about publishing anything—not unless you give me the go-ahead. I think I might be able to help."

"What kind of reporter are you, anyway?"

"I hope I'm an honest one. I did a big exposé on the KGB a couple of years back you may have seen."

"Are you the guy who brought out that Soviet defector—whatsisname?"

"Barisov. Viktor Barisov. Yes, I am."

"I read something about that." Maguire paused to reflect. Then he said, "When are you coming down?"

"How about tomorrow?"

"Make it Wednesday. Wednesday's my day off."

Chapter

3

WASHINGTON, D.C.

The Washington bureau of *The New York World* was in a nondescript glass-and-concrete edifice on Fourteenth Street, midway between the National Press Building and the scrofulous cluster of massage parlors and porn theaters a few blocks north. Hockney got into the office just before ten, after a protracted breakfast at the Hay-Adams with Dick Roth, who worked with Julia on the staff of the Senate Internal Security Committee. Roth was one of the few people Hockney had encountered in Washington who genuinely seemed to have no personal ax to grind. He lived modestly with his wife and kids in a suburban house in Bethesda. His was the mind behind all of the Committee's most successful exposés, and Hockney felt sure that Roth would know something about Senator Fairchild's dealings with the Miami cop.

Hockney was surprised when Roth explained, over the French toast, that he was as mystified as the reporter.

"It's strange," Roth said. "It just wasn't like Fairchild to hoard these things to himself. In fact, he was always nervous when people called him out of the blue. This Maguire must really have pitched him."

Roth thought for a moment, then added, "But you know something else, Bob? If they were having all these midnight chats over the phone between D.C. and Miami, it's more than likely someone else was listening in."

"You mean the Senator's phone was tapped?"

"Not necessarily. You see, a lot of these intercity calls are swept automatically—by our own NSA, or by that big electronic vacuum cleaner the Soviets have set up on the roof of their embassy. To get rid of the trash, their computers are set up to isolate certain key words—hundreds, maybe thousands of them. When somebody drops a key word on a long-distance connection, the tape recorders start rolling right away."

"You mean if I called you from New York and said I'd just had lunch with Teófilo Gómez from the Cuban Mission, we'd be on tape?"

"More than likely. Of course, the NSA collects so much junk it probably takes months to go through it."

Hockney was thinking that if someone had eavesdropped on Fairchild's phone calls from Miami by monitoring the microwaves, then it was possible that his own brief conversation with Jay Maguire was on tape.

He found the *World* bureau in its usual state of cheerful chaos. He retrieved the mail that had piled up in his pigeonhole in the reception hall, and threaded his way through the desks in the bullpen to his glass-walled corner office.

"I love the tan!" Lisa, the bureau's girl Friday, called out to him.

He found Jack Lancer lounging against the door of his office. The younger reporter was good-looking in a loose-boned, gangling sort of way. He was wearing pressed—overpressed—blue jeans and a plaid shirt. His tie hung as low as a hangman's noose.

"Welcome back," Lancer said. Since Lancer had lately been affecting a cool, ironical manner toward his boss that bordered on downright rudeness, this note of bonhomie made Hockney wary.

"I hope you enjoyed yourself holding the fort," Hockney said.

"Oh, sure. I took every girl I know to dinner at the MB on your expense account." Lancer's face creased in a long, straight-lipped smile that was not so much a smile as a tightening of the tiny muscles at the corners of the mouth.

Then he said, "Ed Finkel's called you three times already. He wants you to get back to him urgently."

Hockney nodded and wandered into his office with no semblance of haste. He could guess what was on the Managing Editor's mind. That would explain Jack Lancer's good humor.

"So what's hot today?" he asked Lancer casually. Normally, he held a conference for the bureau reporters about 11 A.M., to make sure the paper had full coverage of all the major stories. His intention now was to show Lancer that he was not overawed by their Managing Editor, as much as to check on what the young reporter had been up to while he was away in the Caribbean.

"Well, I guess your Fairchild story will be good for a few more headlines," Lancer said. "The FBI Director is scheduled to make a statement this afternoon."

"Uh-huh."

"But the big story is Nicaragua."

Hockney tried not to groan audibly. For months past, Lancer had been running in and out of his office—or more recently, going straight to Ed Finkel in New York—with racy accounts of supposed CIA plotting to overthrow the revolutionary regime in Nicaragua.

"Listen," Lancer was saying. "I've got an inside source. He says the Pentagon has orders to prepare a full-scale invasion, starting with bomb attacks on Nicaraguan airfields."

"Who is this source?" Hockney inquired, wondering if Lancer's latest scoop had come from his friends in the Coalition for Hemispheric Understanding, a pro-Castro lobby that had been holding seminars for journalists and Congressmen.

"Not now." Lancer shook his head.

"I find it pretty hard to buy this invasion stuff," Hockney commented.

"But it's so fucking *obvious*," Lancer objected. "This Administration is scared it's going to lose the next election. It's screwed up the economy, its own people are trying to cut each other's balls off and they've all got a bad dose of penis envy. They're jealous of what the Brits did to the Argentines and what the Israelis did to the Palestinians, and they want to show that they're macho too."

Hockney said, "You ought to be leading a rally." But to avoid getting a second lecture, he quickly added, "Some of what you say makes sense. I can buy some of it. But if you want to do a story on an invasion plan, you'll have to come up with hard evidence. And you'd better have sources we can check."

"I'm working on it," Lancer said with that same irritating smile.

The phone started ringing, and Lancer made his exit as Hockney picked it up.

"You shouldn't eat your breakfast so fast, Bob," Ed Finkel said by way of greeting. "You can get heartburn."

Hockney glanced at the wall clock. Just past ten-fifteen.

"I was following up on the Fairchild story."

"That's what I wanted to talk to you about. We got a lot of readers' complaints over that first piece you filed out of San Juan. They want to know where's the proof that the Cubans were involved."

Hockney guessed that the "readers" who were complaining most stridently were on the staff of *The New York World*.

"*And* Fidel issued a complete denial," Ed Finkel went on.

"Yeah. Well, what would you expect?"

"I'm saying that you're stretching credulity too far to make out that the Cubans would get involved in something as high-risk as the kidnap and murder of a U.S. Senator. I want you to drop that whole line of speculation unless you come up with something solid."

Through the glass wall of his office, Hockney could see Jack

Lancer ambling off toward the exit. It struck him that the conversation he had had with the young reporter was strangely similar to the one that the Managing Editor was now having with *him*.

"I'm looking into it," Hockney said curtly. "As a matter of fact, I'm going down to Miami tomorrow to follow up a lead."

"You're supposed to be our Washington Bureau Chief, not our suntan expert," Finkel observed sourly.

"I've already cleared it with Rourke." The *World*'s Executive Editor, Len Rourke, had raised no objections to Hockney's travel plans. It was just like Finkel to seize on any excuse to make him feel uncomfortable. Since he had been in the Washington job, Hockney had made a couple of futile attempts to conclude a peace treaty with the Managing Editor. He had fixed an invitation to a White House dinner, and hosted a cocktail party at home in Finkel's honor that had been attended by half the Cabinet and a dozen Senators. These social efforts—which had demonstrated Hockney's *entrée* in the capital, as well as the power of the newspaper itself—seemed only to have deepened Finkel's animosity.

"I think you ought to put Jack Lancer on the Puerto Rican story, and concentrate on running your own bureau," the Managing Editor said. "It's not as if there's nothing else going on in the world."

"I'd rather field this myself, Ed. I'm only going to be gone one, maybe two days."

"Have it your own way." Then, brightening, Finkel added, "Tell you what I'm going to do, Bob. I'm going to put Jack Lancer in charge till you get back. That all right with you?"

"Well, Jack's a fine enough reporter," Hockney fumbled, "but I don't think he's any kind of manager."

"It won't hurt to give him some experience."

Hockney thought it would be ungallant to raise any further objections. After all, he was going to be away for only a couple of days. But he did not miss the signal: Finkel would grab the first opportunity that came up to install someone else—maybe

Jack Lancer—in his corner office on a permanent basis. Before he went out to lunch, he gathered up all his notes on the Fairchild case and locked them in his file cabinet.

He spent much of the afternoon trying to tie down some of the other loose ends that had been left trailing by Senator Fairchild's death. He wrote a short profile of the man who had succeeded Fairchild as Chairman of the Senate Internal Security Committee—a liberal from Connecticut who had been conspicuously absent from most of the hearings.

No witch-finder he, Hockney thought. He guessed that the work load for Julia and Dick Roth was likely to decrease pretty fast.

He sifted through a mass of file material on previous outbreaks of Puerto Rican terrorism. He was impressed by the dedication of some of the revolutionaries involved. He read through an old news report of one Puerto Rican terrorist who had blown off his hands while trying to construct a bomb. When the cops arrived to arrest him, he was found trying to tear up his secret address book with the bloody stumps and flush the pages down the toilet. Hockney started jotting down the cases in which a link with the Cubans had been established. He learned that in 1973, the man who was then Director of the FBI had testified that one hundred thirty-five Puerto Rican terrorists had been trained in Cuba. Piece by piece, Hockney cobbled together a backgrounder, including the names of underground Puerto Rican leaders who had traveled to Havana. He calculated it might be useful ammunition in any future dispute with Ed Finkel.

Hockney had to take time out to edit the flow of stories from reporters who had been out all day covering the department briefings. Jack Lancer came in, jacket slung over his shoulder, with the text of a skeptical piece he had written on a State Department briefing on the Soviet military buildup in Nicaragua.

"It's the same snow job they try every week," Lancer said. "Even the briefer doesn't believe what he's dishing out. The reporters who are on the spot say these airstrips the Soviets are supposed to be building in Nicaragua are about as menacing as a YMCA summer camp."

"Okay," Hockney acknowledged, turning his attention back to another piece which asserted that three top members of the Administration had claimed excessive tax deductions.

"Now, *this* might interest you," Lancer went on.

Hockney picked up the sheet of paper that came fluttering onto his desk. He saw that it was the text of a prepared statement by the FBI Director. The FBI chief reported that his agency was mobilizing all available resources in the hunt for Senator Fairchild's killers. He also declared that the Bureau had no proof of any foreign involvement in the Fairchild case.

"So much for the big conspiracy theory," said Lancer. "Unless you know something the Director of the FBI doesn't know."

"All he says is they haven't caught anyone yet," Hockney remarked coolly.

When Lancer had gone, he called Frank Parra's number at FBI Headquarters in San Juan. He was told, politely but firmly, that Mr. Parra was not available and would not be available at any time that day.

He was having a late snack with Julia in their kitchen when the call from Puerto Rico came through.

"No names, okay?" Parra said. "You recognize my voice?"

"Sure."

"I'm not allowed to talk to you," the FBI Agent reported. "I said you were dangerous."

"What about the statement your boss put out today?"

"That's the Party Line. If you knock it, you're out on your ass. Just like the good old days of J. Edgar."

"I don't understand. Did you get any leads?"

"Not yet. But we're on the right track, both of us. None of the insiders in the local groups know a damn thing. You follow me? There's no doubt it was an outside job."

Hockney said, "I may have something. I'll know later this week."

"Okay. Let me know if you do. But don't call the office. Be good—you know what they say? If you can't be good, be careful. If you can't be careful—"

"Don't name it after me," Hockney finished it for him.

MIAMI

Miami International Airport was crowded with Latin Americans. Hockney humped his garment bag and battered briefcase through an excited swarm of people waiting for relatives arriving from Guatemala and El Salvador. A mass exodus from Central America was obviously in full spate. Hockney shouldered his way through to the yellow Hertz bus and rode out to the car park where his rented compact was waiting.

On the drive from the airport to the new Holiday Inn on Brickell Avenue, Hockney noticed how much the city skyline had changed since he had last been in Miami, a couple of years before. It did not present the profile of a defeated city. Plush new condominiums and office buildings rose on every side, like upended trays of ice cubes.

Hockney called Jay Maguire from his hotel room, as they had arranged.

The cop's voice sounded deep and furry, as if he had a cold.

"You're my wake-up call," Maguire explained. "I was on duty until four."

"Something serious?"

"It started off with a routine traffic incident. A Mariel bumped into another guy's car. The two guys get arguing over it. The next thing you know, they've both got shooters out, blazing away. Pretty soon some people on the sidewalk have joined in, both guys are dead and a cop is bleeding his guts out."

"Jesus."

"It's not that unusual. You'll see. This town's like a truckload of nitroglycerin rolling down an old dirt track. You're just waiting for the jolt that will set the whole thing off. Listen, you better give me twenty minutes to get myself together. You got a car?"

"Yes."

"You figure you can find the Miami Marina?"

"I've got a map."

"Okay, there's a place there called the Dockside Terrace. You can tell them you're meeting me."

They showed Hockney to a table near the piano, and he settled into a wicker chair with a high peacock's-train back. The waitresses made a fuss over him as a blond girl with a long nose who vaguely resembled Meryl Streep crooned country-and-Western ditties to the almost-deserted room. A lean broken-nosed man in a plain red T-shirt and black pants came in, and the singer bent down to kiss his cheek.

"Well," the man said to Hockney, "what are you drinking?"

"Oh, maybe a beer." Hockney was thrown slightly off balance by the absence of introductions.

Maguire ordered Black Label on the rocks.

When the waitress came back with the drinks, silence fell between them while she arranged everything on the table to her satisfaction.

Then Maguire said, "What did you think of Senator Fairchild?"

"I thought he was responsible for some damned important investigations," Hockney said diplomatically.

Maguire nodded. "I did too. That's why I called him after he went on TV and said he wanted to expose the Cuban drug rackets." He took a good deep swallow of Scotch and said, "Before we get any deeper into this, I gotta say I got a problem with you. I learned a lot of things in Vietnam, and one of them was that the U.S. media miss the big story. I did some checking on you, and a couple of guys I respect say you're different. My partner turns out to be a big fan of yours. He's a Cuban. He's also a reader. He read your book on that KGB defector, and he says it's his Bible. But we're going to be getting into stuff I haven't even told him, so I gotta be sure that you know when to keep your mouth shut."

84

"I don't think I could have written any of the stories that mattered if I hadn't protected my sources," Hockney said quietly. "That goes without saying."

"Well, let me say this up front. If you don't handle this right, we could both wind up dead."

Maguire paused to see whether Hockney understood that he wasn't just laying it on for effect. The reporter returned his gaze steadily.

"You're talking about what happened to the Senator," Hockney suggested.

"Maybe," Maguire said. "But let me tell you another story. I called the Senator about a certain case—a dope case, right? A while back, the department had a CI who was working on this case—"

"CI?"

"Snitch. We call them CIs down here. Anyway, someone tipped off the suspect that there was this snitch inside his organization. The snitch disappeared. We *think* we found the body about a week later."

"You *think*?"

"The body had been dumped in a canal in southwest Dade, and the alligators had it for lunch. All that was left to fingerprint was the right thumb, and not enough of that for positive identification. They had blown off his face with a shotgun."

"I see." Hockney took a pull on his beer.

"Still interested?"

"You're damned right."

"Well, you might want to have a *serious* drink." Maguire gulped down the rest of his whisky and waved the empty glass at the waitress.

"Sounds like a good idea," Hockney said.

Jerkily, pausing two or three times to get his glass refilled, Maguire told Hockney the story of a Cuban businessman and political activist named Julio Parodi.

"You look out your hotel window," the cop said, "and you can see two new skyscrapers that Parodi helped to build, and one that he part-owns. He's big. He's got a business empire here in Miami. He's Numero Uno with a bunch of rightist crazies who call themselves the Blue Brigade. And it's all built on coke. Parodi's bank launders dope money, and he arranges some of the big shipments from Colombia in person. I hear he owns a nice little mansion on Millionaires' Row in Medellín."

"If you know this much," Hockney butted in, "then why haven't you been able to charge him?"

"You should go and ask the FBI and the other agencies. Now and then, we get a lead. But it never takes us anywhere. Funny things happen. The evidence disappears, or the snitch, or plans get switched around at the last minute. You ask me, I'd say this bird is being protected."

"Protected by whom?"

"By the CIA." He squinted at Hockney and added, "You know quite a few guys in the Agency, right?"

"I know some."

"Well, do you know one named Whitman?"

Hockney shook his head. "I don't think so."

"Whitman's the CIA Station Chief in Miami," Maguire explained. "The chief of the *real* Station, not the one they put in the phone book for the tourists and the nut cases to phone up. He's also a friend of Parodi's. I got a picture of them."

Maguire pulled out his wallet and showed Hockney a blurred snapshot of two large, fleshy men sitting together in the front seat of a car under a palm tree.

"I know there are some dirty people in the Agency," Maguire went on. "Like those guys who sold themselves to Qaddafi. I also know that Parodi used to be on the Company payroll, in the Bay of Pigs and afterwards. Now, I don't know whether the CIA is masterminding his dope rackets, but they're sure as shit involved. Does that sound like a story to you?"

"Is this what you told the Senator?" Hockney asked, confused by the sudden appearance of the CIA. He didn't know how to square that with what had happened in Puerto Rico.

"You haven't heard the best bit," Maguire resumed. "Parodi is also tied in with Castro. He goes to Cuba. Sometimes he just hops on his private jet at Fort Lauderdale. Other times, he goes via Mexico. That means the Cubans must trust him, right?"

"I guess so."

"Pretty funny for a rightist anti-Castro fanatic, huh?"

"Some of this is pretty hard to follow," Hockney said. "You're not claiming that the other government agencies— CIA, FBI—are unaware of this guy's visits to Cuba, are you?"

"Beats me," Maguire responded. "I got my own sources."

Hockney frowned over his drink. Scotch never agreed with him, and he wished he had stuck to beer. He felt he was beginning to flounder in a quicksand in which the Cubans, the CIA, the drug racketeers and rightist fanatics were all mixed up together, and wondered whether this corresponded to any kind of reality, or just to the delirium of a frustrated street cop. But the earnest sobriety with which Jay Maguire outlined his story—even as he knocked back the equivalent of a pint of Scotch—made Hockney reluctant to dismiss him as the victim of hallucinations.

The restaurant was filling up with the evening trade.

"Tell you what," Maguire said. "The Blue Brigade is planning some kind of rally tomorrow. If you want, you can take a look at Mr. Parodi in his own *ambiente.*"

"I'd like that."

There were deep pools of shadow among the trees in the waterfront park beyond their cars.

"Don't get caught in there after dark," the cop warned Hockney. "That's where the shims and the chicken hawks hang out."

"Shims?"

"You know, he-shes. Don't tell me you haven't got any of that up North?"

Hockney woke up with a start as the light flooded through the open windows of his hotel room. He had ended the evening with Maguire at a cheerful bar named Ronnie's, where the live music—from swing to samba, from Cole Porter to Stephen Sondheim—was better than he had heard in a long while. The noise level was impressive; a shelf ran all around the stage, lined with beer and soda cans full of loose gravel, which the patrons were encouraged to shake like maracas.

Hockney's hangover did not make it any easier to decide how to interpret what Maguire had told him. But one thing was clear enough: if even ten percent of what the cop said was accurate, it would not be very smart for him to show up at Parodi's demonstration with a police escort. He thumbed through the phone book and found the number of Parodi's bank.

It was nine-thirty by the time he got an answer from the Cuban's private office. He identified himself, and was left listening to noises that might have come from the sound track of *2001* as he was transferred to another extension. He guessed that there was a direct connection between Parodi's home and the bank.

Finally, a man answered and asked the nature of Hockney's business.

"I would like to interview Señor Parodi for *The New York World*."

"Señor Parodi does not give interviews."

"It doesn't have to be a formal interview. I would like to talk to him about the Brigada Azul." He glanced at the headline in *The Miami Bugle*, which he had flung on the bed on top of a pile of newspapers. "And the immigration issue," he added hastily. The lead story in the *Bugle* was about the uproar in Little Havana over the deportation of two Cuban would-be refugees who had arrived at Key West by boat. He guessed that this must be the theme of the Blue Brigade demonstration.

"Please wait," the man's voice came back.

Now Hockney had to endure loud piped music before he was told, "Señor Parodi is prepared to meet you after the rally. Be at the Bay of Pigs memorial, Calle Ocho and Thirteenth, at seven."

Maguire and his partner cruised along Southwest Eighth, at the tail of a column of Cuban marchers that extended for five or six city blocks. Only a couple of hundred were supporters of the Brigada Azul, whose members were easily spotted, for the most part, because of their paramilitary gear—some were sporting forage caps, camouflage fatigues and combat boots—and their violent slogans. Ahead of the squad car, Maguire could see a couple of youths carrying a huge papier-mâché effigy of Castro, swinging upside down from a wooden gibbet.

The Brigada Azul had found a popular cause. The Newgate Administration, alarmed by the flood of immigrants that continued to pour into the United States from all over Latin America, had decided to crack down. Stemming the tide from Mexico was a hopeless task. Illegal aliens who arrived by boat from the Caribbean made an easier, if more limited, target. The Administration had begun by arresting and deporting Haitians who had fled the poverty and brutality of their lives under the Duvalier regime. Now, sensitive to claims that Castro was exporting criminals, mentally disturbed persons and undercover agents to the United States under the mask of the "freedom flotillas," President Newgate had instructed the INS and the Coast Guard to turn back refugees from Cuba who could not be classified as political dissidents or did not have an automatic right of residence because of relatives legally established in America. It was not surprising that Miami's Cuban community was up in arms. Even the staid *Diario de las Americas,* the main Spanish-language paper, had complained that federal agencies were now being required to act as "an extension of the Communist secret police."

Sensitive to the angry mood in Little Havana, Chief Murchison had ordered the police on the street to keep a low profile. Relations between the police and the Cuban community were still friendly, despite the irruption of the people Maguire called Mariels. The Chief had issued a permit for the demonstration, with two restrictions. The first was that the marchers were to keep to one of Calle Ocho's four lanes as they advanced to the Bay of Pigs memorial. The other was that they carry their banners and placards in their hands—without poles, which might be used as weapons in the event of any violence.

Maguire could see that both these restrictions were being

89

generally flouted. Some of the Blue Brigade marchers flourished their placards on metal-tipped poles which looked as lethal as spears. And the ragged procession ahead of his car had spilled all the way across the street, blocking off traffic. The Sergeant eased his foot off the gas pedal until he was just crawling along at the Cubans' heels, his blue-and-red lights flashing.

A close-cropped teenager in a flak jacket spun around and started walking backward in front of the police cruiser with a jaunty, insolent air.

"Hey," Maguire said. "Hey, did that kid just give me the finger?"

The boy in the flak jacket started yelling to the marchers around him.

"What the hell is he jabbering about?" Maguire asked.

"He says they should make the cops go away."

Flak Jacket's hand dipped like an ice cream scoop, and he made the obscene gesture again.

"Hey, you!" Maguire called through his window. "If you give me the finger again, motherfucker, you're gonna get more than my finger up your ass."

Still grinning, Flak Jacket cantered backward until he had squeezed himself into the protective crush of other marchers. Maguire saw one of their posters. It depicted a mangy little pug labeled INS being dragged along on a leash by a bearded, cigar-puffing Fidel. Other placards in the group had nothing to do with the immediate theme of the demonstration. "FREE CUBA NOW" and "LIBERATE NICARAGUA" were two of the most popular Brigada Azul slogans.

They were still eight or nine blocks away from the goal of the marchers: the tiny *placita* at the corner of Thirteenth Avenue where an eternal flame flickered in commemoration of the martyrs of the Bay of Pigs. There had been no incidents, but Maguire could smell trouble from the way that Flak Jacket's group was behaving. These were tough-looking kids, and it was easy to tell from the way they were strutting and showing off that they wanted action. The cop could also see that a few of them were packing heat. He spotted a telltale bulge at the back of Flak Jacket's jeans, where he had tucked a handgun—probably a cheap Saturday Night Special—under his belt.

As Maguire watched, Flak Jacket swaggered out of the crowd, whirled his arm like a baseball pitcher and sent a crumpled soda can flying toward the open window on the driver's side. The kid's aim was good. Maguire ducked just in time, and the can whistled through the open window, bouncing around in the back of the car.

"Shit," Maguire swore as he rolled up his window. He watched Flak Jacket pushing back into the throng.

"You tell me, Wilson," he said to his partner. "These are your people. They like the cops, right? Then why do I get the feeling we're in Liberty City?"

Martinez tapped his forehead. "These Brigada Azul guys are crazy" was all he contributed.

Flak Jacket danced toward the squad car, stopping only a couple of feet away. Then he sucked in his cheeks and spat a great glob of spittle onto the windshield. It dribbled slowly down the glass, viscous as raw egg white.

Maguire's hand was on the door handle. He was breathing hard, ready to jump out.

"Don't let him get to you, Jay," Martinez cautioned. "That's what he wants."

"What's his bag, anyway? Is he trying to start a riot?"

Before Maguire's partner could respond, there was a tremendous crash from behind them. One of Flak Jacket's friends had rammed the iron-sheathed butt of a pole into the back window, fracturing the reinforced glass. The thick splinters bent inward, like the points of a ragged star.

Maguire's patience cracked at the same moment as the rear window, and he was out of the car, swinging his flashlight like a nightstick. In the blur of people around him, he could not make out the Cuban who had smashed his car window. But he saw Flak Jacket darting among the marchers, and threw himself after the boy, clutching him by the collar.

"¡Me cago en tu madre!" the kid screamed.

"Hit the ground!" Maguire yelled. "Hit the ground, you mother!"

He was trying to get a purchase on the boy, to force him to the ground. But the kid wriggled and squirmed. Maguire made the mistake of reaching to snatch away his gun, and in a flash the kid had slithered out of his jacket and made off into the crowd. The Sergeant was left holding the flak jacket, confronted by a solid wall of Brigada Azul types who made no move to let him pass.

He walked back to the car at a steady, even stride. Martinez, covering him from the far side, looked pale. As Maguire climbed back into his seat, he was conscious of the press of marchers closing in on the cruiser from all sides. There were shouts, and then the echoing boom of fists pounding against the roof of the car. People started to roll the police cruiser back and forth, like the rocket in a children's playground.

Maguire punched out a message to the other patrol cars in his squad on his MDT—mobile digital terminal. The computer screen, mounted between the two front seats, enabled an officer on duty to check a suspect license number within seconds. The MDT was also a means of communicating with Headquarters, or other units, without breaking radio silence. That was why Maguire used his MDT, instead of his Motorola, to communicate with the rest of his squad now. Police radio frequencies were an open secret in Miami—as in most cities—and were commonly scanned by criminals, dopers, terrorists, spies and others with a need to know what the cops were up to, not excluding reporters on the *Bugle*.

"QRX TO 51, 52, 53." As he punched them out, the digits and block capitals showed up bright green on the display screen.

"MY QTA IS CENTRO VASCO RESTAURANT, 8TH AND 22ND."

"QTA" was Police Department code for the location of an officer in need of assistance.

The letters "QSL"—the code for "Okay"—flashed over Maguire's screen three times, in rapid succession. The other squad cars were on their way.

In his rearview mirror, Maguire saw one of Flak Jacket's comrades fiddling with the gas-tank cover, trying to prise it open.

"Back off!" he shouted, aiming his .38 over the back of his seat. "Back, damn you!"

The kid paid no heed. He managed to prise open the cover, and Maguire saw the spark as he tried to light a match. His intent was unmistakable.

Maguire threw the car into reverse and drove back into the crowd, blasting his horn as well as his siren. The marchers behind scattered. Panicking, they stumbled into one another, falling, trampling. Martinez opened his door and held it ajar. The edge of the door caught the boy with the matches between the shoulder blades as he turned to run, and he was flung screaming to the ground.

At the sight of the injured man, the mob around the cruiser turned angrier than before. Maguire, uncaring now who overheard, called the dispatcher on his walkie-talkie.

"Three-fifty, Three-five-oh," he rapped out his identification. "You better tell Field Force Two to get the lead out of their butts. It's turning into a riot."

"QSL."

"Hey, Jay."

Maguire followed his partner's pointing finger, and saw that the procession ahead of them had suddenly thinned out. People were drifting back into the left-hand lane. There was room for them to drive forward.

Half a block farther on, Maguire saw what had happened. The three other cars in his squad were plowing toward them down Calle Ocho, blocking off three of the lanes.

Andy Riggs, the senior black patrolman in Maguire's squad, leaned out his window and made a thumbs-up signal.

"Hey, Magic." Maguire returned his wave. "I never thought a big nigger like you would look like the U.S. Cavalry to me."

Magic grinned and yelled back, "Up yours, honky."

The scene was calm enough around the makeshift platform

that had been set up beside the Bay of Pigs memorial. Hockney, sandwiched into the third row of the audience jamming the little square, was only dimly aware of the disturbance somewhere back along Calle Ocho. Since the speeches were all in Spanish, he caught only a few words. But he was fascinated by the body language of the powerfully built man who had now taken the microphone. Julio Parodi was wearing a silk double-breasted suit that minimized his paunch, alligator shoes and the inevitable heavy gold watch and rings. He gestured so vehemently as he delivered his harangue to the crowd that his face was dripping with sweat. From time to time he pulled the crimson handkerchief out of his breast pocket to mop his forehead.

Then people were applauding, and Parodi took a little bow and climbed down from the platform. He was immediately flanked by tough-looking men in loose jackets whose eyes went everywhere, searching the crowd. They were men who had nothing in common with the aging dreamers and young fanatics who made up the bulk of the audience.

One of them stopped Hockney as he elbowed his way through the crowd toward Parodi, pushing the flat of his hand against the reporter's breastbone.

"Mr. Parodi?" Hockney appealed to the bodyguard's boss. He did not like being manhandled. "I'm Bob Hockney."

"*Mucho gusto.*" Parodi brushed aside his hired gun and pumped Hockney's hand. It was the handshake of a veteran politico—firm enough not to seem wimpish, but not so firm that repeated scores of times, it might result in a cramp.

"You must excuse me for a moment, please," Parodi said. "There has been a little excitement. I must explain something to a man from the Police Department."

Parodi's guards cleared a way for him through the mass of Cubans, and Hockney watched while he engaged in a brief conversation with a man with sad, tired eyes who was wearing an old suit with unfashionably wide lapels.

"*Now* we can go," Parodi said when he turned.

"Was it something serious?" Hockney asked as he hurried along, half a pace behind the Cuban.

94

"Not serious, no. Just some young hotheads who got involved in a fight with the cops. We just ask for understanding. Tempers are running high. We're anti-Communists. We believe in law and order."

Hockney gaped at an extraordinary apparition: a champagne-colored Rolls.

Parodi motioned for him to get into the back seat.

"And now, if you don't mind," the Cuban said, "I thought we would talk in a more agreeable setting."

They settled into a secluded corner of the Mutiny Room, and a strawberry blonde in a wide straw hat and an off-the-shoulder blouse brought them drinks—a daiquiri for Hockney, a straight Scotch for the Cuban. The only table within earshot of theirs was commandeered by two of the men who had ushered Parodi through the rally. Hockney could see a couple of men sitting alone at other tables, bent over newspapers despite the feathery darkness of the room.

"Shoot," Parodi said.

"Well, let's start with the rally. What's it all about?"

"That's easy. I came to this country as a refugee from Castro, right? I want to defend the right of anyone who can escape from Cuba to come to the U.S. the same way. We're not Haitians, for Chrissake. Let me tell you, I think Fidel is going to let more people out because he can't control the situation inside Cuba any longer."

"You mean there'll be another boatlift? Another Mariel?"

"Maybe. And just think what it would mean in the eyes of the world if Uncle Sam, supposedly the leader in the fight against Communism, turned back people who were trying to escape the Communist system. We can't let that happen. Did you listen to my speech tonight?"

"I didn't understand all of it," Hockney admitted.

"Okay. I want you to know I'm setting up a special fund to help pay for people to get out of Cuba. I'm kicking in twenty-five grand out of my own pocket. That's serious money. It's going to be used to charter the boats to bring people off the

95

island, and nobody in Washington is going to stop us."

"I can see you're determined."

"Listen, the Cuban community down here is probably the most determined anti-Communist force in the whole country. That's something Washington should appreciate. We're ready to fight. We showed that in the Bay of Pigs. We're ready to do it again. We'll fight in Cuba, we'll fight in Nicaragua, we'll fight wherever we can hurt Fidel. Cigar?"

Hockney accepted a cigar that looked about the size of a medium-range missile. He examined the band and saw it was a Montecristo.

"You smoke Havanas?" Hockney said.

"I don't discriminate against the Cuban people," Parodi said. "Just the bastards who are sitting on them."

"You mentioned Nicaragua," Hockney prodded.

"Sure. We have some Nicaraguans in the Brigada Azul, patriots who want to kick out the Communists. They train in our camps. If you want, you can take a look."

Hockney was amazed at Parodi's openness, and the fervor of the anti-Castro opinions he expressed. The man was altogether different—or so it seemed—from the intriguer that Maguire had described.

"Well, yes," Hockney said. "I'd be very interested to visit one of your camps."

"I'll try and set it up for tomorrow. I'll tell you this. We're the best thing Langley has going for it in Central America."

At this point the Cuban winked, and with the drooping eyelid, it seemed that his whole face contorted into a rather unpleasant leer.

Hockney began to feel distinctly uncomfortable.

He decided to jump in at the deep end. "There've been stories that Castro is mixed up in the drug traffic in this town," he said.

"It's possible," Parodi said, apparently unfazed.

"There are also people who say that your bank has been used to launder drug money."

Parodi did not lose the urbane smile he had assumed, but he

grabbed Hockney's wrist so tightly that his grip felt like a tourniquet.

"You bring any asshole who says that to me," the Cuban hissed, "and I'll straighten him out. You probably got that from one of those Anglo snobs who are always trying to heap shit on any Cuban who manages to make it on their turf—or what they *think* is their turf. If you want to talk about laundering dope money, you go talk to the big, snotty-nosed Anglo banks"—he named a few—"and you'll find they're all in it up to their eyeballs. *None* of them are clean."

As he waited for the Cuban to simmer down, Hockney realized he had gone too far.

He was grateful for the interruption when two striking young women came sashaying across the room, right up to Parodi's table. He was conscious that most of the men in the room—even the taciturn pair hiding behind their newspapers—were looking at them.

The leggy brunette was wearing a long black evening dress that left most of her back exposed. The redhead wore a yellow pant suit that clung to her breasts and thighs. The choker around her neck sparkled with what looked to Hockney like diamonds and rubies. If they were imitations, they were damn good ones.

Parodi motioned with his cigar, and they slid into the empty chairs on either side of him.

"Meet Gloria," he said, introducing the redhead. From the way she was running her hand down the Cuban's back, it was plain to Hockney they were old friends. In the circle of light from the lamp between them, he could see that if she removed some of the excess rouge and the caked eye shadow and let down her hair, she would really be quite beautiful. Her cute little snub nose made her look kittenish.

"This is my friend Sonia," the redhead said, introducing the other girl. The brunette seemed very young too, but from her glassy smile and her slow speech, Hockney guessed she was on drugs.

"Bob is a reporter," Parodi announced.

Gloria pouted, and Hockney said, "Have you got something against my profession?"

"It sucks," she said candidly. "A few weeks back, one of the TV networks staked out the lobby of one of the hotels. They got their lousy story. They also got some of the girls busted." She opened her crocodile bag and popped a pill into her mouth.

"We're going to have a party back at my place," the Cuban said to Hockney. "You're included if you want to come along."

"Thanks," Hockney said. "But the lady says she doesn't like reporters."

"She's just kidding around," Parodi reassured him.

But when he looked into Gloria's eyes, Hockney could see that she wasn't. What he read there was not so much distaste as fear.

"Some other night," he cried off.

He left feeling faintly absurd. The manner of his departure reminded him of the tabloid reporters who exposed massage parlors and vice rings, regaling their readers with every detail up to the moment when—so they declared—"I made my excuses and left."

Maguire sounded frosty when Hockney called him at about breakfast time. .

"I hope you had a good time," he said.

"You're not offended, are you?" Hockney asked, worried by his tone. "I told you I wanted to take a look at Parodi close up."

"I'm not offended," Maguire snapped. "It's just that while you were listening to the speeches, I just about got my balls busted by some of those shitheads in the Blue Brigades. It was on TV. They called it police brutality. They got the cameras there just in time to show some cops going in with nightsticks. Naturally, they missed the guys who tried to drop a light in the gas tank of my car."

Hockney tried to make pacifying noises, but the cop brushed them aside.

"So what did you make of our friend?" Maguire asked.

"I'm confused. He talks like a Cold War crusader. He's going to take me to see one of his training camps."

"If you're not careful, they'll use your ass for a target," Maguire promised him. They agreed to talk at the end of the day.

It was an odd kind of Friday which left Hockney seriously concerned that he was on a wild-goose chase. He called the office to say he would be back at the weekend. Jack Lancer was out, working on some investigation, so he had the call transferred to Finkel in New York.

"No hurry, Bob," the Managing Editor said to him. "Jack is doing just fine. How about you? Are you getting anywhere?"

All Hockney could say was "I'm working on it."

"Well, take all the time you need."

The way Finkel said it made Hockney feel he should have flown back to Washington the night before. Something was definitely cooking.

He called Julia, as he had done the previous days.

"Your friend in Puerto Rico tried to reach you," she told him. "He wouldn't give a name, but he said you would know who it was."

"I know," he confirmed. It had to be the FBI man, Frank Parra.

"He said to tell you he's been kicked sideways, to New York."

"Oh, hell." Parra had struck Hockney as the one man who might be able to handle the Puerto Rican end of the Fairchild case. He wondered if the FBI Agent was being transferred because his boss was aware he had talked to a *World* reporter.

Parodi kept his promise about the training camp. He showed up at the hotel in person just after 10 A.M., complete with his champagne Rolls and his gargantuan chauffeur. Hockney brought along his camera, a new miniature model that fitted comfortably into the pocket of his linen jacket.

"Do you mind if I take pictures?" he asked the Cuban when they arrived at the camp, walled off by barbed-wire fencing on a private estate on the edge of the Everglades.

"Take all the pictures you want," Parodi said. "We want people to know we mean business."

The Cuban's offer, as it turned out, was not entirely literal. They let him photograph a mixed team of Cuban and Nicaraguan exiles wading through the swamps and shooting at metal targets that sprang out of the brush at the touch of a button. One of them looked like Fidel; another, a black guerrilla with a rifle. In these exercises, the Blue Brigade recruits—some of them former members of Somoza's National Guard—used Colt AR-15s, which could be bought, cheaply and legally, in plenty of gun shops in South Florida.

They did not let Hockney photograph a second team that was training with special weapons—assault rifles fitted with grenade launchers, laser guidance systems or bullets with apple-green tips which, according to the instructor, could penetrate an armor-plated car.

Parodi borrowed a rifle from the instructor and aimed it at Hockney's chest. The reporter looked down and saw a small red circle of light over the left side of his shirt.

"The red dot is what you hit," Parodi said, grinning. "These lasers are a big deterrent. I tell you, it makes a guy think twice about picking a fight when you show him that little red dot."

"I bet," Hockney concurred, swallowing to ease the sudden dryness in his throat.

Then Parodi showed him a barrackslike building fitted out as a gym.

"Our boys practice the hand-to-hand stuff and the dirty kills in here. The Chavante armlock, the Ganges groin gouge, the Cantonese corkscrew. Take a swipe at me."

"What?"

"Go on—throw me a punch."

Hockney stared at his host uncertainly. Despite his massive build and his broad shoulders, Parodi looked desperately out of shape. He certainly did not look like any sort of paracommando.

"Go on," the Cuban urged again.

Hockney swung his right fist forward. In an instant, the Cuban had cupped Hockney's right elbow underneath with his flattened left hand, and brought the palm of his right hand down on Hockney's wrist. Parodi had the reporter's right arm pinioned in one crisp motion. He applied only moderate pressure, but Hockney yelped with pain. He felt sure that his elbow had been snapped from its socket.

Parodi released his grip and patted Hockney's cheek, as he might have patted a child or a dog. "That's the favorite trick of the *panmo* wrestlers in Brazil," he explained, as the reporter nursed his elbow. "It's the best way I know to break a guy's arm. The elbow isn't built to take that kind of strain."

As they walked back to the Rolls, Parodi winked. "I learned that stuff in the Agency," he said.

Hockney had counted about twenty men in the training camp.

"You really think you're going to overthrow Castro or the Sandinistas with a couple of dozen fighters?" he asked Parodi as they glided back toward Miami. Cushioned by the big car's shock absorbers, he could hardly feel the dips and bumps in the road.

"Didn't you read Mao?" the Cuban responded. "One spark can start a prairie fire."

The pain in Hockney's arm had faded to a memory, and he risked another leading question.

"Julio, aren't you worried that Fidel has penetrated your operation? I've heard there are DGI agents inside most of the exile groups."

Parodi took the question in his stride. "That's mostly true," he said blandly. "But we've got our agents too. A whole network inside Cuba, waiting for the signal to rise."

"Your own network? You mean the Brigada Azul? Or the CIA?"

Parodi's response was a wink—the wink that made him look as if he were sharing some gross obscenity.

Then the Cuban said, "There are some things it's better not

to talk about. That's the Cuban national vice. Talking too much. *Se hace correr la bola.* You know what that means?"

Hockney shook his head.

"We make rumors spread as fast as a fucking football moves around the field."

The visit to the Everglades gave him *something* to play with, Hockney reflected when he got back to the hotel. He banged out a short feature, with lots of color, on the Blue Brigade and Julio Parodi and expressed it to New York, together with the film from his camera. The piece was no literary masterpiece, even though he devoted a paragraph to describing the peculiar stench of rotting mangroves. And he was very much aware that he had been sidetracked from his initial purpose: to trace the connection, if there was one, between Senator Fairchild's death and the object of Jay Maguire's suspicions.

He kept wondering why Parodi had put on such a show for him, all but announcing over a public-address system that he was running an operation for the CIA. Was it just the "Cuban national vice" at work, or was Parodi flaunting his cover? It occurred to Hockney that one way to get the answer was to ask Parodi's CIA friend, the fat man in the snapshot Jay Maguire had shown him. After a couple of calls to Washington contacts, he got a Miami phone number that turned out to belong to the Gator Lumber Company. The woman who answered professed never to have heard of a Mr. Whitman. Hockney drove out to the place—a squat, almost windowless block, behind an electrified fence, that looked like an enormous pillbox. The security guard turned him away, claiming, once again, that there was no Mr. Whitman at the Gator Lumber Company. Hockney realized that if he was going to get to the bottom of *that,* he would have to use his Agency connections in Washington.

Maguire stole an hour or so away from his shift that evening to eat *chuletas de cerdo* with Hockney at the Centro Vasco. Hockney became very conscious that the cop was more reserved than before. He seemed tense and edgy. Hockney became more and more frustrated as they ground their way through the meal, the cop giving monosyllabic replies to his questions or ignoring them altogether.

"Jay," Hockney finally burst out, "I know you're mad at me for some reason. I think it's because you have a feeling that Parodi has suckered me. Well, he hasn't. I just don't know where to go next. You've got to steer me in the right directions. I know you're holding back. If you don't open up, I won't be able to help."

Maguire's reply astonished him.

"Do you ever get to go to Havana?" the cop asked, without looking up from the remains of his rice and beans.

"I don't know if they'd let me in," Hockney said. "I've never applied for a visa."

"I can give you an address," Maguire said. "It's a place in Havana where Parodi goes. Do you have a piece of paper?"

Hockney rummaged through his pockets. It was ridiculous: a newspaperman without anything to write on. Finally, he found a bank deposit slip in his wallet.

Handing it to Maguire, he said, "Sorry. This is all I've got."

"That's okay," the cop replied. "You can take this as a down payment."

Maguire scrawled an address on the back of the slip. His letters were big and ungainly, like a schoolkid's, with great loops on the ys and gs.

"Don't ask where I got it," the Sergeant warned Hockney. "But if you have a way to do it, check it out."

Chapter

4

MIAMI

Arnold Whitman detested Sunday evenings. They always seemed to bring on a drab melancholia. This had something to do with the fact that the weekend was nearly over and he had to face the office, with its impossible demands, once again. It was bound up, too, with his sense of the passage of time, with his compulsive need to make a reckoning of what he had gained, and what he had lost—not merely during the week that was gone, but through the whole course of his life. On the quiet days, the Sundays when he was not on duty, or playing golf, or entertaining people at dinner, he would sit by himself and balance the books, and each time, he found that his losses had grown.

Whitman was sitting in his five-year-old Saab in the middle of the Rickenbacker Causeway, waiting for the bridge to be lowered. He watched a yacht with a bright pink hull drift past in the direction of the setting sun. A curvy blonde in a bikini waved from the deck at the motorists stranded along the causeway for her convenience.

"Fuck you," Whitman muttered under his breath, which

came noisily, as if through blocked passages, as fat people's breath is apt to do. Arnold Whitman was not merely fat. He was huge. He was built like a six-foot-four Buddha, and the resemblance was enhanced by the high bald dome of his head.

When the Agency had offered him the job of Station Chief in Miami, he had jumped at it, partly because he felt a warm glow of nostalgia when he thought back to the days when he had swaggered into Sloppy Joe's for a liquid breakfast after staying up all night to run a maritime raid into Cuba, the days when he had believed, with missionary passion, that he had the power to *change* things. In the early sixties, he had known how to play the Cuban exile community like a harpsichord. Even the flimsy cover that the CIA Station in South Florida used—the Gator Lumber Company—took him back to those times.

But there was another attraction in the Miami job. He had seen it as an easy slide into a cozy retirement in the sun, downhill all the way. Fate had worked differently. He found that Miami had turned into the Casablanca of the Caribbean. Every secret service in the hemisphere—and many from outside—was engaged in its murky intrigues. Émigrés from all over the Latin world conspired in its bars and nightclubs, together with the drug traffickers, arms merchants and shady financiers. On top of which, the Newgate Administration seemed bent on pursuing a secret war against Cuba. Some people at Langley seemed to think it would be an easy job to rehire contract employees in the Cuban community who had been dropped from the Company payroll when the Nixon White House, in 1973, ordered the CIA bases in the Florida Keys closed down for good. Whitman knew, firsthand, how much things had changed. He had revisited some of the hidden coves where the Agency had once based its private fleet of revved-up boats, used for secret landings in Cuba. He found that new roads and apartment houses and fishing resorts had taken over: the triumph of concrete over mangrove, of developers over secret agents.

It was not just the landscape that had been transformed. Whitman had found that many of the old CIA hands in Little Havana had not forgiven their former employers for abandoning them. Even those who were still enthusiastic about trying to "liberate" Cuba, or at least pull Fidel's beard, had powerful personal reasons for not getting involved. They were older; they had kids and middle-age spread. Many had built up their own businesses and lived in three-hundred-thousand-dollar houses in Coral Gables. More than a few of them were mixed up with drugs.

Whitman did not find the dope connection particularly shocking. He knew any number of rightist exiles who thought that drug dealing was perfectly justified if it helped to support their political causes. He knew that in old Havana, in Batista's (and Meyer Lansky's) day, there had been little social stigma involved. Cocaine had been as freely available as Chivas Regal, maybe more so. He had heard of affluent Cubans who rubbed it into their genitals in the—unverifiable—belief that its reputed aphrodisiac powers would thereby be increased.

Arnold Whitman had no objection to working with dopers, provided they had enough to offer. His attitude had resulted in one major row with his FBI counterpart in Miami, when he had asked the Bureau to stop snooping on one of his agents.

"But we know that this guy is one of the biggest cocaine suppliers in South Florida," the FBI man had objected.

"The coke gets in anyway," Whitman had explained patiently. "A chance to get deep inside Castro's intelligence networks comes about once every ten years."

What worried Whitman most about using criminals as agents was that psychologically, they could never be expected to stay loyal to a single employer; there was always the chance they would end up robbing the till. "The specialty of a spy or a double agent," Whitman had once lectured a class of young intelligence officers, "is the betrayal of trust. The difficulty in running a double agent is that once he becomes habituated to betraying the trust of people who are close to him—the people on whom he is spying—he may find it just as easy, emotionally, to betray you."

The man Whitman was on his way to visit was both a doper

and a double agent, an expert in betrayal who almost appeared to live for the thrill of stabbing people who trusted him in the back. Whitman believed that what this agent had to give was so valuable that it was worth running the risks—and suffering the occasional embarrassment—in order to keep possession of it. It was not often, in recent years, that the Agency was presented with a source who was in personal contact with Castro's intelligence chiefs, so trusted by them that he was used in the most sensitive undercover operations. When you found a source like that, you didn't blow it, and you sure as hell didn't allow a couple of dumb cops in the Miami Police Department to put him away for bringing in a little coke on the side.

At the same time, you didn't expect him to set out to get his name in the newspapers.

The fat Sunday edition of *The New York World* lay on the passenger seat, next to Whitman. The Review section was on top, folded open to an article headed "CIA TRAINS RIGHTISTS IN FLORIDA FOR NICARAGUA, CUBA INVASIONS." The article, accompanied by some incredible photographs of members of the Brigada Azul wading through the Everglades or taking pot-shots at metal dummies, occupied the best part of a page. Whitman had begun—as he always began with newspaper articles—by studying the reporter's name. He recognized the by-line at once. Robert Hockney was the man from the *World* who had been trying to phone him at the Gator Lumber Company.

What Whitman found unbelievable was that Julio Parodi had apparently led Hockney around by the hand and shown him all over the training facility. The fact that Parodi was shooting off his mouth to the press intensified Whitman's concern that he had allowed the Cuban agent too loose a bridle. Parodi was getting noticeably more vain and offhanded; witness the way he had insisted on naming the place where they were going to meet tonight. Whitman decided he would have to remind the Cuban who was the boss.

The venue Parodi had picked was typical of the man—typical of that self-indulgent sloppiness which made it easy to understand why he had drawn the suspicions of the Miami police, and hard to grasp how he had avoided being caught out by his Castro contacts before now. It was a swinging Italian disco/restaurant named Stefano's. Whitman could see the sign looming up to the right. True to form, Parodi had left his champagne Rolls parked close to the door: more self-advertising. As Whitman got out of his own car, he spotted Parodi's goon lounging nearby, dragging on a cigarette.

It was early for Stefano's. But as Whitman strode past the triangular bar, he saw a few single girls—one of them stunningly attractive—nursing drinks, waiting for the place to fill up. The band would not come on until later, but the decibel count from the hi-fi was sufficient for Whitman to feel that his eardrums were bruised by the time he located Parodi's table and pulled back a chair.

"We're not here to disco," the CIA Station Chief complained, leaning across the table to make himself audible.

Parodi was wearing his playclothes: an off-white suit of raw silk, and a crimson shirt unbuttoned to display his gold chains and a curly tuft of gray hair.

"I assume you've seen the *World*," Whitman said, dropping the Review section on the table. "What the hell were you trying to do, playing footsie with reporters?"

"The man was looking for a story," Parodi said urbanely. "I gave him a story. It stopped him nosing around."

"You're crazy," Whitman said, shaking his head.

"Listen, everybody's happy. The Brigade kids are happy. They got their pictures in the paper. My friends on the island are happy. This proves I'm a big guy with the anti-Castro crazies. So what are you upset about?"

"Stop pissing around." Whitman did not swear often, and when he did he sounded as if he were trying to talk with his mouth full. "Look at that headline," he specified. "The Company's name is smeared all over this crap. We're going to have Senate committees and reporters climbing all over us. Langley is mad as hell."

Parodi was engaged in circumcising one of his mammoth

cigars with an extraordinary device that looked like a pair of gold shears. His casual air was starting to infuriate the CIA man.

"I still don't see your problem," the Cuban said once he had trimmed and moistened the end of his cigar to his satisfaction. "We both know the Company isn't running that camp. The camp belongs to me. The Brigade belongs to me."

"And you belong to us," Whitman broke in. "If you start forgetting who owns you, you won't be worth a rat's ass." He saw the waiter approaching, and fell silent.

"What are you drinking?" Parodi played the gracious host.

"I want a daiquiri. But not too sweet. *Poco azúcar.*"

Force of habit had made Whitman shunt his chair around so that he was facing the door, with the empty bandstand at his back. The brunette he had noticed at the bar came rippling over to the next table. He noticed that she was not wearing a bra. But the steady look he gave her was not one of appreciation.

They both sat silent until the waiter came back with the drinks.

Whitman tasted his daiquiri and said, "It's too sweet."

"I'll order another."

Parodi snapped his fingers at the waiter, but Whitman was already pushing back his chair.

"We can't talk here anyway," the CIA man said. "Get up. We're leaving."

Whitman was halfway to the door by the time the Cuban had reluctantly hauled himself to his feet, shrugged to the waiter and started padding after him.

Outside, Parodi's chauffeur stood waiting by the open door of the Rolls.

"Forget it," Whitman instructed Parodi. "We'll take *my* car."

"We can go to my apartment," the Cuban suggested. "It's only five minutes from here."

"We'll take a drive," the CIA man countered. "The night air might help you to think straight."

They both got into the Saab. Parodi's knees were bunched

up against his chest in the cramped space, but Whitman made no offer to roll his seat back.

"We'd really be much more comfortable at my place," Parodi tried again.

"You've got to be kidding," the CIA man snapped. "Every goddamn government agency in town has your mattress room bugged."

"I've got thirty thousand dollars' worth of debugging equipment in there," the Cuban objected with an air of wounded propriety.

"From the animal noises your hookers fake," Whitman observed drily, "I can tell you it doesn't work."

As they drove over the causeway toward the downtown area, Whitman could sense that the Cuban was starting to lose his poise. That suited his purpose. He steered the car through a residential district of one- and two-story houses faced with pink, green and white stucco, each with its patch of garden. Some of the streets were dotted with palms and shade trees, oleanders and the occasional Norfolk pine. It was a typically Latin part of Miami, an area of hardworking lower-middle-class families. Whitman circled back and drove along a winding road by the Miami River. There was enough light to see the sign that identified NW 16 STREET.

Whitman slowed the car as they neared number 2400. It was a four-floor red-brick–and–concrete block, with washing hanging from the balconies.

"Are you crazy?" Parodi hissed. "You can't stop here."

The Cuban was visibly agitated. He dropped his cigar, and ash crumbled down the front of his white suit. He went fishing for the stogie between his knees, and when his head came up, Whitman could see the beads of moisture on his forehead.

"Cõno," the Cuban swore. "Let's get out of here before somebody sees us."

Whitman lingered a moment longer before he put his foot down on the gas pedal and made a sharp left at the next corner.

"I'm asking you, Arnie," Parodi said, recovering his composure once the apartment building was out of sight. "Why the fuck did you drive down here?"

If there was one thing Whitman hated, it was for people to call him Arnie.

He didn't say anything until they were a safe distance away from Northwest Sixteenth Street. Then he stopped the car, turned off the engine and swiveled to look the Cuban directly in the eyes.

"I want you to understand something, Julio," the CIA man began. "I could have dumped you there and honked my horn just to show your friends inside who you're working for." Whitman was familiar with what went on in the building on Sixteenth Street. There was an apartment on the top floor that was used by the DGI as a safe house. It was leased by an elderly Cuban who worked for a local cigar company—a very fitting contact for Julio Parodi. Whitman knew that Parodi had visited the apartment a couple of times to send messages to Havana, although most of his meetings with the DGI took place outside the United States. Parodi always reported the meetings that took place on Sixteenth Street. Whitman was sure of that, because he had taken the precaution of having the apartment bugged. But he could never be sure how much more was being exchanged hand to hand, on bits of paper.

"*Carajo,*" Parodi said with feeling. "You could get me killed. If the Cubans knew I was talking to you . . ." He made the gesture of slitting his throat. Then he stuck his cigar into his mouth like a pacifier.

"I'm trying to make a point, Julio," Whitman explained. "Now you've got a nice life. You're a very wealthy man. I don't know anybody up at Langley who lives like you. You're a big man in Little Havana. And even Fidel loves you. It would be a pity to spoil everything because you're lacking in discipline."

"What are you saying?"

"I'm saying button your mouth. In fact, get out of sight for a while. Take a trip, starting tomorrow. Can you arrange a trip to Havana?"

"I was there just two weeks ago," Parodi said. "I've got to be careful. People here might start to notice something, people in the Brigade."

"We want you in Cuba," Whitman said, with the edge of command in his voice. "I'm not discussing this with you, I'm *telling* you. Have you found my wavelength yet?"

Parodi sat quiet, stripping loose tobacco from the end of his cigar.

"Don't dry up on us now, Julio. You've been living on credit for a while now. Don't forget who's keeping the cops and the Bureau off your back."

"They haven't got a goddamn thing on me that would stick in court," the Cuban said contemptuously.

"But *we* have, Julio."

"*Te jodistes,*" Parodi said passionately.

"I know."

As they rode back to the causeway, the silence that fell between them was deeper than before. Whitman felt a degree of quiet satisfaction. Fear was the only sure way he knew to keep Parodi honest, and he thought he had managed to instill a little that night. In Top Secret intra-agency memos, the agent was sometimes referred to as "Daiquiri"—yet another of those alcoholic monikers some drunk in Washington dreamed up. Whitman preferred the original code name the Agency had assigned to Parodi: AMTRAK. The humorless bureaucrat who had come up with that one had picked it because it was a combination of letters starting with AM, the old CIA serial for Cuban assets. But Whitman appreciated the unintended pun. The code name suggested you'd be lucky to get to your destination on time, and you might miss the train altogether.

NEW YORK

Hockney was sitting in a cheerful whitewashed room hung with dried red peppers and peasant rugs on the corner of Seventy-seventh Street and Second Avenue. The Csarda was exactly the way he imagined an old country inn east of the Danube should be, and "country inn" was what its name meant in Hungarian. He watched Len Rourke wolfing down everything that was placed in front of them, starting with the *lecsos kolbasa*—generous slices of garlic sausage swimming in tomatoes, green peppers, onions and, of course, paprika—through the veal *paprikás* to the *palacsinta,* jam-filled crepes sprinkled with walnuts. The gargantuan portions defeated Hockney. They were on their third bottle of Bull's Blood by the time the Executive Editor of the *World* leaned back in his chair, rubbed his flat belly and called for coffee.

"The Hungarians really know how to eat," Rourke said approvingly.

"Well, you certainly did them justice," Hockney observed wonderingly. The last time he had dined with his editor, Rourke had picked at his food with utter indifference. And Rourke looked thinner than ever. His narrow, stooped shoulders and the hollows under his cheekbones gave him a wasted, cadaverous look. Yet he had grabbed at his food with the excitement of an alcoholic approaching the first drink of the day.

"That operation seemed to change my whole metabolism," Rourke explained, noting Hockney's curiosity. "The night they let me out of the hospital, I ate four sirloin steaks—*four*—and about five pounds of potatoes. The doctors say not to worry. It happens to some people. I'll get back to normal in a couple of weeks."

Rourke was unnaturally flushed, and his hand shook as he tried to light a cigarette. He had had his bypass operation barely a month before.

"I can't stop thinking about it," he said to Hockney. "I told the doctors I wanted to understand everything that was happening to my body. They let me watch the X-ray picture on a videoscreen while they were trying to open up one of the arteries. They injected nitros with a tiny, tiny needle. I didn't feel a damn thing to begin with. Then there was an explosion inside the artery—it showed up on the screen like a cloud of ink squirted out by a squid—and I was lying there wondering what this had to do with me. And then the pain started. They told me later it lasted about twelve seconds. I can't describe that pain to you, Bob. It felt like a shooting star."

Rourke's teeth chattered a little as he talked, as if he were chewing nuts. He always sounded that way when he was nervous or excited.

"Something like that changes you, Bob," Rourke went on. "It makes you realize that you don't have forever, you know? It forces you to decide what *really* matters."

Hockney listened closely, and the sympathy in his face was genuine. He had always liked this man, even if he was a weak editor, too ready to let himself be bullied by Ed Finkel. He also understood that if there was a sermon in Rourke's words, it was intended for *him*. He had flown up to New York from Washington to protest the way that Finkel and Jack Lancer had handled the story he had filed on the training camp in the Everglades. They had singled out a single reference to Julio Parodi's past association with the Agency and presented the piece as if it were an exposé of an illegal CIA operation.

Rourke had already made it plain that he was not disposed to play umpire in another office row. He wanted to talk about other things.

"Why are you so interested in this Fairchild story?" Rourke was asking.

"Well, I always liked whodunits," Hockney said. "I can't prove anything yet, but I think there's a lot more involved than just some Puerto Rican crazies who didn't like the way the Senator talked about their movement." In a cautious, sketchy way, not mentioning names, he explained the possible Miami connection. "I may have to go to Cuba," he concluded.

Rourke stubbed out his half-smoked cigarette, and immediately put another into his mouth. It was a perplexing habit that did not reduce the amount of nicotine he consumed; it merely raised the cost.

"You're not happy running the Washington bureau, are you, Bob? I'd like you to be frank."

"Well—I guess I do miss being able to run around the way I used to."

"I can understand that," Rourke nodded. "You're not a deskman. You never were. Do you think the Fairchild case is worth pursuing further?"

"I'm sure of it. I may not be able to make this sound convincing, but I know it will pay off. You can smell these things."

"Okay." Rourke exhaled, and a smoke ring like a figure-8 on its side—the sign of infinity—wafted up toward the ceiling. "It's time we sent somebody top-notch to Cuba. I'm sick of the crap we're getting from that stringer in Havana. Ed Finkel was telling me this afternoon that the Cubans are interested in arranging for five or six senior editors to go, full access guaranteed. Ed was proposing that we nominate Jack Lancer. I don't see why you shouldn't go instead. Are you interested?"

"When does this junket begin?"

"In a couple of weeks."

Hockney started thinking about what Jack Lancer would file if he made the Cuba trip. *Jack wouldn't recognize a DGI agent if he went to bed with one*, Hockney reflected. But what decided him was the scrap of paper that Jay Maguire had given him in Miami, the bank deposit slip with a Havana address on the back.

"I'd like to go," Hockney said.

"All right," Rourke replied. "I'll try to fix it. Now, there's one more thing, Bob. It's healthy to have disagreements inside a newspaper. But I get tired when personal feuds wind up in my in tray every day of the week. Finkel wants you out of the Washington job. You know that."

"He advertises the fact."

"Yes, he does. Now, I'm ready to back you up. Up to a point. You've got to make up your mind whether you want to hold on to the Washington job. If you do, you can't just go whoring off after every story that comes up. But I get the feeling you might be happier if you went back to what you used to do. You're one of the best goddamn investigative reporters I've ever come across, Bob. Maybe you should have stuck to that."

"You could be right."

"We don't need to make any decisions now. Go see Castro, and then we'll talk some more."

MIAMI

On the day that Hockney flew up to New York, Julio Parodi had left his Key Biscayne apartment before 9 A.M. Instead of using the familiar Rolls, he had Mama Benitez drive him downtown in a powder-blue Dodge. He alighted at the corner of Flagler and Twenty-fourth, and hurried into a three-story building whose inconspicuous sign read, "CAMAGÜEY INTERNACIONAL, S.A."

He exchanged a few words with the security man in the ground-floor shop, where racks of handguns and rifles were on display behind reinforced glass. Then he loped up the stairs to the Manager's office on the second floor. When the Manager had discreetly withdrawn, it did not take Parodi long to conduct his business. He dialed out on his private line. One of the calls was to an obscure air-freight company in Fort Lauderdale. Another was to the local representative of an even more obscure import-export firm that operated out of the Colón Free Zone in Panama. The final call was to Aeroméxico, to confirm a one-way first-class reservation for Mexico City for the same day.

"You will be gone for some time, Don Julio?" the Manager inquired when Parodi summoned him back to his office.

"Not long, Felix. I have every confidence in you."

Parodi's next stop was at a bank in which he held the controlling interest—although prudently, he had had most of the stock registered in the names of various relatives and employees. From the bank, Parodi drove direct to Miami International Airport. Bag in hand, he made a local call from a quiet phone booth down the concourse from Aeroméxico's departure lounge. His conversation would have baffled the casual eavesdropper. Leafing through a pocket edition of a Spanish-language dictionary, he dictated:

"Página sesenta y nueve, línea doce. Página treinta, línea cuatro."

It was a laborious way of transmitting a message, but it was bugproof—unless somebody listening in happened to know what edition of what book the people on the line were using. When he had finished reading off his dictionary references, the man at the other end of the line said, *"Listo."*

Parodi's arrival in Mexico City a few hours later was not recorded. Two obliging officials in dark suits met him at the plane and escorted him past Immigration and Customs. No one asked to inspect his luggage. There was no record of his departure from the Mexican capital. But three days later, a heavyset man with a small leather suitcase and a passport that identified him as a Panamanian national boarded an Avianca flight for Medellín.

MEDELLÍN, COLOMBIA

Marijuana is a lazy man's crop. It sprouts like weeds, maturing in only three or four months. Cocaine requires more patience. It may take three years before a coca tree comes on tap. But once it starts producing, a single coca tree is as good as a gold mine. It is possible to harvest the leaves several times a year, for up to forty years—as long as an average man's working life. The leaves of the coca are ground into a paste that is taken for refining to one of the hundreds of laboratories concealed in the Amazonian rain forests of Colombia, in the *llanos* on the eastern side of the Andes, in Bogotá, Cali and Medellín. Once distilled, the pure cocaine is taken to cutting rooms where it is mixed with cheaper substances, like lactose. In old-fashioned cutting rooms, female workers are required to work nude, to reduce the possibility that they will try to conceal a pinch or two of valuable white powder about their persons. The cocaine will be cut, or "stepped on," many times before it reaches the street consumer in Miami or New York. A kilo of uncut coke may fetch twenty-four thousand dollars in Colombia. Stepped on repeatedly, that same kilo will produce between twelve and twenty pounds of snow, with a street value of three hundred thousand dollars or more. It is not difficult to understand why people kill for cocaine.

Behind the high walls of one of the cocaine palaces along Millionaires' Row in the city of Medellín, beside an Olympic-length swimming pool shaped like a porpoise, a young Colombian who called himself Demetrio had come to pay his respects to Julio Parodi.

Demetrio had the props of his trade. He arrived in a white Mercedes convertible with a flashy blonde, who peeled off obediently to sun herself out of earshot on the far side of the pool. The Colombian wore a showy watch, a considerable amount of jewelry and designer jeans. He walked with a slight limp, supporting himself on a black cane with an ivory grip.

But when Parodi embraced him, he addressed the young Colombian as "Comandante."

Demetrio was one of the commanders of the northern front of the April Nineteenth Movement—the M-19. He had developed his limp after he caught a stray bullet during a shoot-out at sea, when the Colombian Navy intercepted a rusty old tramp steamer the M-19 was using to ferry Cuban-trained guerrillas to a lonely anchorage on the Pacific coast. Despite his wound, the authorities had failed to identify Comandante Demetrio. Or chose not to. He was the nephew of one of the Republic's most important generals, and he had some extremely influential business associates.

"Have you got the stuff?" Parodi asked him.

"I brought a sample," Demetrio said. "You can inspect the rest at the farm, when the exchange is complete."

The Colombian unzipped his Italian-style shoulder bag, pushed his automatic to one side and removed a package the size and shape of a tobacco pouch. He offered it to Parodi.

The Cuban unwrapped the oilcloth, took a pinch of the white powder between thumb and index finger and transferred it to the palm of his left hand. He noted approvingly that the powder shone in the bright sunlight. If it had already been stepped on, grains of lactose or other additives would have shown up dull, like flour among sugar crystals.

Gingerly, Parodi rubbed the powder against the film of moisture in his cupped palm. The coke turned clear and mushy.

"Excelente," Parodi commented. *"Espere un ratito."*

Demetrio hobbled around the pool to where his girlfriend was sunbathing, face down. Parodi went inside the villa. A piece of tinfoil on a stand was ready for him in the kitchen. He built a tiny mound of white powder on the foil, then lit a long wooden match and held it underneath. The heat caused the cocaine to vaporize. Little by little, it turned into a twisting ribbon of smoke, leaving only a stain behind on the tinfoil. The stain, Parodi observed, was the palest shade of yellow. That pleased him. The more that cocaine has been cut, the darker the stain appears.

He prodded around inside Demetrio's package with his finger, and found a few minute lumps among the powder. That pleased him too. Addicts became very much excited when they found "rocks" like these in their coke, thinking it meant the stuff was one hundred percent pure. Practiced distributors like Parodi would strew a few lumps of solid cocaine into snow that had been stepped on until it was less than ten percent pure in order to command top prices.

"Macanudo," Parodi declared when he rejoined Demetrio outside. His eyes flicked across to the blonde, who had unhooked the top of her bikini.

"It's all the same quality," Demetrio said casually, sounding already bored with the whole transaction.

"How much have you got?"

"The full consignment. Four hundred Ks."

It was a large shipment, but by no means the largest that the two men had arranged together. The value agreed on was ten million. Parodi would pass on the coke to a South Florida associate for cutting, and collect eight or nine times the purchase price from distributors further downstream.

"I brought a deposit," the Cuban said, opening the leather suitcase to display neatly stacked wads of hundred-dollar bills.

Demetrio did not bother to inspect the money.

"I want to see the guns," he said. "When are they arriving?"

"First light tomorrow. Or the day after. It depends."

"All right," the Colombian said. "I'll meet you at the farm. We have plenty of grouper, if you're interested."

"How much?"

"All that your boat can handle."

"Square grouper" was the slang that Caribbean fishermen used to describe the bales of marijuana they sometimes hauled in place of other kinds of catch. Parodi was not very much interested in pot. The profit margin was less than on coke and heroin. Marijuana was a lot bulkier—increasing the risk of getting caught. Still, he would have an empty hull after the arms drop had been completed, and Julio Parodi hated to miss an opportunity to increase his earnings.

"I'll take a look," he said. "I assume my credit is still good," he added, grinning, as he closed the leather bag and handed it to Demetrio.

Their deal was not particularly big by South Florida standards. A year or two before, Customs inspectors at Miami Airport had intercepted a consignment of cocaine with a street value of almost a billion dollars.

What made Parodi's business relationship with Comandante Demetrio different was that the Cuban was trading guns, rather than money, for Colombian dope. Parodi had not wasted a single hour worrying about the risk of a double cross. He knew that Demetrio would honor their agreements, not because the Colombian was a Marxist revolutionary, but because the two men had originally been introduced by a senior official in the DGI.

It was two days later, at 6:15 A.M., that the twin-engined plane from Fort Lauderdale made a bumpy landing on a strip that had been hacked out of the scrub. Even at that early hour, you could feel the stifling heat coming down through the low gray cloud ceiling. The landing strip was on a farm near Manaure, on the Orgeguaza River. The Colombian had posted lookouts on the rough country road that zigzagged back to the dusty port of Riohacha.

Parodi had taken that road in the middle of the night, swerving and snaking after the taillights of an old LTD driven by one of Demetrio's men. Behind Parodi's car, bunched together too closely for safety, had followed a new Volkswagen van, a near-new Toyota pickup and an ancient hearse—an oddly assorted convoy to transport part of the cargo from a tramp steamer docked in Riohacha. Bringing up the rear was a furniture-moving van. The larger of the crates unloaded from the freighter *Catriona*, registered in Panama, contained Belgian-manufactured FAL automatic rifles. The smaller ones contained 7.62mm ammunition, a thousand rounds to each box. The guns and the ammunition had been supplied from a warehouse in the Colón Free Zone of Panama with which Parodi had had numerous dealings.

The Colombian had broken open a couple of crates after the convoy arrived at the farm. He had found the contents to his satisfaction. With the aid of a tractor, the boxes had been transferred to the hold of a cargo plane "borrowed" from Aeropesca. When the new consignment arrived from Florida, the Aeropesca plane would be used to fly most of the weapons to M-19 guerrillas in the south. Parodi was supplying the means to launch a new insurrection.

The Aeropesca pilot waited nervously, pistol in hand, for the plane from Fort Lauderdale to complete its landing run. A dozen oil drums were lined up at the edge of the strip, ready for the refueling. Six M-19 guerrillas, armed with a variety of American-made weapons, stood guard around the landing site.

One of them was the blonde who had accompanied Demetrio to the villa in Medellín. She looked different now, with her hair tied back in a ponytail. Like the other guerrillas, she wore a beret and fatigues.

The pilot from Fort Lauderdale, a freckle-faced American, jumped out of the cockpit.

"You're a day late," Parodi reproached him.

"Had to take evasive action," the American explained. He gasped a little as the still heat enclosed him. "I thought the Colombian air force was on to me," he went on. "Guess I threw them off the scent."

Parodi took him to one side and counted out fifty thousand dollars in large bills. The Colombians got on with the unloading. Some of the crates they pulled out of the small plane were the length of a man's body.

Demetrio picked up a crowbar and prised one of the crates open. It contained a heavy metal tube with a telescopic sight mounted on top. The M-67 recoilless rifle had been one of the American Army's standard antitank weapons for many years, until it was replaced by the M-47 guided missile. Firing fin-stabilized HEAT rounds, weighing more than nine pounds apiece, it had a range of more than two thousand yards. Its main attraction, from the point of view of the guerrillas, was that it could be fired from the shoulder by a single man.

The other crates contained a lighter antitank rocket, grenade launchers, mortars, two dozen M-60 gas-operated, air-cooled machine guns and a hundred AR-15 assault rifles, all exported by the arms company in Miami under a fake end-user certificate.

"Are you happy?" Parodi asked Comandante Demetrio.

"*Satisfecho*," the Colombian acknowledged.

The blond guerrilla came over, hoisted the recoilless rifle onto her shoulder and made a play of gunning down an imaginary tank.

"*Basta*," Demetrio reprimanded her. "We'll get a shot at the real thing soon enough."

Parodi lit a breakfast cigar—the best cigar of the day—as

he watched the Colombian team set to work moving the new arms consignment on board the Aeropesca plane. It struck him, not for the first time, that there was a certain genius behind this drugs-for-arms barter trade that the Cubans had orchestrated. It enabled Colombia's revolutionaries to finance their own insurrection many times over. The profits from the hash and cocaine they supplied could be skimmed to finance arms purchases for guerrillas all over the hemisphere. Since the guns that Parodi and other dealers supplied were of Western origin— whenever possible, American-made—the risk that the Cubans or their Soviet big brothers could be held liable for arming terrorists was minimized. Not to mention the fact that the drugs that got through to the United States contributed to what one of his friends in Havana liked to call "social decomposition."

The pilot from Lauderdale shuffled up, dabbing at his neck with a handkerchief, and said, "Are you flying back with me, sir?"

"Not this time," Parodi replied.

"Okay. Good hunting."

Parodi watched him board his plane, taxi to the end of the landing strip and take off, barely clearing the trees.

He swatted reflexively at a buzzing mosquito close to his ear.

The loading operation completed, Demetrio came back and shook his hand. "I may have more for you in about a month," the Colombian said. "Can you handle it?"

"How much this time?"

"Six hundred, eight hundred Ks."

"No problem."

"Okay. *Hasta la victoria siempre.*"

THE WINDWARD PASSAGE

The Captain was not entirely happy about Parodi's presence on the boat that had been rebaptized *Zar de Colón*. It gave him the feeling that he was no longer the master of his own vessel. But after the cargo had been loaded, and the boat slipped its lines, the Cuban disappeared into the First Mate's cabin and did not reappear until dinnertime.

The voyage was uneventful until the *Zar de Colón* was more than halfway through the Windward Passage, the forty-mile stretch of limpid blue water between the eastern tip of Cuba and Haiti.

Parodi came up onto the bridge to watch the dumpy Cuban patrol boat closing in on them.

"It's the *Cañonera*," the Captain announced. "*Coño*. They don't recognize us."

Parodi borrowed the Captain's binoculars. He could see men in uniform on board the Cuban Coast Guard cutter, manning the machine guns that were mounted fore and aft.

The voice of the Cuban commander crackled over the *Zar de Colón*'s radio, advising the skipper to heave to for inspection.

"Do it," Parodi said.

His order was unnecessary. The Captain, who had met the Cuban gunboat many times before, had already set his engines full astern. It took several minutes before the tramp steamer came to a complete halt.

Six armed Cubans from the *Cañonera* rowed alongside, and the crew of Parodi's boat helped them on deck.

It was routine practice for the Cuban Coast Guard to intercept drug boats in the Windward Passage and the Yucatán Channel, to the east of the island. The Cubans imposed tolls for the use of their territorial waters. These imposts were regarded as matter-of-factly by experienced dopers as a commuter driving between Manhattan and Long Island might view the tollbooths on the Triborough Bridge. The basic tariff, in this case, was twenty cents for every Quaalude pill on board, ten dollars for every pound of marijuana and ten percent of the purchase price for every kilo of cocaine—two thousand four hundred dollars and up. Payment was sometimes demanded on the spot, on penalty of confiscation of the cargo and the boat, and the imprisonment of the captain in the wing of the Combinado del Este prison that was reserved for foreigners. But dopers who were known to the Cuban authorities could run a tab. Regular traffickers who knew the ropes were allowed to make payment later, to Cuban agents in Panamá, the Bahamas, or Miami.

The exact amount of the dues imposed depended on whether the Cubans provided additional services. For an extra fee, drug boats were permitted to hole up in Cuban ports for repairs and overhaul. Some were licensed to use the Cuban flag on the high seas. Sometimes, the Cubans were willing—for a price—to provide a naval escort to shepherd the dopers' mother-ships to rendezvous-points in the Bahamas, like Cay Sal, where their cargoes were off-loaded onto zippy "cigarette boats" for the last part of the voyage to South Florida.

Julio Parodi's credit with the Cubans was unusually good.

"I didn't recognize the boat," the captain of the *Cañonera* apologized after he had checked Parodi's credentials in an exchange of coded radio signals with his base.

"Don't worry about it," Parodi said patronizingly. "We're going ashore."

The Cuban gunboat escorted the *Zar de Colón* along the northern shore of the island, to a secure anchorage screened by the archipelago of Camagüey.

"I'm leaving you here," Parodi said to his captain. "You understand the rest of the instructions?"

"Seguro," the Captain replied. "There's nothing to it."

CUBA

Parodi walked barefoot along the strip of white sand between the palms and the water's edge, drinking in the fresh salt air of Santa María del Mar. The villa was set on a rise beyond the palms. From the beach, he could see the flash of bougainvillea and orange and white hibiscus around its wide veranda. Before the Revolution, the villa had belonged to one of the wealthy *criollo* families. Now it belonged to the Ministry of the Interior.

It was one of scores of palatial beach houses at Santa María and at Varadero, farther east along the coast road, that were reserved by the Cuban secret service for special guests.

The accommodating maids at the villa, Parodi knew, were supplied by the Vice Squad of Cuban State Security. This extremely active department had been founded in the sixties under the supervision of Colonel Ivan Macharov of the Soviet KGB, a man who was celebrated for his prowess in running male and female sexual operatives—"ravens" and "swallows." The first Cuban appointed to head the Vice Squad had quickly earned the nickname of "La Puta Militante"—The Militant Whore. The sobriquet had stuck to some of his successors. The Vice Squad controlled hundreds of hookers, including homosexuals and lesbians. They were classified not only according to their sexual specialties, but according to their intelligence targets. So there were *putas diplomáticas,* used in efforts to blackmail and entrap diplomats and visiting Congressmen; *putas técnicas,* who had been given the necessary schooling to recognize the value of technical and scientific information, and *putas marineras,* at the bottom end of the scale, who picked up foreign sailors.

In his bedroom the night before, Parodi had enjoyed the favors of one of the maids, a sexy *mulata* who drifted around the villa in an apron and little else. She had boasted to him of how she had been summoned to entertain an influential American Congressman at one of the resort hotels. The Congressman was presumably unaware that his bedroom was wired for total visual and auditory surveillance. Since he was well known as an admirer of the Cuban regime, it was unlikely that any use would be made of the photographs in any imminent future. They would be held in reserve—insurance against the day when he might change his mind and require an extra incentive to return the favors he had received in Havana.

Parodi walked until he was only a few paces away from the guard who was leaning unobtrusively against the royal palm that marked the limit of his private beach. There was no fence, no barrier; just a sign on the tree that read, "ENTRADA PROHI-

BIDA." The spiky fronds of the royal palm described a near-perfect circle, like the vanes of a windmill.

Parodi exchanged a few pleasantries with the guard and started trekking back along the sand, walking in his own footprints.

Then he heard the maid's voice.

"*¡Venga, señor!*" she called as she ran down from the house. "*Ya viene el comandante.*"

Parodi buttoned his shirt, pulled on his canvas shoes and followed her back to the villa.

A tall, dark-skinned man in fatigues without badges of rank was waiting for him on the veranda. Sighting the newcomer, Parodi experienced a moment of dizziness, like an acrobat, attempting an enormously difficult feat without a safety net, who had chosen the wrong moment to look down.

It made no difference how many times Parodi met Calixto Valdés. There was always this moment of fear.

It did not subside until after the dark Cuban, evidently in high spirits, had clasped Parodi in a welcoming *abrazo*.

Drawing back, Valdés feinted at Parodi's belly three, four times.

"*Gordito,*" Valdés mocked him playfully. "You should have spent more time in the jungle with our Colombian friends."

Valdés knew the jungle. He had been with Castro in the early days, in the Sierra Maestra, where he had won the coveted title of Comandante. His exploits since the revolution were legendary. Posing as a CIA man, he had infiltrated the mountain headquarters of one of the surviving anti-Castro leaders and shot him in the face with a magnum loaded with cyanide bullets. He had worked with the PLO in Beirut and Damascus, and had led a Palestinian raid into the Israeli-occupied Sinai in 1970. He had directed a team of DGI officers who helped the North Vietnamese to interrogate American POWs. He had fought with the Sandinista guerrillas in the field during the Nicaraguan civil war. He shuttled back and forth from Managua to Luanda, from Paris to Aden, to maintain liaison with the "liberation movements" that sent their best recruits for training in Cuba.

His speed and stealth, more than his complexion, explained the sobriquet by which he was widely known in the DGI: "La Sombra," or The Shadow.

As head of Bureau 13, Valdés was one of the most powerful men in the DGI, with automatic access to General Abrahantes, the Vice-Minister of the Interior, and to José Joaquín Méndez Cominches, the director-general of the DGI. His job involved doing business with many people whom Valdés regarded with secret contempt—with doctrinaire fanatics; with criminals, turncoats and mercenaries. There were mercenaries like the colonel in Panama who was an indispensable supply link to the guerrillas in Central America, but could be managed only by a combination of blackmail and bribery, in ever-increasing doses. There were turncoats and criminals like Julio Parodi. Valdés was far too professional to allow personal repugnance—let alone any vestige of bourgeois morality—intrude on his dealings with such people, as long as they remained useful.

So Valdés flung his arm around Parodi's shoulder as they strolled toward the living room, as if they were the closest of friends.

"I hope your voyage went well," Valdés said.

"There were no incidents."

"Good, good. We have to move on to more important business. I brought two friends I want you to meet."

Two men were waiting for them in the living room.

"This is Teófilo," Valdés said, introducing a squat, sallow-faced man with a droopy mustache. "Teófilo works at our Mission in New York."

Teófilo pumped Parodi's hand.

"And this," Valdés went on, "this is Compañero Favio. He expressed a special desire to make your acquaintance."

Valdés gave no further explanation of the tall, fair-skinned man with inquisitive eyes who now came forward. But Parodi could see at once that Favio was not a Cuban, even though his face was weathered from long exposure to the Caribbean sun and he spoke Spanish like a native of Havana. Parodi guessed that Favio was East European, probably Russian.

"Tell us about your last conversation with Mr. Arnold Whitman," Valdés instructed him.

Parodi summarized the conversation he had had in the CIA man's car. Valdés and the others seemed especially interested in Whitman's efforts to find out what the Cubans would do in the event of an American-backed uprising in Nicaragua.

"That confirms what we are getting from other sources," Valdés commented.

The man from New York nodded. "The Americans are planning to attack," Teófilo commented. "Every few days, the State Department puts out a new story about how Nicaragua is the base for the guerrillas in El Salvador and Guatemala. But there is no popular support in the United States for military action anywhere in Central America. If the Newgate Administration risks it, the response will be a protest campaign on the scale of the anti-Vietnam demonstrations or the nuclear-freeze movement. The United States will be paralyzed."

"So what do I tell Whitman?" Parodi asked.

"You can give him what he wants." Valdés glanced at the Russian, who signaled approval. "It's chicken feed, and it will help you to keep the trust of the CIA."

"Whitman was also asking about the Fairchild kidnapping," Parodi went on.

"Tell him we're angry about it," Valdés responded. "Tell him that the Puerto Ricans got out of hand. Don't worry," he reassured Parodi, "the Americans won't be able to prove anything."

"I saw your name in the American newspapers," the man from New York observed to Parodi.

"Whitman complained about that. He told me I should stay out of sight for a while."

"He's right," Valdés said. "You're becoming too well known. I want you out of sight too. *When* you've finished your assignment. Now, tell me this. How much money are you going to make from your latest shipment?"

Parodi looked studiously vague. "I'm not sure," he said. "Maybe ten million, after expenses."

"Always the little capitalist," Valdés purred. "You'll make at least five times that. I was looking over the accounts. I see that you owe us about nine million already on past shipments that we helped you with. I wouldn't like to think that you're the kind of man who forgets his debts."

"No, really, I swear to you—" Parodi began to protest, but Valdés silenced him, firm but still friendly.

"That's all academic," the head of Bureau 13 explained. "Because we are going to settle up in the following way. You are going to arrange for certain deliveries of cash and weapons to be made, totaling twenty million dollars. The first deliveries will be made within the next two weeks. That will give you time to arrange for the resale of your present shipment. These deliveries will be easy for you to arrange, because for the most part they will be inside the United States, mostly in the New York and Miami areas. And in the case of New York, Teófilo here will be able to assist you through his own networks. We know you have the facilities to do what is involved."

"Twenty million." Parodi repeated the figure slowly, as if stunned.

"We will repay half that amount if the operation is successfully concluded," Valdés said. "I am sure you understand that you ceased to be an independent operator from the moment you entered into your understanding with us. You are in the position of the manager of a trust fund. We are not unreasonable about this, you know. We have no wish to deprive you of the creature comforts to which you have become accustomed. We are just requesting that you fulfill your side of the bargain. Is that understood?"

"Yes," Parodi replied cheerlessly. He added, "I suppose you realize this will make it impossible for me to go on living in Miami. The Americans are bound to find out in the end."

"We have taken account of that." Valdés waved his arms around the tastefully furnished room, full of Spanish Colonial pieces. *"Tu casa,"* he said. "You will live *here*."

Parodi looked less than overjoyed at the prospect of returning to the cradle of Latin American socialism on a permanent basis.

"Well," Valdés resumed, "Compañero Favio is anxious that we all have a meeting of minds on the execution of what the leadership calls the Monimbó Plan. This discussion, needless to say, is not for the benefit of Mr. Arnold Whitman or *The New York World*."

"Of course." Parodi's nervousness grew at the realization that Valdés was preparing to share with him the specifics of a plan that he had hitherto understood only in blurred outline.

"The objective," Valdés said, "is the paralysis of the United States through a social revolt that will make it impossible for the Newgate Administration to pursue any coherent foreign policy—or respond to any crisis developing abroad—and will also increase the likelihood of the defeat of President Newgate's party in the next American elections. We did not need to create the conditions for a social revolt in the United States. Those conditions have been created by the Americans themselves. The reactionary economic program of the Administration is adding to the racial and class polarization by producing higher unemployment, welfare cutbacks and a decline in housing and education in the inner cities. The tensions are increased by the pressure of immigration. The United States, beyond any other country in the world, had lost control of its borders. A million illegal aliens are flowing in every year, competing with the American underclass for scarce jobs. We can read all of this in any American newspaper any day of the week."

He paused as Parodi offered cigars around the room. Only the Russian accepted.

"In other words," Valdés continued, "we do not have to look for explosives. We have only to look for detonators. We saw the potential in Miami in the spring and summer of 1980. *You* were there . . ."

"Yes," Parodi agreed.

"You saw the force of hatred that was unleashed in those riots."

"Yes." He remembered how the whole country had been stunned by the savagery of the attacks on individuals in the Miami riots: the white boys who had been caught in Liberty City at the wrong time, dragged from their car and stabbed over and over with a screwdriver; the man who had had his tongue cut out; the lunatic driving his car back and forth over a man's body. The commission report that had come out two years later had listed all the sociological factors which might have contributed to the riots, but had not really come to terms with that depth of hatred.

"The effect of the Miami riots was limited by the lack of an organizational weapon," Valdés went on. "Some of the arsonists knew their job. But the disturbances were basically confined to the black ghetto, and did not ignite a nationwide response. We believe that if we select the right situations and the right timing, we can repeat the Miami experience on a scale that will make those upheavals look like a summer camp. We have many assets in the United States. We have influence over militant organizations in the minority communities. We have trained thousands of Americans in Cuba through the vehicle of the Venceremos Brigades and the Antonio Maceo Brigades. We have our own agents in the Cuban exile community. We have friends and agents among the religious organizations, the media and the American Congress. With all of these assets, we can continue to build the climate for a major eruption."

"You're talking about acts of sabotage? Terrorism?"

"Catalytic acts," Valdés repeated. "The rest will happen without our having to lift a finger, like an inevitable chemical reaction. The Americans will be unable to grasp what is happening to them, because the Americans—despite all their claptrap about the dignity of the individual—no longer believe in individual responsibility. A riot breaks out, people are killed and their jurists and professors say it was not because individuals committed murder, but because of some statistics in an economic yearbook. A man tried to assassinate the American President, and their court decided he was not responsible because he was not in full possession of his mental faculties. A so-

132

ciety that does not make individuals accountable for their actions has lost the ability to preserve itself from what they may do."

"You're turning into a philosopher," the Russian observed, with a wry twist to his mouth. "You may be confusing our friend, and I would like to hear his opinions."

"Of course," Valdés said, picking up the thread. "We have teams—some of them inside the United States, some ready to go there—whose members are completely unknown to the American authorities. This is our hidden force, our Monimbó brigade. When these people strike, the police and the FBI will have no warning. They will flounder about, rounding up the usual suspects, just as they have been doing in Puerto Rico since Senator Fairchild's death. We will have the advantage of total surprise.

"We have studied many alternative scenarios," Valdés explained. "Teófilo suggested, for example, that we might consider blowing up the new computer center outside Baltimore that houses the records of the whole U.S. Social Security system. It's an easy enough target. If you parked a delivery truck near the entrance with five hundred pounds of explosives on board, you could disrupt the workings of the entire system. Imagine the impact once people stopped receiving their Social Security checks. A nice twist would be to have a rightist organization—perhaps the Klan—claim responsibility for such a bombing. We examined the potential for unleashing weapons of ultimate horror—bacteriological agents, for example. We discovered that it is possible to order *Pasteurella pestis* by mail from a culture collection in Maryland, if you write in on the letterhead of a medical-research outfit."

"Pasteurella pestis?" Parodi queried.

"Bubonic plague."

"My God," Parodi breathed.

"We rejected that idea," Valdés told him. "But the ease with which we were able to conduct a dry run is an index of the extraordinary vulnerability of the United States."

Valdés gave Parodi a long, searching look. "You're wondering why I am telling you all this," he said. It was not a question. "The reason will become clear in a moment. It was agreed, at the highest level, that we would simplify the plan and home in on two targets in the United States. New York"—he paused— "and Miami. The two operations will be separated by a period of several weeks. If they are executed properly, their effect should be felt all over the United States. The details of the New York operation do not concern you, except insofar as you will be required to make those deliveries. In the case of Miami— well, it's your city. You understand that it also has a very special importance for Fidel."

"Yes." One of the minor services that Parodi had performed for the DGI was to arrange for the making of some rather professional videotapes depicting the life of the Cuban community in South Florida. He was given to understand that they were for the personal entertainment of El Líder Máximo, Fidel Castro, himself. Valdés had since told him that in the midst of his bouts of insomnia, Fidel would sit up alone contemplating the footage that showed his "godchildren"—as he sometimes called the Cuban exiles—at work and at play. The economic success of the Cuban community in Miami was a malign obsession with him; he would spare no effort to spoil that. So Parodi had no difficulty in understanding why Castro had singled out Miami as a target.

"Let me ask you this question," the Russian intervened again, his cold, enigmatic gaze fixed on Parodi. "If riots began again in Miami, and blacks attacked Cubans—let us say, Cuban shopkeepers—how would your Brigada Azul respond?"

"They would shoot back," Parodi said without hesitation.

"And if there were another boatlift from Cuba under way when the riots erupted, what effect would that have on the local authorities?"

"You mean the law-enforcement agencies?"

"Exactly."

"They would be swamped. Overrun."

"Hmm." Favio puffed on the Double Corona Parodi had given him. "This is really a very fine cigar," he said.

Parodi could hear the distant boom of mortar fire as the Russian-made jeep sloshed through the red mud of a narrow trail inside the training camp up in the rugged, forested terrain of the Sierra de los Órganos. Over to the right, through pines and a few yagruma trees, Parodi could see men and women wriggling on their bellies through an obstacle course, trying to dodge percussion grenades.

"They'll be fighting in Guatemala soon," Valdés said. "Some of them couldn't even read and write when they arrived here. Now they know how to fire Stalin organs." These were huge Soviet rocket launchers with forty tubes.

The camp was named after Camilo Cienfuegos, a hero of the Revolution whose popularity had rivaled Castro's before his early, and still disputed, death. It covered more than twenty-five thousand acres. In fact, its electrified fences and watch-towers screened not a single camp, but many. The Central Americans had their own special facilities where they were learning to operate in units of up to brigade strength. There were also trainees from all over Europe and the Middle East.

Many of the military instructors at the Campo Camilo Cien-fuegos were veteran members of Cuba's Special Forces, the elite corps of paracommandos that had supplied shock troops for the campaigns in Angola and the Ogaden desert. When Fidel Castro had created the corps in 1962, he had called it his "Army of Solidarity," and had told its members that they had a special mission to fight at the side of "the forces of liberation" all over the world. Commanded by Colonel Patricio de la Guardia, the Tropas Especiales had sent units to Nicaragua to assist in the suppression of "counterrevolutionary" elements. Others oper-ated in the field with the Central American guerrillas, wearing the same uniforms.

Parodi saw a derelict DC-4 in the distance, over toward the Monte Oscuro. It had been used for practice hijackings. Many Palestinian terrorists had mastered their trade in the Camilo Cienfuegos camp in the seventies.

Parodi took a sidelong glance at Valdés. The Cuban's eye-lids were closed, his arms folded, his breath coming deeply and evenly, as if he had dozed off in the sun in the back of the jeep. At the instant Parodi looked at him, Valdés jerked awake, as if he had been physically touched. The expression in Valdés' dark, startled eyes gave Parodi the unpleasant sensation that he had just disturbed a wild animal asleep in a cave—maybe a jaguar. The kind of animal that would try to tear your throat out if it felt threatened.

All Valdés said was "We're there."

The jeep had slowed at the entrance to a compound that looked different from the others they had passed. It was defended by a high, blind wall, not merely an electrified fence and a few coils of barbed wire. The guard in a closed booth beside the steel gate checked and rechecked Valdés' pass. The only identification on the gate was a number painted in neat black figures.

"Welcome to Monimbó," said Valdés. "*Our* Monimbó."

Inside the gate, Parodi saw four or five Quonset huts ahead. They looked like halves of gigantic tubes. The driver stopped in front of one of them. It was like a schoolroom inside. There were rows of desks, facing a blackboard; a small movie screen and a display board on which the map of a city and many aerial photographs, stapled together, had been pinned. There was something familiar about the amebalike sprawl of the city, with all its bridges and islands and the winding river. Parodi realized that he was looking at Miami, viewed from higher up than his penthouse on Key Biscayne.

There were about a dozen people in the room—blacks, Hispanics and two or three light-skinned Caucasians who looked like Americans. A Cuban instructor in fatigues had been pointing out something on the map as they came in. Two of the students were standing with him, as if they had been called upon to explain something. He was tall and blond, wearing faded denims. When he had landed from a cruise ship at San Juan, he had been traveling under the name of Mitchell Lardner. He was more familiarly known as Beacher.

For half an hour, Parodi answered questions from the class:

136

about the geography of Miami and the surrounding area, the character of various community leaders, the tactics of the police force and its radio communications system, the accessibility of the canals that carried water to the city from Lake Okeechobee and of the high-voltage lines running from the Turkey Point power station.

At the end of the grilling, Valdés took Parodi and Beacher aside and made more elaborate introductions.

"I want to be sure you two understand each other," the head of Bureau 13 said to them. "If there is anything—anything at all—that Beacher needs in Miami, you will supply it to him," he instructed Parodi.

It was at their last meeting before Parodi took the plane to Mexico City, in an anonymous modern building in Vedado, that the problem of Robert Hockney was raised.

"I talked to our people in the Foreign Press Bureau about Hockney," Valdés informed the drug trafficker. "He's dangerous. He did a lot of damage to our Soviet friends. Don't think he'll give up just because you gave him a false scent."

"What do you suggest?"

"The same as Mr. Whitman. Keep away from him. As it turns out, I may be able to fix things for you."

"How is that?"

"Robert Hockney has applied for a visa to come to Havana."

"Are you going to give it to him?"

"Naturally."

Chapter

5

WASHINGTON, D.C.

In Washington, a city obsessed by pecking orders, there are many ways of assessing status. Perhaps the most reliable is the treatment afforded to guests by the *maîtres d'hôtel* of the capital's more fashionable watering holes, which vary with the political season, from one presidency to the next. In the years of the Newgate Administration, there were two restaurants, beyond the rest, where those who wished to assert their place in the registers of power and privilege were eager to be seen at lunchtime. The Jockey Club, in the sedate Fairfax Hotel, was favored by Californians from President Newgate's kitchen cabinet. The Maison Blanche, or "MB," in a cement block on F Street that looked like an unfinished building, was patronized by Washington's *other* government: editors, columnists, TV reporters, network producers. In a city that lives for politics and news about politics, these are the only elites that are universally recognized. In authentic, multidimensional cities—in New York or Chicago, Paris or London—journalists are never deferred to in the same way as in Washington. As commentators on society, they may be taken less seriously than novelists, playwrights, philosophers, artists and even movie actors. As a privileged class, they are outshone by bankers and captains of industry, dress designers and real estate moguls, sports heroes and most certainly movie stars. But in unidimensional Washington, the press corps does not have to share its prerogatives, its place in the sun. And in the time of the Newgate Administration, the regulars at the MB deferred to no one, with the possible exception of Georges, the establishment's silkily professional maître d'.

On one of those muggy, subtropical days in Washington when even the lightest seersucker suit seems to be made of rubber, Hockney slipped into the sanctuary cool of the MB, shook hands with Georges and was shown to his usual table toward the back of the restaurant, against the wood paneling. Art Buchwald was already holding forth at *his* regular table, which commanded a view of the whole room; the humorist was the only patron of the MB who was allowed to forgo the mandatory necktie.

Hockney's guest had not yet arrived, so he settled into his place and ordered a Campari. Hockney's attention turned to a woman Georges was shepherding to a nearby table. She had fine, regular features, a slightly upturned nose, a lustrous, pearly skin and a mane of ash-blond hair that betrayed no hint of the bottle. She had a narrow hourglass figure, good legs, neat, well-turned ankles. Each step she took, each little wave to friends in the restaurant was performed with the studied control of a ballet dancer. Yet she managed not to convey the impression that she was putting herself on show. The whole effect was provocative, but not bold.

She favored Hockney with a little flutter of the wrist, and something more. He rose to greet her as she approached his table.

"Bob, it's wonderful," she said. She had a fairly deep, throaty sort of voice. Her pronunciation was mid-Atlantic; you didn't miss a single consonant. "I've just heard you're coming on the Cuba trip."

"Yes, I got drafted too," he said, smiling, making light of it. "But I'm still waiting to find out if the Cubans are going to give me a visa."

"I'm sure there *can't* be any problem," she said, examining him with her big gray eyes. "They read the *World* in Havana too. Last time I saw Fidel, he quoted one of your stories."

"I guess I should be flattered. Can I buy you a drink?" He gestured to the empty place opposite him.

"I'd love to, sweetheart, but I've got people waiting." Her tone made the words sound whimsical rather than vapid. She presented her cheek to be kissed. "If there *should* be any problem," she told Hockney, "give me a call and I'll talk to Teófilo."

"Teófilo *Gómez*? Is *he* handling the arrangements?" Hockney was familiar with the name of the Minister-Counselor at the Cuban Mission to the United Nations in New York. Teófilo Gómez was a fixture at liberal dinner parties, much sought after by the kind of moneyed hostesses who liked to show off their social conscience in the way they might show off the latest Saint Laurent. Teófilo Gómez was also a spy. Under his diplomatic cover, he controlled the DGI network in the United States. Hockney doubted whether the beautiful woman standing in front of him knew what the initials DGI stood for, and the way she replied confirmed his doubts.

"Teófilo is *such* a sweet man," she said. "And he can fix absolutely *anything*."

"I'll bet."

"Well, listen. Give me a call anyway. I can't wait to show you the sights of Havana."

Hockney watched her glide away to a table where a couple of network producers and the Deputy Secretary of State were waiting. He was fond of Angela Seabury. She was co-host of a network magazine program. He had been interviewed once on her show. Angela insisted that she was interested in increasing the "serious" content of the show, and had done interviews with several world leaders, including Margaret Thatcher and Fidel Castro. She went at everything with high enthusiasm, but also with an insouciance that was startling in a network correspondent whose contract was worth almost a million dollars a year. To have gone to Havana to interview Fidel and to be on intimate terms with Castro's spy chief in New York without quite knowing what the DGI amounted to was only one illustration of that apparent naiveté.

In the year he had known her, he had felt flattered and mildly excited by the air of tacit invitation she extended to him. She might be the wrong side of forty, but she was an exceptionally attractive woman, and if he had so far resisted the temptation to start an affair with her, he suspected that there were many others who had not. He wondered now whether Teófilo Gómez was among their number.

He glanced over the menu, mentally weighing the relative merits of veal and a seafood salad. When he looked up, the first thing he saw was Jack Lancer's Navajo belt buckle, featuring some kind of winged snake. The young reporter had actually changed into a pair of slacks. They did not match his jacket, but marked a definite concession on the part of someone who always turned up at the office in jeans. Lancer had rounded off his outfit with a clip-on bow tie, his equivalent of a Mickey Mouse badge. His scuffed shoes were in no better and no worse shape than those of most of the media regulars at the MB. Reporters are not the mainstay of the shoe-polish industry.

"I know I'm late," Lancer said. It was not an apology.

After his dinner with the *World*'s Executive Editor in New York, Hockney had concluded that it would be expedient to try to achieve a truce with Jack Lancer before he went off to Cuba—always assuming the visa came through. He was pretty sure that the gesture of buying Lancer lunch at the MB would mean nothing to the younger reporter. He had really chosen the locale for his own benefit; he felt secure here, as if he were on his own territory. Lancer, for his part, looked less than overawed. On the other hand, he was distinctly agitated. "Vodka-rocks," he rapped out his order when the waiter came, obviously wanting to get the rituals of the lunch out of the way.

Lancer's patience ran out before they had placed their food order.

"I got the Nicaragua story," he announced. "It's a damn sight bigger than I thought. I got *everything*, Bob. Names, documents. It's all there."

"Tell me."

"Read it for yourself." Lancer pulled a few typed pages from his pocket. That was one thing he and Hockney had in common: in the age of the word processor, they still liked to write on battered portables.

Hockney skimmed over the piece, then backtracked and went through it line by line.

"This is quite a story," he said.

"I'm glad you agree it's newsworthy." Lancer tried to flatten the wild curls at the back of his head with the palm of his hand. He could hardly keep still. While Hockney was reading, he was fidgeting in his seat, kneading bread, tracing patterns on the tablecloth with his fork.

Lancer's article described a White House plan to invade Nicaragua. The story included long quotations extracted from something called Presidential Review Memorandum 83— PRM-83. The memo claimed that the survival of a leftist government in Managua was "a standing humiliation for the United States and a source of aid and succor for every revolutionary group in the hemisphere." The memo sketched out a plan for a full-dress invasion to be mounted from neighboring Honduras. The troops would be supplied from a variety of rightist exile groups, supplemented by mercenaries hired by the CIA. The invasion attempt would be supported by air strikes, to be flown by American pilots in planes whose markings had been painted over. The strike across the border would be accompanied by terrorism and sabotage in Nicaraguan towns, directed at Sandinist leaders, Cuban advisers and the Palestinian camp on the outskirts of Managua. The memo urged that Nicaragua's air bases be hit simultaneously in Israeli-style lightning raids.

"Where's the original?" Hockney asked.

"I can't produce the original," Lancer told him. "My source could be blown."

"What do you mean?"

"Since the last leak investigation, they've been making copies of hot documents according to this new system," Lancer explained. "They insert a minor typo in each copy—something you wouldn't notice, like a comma in the wrong place: that sort of thing. If a copy leaks out, they can tell where it came from."

"I wasn't proposing to hand the document over to the FBI," Hockney said curtly. "I'd just like to see it for myself."

The waiter was hovering nearby. Hockney gave him their order fast, to get rid of him.

Lancer shook his glass of Stolichnaya, so that the ice cubes rattled.

Hockney looked at him and said, "Are you sure this document is authentic?"

"I read it myself."

"How do you know it hadn't been doctored?"

"I trust my source," Lancer said doggedly.

"Then would you mind telling me your source?"

"Yes, I would mind."

"Well, I have to say this, Jack. This PRM–Eighty-three stuff rings false to me. All the opinion polls show the last thing the electorate wants is a military adventure in Central America. That would be political suicide for this Administration. Newgate's people know that. They're not going to go and cut their throats before the next elections."

Lancer shrugged. "That's your judgment," he commented. "Ed Finkel thinks different. He thinks this story is as big as the Bay of Pigs, and could be as big as Watergate."

"I'm glad to hear that Ed hasn't lost his sense of romance," Hockney remarked sourly, annoyed that Lancer had gone to the Managing Editor over his head. "But I'm also sure that Ed would want to do some checking before we leap into print on page one with a story about a White House document that nobody but you has seen."

"Go ahead and check with your White House friends," Lancer said contemptuously. "But I wouldn't count on them baring their breasts to you about how they're planning to invade an independent Latin American country so they can pull Castro's beard."

On a sunny day in Washington, even the massive gray pile of the old Executive Office Building, with its improbable columns and curlicues and stepped facade, can start to resemble a rather grand, if faded, Victorian beach hotel. Hockney had no eye for the architecture—or for the ragtag demonstrators who had erected a mock shantytown in Lafayette Park across the street to protest welfare cuts—as he loped up the steps to the main entrance. At short notice, he had managed to set up an interview with Blair Collins, the Director of Central Intelligence. The initials PRM-83 had worked like a charm.

Collins spent more time in his office here, conveniently close to the White House, than at Agency headquarters in Langley, Virginia. They sat around the table in a chamber that looked like the boardroom of a nineteenth-century shipping company—Hockney, Director Collins and a dapper little man named Quayle, fastidiously attired in a three-piece suit and a custom-made shirt, white on white. Quayle had been introduced as the chief of the Cuba Operations Group at Langley. The acronym COG had a businesslike, ratcheting sound, and the impression Quayle made was also businesslike and mechanical. His speech and his body language were clipped and exact. His hair was oiled flat against his skull. His chin and the back of his neck gleamed pink from the razor. By contrast, the Director of the CIA appeared donnishly disheveled. He wore a rumpled charcoal-gray pinstripe and a droopy bow tie, carelessly knotted. His face sagged a bit, like a basset hound's, and the resemblance was enhanced by the moist eyes, pink-rimmed, that contemplated the world through horn-rimmed lenses.

"What do you know about PRM–Eighty-three?" Collins snapped at Hockney.

"It's a plan to invade Nicaragua."

"Horsefeathers." Collins set to tamping his pipe. He looked

somewhat relieved. He said, "Somebody's sold you a pup."

"But you admit there is a PRM–Eighty-three."

Collins glanced at Quayle before saying, "You know what a Presidential Review Memorandum is? It's an options paper, nothing more, nothing less. It's not an action plan. In any case, nobody around here is planning to invade Nicaragua."

"Well, then"—Hockney paused—"I guess you'd have no objection to letting me take a look at the real PRM–Eighty-three."

"Come off it, Bob. You don't have a Goldline clearance. You'll just have to take my word for it. Your man was given a bum steer."

"I don't see how you can ask me to buy that if you're not willing to tell me what's in the real document," Hockney objected.

Blair Collins sucked at his pipe. He said, "What I'm about to tell you does not go outside this room. PRM–Eighty-three is an overview of this country's position in Central America. A kind of balance sheet. It also lists some of the options that might be available to us for dealing with Castro. The possibility of military intervention is discussed, and is totally rejected. We are not entirely insulated from the mood of the country up here."

"Then what's so touchy about this memo?"

Collins blew down the stem of his pipe, trying to clear a blockage. A pipe was a wonderful accessory for a committee-man. The mechanics of filling and lighting and cleaning it allowed you lots of time to think up answers, and gave you something to do with your hands.

Collins finally said, "PRM–Eighty-three reflects some of our sources and methods. If the full text were released, some of our agents and assets would be blown. People's lives would be placed in jeopardy. Does that make it clear to you?"

"Not exactly," Hockney replied. "Are you telling me that the version Jack Lancer got hold of bears no resemblance to the original?"

"I'm telling you the *World* got a doctored version. I'd love to know how."

"Me too," Hockney admitted.

"You know that Lancer hangs out with a Cuban-front group," Quayle interjected.

"You mean the Council for Hemispheric Understanding? Yes, I know about that."

"Those are the creeps who fed the *World* that plant about how we were supposed to be training torturers in Central America," Quayle added for the Director's benefit. "Their handouts read like they've been translated from Spanish—Cuban Spanish."

"Is the *World* really going to run this Nicaragua bullshit?" Collins asked, blowing a great cloud of smoke in Hockney's direction.

"It's not up to me," Hockney said. "I wish you could give me something more to go on."

"The fact one of your people fell for a forgery doesn't give you the right to examine Top Secret documents," Quayle said sourly.

"I'm sorry," Director Collins added, more gently. "All I can do is warn you that if the *World* runs with that story, you're going to have egg all over your faces."

When Hockney had left, Blair Collins turned to Quayle and said, "Do you think the Cubans got hold of the original document?"

"No." Quayle shook his head. "Why wouldn't they release the real thing, if they had it?"

"The *World*'s version is sexier."

"But maybe less damaging, from our point of view, in the longer term." The most sensitive section of PRM-83—the version that had been approved by the National Security Council on Monday—concerned not Nicaragua, but Cuba. It mentioned the rising strength of a secret resistance organization inside Cuba that sought to remove Castro and break the Soviet grip on the island. The information had come from a source the CIA regarded as a uniquely important asset: the agent code-named Daiquiri. It was better, in Director Collins' opinion, to risk a major political uproar over a fictitious plot against Nicaragua than to release material that could help the Cubans to identify and eliminate a source as valuable as Daiquiri. Anyway, there was the chance that the *World* would suppress the PRM-83 story. You could smell it a mile off.

Later that afternoon, Collins slipped across to the Oval Office to tell his old friend the President about it. He also took the President some new pictures taken from a spy-in-the-sky satellite. They showed Soviet MIGs on the ground at Puerto Cabezas, on Nicaragua's eastern coast, and a new batch of Palestinian terrorists arriving from the Middle East.

President Newgate glanced at the photos and tossed them wearily aside.

"Maybe we ought to do what the *World* says we're planning to do," Newgate said quietly. "Since we're going to be blamed for it anyway."

Director Collins couldn't think up any rejoinder to that. Neither of them was getting any younger. The President was past seventy, and his chance of getting reelected seemed to be retreating day by day. If they were going under, it might as well be with a bang instead of a whimper. The thought flitted lazily around the corners of the Director's mind. He brushed it away and said, "What do we do if the *World* runs the story?"

"Oh, we'll deny it. I'll deny it. That won't make any difference. The people who want to believe it will do so just the same. And denials never catch up with the dramatic value of a headline. The Russians have a saying about that, don't they?"

" 'What is written with a pen,' " Blair Collins quoted, " 'cannot be cut out with an ax.' It's nearly true."

"Well, we'll live," Jerry Newgate went on. "As long as we don't get blown off course by the little things. The objective is Cuba. If we can deal with Cuba, Central America will fall into place. I remember we sat in this room the day after my inauguration and we talked about that, Blair. I remember saying to you that if we could deal with two men—Castro and Qaddafi— then the foreign policy of this Administration could be counted a success."

"We nearly got Qaddafi," Collins observed. "And there's

147

movement inside Cuba. I wouldn't give up hope on that front. Not at all."

About the same time, Hockney went back to the *World* bureau—after failing to get any further leads out of the White House press office and his contacts on the NSC—and found Jack Lancer lolling in the swivel chair in the corner office. Hockney's office.

"Looks like I missed the *coup d'état*," Hockney remarked.

Lancer took his time about moving his sneakers from the top of the desk. "Guess what?" he said exultantly. "Two FBI gumshoes showed up here, asking to interview both of us about that PRM."

"So what happened?"

"I asked them if they had a warrant. They said no, it was a matter of voluntary cooperation for the sake of national security. I told them they had to check with Finkel, and Ed told them to go screw. You know what else he said?"

"Hit me," Hockney responded with the resignation of a blackjack player who knows he is about to go over.

"Finkel says the fact the Bureau is putting out a security alert proves that our story is authentic."

Hockney did not like the way he said "our."

"Finkel's going to run it, Bob," Lancer went on. "Unless you can come up with proof of forgery. He says it could be a Pulitzer."

Lancer started to get up from the desk. Hockney glanced at the cigarette stubs he had left floating in a cup of cold coffee. He said, "Don't mind me" and swung back out the door to read the wire-service dispatches.

Unfortunately for the Newgate Administration, the first high official to appear, live on camera, to comment on the *World*'s account of PRM-83 the next morning was the Vice-President, who was not consulted on many things, including this particular memorandum, and whose relations with the Chief Executive had chilled since he had made it clear he was going to throw his own hat into the ring at the primaries. The cameras caught up with Vice-President Morgan at Andrews Air Force Base, as he deplaned after a week in Texas making speeches to the party faithful.

"Hi, uh, great to see ya, great to see ya," the Vice-President kept repeating into the microphones. When caught without a double-spaced prepared text, he sounded faintly dazed.

Several reporters vied with each other to get in the first question about the supposed invasion plan.

"Well, uh, I'm not aware that we're gunning to attack anybody," the Vice-President fumbled. Then he added brightly, "But you know, uh, when a few guys get together, shooting the breeze, you get a few crazy ideas floating around."

A light rain started at that moment. The White House press secretary, watching the videotape later in the day, remarked that the weather had been providential. One of Morgan's aides had rushed forward with an umbrella and hustled his boss away into a waiting limousine.

After that, the official denials came thick and fast, ending with a personal assurance from the President that night that his Administration was not planning to embark on a new Vietnam War in Central America. But the damage, as Jerry Newgate himself had predicted, had already been done. In Havana, Fidel Castro seized the opportunity to hold a mass rally to pledge undying support to the Nicaraguan Revolution. In Managua, the Sandinist regime called for "increased vigilance" against "counterrevolutionary elements" working in concert with the CIA. In New York, several Third World countries lined up to sponsor a resolution attacking American imperialism.

By nightfall, rowdy brigades of demonstrators, some equipped with candles and torches, had begun to converge on the White House, and busloads more were rolling in at ten-minute intervals from Boston, Baltimore and all points south. The rally was still going strong when a dapper, slightly pudgy Cuban arrived on the early shuttle from LaGuardia the next day. He enjoyed the spectacle. He made a mental note to offer a bonus to the agent who had planted the Cubans' version of PRM-83 on *The New York World*. Teófilo Gómez skimmed through the morning edition of the *World* again as he rode to Capitol Hill in his taxi. He had told Havana that he thought the forgery was too crude to be accepted by a major American paper, that they would have to feed it to one of the Central American rags. The gullibility of Americans in one respect never ceased to surprise him: they would believe almost any charge against their own government.

Angela Seabury looked more like a businesswoman than a TV star the same morning as she opened her briefcase for inspection in the lobby of the Rayburn Building, next to the Capitol. She was wearing a navy-blue pinstripe suit, a blouse that buttoned up to her throat and sensible shoes. The guard smiled at her appreciatively, took a perfunctory look at the books inside her bag—the kiss-and-tell memoirs of a Hollywood sex symbol and a travel guide to Cuba—and waved her through. Angela squeezed into a crowded elevator and rode up to the third floor.

During the last confrontation between Washington and Havana, the Newgate Administration had closed down the Cuban Interests Section on Sixteenth Street, which had operated under the umbrella of the Czech Embassy. Since then, the office of Congressman Coleman North in the Rayburn Building had come to be widely described as the Honorary Cuban Consulate. Coleman North was a second-term Democrat from California, and no admirer of President Newgate. North was an enthusiastic sponsor of the proposed amendment banning CIA operations against Cuba and Nicaragua. In his third-floor office, he received a steady stream of visitors from Havana.

A spruce young man with a bushy mustache intercepted Angela in North's outer office.

"Coleman's at the rally," he told her. "Did you see it? They say they're expecting a hundred thousand people."

Through the night and into midmorning the buses chartered

by the Brotherhood for Peace had continued to stream into Washington, bringing protestors from as far afield as Pittsburgh and Atlanta.

"I saw it," Angela said. "It looked like the White House was under siege."

"This is going to be even bigger than the nuclear-freeze movement," the aide went on enthusiastically. "Newgate won't know what hit him. It must make you feel good to be a member of the Fourth Estate when you see the effect of one newspaper article. Jack Lancer is one helluva reporter."

"Yes, he is," Angela agreed.

"And you're going to Cuba, right?"

"I hope so."

"I wish to hell I was going with you. But I can't get out of the office even for five minutes. We're planning demonstrations in more than two hundred cities."

A couple of girls pushed by, staggering under the weight of piles of petitions.

Angela took advantage of the interruption to say, "Is Teófilo here?"

"Yeah, sure. He's using Coleman's office."

The aide rapped lightly on the door and threw it open for her. "Be seeing you," he called out as he charged back into his own cubicle.

A short, olive-skinned man with a thick mustache and curly black hair, his paunch minimized by his beautifully tailored Italian suit, jumped up from behind Congressman North's desk. He greeted Angela with warmth that exceeded even the traditional cordiality of a Cuban *abrazo*, kissing her on the side of the mouth. With his arm around her waist, he guided her to the leather-upholstered chesterfield.

"It's all arranged," he reassured her at once. "You're leaving tomorrow."

When Coleman North had first invited Teófilo Gómez to make himself at home in his office on Capitol Hill, the Cuban had taken him at his word. Gómez flew down to Washington from his base in New York once or twice a week, on average. The Congressman's office was a very convenient place to conduct private conversations. Under an edict of the late J. Edgar Hoover which no subsequent FBI Director had cared—or dared—to rescind, Congress was hallowed ground, off limits to Bureau Agents.

Angela knew Gómez in his public role, as a counselor to the Cuban Mission to the United Nations in New York. At a series of cocktail parties in Manhattan, she had found that his natural vivacity and quicksilver charm more than made up for his lack of obvious physical endowments. Gómez had been suave but insistent in his courtship, and it had not taken long for their relationship to develop into something more than friendship.

Their affair had been intense for about a week. Then they had drifted apart again, without any sense of loss on either side. Angela knew, from her first observation of the Cuban, that his hobby was collecting American women. She recognized, and delighted in, his unapologetic desire to satisfy a physical compulsion without emotional complications, because it matched her own.

Angela had given no real thought to the likelihood that her dalliance with a Cuban diplomat might have earned her a place in the files of the FBI or other government agencies. She had given no thought at all to the probability that it had brought her under the intense scrutiny of the DGI, because she did not know what those initials meant. She would have been surprised to learn that the sometime lover who was being so helpful about arranging interviews in Havana was the Station Chief of Castro's secret service in New York.

"Can I offer you some coffee? Or perhaps a drink?"

Teófilo's question brought it home to Angela that it was unusual for a foreign diplomat—let alone a Cuban—to be permitted to use a Congressman's office as if it were his own. But the thought passed quickly. The setting made their meeting feel very aboveboard, even very *American*.

"No. Thank you," she hastily declined the offer.

"Your group will be leaving from Mexico City tomorrow,"

Gómez told her briskly. "A special charter has been arranged. Of course, you know that five or six other journalists are going."

Angela nodded. A Cuban Government agency called ICAP had taken the initiative in inviting selected editors and correspondents to Havana. In her case, the invitation had been conveyed by Teófilo in person. But it had been made clear to everyone invited that "exceptional" facilities would be provided in Cuba. As Teófilo Gómez now explained to her, the timing of the trip could not have been more auspicious. The revelation by the *World* of the White House plans for an attack on Cuba and its Central American protégé meant that the Cubans were more anxious than ever to let their views be known to the American audience.

"Lancer is a brilliant reporter," the Cuban commented.

Angela agreed politely, but the Cuban could pick up the note of demurral in her voice. She had met Jack Lancer at parties, but did not care for him overmuch.

"Jack Lancer may actually have stopped a war," Gómez went on. "But don't worry"—he patted Angela's arm—"you'll get your exclusive too. I've just returned from Havana. Confidentially, I can tell you that Fidel is delighted you are coming. He remembers you fondly. He has ordered all departments to provide you and your team with anything you may require. All doors will be opened—Abracadabra!" He made a flourish with his hands and laughed.

"And the interview?" she pressed Gómez anxiously.

"It's all been fixed. Fidel will give you whatever time you need."

"Away from the other reporters?"

"All by yourself." Gómez stroked her knee. "I should be jealous," he bantered. "Fidel is a very seductive man."

"I was hoping we could go to his private island. It would be more"—she hesitated—"more *visual*."

Gómez made a pretense of clucking. "There is no private property in Cuba," he said in parody of an outraged moralist. Then, in a confidential hush, he added, "Fidel's agreed to that too."

"That's marvelous, Teófilo."

The Cuban stood up and made a show of leafing through some papers on the desk.

"I'd like to ask you about one of the other correspondents in the group," he said casually.

"Yes?"

"His name is Robert Hockney. He's Jack Lancer's boss in the Washington bureau of the *World*. What do you think of him?"

"Bob?" A smile plucked at the corners of Angela's lips as she formulated her reply. "I like him. I think he's a good reporter. I think he's honest."

"He's not very sympathetic to our problems. I looked up some of his articles. In recent years, he seems to have started to imagine that the Soviet Union and Cuba are responsible for all the ills of the world."

"Oh, Bob isn't *that* dogmatic," Angela defended him. "I think he writes the truth as he sees it."

"I understand that he is quite fond of the ladies."

Angela did not like the sidelong glance that Teófilo gave her.

"My impression is he's happily married," she responded. "He has a beautiful wife who works for one of the Senate committees. I understand Julia is expecting a baby."

"Really?" The Cuban looked genuinely interested, and that added to Angela's growing sense of unease. She could not imagine why he should care whether Julia was pregnant or not. Angela had heard the news herself only the night before, when she had—literally—bumped into Julia on the steps of the Dirksen Building. Julia had looked radiantly happy. Now Angela felt, without knowing why, that it was somehow wrong, somehow dirty, to be discussing any of this with Teófilo Gómez.

"You know Hockney quite well, don't you?" the Cuban persisted.

"We're friends. Only in the platonic sense, of course."

"Of course. But I understand he's not very popular among your colleagues."

"I wouldn't say that. It's a pushy business. People are always jostling each other for position. There's a lot of jealousy."

"But there are some of your colleagues who say that Bob Hockney works for the CIA." Gómez showed her a back issue of a magazine with a lurid cover that depicted CIA Director Blair Collins as an octopus with his many tentacles squeezing the life out of Nicaragua and other Third World countries. "There's an article about Hockney in here."

Teófilo Gómez did not see fit to mention that he had dictated the text of the article, line by line, over the telephone to one of the editors of the scandal rag, which called itself *Whistle-Blower*.

Angela glanced at the article, which seemed to be mainly about Hockney's involvement with a KGB defector and the series of pieces he had written on a Soviet disinformation campaign in Washington.

"I think this is just sour grapes," she commented, handing the magazine back to the Cuban. But she recalled that she had seen copies of *Whistle-Blower* before, on the desk of her producer, Simon Green, and that Green had once used the same article as a reason for not including Hockney in a talk show.

"So you think that Hockney should be allowed to join the group?" Gómez was asking.

"Why not? That would prove that Cuba doesn't only give visas to people who are going to say what you want them to say."

"My reasoning exactly," Teófilo said, beaming. "That's the advice I gave my government."

Gómez did not explain that the decision to admit Robert Hockney had been taken the week before, after he had met with Julio Parodi and Calixto Valdés in Havana, and that it had been taken for reasons that had nothing to do with the other journalists who had been invited.

Angela still felt troubled as she emerged into the outer office, now as bustling and crowded as a rush-hour railway station. A dozen people were hovering around the receptionist's desk, while the young man with the mustache worried at them like a sheep dog. A pale, strung-out girl who wore her lank hair tied up in rubber bands got up from a straight-backed chair as

Angela left the Congressman's office. The girl shuffled into Teófilo's sanctum without knocking.

"I'm sure I've seen that girl before," Angela remarked to the receptionist.

"Oh, that's Elaine Zweig. *Whistle-Blower* magazine."

Angela's unease, at that, became something crawling and palpable and many-legged, like a centipede between the sheets. When she got back to the studio, she tried to call Hockney to tell him about her conversation, but his extension was steadily busy, and later, back at her apartment, she got caught up in the swirl of last-minute packing and drafting a neighbor to look after her cats and her Ficus trees.

MONIMBÓ, NICARAGUA

The same morning that Angela made her call at Congressman North's office, Jesús Díaz, whose nickname "Monkey" had stuck even though he was now a lieutenant in the Revolutionary Armed Forces, came home to the Indian *barrio* of Masaya, the City of Flowers. He came in a jeep at the head of a small military convoy, chugging along the road from the capital through a lush, unbelievably green tropical landscape. The cane fields and banana groves were obscured for much of the time by thick black diesel fumes spewed out by the *guaguas*, the rickety red-yellow-and-green buses that plied the route.

Monimbó had not changed much. Artisans and peddlers still hawked embroidered shirts, tablecloths, hammocks, straw mats and wood carvings around the triangular plaza with its waterless fountain and its monument to the Revolution. The church of Don Bosco stood where it had always stood, a faded watercolor yellow, pockmarked with bullet holes from the battle that had raged around it during the civil war. Nearby was the school—the Colegio Salesiano—where Fidel had made his speech years before, on the first anniversary of the Revolution.

The Cuban colonel from the Ministry of the Interior glanced sharply at the young lieutenant as they drove around the apex of the triangular plaza.

"His house is *there*," Monkey Díaz said, inclining his head at a narrow, dusty street that opened off the plaza.

The Cuban, like all of his comrades attached to the secret police, wore a Nicaraguan uniform without badges of rank. Monkey Díaz had felt honored, on that day in 1980, when he had been singled out to attend the Cubans in Monimbó. He felt no sense of honor at being called on to serve today. He knew they had picked him because he was an *indio,* a native of Monimbó, who was of the people and whose authority might therefore be accepted with less resentment than the word of a stranger. The men who now owned the country had reason to value those qualities. Monkey had heard rumors of what had been done to other *indígenas*—the Miskito Indians on the east coast: terrifying reports of villages that had been razed and mass graves heaped with corpses.

There had been bombings. A bomb had even been planted in Las Colinas, on the southern flank of the capital, outside the compound that housed the Cuban Mission—a cluster of a half-dozen whitewashed bungalows with red-tiled roofs, screened by barbed wire and sentry posts. There had been another bomb at Sandino Airport—an ugly one, a nail bomb left in a car outside the office of Executive Charter Airways, which operated an air taxi service between Managua and Havana. Not many people knew that this obscure charter outfit was a wholly owned subsidiary of the Cuban secret service. Evidently, the bombers knew; a Cuban pilot and a DGI officer were killed in the blast, their faces turned to currant jelly.

These incidents, Monkey was aware, had made the Cubans extremely jumpy. Now the government-controlled radio broadcasts were full of a new *yanqui* plot to invade the country. Posters calling on the citizenry to be ever vigilant, and to report any suspicious behavior by neighbors, even by relatives sharing the same hearth, had gone up on the walls. And the lists had been drawn up—lists of "social enemies" and suspected counter-revolutionaries. Monkey had heard talk that the compilation of these lists had been carried out under the watchful eye of General Caldeiro, the top Cuban intelligence officer attached to the Ministry of the Interior.

His jeep pulled up on the side of the plaza and they began walking—Monkey and the Cuban colonel and a couple of soldiers with Kalashnikovs—toward a little hole-in-the-wall that the man called the Licenciado used as shop and kitchen and bedroom and lecture theater, all in one. The Licenciado had been accused of spreading counterrevolutionary propaganda. Monkey did not know the name of his anonymous accuser. Whatever had prompted the informer, he had succeeded in placing the Licenciado's name on the List. This meant that the Licenciado had been classified as an enemy of the revolution who was to be arrested and held in a detention center, after which—¿quién sabe? Monkey was aware that in these times of revolutionary vigilance, more than a few people had disappeared for good after the soldiers or the secret police had come rapping at the door.

They had ordered Monkey himself to make the arrest, and he had not dared to refuse the assignment, even though the Licenciado was the closest thing to a father he had known, and one of the few men who commanded his respect. It came flooding back to Monkey now, as he caught sight of the old man sunning himself in the frame of his open door, his big, unwashed, ungainly toes sticking right out into the street as he sprawled on some hazardous arrangement of rugs and boxes. Monkey remembered an outing with the Licenciado when he was just a kid who had never been outside the *barrio,* a magical day when the old man had taken him on a bus to visit the Huellas de Acahualinca. The *huellas* were the country's most revered landmark—clear, deep footprints in petrified clay on the shore of a lake, on the northwest side of the capital. The Licenciado had wrapped his long arm around the boy's shoulder and murmured, "Be careful where you walk, because your steps may outlive you."

"*¿Qué tal, Mono?*" the old man now greeted the young lieutenant as he stood in front of the doorway, blocking the sun. "*¿Qué dices?*"

Monkey had difficulty finding words. The Licenciado made it easy for him. The sight of the Cuban colonel hovering behind Monkey Díaz had made everything clear to the old man. He hauled himself to his feet and, leaning on his stick, came out to join them in the street.

"All right," he said, "which way do we go?"

In the old days, it had been the Licenciado who had spoken loudest in favor of rising against the dictator. But in recent months, he had started talking a different way. Mostly, what he had to say took the form of a dialogue with the ruined bust of Don Pedro Joaquín Chamorro, the great liberal editor murdered under the dictatorship, in the plaza. People would gather around and listen as he pointed out that, years after the Revolution, the poor were no better off than before, a man was no freer to speak his mind, the *indios* were bullied and tormented as badly as in the days of the Conquistadores and the yoke of the *yanquis* had been replaced by that of the Cubans.

The Licenciado was bundled into the jeep with Monkey. The old man had a dreamy, vacant look, and said nothing for ten minutes or more as they bumped back along the highway.

Then suddenly his bony arm shot out, ragged and long and straight as a scarecrow's.

"See that?" he said to Monkey, pointing to a tree beside the road. Monkey followed his pointing finger, and saw the scorched brown trunk of a dying tree. It had only a few brown leaves, but it was enveloped by a thick green vine.

"*Mata-palo,*" the old man said. "That is what the Cubans are—*mata-palo.*"

The Cuban colonel swore and slapped the Licenciado across the mouth, hard enough to split his lower lip.

Monkey Díaz winced, and stared back at the vine they called the Tree-Killer.

The *mata-palo* grows parasitically. Little by little, it strangles the tree that enables it to climb up from the ground. It survives its bearer, extending its creepers laterally over great distances. Like the banyan, it puts down fresh trunks, their roots ready-formed, into the ground. It flourishes while its host dies.

It was at that moment that Monkey Díaz decided he was going to fight against the Revolution. It might have been because of the Licenciado's arrest, or the brutal slap from the Cuban colonel, or his new understanding of what the *mata-palo* symbolized. When the idea came, it was fully formed, and it filled his mind as light fills a darkened room when the switch is thrown. To fight the Revolution, he had first to escape. To the United States, where—according to the Sandinist broadcasts—there were many people who were planning to wage war on the Nicaraguan Revolution.

It did not occur to Monkey at this point that he had anything to tell the Americans that they did not know already. He had met many Cubans, yes; but the Americans would know all about that. He had heard Fidel Castro make an extraordinary boast in a secret speech in a schoolhouse in Monimbó; but the Americans would know all about that too. How could a seventeen-year-old boy—as he had been then—know more than the *yanquis*?

Chapter

6

EN ROUTE TO HAVANA

"Mind if we swap places for a while?" Hockney asked.

Angela Seabury's producer showed by his facial contractions that he considered the suggestion an insufferable intrusion. But he unbuckled his seat belt, picked up his wineglass and surrendered his aisle seat on the Cuban executive jet that had just taken off from Mexico City.

"Simon can be such an old woman," Angela said apologetically as Hockney took his place beside her.

"What's this? Your homework?" He commandeered the folder of clippings she had laid out on the folding table in front of her. He glanced at the text of Barbara Walters' celebrated interview with Castro, a series of articles on Cuba that had run in the Washington paper and a batch of magazine pieces that Angela's researcher had collected for her. At the bottom of the pile was a copy of *Whistle-Blower* magazine.

"I see that I'm included in your dossier," he commented, flicking the issue open to an article titled "JET-SET REPORTER FLAKS FOR CIA."

"Nobody takes that stuff seriously," she said reassuringly, although she knew at least one person on the charter flight who did—her own producer, Simon Green.

"I find it rather flattering," Hockney said urbanely. "And it shows that McCarthyism isn't the exclusive domain of the right. But I guess it must have taken all your influence with Teófilo to get me onto this plane."

"It's funny," she said, recalling the milling crowd in Congressman North's office. "Guess who I saw going in to talk with Teófilo? Elaine Zweig of *Whistle-Blower* magazine."

"That's hardly surprising," Hockney remarked. "A lot of their stuff reads as if it was translated from Spanish. Frankly, what a smear sheet like *Whistle-Blower* puts out worries me a lot less than these other articles." He made a gesture that encompassed the whole stack. "How often do you read about what happens to critics of the Castro regime? Did you come across a single reference to the DGI?"

"Oh, come on, Bob." Angela was beginning to grow impatient with him. "The plight of the political prisoners was one of the first things that Barbara raised with Fidel. I took that up with him myself."

"Accepted," Hockney said. "And Fidel conned you with some spurious figure, a fraction of the real number he's holding in jail. As for the DGI . . ." She looked puzzled, so he helped her along by adding, "The Cuban secret service. Teófilo's employers. And as it happens, one of the most active intelligence services in the Soviet Bloc."

"What are you saying?"

"I'm saying that we wouldn't give any awards to a correspondent who went to Nazi Germany and then failed to mention the Gestapo or the concentration camps in his reports. Although of course there were lots of correspondents like that in the thirties."

"Bob, that's outrageous," she protested. "You can't make a comparison like that."

"Can't I?" he said thoughtfully. He showed her the book he

had with him, a copy of Carlos Montaner's *Informe Secreto sobre la Revolución Cubana*. "This is *my* homework," he went on. "I've been trying to brush up my schoolboy Spanish." Over the past week, he had sat down with Julia at the breakfast table every morning, painfully rehearsing basic Spanish conversation. He had got to the point where he could handle a waiter, but he had needed a dictionary to get beyond the first page of Montaner. "The book tells some charming stories about the Cuban Gulag. Montaner describes the case of a journalist who was trampled by jackbooted guards day after day until they left him for dead. He tells about a hero of the Revolution who had his prisoners asphyxiated in a hermetically sealed truck. I wonder why nobody knows about Teófilo's organization but everyone knows about the CIA. Valladares says it's because there's a conspiracy of silence."

That puzzled look came over Angela's face again.

"Valladares is one of Cuba's greatest living poets," Hockney elaborated. "They kept him in jail for twenty-two years after the Revolution. In a letter smuggled out of his security prison, he said that the fate of political prisoners in Cuba today is like that of the Christians who were persecuted in pagan Rome. He says the full extent of the barbarism will only be understood after there have been untold numbers of martyrs. And then their blood will be on our conscience."

Angela shuddered and sipped her wine. "That's pretty grisly stuff," she commented. She glanced at the book and added, "I guess they won't let you bring that into Cuba."

"You're right," Hockney agreed. He slipped the book into the seat pocket in front of him. "Maybe some *apparatchik* will find it and be converted," he said, trying to lighten the tone of the conversation.

As he chatted with Angela, it struck Hockney that more than two decades after the Bay of Pigs and the missile crisis, Cuba continued to occupy a unique place in the American psyche. Why was it that young militants who understood that the Soviet Union was controlled by a corrupt, backward-looking oligarchy which was ready to appeal to the lowest political emotions among its own population—anti-Semitism and crude jingoism—to divert attention from its failures could still find romance and hope in Cuba?

A whole folklore had grown up, compounded of tales—many of them true—about the United Fruit Company; coups and assassination plots masterminded by the CIA; America's complicity in shoring up strutting generals and oligarchs. It had got to the point where Hockney found that some of his colleagues were automatically hostile to any Latin American leader who was naive enough to declare himself a friend of the United States. A Third World leader who wanted the American media on his side would be well advised, in Hockney's observation, to begin by attacking the United States.

Then, too, Castro had somehow managed to retain some of the glamour that had surrounded him when he descended from the sierra as conquering guerrilla chieftain. It did not seem to matter to his admirers that his every move was taken with the endorsement—or at the active instigation—of the Soviets, who subsidized his regime to the tune of millions of dollars a day, and had inserted their advisers into key positions in every significant department of government. Charmers like Angela's friend Teófilo oiled their way around, dropping the occasional disparaging remark about those tedious Russians, and this was seen as some daring declaration of independence.

Hockney wondered what it would take to shock Angela—or harder still, Jack Lancer—out of their roseate view of Cuba. The evidence that the Cubans were up to their necks in revolutionary terrorism around Central America had not done it. The proof that the Cubans were equally embroiled in spreading the drug poison in the United States would probably not do it either, even if he managed to acquire such evidence.

Hockney shared none of these reflections with Angela.

He just said, "Tell me about the hotel. Did you stay at the Riviera last time?"

"Oh, you'll love it," she gushed, relieved to be back on soft, neutral ground. "It's a big blue thirty-story pleasure dome, built by gangsters, the people who rubbed out that famous New York mobster."

"Anastasia?"

"Yes, that's the one. It's so hideous—the aesthetics are pure Miami Beach—that you can't help but *adore* it."

HAVANA

The Riviera Hotel, it transpired, was on the southwest flank of the Vedado district, overlooking a broad beachfront boulevard called the Malecón. As the journalists climbed out of the small fleet of government limousines that had collected them from the airport, Hockney felt salt spray against the side of his face from the waves that were breaking over the seawall. Farther up along the Malecón he could see a sandbagged antiaircraft emplacement and a platoon of militiamen drilling near the abandoned, dilapidated shell of the American Embassy.

While a solicitous Cuban official bustled around the reception desk, making sure that all the journalists collected their hotel *tarjetas*—identity cards—Hockney strolled away into a cavernous bar with tall mirrors, leather-upholstered banquettes and lots of empty tables inexplicably garnished with little placards that announced, "RESERVADO." He remembered what Angela had said about mobsters. It was easy enough to picture a Meyer Lansky at one of the deserted tables, cutting a deal in the shadows.

The spindly old man who worked the levers and buttons inside the elevator cage looked like a survivor from those colorful times. But he had made his adjustments. Respectfully but firmly, he insisted on inspecting each journalist's *tarjeta*.

Angela and Hockney looked at each other's door keys.

"I see they gave you a penthouse," Hockney commented.

"The triumph of video technology," she joked. Hockney's

room was two floors below, and—as he soon discovered—you could get a sea view from it only by clambering out onto the minute balcony and craning precariously around the edge. "Come and have a drink as soon as you get settled in," Angela invited him. After inspecting his lodgings, Hockney was grateful for the invitation and went up before he had bothered to unpack.

Angela's door was open. He found her standing with her cameraman on a wide terrace with a magnificent view of the ocean. Hockney had run into the cameraman in Vietnam, and respected him as a pro who was ready to take hair-raising risks without being any sort of war freak, and would come back with the most haunting shots without ever moving the bodies around—more than could be said for some of his competitors. Russ Tyrrell was a weathered, sandy-haired Australian, and the tracery of fine red lines on his face told you at once that he had emptied a few serious drinking establishments in his day.

"Did you trip over any wires on the way in?" Tyrrell chaffed him. "Last time we were here, I found bugs all over the place. There were even a couple in the john. How about that, eh? I lifted up the top of the tank, and there was a mike just looking at me."

"Are all the rooms bugged?"

"I dunno. But I'd sure bet *yours* is."

"Come on, Russ. Why would they bother?" Angela interjected.

The Australian shrugged. "Why don't you ask Fidel?" he suggested.

A voice called out from behind them, and they all turned around. A young, slightly built man with frizzy hair was walking across the living room. He was wearing a khaki bush shirt with a row of pens in one of the breast pockets.

"Brad." Angela went in to greet him. "It's wonderful to see you. Do you know Bob Hockney from the *World*?"

The two men assessed each other, and it seemed to Hockney that the newcomer's stare was far from friendly. Hockney knew

166

a fair amount about Brad Lister. He was an extremely rare phenomenon: an American private citizen living in Cuba. Despite his boyish looks, Hockney knew that Lister had been living in Havana since at least the late sixties, seemingly unimpeded through successive blowups between the Cubans and the Americans. Lister had servants, and frequented the hard-currency stores where such luxuries as imported cigarettes and blue jeans and shampoo that did not make your hair fall out were for sale. Such items could be sold on the street for four or five times their initial price.

Lister's by-line appeared infrequently in the *World*, and Hockney had questioned his ambiguous relationship with the Cuban authorities. But Ed Finkel, the paper's Managing Editor, had protected Lister, on the ground that the stringer was indispensable. He had sources in Havana that nobody else could tap—at any rate, not on a regular basis. And as far as visiting correspondents were concerned, Lister was a godsend. When all else failed, he was the man who could extract the missing camera from Cuban Customs, arrange the impossible interview with the reticent government official, the permit to the restricted zone or the introduction of a complaisant Cuban girl (or boy) without sexual inhibitions.

"I've heard a lot about you," Brad Lister was saying to Hockney.

Hockney mumbled something inane and watched Lister turn his full attention to Angela.

"How do you like the hotel?" Lister asked her. She was at the phone, dialing a number that seemed to be steadily busy.

"It's fine," she replied. "If I can ever get Room Service."

"Here, let me do that." With a smile, Lister took over the phone and tried a different number. Someone answered straightaway. *"Espere un momentito,"* he murmured into the receiver. "What do you all want?"

Russ Tyrrell was not too far away to catch that. "Scotch!" he yelled.

"I want something tropical." Angela yawned and stretched

167

her arms wide as she arranged herself on the sofa in the living room. The humidity, after the cramped ride on the plane, was making her drowsy.

Lister ordered daiquiris.

"I guess what they say about you is true," Hockney remarked to him.

"What's that?"

"You know how to fix things."

When the waiter came with the drinks, Lister nodded to him with friendly recognition. He had met Antonio years before, although the Cuban had not been wearing a white jacket in those days. Antonio had been occupying a desk in a modern, anonymous building near the corner of M Street and Second Avenue in Vedado. Like most of the hotel staff at the Riviera, Antonio was employed by the secret police—the Departamento de Seguridad del Estado, known to most Cubans as the G-2.

Since he was part of the system, Lister understood that in *el estado policiaco* (as Cuban dissidents called it) foreigners were not admitted to a real country. They were led along a narrow tube, hermetically sealed and walled with two-way mirrors. Part of Brad Lister's function in the Foreign Press Bureau of G-2 was to divert the attention of American correspondents from the confining walls of that tunnel. Lister was good at his job. Before Angela and Hockney had left Washington, he had spent many hours in the building on M Street studying the copious psychological profiles that were stored in the G-2 computers.

These files were updated several times a year. The Bureau's analysts carefully noted any signs of a shift in the subject's political attitudes, his range of contacts, his relations with colleagues and friends. Brad Lister, glancing over Hockney's file, had found it interesting that Julia was expecting a baby. Journalists, in general, were not good targets for sexual entrapment and blackmail, since so many of them—Lister had found—were sexually promiscuous, and unabashed about it. Especially on foreign trips. But when a particularly gross perversion was involved, or there were special emotional factors, the "honey trap" was still worth considering.

Brad Lister had talked this over with Colonel Oliveira.

As Lister watched Angela reclining on the sofa, he recalled Oliveira's words about *her*.

"She's a *ninfo*, no?" the Cuban had suggested after skimming through an updated list of Angela's lovers. The list included Senators, movie producers, network bosses and a sports promoter.

"I think the American term is starfucker," Lister had commented acidly.

"Teófilo had her in New York," Oliveira had reflected aloud, his gaze lingering on some publicity stills of Angela that the network had released. "She's got nice tits," he added. He puffed out his chest and said, "I'd like to meet this one myself."

As he sipped his daiquiri in Angela's penthouse, Lister could feel the bulk of the envelope that Oliveira had given him, inside the pocket of his bush shirt. It contained three thousand dollars—not a munificent sum, since the Foreign Press Bureau had omitted to pay Lister his retainer in more than two months. Still, converted into imported goods for resale on the black market, three thousand bucks was a tidy amount.

"I'm counting on you not to screw up," Oliveira had cautioned him. "This is one of the best opportunities we've had in years. Keep them happy. And watch Hockney the way you would watch a tarantula. *Que no se chupa el dedo*, ha?"

Loosely translated, Oliveira's final instruction meant "Don't suck your thumb."

"The official program doesn't start until tomorrow," Lister was saying when Hockney strolled back in from the terrace. "I thought you might like to meet some Cuban friends of mine, people who won't give you any bullshit."

"Fine," Angela replied.

"You remember the Bodequita del Medio? The place that looks like a wine cellar in the Old Town, near the cathedral?"

"Oh, yes. It reminded me of an Old World grocery store."

"I made reservations," Lister explained. "A friend of mine named Manuel—Manuel Oliveira—said he would join us. You'll like him. He's very engaging. And he's not afraid to speak his mind."

"What does he do?" Angela asked.

"Manuel's a psychologist." This description of Colonel Oliveira's profession was not light-years removed from the truth. His work was based, in large part, on character analysis.

"How does that sound to you, Bob?" Angela said, turning to Hockney.

"Well, I was thinking of going to the Floridita to have a drink with Papa Hemingway's ghost," Hockney demurred. In fact, he was less than enthralled by the prospect of being chained to Brad Lister for the entire evening. He preferred to go out and sniff the air by himself.

"Say, I reckon that's not a bad idea," Russ Tyrrell chimed in at that moment. "We could do some filming at the Floridita. It could make a nice opening shot."

Brad Lister made a face. "The Bodeguita's associated with Hemingway too," he pointed out to Hockney. "He used to go there all the time. For the *mojitos*."

"More people have heard of the Floridita," Russ Tyrrell insisted, seeming to enjoy upsetting Lister's arrangements.

"It's probably too late now to get reservations," Lister held out stubbornly.

"Oh, give it a try, Brad," Angela said, surprised that the stringer appeared to be seriously put out by something as trivial as a change of restaurant. "We know you can fix anything."

If Angela had been able to witness the scene at the Floridita an hour or so before their arrival, she might have understood the reason for her guide's disquietude.

It had started out as a fairly typical evening. The air conditioning was on full blast. A couple of Canadian tourists and an elderly man in a gray suit of expensive cloth that had worn shiny at the elbows were sitting in front of the massive black wooden bar, near the bust of Hemingway and a mural depicting eighteenth-century Havana. In the dining room, waiters in hand-me-down tuxedos hovered around a mostly Cuban clientele. The women were dressed casually, in pants or cheap print dresses. A young couple were engaged in changing their baby's diaper; its howls were not entirely drowned out by the transistor radio they had blaring on their table.

The waiters presented the customers with enormous, poster-size menus.

Regulars rarely bothered to glance at it. The menu was for show. Anyone who ordered something other than one of the waiters' three "suggestions" was likely to get the stock reply *"No hay."* The worst news that evening was the announcement *"No hay limón."* In the absence of lemon juice, even the Floridita's famed daiquiris were out.

Yet many of the Cubans in the restaurant were stuffing food into doggie bags to liven their fare at home the next day. Even the rolls, which had the taste and consistency of plaster of Paris, were scooped up. The process was a familiar sight at Havana restaurants, where many diners came equipped with a heavy plastic bag—*el nylón*.

Forty minutes before Angela's party arrived, a large, unmarked van pulled up at the back entrance to the Floridita. Several men started unloading crates of food and drink.

Fifteen minutes later, a dozen well-dressed couples, some with children, streamed through the main entrance. The manager received them obsequiously, and started whispering urgent instructions to his waiters. The Canadian tourists were annoyed when they were told that there was no seating for them in the dining room after all, because of a "private party." The family with the howling baby was given twenty minutes to finish dinner and settle the bill. By the time the American reporters arrived, the place looked as lively and prosperous as it must have seemed in the days when Hemingway propped up the bar.

"It's perfect," Angela purred.

She enjoyed talking to Lister's Cuban friend, Manuel Oliveira, who told a couple of funny stories about the Russian advisers in Cuba that reminded her of the jokes Anglo South Africans told about van der Merwe, the archetypal dumb Boer. The Cuban made her very conscious of being a woman. There was nothing furtive about the way his very dark, liquid brown eyes ranged from her face to her body, or the way he let his thigh brush hers under the table. Oliveira was a cheerful predator, giving fair warning of his intentions, and was attractive and lively enough for her not to shy away.

Hockney was equally conscious of how Oliveira was looking at Angela. All the same, he found it hard to dislike this cordial, expansive Cuban who managed, as he talked, to make everyone at the table feel that some part of what he was saying was addressed exclusively to *him*.

Hockney asked Oliveira about the Cuban attitude toward drugs.

"Oh, I'm afraid we are rather puritanical," the Cuban replied. "Our Revolution is still young, and like your Puritans in early New England, we have our share of moral crusaders who burn with an unyielding light. As Fidel says, our Revolution is still in its kindergarten phase. There is a wing at the biggest security jail—Combinado del Este—that is reserved for foreign drug-runners who are caught trying to smuggle their goods through Cuban waters."

Later, when they were drinking small, sweet cups of strong Cuban coffee, Hockney asked Oliveira about Santa María del Mar.

"It's charming," he said. "One of our most popular beaches."

"But there are private villas, too."

"Oh, yes. As a matter of fact, some of our most senior government officials have weekend places there. Then there are guesthouses. Some of them were made available to officers who fought in Angola as a reward. I have a place there myself. I would be happy to invite you—all of you"—he extended the invitation to the whole table—"if you have time during your stay."

"Does it take long to get to Santa María?"

172

"Half an hour. Maybe forty minutes. You have to go through the tunnel, then east along the coast road. I believe there are buses."

"Is it possible to hire a car in Havana?"

Oliveira looked skeptical. "Possible, but not easy. And you know, most of the drivers report to the G-Two. If you want to go to Santa María," he volunteered, "I would be delighted to lend you my own car."

"You're very generous," Hockney said to the Cuban. *Too* generous, he was thinking. In a society where people were watched as closely as in Cuba, a man who talked as openly as Oliveira had to be either crazy or connected with the secret police. He agreed to meet Oliveira for a cocktail before lunch the next day, while the other reporters went off to the Playa Girón to listen to speeches about the new Bay of Pigs that the Newgate Administration was supposed to be planning.

Hockney spent most of his morning wandering around Vedado. He strolled up the Malecón, past the disintegrating facade of the deserted American Embassy. He observed that the fifth-floor balcony hung at a precarious angle, seemingly about to fall. The stonework was cratered and chipped. In places, the aluminum casings of the windows had worked loose from their moorings. The entire building was listing dangerously to the left. Someone had tied a rope around its middle, as if to hold the crumbling edifice together. The effect was surreal.

He found a taxi and rode out to the Plaza de la Revolución. The vulgar, pompous modern building that housed the Palace of the Revolution was vaguely reminiscent of the U.S. Supreme Court building, which Hockney guessed must have served as the original model. There was a considerable amount of activity in the plaza. Bands of schoolchildren were marshaled like army platoons in front of the palace, under the supervision of unsmiling Party youth organizers. Uniformed guards were massed around the steps leading down from the palace.

"The people love you, Fidel!" the schoolchildren chorused

as a familiar bearded figure in battle dress hurried down the steps, through the ranks of his guards and into the back seat of a black armored Zil limousine.

From the other side of the great plaza, Hockney watched the big car moving past the throng like a flagship being convoyed across the high seas. The Zil was surrounded on all sides—left and right, front and back—by other cars. Hockney counted nine of them, each carrying four men. At the rear of the convoy he saw three military trucks with about a dozen guards, equipped with automatic rifles and grenades, in each. Ahead of the little cavalcade, the road had been cleared of traffic, the side streets cordoned off, and bystanders were being methodically screened by G-2 agents. Hockney slipped away as he saw two tough-looking men working their way through the crowd toward him. They had approached a young man who had his shirttail hanging outside his pants, and were frisking him.

In the hotel bar, just after noon, Hockney described the scene to Oliveira.

"Yes, of course," the Cuban said. "Fidel has become more and more worried about security. The guards you saw belong to Unit Forty-nine."

"Unit Forty-nine?"

"The official name is the General Department for the Personal Protection of Leaders. But from the early days, everybody calls it Unit Forty-nine. It may well be the largest private bodyguard in the world. Fidel has four thousand men who watch over him. Raul, his little brother, has five hundred. They go with Fidel everywhere. If he visits a factory, they send the workers away for a couple of hours so they can check everywhere for explosives. One of those guys you saw with Fidel is a professional baseball catcher. His job is to catch a bomb if somebody throws one and—you know—toss it back."

Oliveira chuckled as he mimed the action of lobbing back a grenade at the place whence it had come.

"But everybody is nervous these days," Oliveira continued. "Fidel is nervous, and that makes everybody around him jumpy. It began to get really bad when the woman—Celia Sán-chez—died. You know about her?"

"Wasn't she Fidel's mistress or something?"

"Mistress?" the Cuban shrugged. "I don't know about that. She wasn't pretty, you know. But he depended on her. She was his *madrina*, you know. His godmother. Up in the sierra, she was always beside him. She would wash his feet when they were tired from a day of marching. She was the one he could confide in. She was also a priestess in the religion, an *iyalocha*."

Hockney's expression showed that Oliveira had lost him.

The Cuban chuckled again. "You'll never understand the Cubans until you understand the religion—*santería, lucumí*. It started with the Yoruba people in Nigeria. They brought it to Cuba when they came as slaves, and it survived. It is stronger with many of the blacks—*and* many of the whites—than Catholicism. Celia Sánchez was a priestess in the religion, a priest-ess of Obatalá. She initiated Fidel into it too. You'll see that he wears two watchbands on his left wrist sometimes. One is to conceal his *collar,* his ritual bracelet."

"You mean Fidel believes in some kind of voodoo?"

"I don't think Fidel's a believer. Many of the *batistianos* be-lieved in the religion; they relied on it. Fidel tries to use it to get some popular support. But his relationship with the woman went beyond that. He depended on her. You should have seen him when she died—he was white as mutton fat, sweaty, insom-niac. Since then, he's been haunted by fear of assassination."

Hockney wondered again whether the Cuban was talking so freely because he was crazy, or a genuine opponent of the re-gime, or a secret policeman laying some kind of trap. Whatever the case, Oliveira was good value.

One thing that Colonel Oliveira did not choose to tell Hock-ney was that at the very moment he had watched the armored Zil leaving the Plaza de la Revolución, Fidel Castro was thirty kilometers south of the capital, in the new Soviet bunker com-plex that irreverent Cubans living in nearby Bejucal referred to as "La Cuevita"—The Rathole. The bearded man in the black limousine was a dead ringer for Fidel, at least from a distance. Close up, it became apparent that he was slightly shorter than El Líder Máximo, his eyes were closer-set and his beard needed filling out. But distance and the props—the cigar, the combat fatigues or Russian-style uniform, the cap, the revolver at his hip—brought off the illusion.

"I'll be very frank with you," Oliveira was saying to Hockney. "This kind of story amuses you, no?"

"Of course," Hockney agreed, wondering what was coming next.

"I can tell you many things that might amuse you," the Cuban went on. He made a show of looking around the bar to see whether anyone was listening in. "But hotels are not a good place to talk *en serio*. What would you say to a little drive?"

Hockney shrugged. He had nothing better to do.

To his mild surprise, the Cuban drove him in his battered fifties Plymouth—most of the cars on the streets looked as if they belonged on the set of a vintage Hollywood movie, the kind that has scratches and blobs on the worn celluloid—to an enormous recreation park somewhere south of Vedado. Hockney learned that it was called the Parque Lenín, and that it stayed open in the evening so that families could bring their kids to look at the animals in the zoo and to enjoy the carousels and fun houses. The main attraction for the children, it seemed, was the ride on the Dumbo the Elephant cars.

"I'm glad to see that *yanqui* culture isn't altogether extinct," Hockney remarked. "We could be at Disneyland."

"Shall we?"

Hockney was startled when the Cuban took his elbow and steered him to the gate.

"This is absurd," Hockney laughed after they boarded their car and began to swoop and roll. He was holding on to one of the dopey elephant's ears, squeezed up against the side of the car. The cars were not built to hold two adults.

"It's a little unorthodox," Oliveira said, "but I wanted to ask you a serious question. What are you looking for in Cuba?"

The sudden shift in tone alarmed Hockney.

"You needn't worry," Oliveira reassured him. "You can talk to me openly. You see, I have certain connections—oh, yes, I can see that you guessed that already. I have respect for you. I know you are a clever man. I can tell you that I have a very important job in the state security apparatus, and I am supposed to be keeping you under close watch."

"Why?"

"What does it matter?" Oliveira said offhandedly, as their car made another swoop and Hockney saw a pair of fat Cuban women, their hair in curlers under see-through plastic wraps, waiting to put their kids onto the ride. "We have a law of *peligrosidad* in this country. It is very enlightened. You are liable to be detained if you are considered a dangerous man. You are most obviously a dangerous man, Mr. Robert Hockney."

Hockney tried to say something, but the Cuban shouted back into the wind, "Let me explain, please. I know you have certain connections too. I know you helped the Russian, Barisov. I think you can help me too. I have had enough of our glorious Revolution. I want to get out. But not on a leaky shrimper with the *gusanos*. You can help me."

"What do you want me to do?" Hockney asked, yelling as hard as he dared. Oliveira's voice came and went in gusts. Then their car clanked to a stop, but Oliveira muttered something to the attendant and the women in curlers had to wait for the next Dumbo.

Hockney was not automatically inclined to trust Manuel Oliveira, and the Cuban must have sensed it, because he said, "I want to prove my intentions to you. Tell me what you are looking for, and I will make it possible. I have that power."

Hockney considered for a moment, then shouted, "I'll think about it."

"I can also give you some papers," Oliveira roared into his ear. "You can give them to the right people in Washington. You know Mr. Blair Collins."

"You want me to smuggle documents out of Cuba?" Hockney gasped, astounded.

"It's safe, perfectly safe," Oliveira insisted. "Nobody's going

177

to search your group. Fidel wants the best possible relations with the American media. I know about these things."

When they finally got off the ride, Oliveira led Hockney to a stand that sold *bocadillos* and sodas. Hockney sipped at a sickly-sweet, slightly fizzy fruit drink and thought over Oliveira's offer.

Then the Cuban observed, "It's only natural that everybody is interested in Julio Parodi," as nonchalantly as if he were commenting on the weather. Later, it was plain to Hockney that he should have shied away at that moment, broken away and taken cover, as deep as he could burrow. But it was his first, impetuous reaction that won out, the little voice inside that said, *Dammit, I don't know what Oliveira's game is, but since it seems he knows everything anyway, I may as well find out how far this will get me.*

So Hockney drove with Oliveira eastward from the capital, through a long tiled tunnel with abandoned tollbooths—relics of the evil times before socialism—past the fortress of La Cabaña and out along the coast road to the address that Maguire had given him in Miami. The house overlooking the ocean was called the Villa Yagruma. The Cuban explained that the *yagruma* was the island's national tree, and had magical significance for people involved in the Afro-Caribbean religion. The Villa Yagruma was screened from the road by shrubbery and high walls with what looked like razor wire on top. Apart from that, there was no indication of unusual security precautions. A young man in a white shirt and black pants opened the door to Oliveira. He did not appear to be armed. But he snapped his heels to attention when he recognized Hockney's companion.

"Welcome to the Villa Yagruma," Oliveira said, when they had made themselves at home in the living room. "I hope it satisfies your curiosity."

When Hockney tried to remember what had happened during the rest of that afternoon and evening, he could summon only fragments of conversation, glimpses of the white, sandy beach and of an earthy, voluptuous woman, lit up only briefly, jerkily, as if caught under a strobe light. He could remember Oliveira saying something about Parodi as he poured drinks—that Parodi had been to Havana, and had stayed at the villa, but that the Cubans distrusted him because he was the CIA's man. He remembered a full-bodied, dark-skinned woman in a skimpy dress, who was brought in when he had nearly finished his first drink. She giggled and talked, mostly in sign language, about Parodi's sexual prowess. He remembered the girl shriek-ing with laughter as she tore at the buttons of his shirt, at his fly, shaking hands with his cock as he had seen dockside whores do in Saigon and Marseille. He remembered weakly protesting, but all the strength seemed to have been sapped from him. He remembered sinking deeper and deeper into the sofa, rolling off it onto the floor, hoping the fall might help to revive him, but finding his eyelids weighed down as if with lead.

Then the lights and the scuffles, the harsh voices, the girl being bundled out of the room, someone laughing mirthlessly at his nakedness, throwing his clothes at him in a crumpled ball, and a man in uniform with a bald, narrow head like a mahogany skull slapping him again and again, his big hand moving with the regular, mechanical rhythm of a windshield wiper. Then he was being manhandled into some kind of truck, and there was a long ride to a place Hockney could not identify, a place of echoes and clanging doors. Where was Oliveira through all of this?

Hockney was trying to find Oliveira among the images that flicked through his mind like slides inserted in a projector up-side down, sidewise, in no perceptible sequence, but what was happening inside his head was worse than a headache. It was as if they had burned out some of his brain cells, leaving his memory and his analytical faculty punctured full of holes like a Swiss cheese.

"Oliveira?" he croaked at the ebony skull he could make out indistinctly behind the light on the desk that was hurting his eyes.

"Oliveira is under arrest," said Calixto Valdés. "We are not here to discuss Oliveira's case. We are here to discuss yours."

They drugged me, Hockney thought, in dumb realization. *It must have been in the drink.*

"I'm a journalist," Hockney mumbled, as if here, in a windowless cell in the bowels of a Cuban prison, American press accreditation could be trusted to cast a magic circle around him.

The Cuban snickered. His English was not as good as Oliveira's, but his tone filled in the gaps in his vocabulary.

"Not journalist," Valdés said. "All the journalists were at Playa Girón. You come to spy."

"It's not true," Hockney argued. The effort to get each word out was so great that it made him want to throw up.

"We have the proofs," Valdés chastised him. He passed a sheaf of papers across the desk.

Hockney had to make a conscious effort to mold his hands into the right shape to receive them. The papers seemed intolerably heavy. He squinted to read the top page. The letters swirled before his eyes, repeated not just once, but two or three times. The words were in Spanish. There was a red stamp at the top that said SECRETO. That was all he could make out.

He had no recollection of these papers.

"I—never—saw—them—before"—he ground his statement out.

"Spy," Valdés charged him again. "Oliveira sold you state secrets for the CIA. We found the *documentos* among your clothes."

Hockney looked at the top page again, and still could not recall anything about these documents. Then a snatch of conversation came swimming back, and a crazy scene on the Dumbo the Elephant ride. Oliveira had offered him secrets, to take to Blair Collins. Had he accepted the offer, or had these papers been planted on him?

Calixto Valdés took back the documents and placed another sheet of paper on Hockney's lap.

"Your confession," Valdés said. "You will sign."

Hockney felt an overwhelming desire to sleep. He had actually started to slide from the chair onto the floor when someone standing behind gave him a swift, painful jab in the kidneys.

"Sign," Valdés repeated.

"I—have—to—sleep," Hockney gasped.

"Sign. Then you can sleep."

Hockney took the pen, but it slipped from his insentient fingers. The clatter of the pen against the flagstones made him dimly aware of what they were seeking to do to him.

"No," he mumbled. "Not sign."

"Three hours." Valdés nodded to the man standing behind the prisoner. "We resume in three hours. He will sign then."

Angela thought little of it when she called Hockney's room before dinner and got no reply. She had noticed his absence from the rest of the group when they rode out to the Bay of Pigs in a big Russian-made bus whose air conditioner worked intermittently, and put that down to Bob's characteristic working habits. He was a loner, always had been. She guessed he had found something to keep him busy. What she wanted most, after the long, dusty trip, was to take a languorous bath. She poured in a generous dollop of milk bubble bath, and the luxurious tiled bathroom was filled with the fragrance of Fidji.

Her mind slipped away from any thought of Hockney. When she had dressed for dinner and Brad Lister arrived to take her to the hotel floor show, Lister said that she and her team were to stay in their rooms the next day. Fidel might summon them at any moment.

"What happened to your friend the psychologist? Oliveira?" Angela asked idly later on, in between a *guajira* combo and a peroxide blonde singing old American songs with a vaguely torchy flavor in an accent you could have cut with a cleaver. She had been quite taken by the elegant, intensely masculine Cuban who had joined them for dinner at the Floridita. Lister made some insignificant comment about the pressures of Oliveira's work.

The next day was as exciting as she could have hoped. It really began about eleven, when Russ Tyrrell and Simon Green, her producer, were playing poker on her terrace and she had just succeeded, after about three hours of waiting, in getting a phone call put through to New York. She heard an imperative rap at the door and called out, "Russ, would you get that, please?"

Tyrrell yanked the door open and found himself looking at a tall, heavyset man in green fatigues. The uniform was freshly starched, but failed to contain the roll of loose flesh around the man's waist; one of the buttons had popped open. He wore a heavy revolver at his hip. The beard was scraggly and mostly gray; it made the man look rather older than he appeared in photographs. That, and his singularly pale complexion. The face, Tyrrell thought, was the color and texture of wet cement. It made it seem that Fidel Castro had not enjoyed the sun on his tropical island for quite some time.

"Mr. President," Tyrrell stammered as Castro blew a puff of cigar smoke past his ear.

"You can call me Fidel," the Cuban leader announced in a stage-Latin accent as he swaggered into the room as if he owned it. "You may all call me Fidel."

The Australian cameraman could see armed guards milling around in the corridor outside, eight or nine of them at least.

Castro's surprise appearance had its predictable effect on the Americans in the room. Angela dropped the phone in her excitement. Simon Green forgot about his four queens. They were both magnetized.

"I must apologize for keeping you waiting," Fidel began in rapid-fire Spanish. "As you must be aware, your President Newgate has been keeping me a little busy. He is sending spy planes over my country every day. The sonic boom keeps people awake at night in the city. Perhaps you heard it last night. Well, perhaps you would like to ask me some questions."

It took them a few minutes to get the camera and the sound equipment set up. Then, with Lister translating, Angela ran through a list of prepared questions, starting with Nicaragua and the reported resumption of CIA covert operations against Cuba. Mindful of some of Hockney's strictures about their colleagues' reporting of Cuba, Angela had prepared a few questions that were far from soft lobs—on the Cuban role in training terrorists; on a recent espionage case involving Cubans in New York; on the plight of political prisoners.

Fidel sidestepped some of these, but on the topic of political prisoners he was obligingly candid.

"Of course we have political prisoners," he said. "The Revolution does not have the right to cut its own throat by allowing people to conspire to reverse the course of history. We have fewer political prisoners than we had in the years just after the Revolution. And I will tell you this. If these people want to leave, we are ready to let them leave. We don't care what they do in Miami. The port of Mariel is open. They can go. All of them."

"Excuse me," Angela broke in. "Did you say the port of Mariel is open again? Does that mean that there is going to be a new boatlift of Cuban refugees to the United States?"

"As of today, Mariel is open," Castro confirmed.

Angela realized she had just been handed a major news exclusive. "I am sure you are aware, Mr. President," she went on, "that the Newgate Administration in Washington has announced that it is not prepared to admit immigrants from Cuba who do not have a clear right to political asylum. The Administration has made the claim that your government used the last boatlift—the so-called Freedom Flotilla—to ship out hardened criminals and psychiatric cases."

Fidel shrugged and took a drag on his cigar. "That is not my problem," he said. "That is a problem for the United States. And for the poor reactionary fools who are still duped by the United States into believing that it offers them some kind of hope."

After a couple of hours, the Cuban leader left as abruptly as he had arrived, with a promise that he would arrange a trip for Angela to the island where he sometimes went spearfishing. He parted from the men with backslaps and *abrazos*. He took Angela's hand and squeezed it gently, holding it for what seemed like a long time, staring deep into her smoky gray eyes. Then he was gone, and she was left to spend the rest of the day trying to work out arrangements for transmission of the interview to New York in time to be excerpted for the late-night news.

When all the work had been done, Brad Lister was there, solicitous as always. He had set up another dinner, with a Cuban writer who had fought in Angola and Ethiopia.

Lister waited until she had dialed Hockney's room number and listened to the phone buzz a few times before he cleared his throat and said, "Look, I guess you'd better know about this. Hockney's in trouble."

"What sort of trouble? Why didn't you tell me before?"

"I only heard tonight."

Russ Tyrrell strolled over to listen in. After a few beers, Tyrrell was in a belligerent mood, and Brad Lister did not like the way the big Australian pushed right up against him.

"Bloody hell," the cameraman said. "What's happened to Bob?"

"He's under arrest," Lister explained nervously. "He could be charged with espionage. It seems he was found with secret government documents in his possession."

"Flaming shit," Tyrrell erupted. "It's a setup. Has to be."

"But why?" Angela asked. "Why would they want to frame Bob?"

"You just come with me for a minute, love," Tyrrell said, taking her arm. He guided her into the bedroom and shut the door so that Lister could not hear their conversation.

"Now, tell me," he went on. "Do you think Bob is a CIA agent?"

"No. Of course not."

"Well, then, whatever happened, it's up to us to get him out. This is supposed to be a group junket, remember? We've all got to stick together."

"You're right," Angela said decisively. "Let's try to round up everybody else. We'll find out where they're holding him, and lodge a formal complaint. Maybe somebody should call the *World* in New York." Her brow wrinkled. "It's hard to understand, though. I mean, they've arrested an American correspondent and simply held him for twenty-four hours."

"You can see why they don't have any Watergate dramas in the Cuban press," Tyrrell observed sourly. "What did Fidel say to you in that interview?"

"He said the press isn't needed as a watchdog in Cuba," Angela quoted from memory. "He said the people themselves stand guard over the civic virtues, and will deal with anyone who transgresses."

"Yeah," Tyrrell said. "I s'pose that just about says it all."

Hockney had not slept for more than twenty minutes at a stretch. He knew that much because he had counted off the minutes during the intervals when he lay awake, in the middle of the night, waiting for the guard to come back and hammer on the metal door of his cell. The guard came past every twenty-five minutes. Inside the cell, which had the dimensions of a tomb—three feet wide, eight feet long, twelve feet high—the noise was deafening. He had tried cupping his hands over his ears until his arms began to ache. Now he lay on his side on the stone floor, waiting for the ringing that still echoed inside his head to start all over again.

There had been none of the darker horrors: no beatings or other physical torture, electrodes, truth serums. Just the noise, and the lack of sleep, and three or four sessions in the interrogation room, and the lack of any other distractions. The only furniture in the cell was a stinking bucket, Hockney's latrine, which nobody bothered to empty. The only light that reached him in his confinement came through the crack at the foot of the door.

But his captors had one more weapon to use against him: his own imagination. Once, somewhere between midnight and morning, he had heard the tramp of booted feet and the panting and snarling of dogs. Then the jangle of keys and the clash of metal as a door somewhere on the same level was flung open. Then the pleading and cursing of another prisoner, soon to be swallowed up in screams.

Hockney had had time, once his head had cleared sufficiently, to think over everything he had heard and read about

Castro's jails. He knew that there was a kind of color code among the prisoners. The men who were made to wear yellow uniforms—the *amarillos*—were political prisoners, denied all privileges, regarded as persons beyond redemption. Gray-blue uniforms were worn by common criminals. The most unregenerate captives, in the eyes of the regime, were those who refused to wear either yellow, which was identified with Batista's soldiers, or blue, and were left to endure the extremes of heat and cold in their undershorts. They were called the *calzoncillos*— the Underpants Brigade. Hockney belonged to none of these categories. They had left him in his own clothes. He felt soiled and sticky, badly in need of a shave and a shower.

Something his interrogator had said during their last session had made him aware that he was being held neither in La Cabaña, the old fortress on the rock, nor in Combinado del Este, the big security prison where foreigners were usually taken. He was in the building called the Villa Marista, because it had once housed a school run by the Marist Brothers.

He heard the rattle of keys against the lock, and a guard with a broken nose came to hustle him back to the interrogation room.

"I don't think you are treating this seriously enough," the Cuban behind the light said to him. "You must know there are very strict penalties for crimes against state security in Cuba. Your friend Oliveira could face the firing squad. But you are very fortunate. We are prepared to let you go. As soon as you sign the confession."

Again the proffered sheet of paper, and the pen.

Hockney shook his head, and felt the ache in his neck grow worse.

"Have it your way," the interrogator said, as if suddenly bored with the whole business. "I'll repeat the offer one last time. Sign the confession, and you have my promise nothing will be done with it. Nothing will happen to you."

"I can imagine," Hockney commented.

"Very well. It seems a pity, though. This means you're finished. Your career in journalism is finished. Your marriage is finished. You're washed up."

"My marriage? What the hell are you talking about?"

"These will interest you." Calixto Valdés removed some glossy photographs from a large envelope and handed them to the reporter. They showed him cavorting with the dark-skinned girl from the Villa Yagruma in a variety of compromising poses—or rather, it showed the girl cavorting, since Hockney was usually underneath, his face partially obscured, looking less than energetic.

"Not very imaginative," Hockney said.

"You mean your technique?" For the first time, the Cuban grinned.

"No. I mean yours. You can't scare me with that kind of blackmail."

"Such a pity," Valdés repeated as he sealed the photographs inside the envelope. He showed Hockney the address on the outside. The envelope was addressed to Julia at their Washington apartment. "These will reach your wife before you do," Valdés explained. "I know how liberated you all try to be in the United States. This will be an interesting test of how far your permissiveness extends between man and wife."

The Cuban leaned back to examine Hockney's response.

"You shit," Hockney breathed.

He *knew* it was the oldest trick in the world, yet the thought of those pictures reaching Julia scared him more, in a way, than all the stuff about espionage charges. Julia was more vulnerable than before, now that she was bearing his child. They had got through a choppy passage, and this was something that could throw the marriage into a whirlpool. Yet he did not intend to let himself be intimidated by this crude setup.

Calixto Valdés sighed and got up from the desk.

"Well, the decision is yours," he said. "*Hasta luego,* Mr. Hockney."

Hockney sat there for a moment, waiting for the guard to take him back to his cell.

"Don't you understand what I'm saying?" Valdés demanded. "You're free to go back to Washington. And whatever is left of your life there. Your visit to Cuba is over."

Chapter

7

MIAMI

"There's that girl again," Martinez said to Sergeant Maguire as they cruised past Mama Lucy's in Overtown.

They watched an emaciated white girl in a loose cotton shift stumble out of a Lincoln parked in a vacant lot. She had huge black circles around her eyes, like a raccoon. She staggered a few paces, bent over and spat on the ground.

"Aw, shit," said Maguire. "It makes you want to throw up."

The girl caught sight of the patrol car and started scuttling away to the far side of the lot, like a thing made of matchsticks and wires.

"Are we gonna do the right thing? Are we gonna pick her up?" Martinez asked.

"Uh-uh," Maguire grunted, and put his foot down on the gas pedal. The girl was of an age when a lot of kids were still at home playing with dolls. She had run away from home, fallen in with a pimp who pumped her full of heroin and ended up in the roughest whorehouse in Overtown. Two days before, Maguire and Martinez had found her while checking out a report of a sexual battery. They had spent the best part of a night tracking down her family, poor but respectable people in Fort Lauderdale who had welcomed her back with tears and embraces. As soon as she was left alone, she had run away again.

There were days when it seemed to Maguire that what he was up against was a blind, formless monster composed of countless ravening mouths. Those whom it swallowed rarely came back. So he let the girl hobble away toward her next fix, wondering how many years she would survive on these streets.

It was the kind of day when Maguire asked that question about himself. He had had two fights with the higher-ups in the Department in the space of as many days. The first was over Julio Parodi. He had been given a direct order to get off the Cuban doper's tail. The way the order was expressed made Maguire certain that Parodi was being protected by powerful outside interests—no doubt the CIA. The order had come after Maguire had tried to shake down Felix Rey, the manager of Parodi's arms business. There seemed to be a lot of activity around the offices of Camagüey Internacional these days.

But the Captain had told Maguire, "You're way out of your league."

"I hear you" was all Maguire had said. He still had his own lead into Parodi's network—the hooker, Gloria—and he wasn't planning to share her with anybody else. He had learned from Gloria that the Cuban was back in town after a foreign trip and that Parodi was in a state of high agitation, working on something big. Maguire was counting on Gloria to find out what was going on.

Then there had been the row over Magic. The Intelligence Unit had asked for the black cop from Maguire's squad to help out with an undercover surveillance operation. Magic had been happy enough to go along with the idea.

"Hey, I could get my gold shield yet," he had announced cheerfully to the Sergeant.

But when Maguire found out the nature of the operation, he had protested. They wanted to use Magic to listen in on some of the meetings that the Black Fedayeen were holding around the city.

"You're crazy to let this go through," Maguire had complained to the chief of Patrol. "Magic is known all over the town. You'll be putting his ass on the line."

"Intelligence says he'll be okay," Maguire was told. "This isn't his usual scene. This is a political crowd. These aren't the pushers and the muggers."

Maguire had remained skeptical. But he conceded that the decision should be left up to the black cop himself.

"It sure beats chasing niggers into The Hole," Magic said.

So while Maguire cruised Overtown, thinking over who might hire him if he turned in his shield, the cop he called Magic was strolling into a dusty lot near the junction of Sixty-first Street and Second Avenue, on the fringes of Liberty City. Magic was wearing street clothes, his hair frizzed up as far as it would go, his .38 concealed in a leg holster just above his ankle. He had backup: a second black undercover cop, borrowed from Metro-Dade, was already standing near the back of the crowd.

The lot was behind a ramshackle shingled house which the Black Fedayeen were using as their headquarters. The house had become the base for a floating population of revolutionaries from Northern cities. Commander Ali, the Jamaican-born activist who led the Black Fedayeen, had encountered more difficulty in recruiting followers in Miami than in Washington, New York or Chicago. His rhetoric about the Islamic Nation and the Jihad was too exotic to most of his listeners in South Florida to make much of an impression. He struck a more responsive chord when he took up local issues, and one of the most sensitive was the competition for jobs and housing between the Miami black community and recent immigrants.

Now the word was spreading that a new influx of Cuban refugees was about to start arriving in South Florida. Some of the people who were gathering in the lot at Sixty-first and Second had seen Fidel Castro announce in a TV interview with Angela Seabury that the port of Mariel was going to be thrown open again to anyone who wanted to leave Cuba. Nobody knew how the Newgate Administration would respond. But few people believed that the President would risk the wrath of the Cuban community in the United States—and the charge that his public attacks on the Castro regime had been hypocritical—by sending the new refugees back. The man who called himself Commander Ali was smart enough to recognize that a new Cuban boatlift could be the fuse he needed to set the community alight.

Magic threaded his way into the midst of the crowd and surveyed the scene around the back porch of the house, which was being used as a platform. The Jamaican took his stand at the top of the steps, dressed in a white skullcap and flowing robes. Eight or nine armed men, wearing berets and paramilitary gear, lined up at the foot of the porch.

The Intelligence Unit had given Magic the bare bones of the Jamaican's biography. What Magic had not been told was that Commander Ali planned no major operation without consulting the Cubans.

"Allah-u-Akbar!" the Jamaican yelled at the crowd.

There was a ragged response from part of the audience.

"Today we face a new emergency," Commander Ali announced. "The fascists in the White House want to deal with our brothers in America the way they instructed their Zionist puppets to deal with our Palestinian brothers in Lebanon. President Newgate thinks he has found the solution for the black people of America. That solution is genocide. It starts as creeping, economic genocide. It will escalate to physical warfare. And when that day comes, we must be prepared. The only answer to what *they* have planned is to beat them to the draw."

"Right on, brother!" several people shouted. The gathering responded to the Jamaican with a forest of clenched fists. Some were clutching guns. Magic waved his arm and bellowed approval like the rest.

"It is no sin to kill the oppressor," the Jamaican went on. "It is no sin to kill the infidel. The Holy Koran teaches us that the infidels are criminals of the earth. It is no sin to attack an American, because no American is innocent as long as the United

States is bent on the destruction of the holy Nation of Islam throughout the world, and the genocide of our brothers in America. We know that victory is with our cause, because this is the revelation of God Almighty in the Holy Koran. But just because the final victory will be ours, that don't mean we can sit around on our asses waiting for everything to be dished out to us on a plate. The wrath of Allah will surely come upon us if we are not ready to take the sword into our own hands. I have been sent to lead you in this holy cause."

There were mingled shouts of "Right on!" and "A-men!"

"Now, the fascists are very cunning," the speaker resumed. "Here in Miami, they are using the Jews and the Cuban renegades to perpetuate the exploitation of our brothers in the black community. More of these renegades, these worms from Cuba, are coming to steal our jobs and our homes and sow division among us."

Magic experienced a slight burning sensation, and glanced over to his left. A man in blue denims was studying him. As their eyes met, Magic felt the shock of recognition. The big, muscular black to his left was a familiar figure in Overtown, a neighborhood enforcer who usually hung out around The Hole. Magic did not waste time trying to figure out what Blue was doing off his own turf, at a Black Fedayeen meeting. He started moving, crabwise, toward the back of the crowd, looking around for the second undercover cop.

"Hey!" Blue called after him, through the chorus of applause for the man on the porch. "Hey!"

Magic spotted the second cop, lounging by the broken-down picket fence that divided the yard from the neighboring lot.

"Hey!" Blue shouted, louder than before.

People turned to examine the object of his interest.

Magic started to run.

He heard his pursuer call out, "Stop the man! He ain't no brother! He's a pig spy!"

Commander Ali observed the commotion and interrupted his tirade.

"Now listen up, brothers," he boomed into his microphone.

"The enemy is among us. Arrest the spy and bring him to me."

The other undercover cop had already slipped over the fence. Strong hands clutched at Magic as he tried to follow suit. Someone tried to drag him back by his left leg. Magic saw the gleam of metal, and lashed out with the leg that was free. There was a crunch of bone as the toe of his boot connected with his pursuer's chin. He flung himself sidewise to avoid another attacker, and barreled into the fence. The rotting wood splintered and gave way under his weight. The black cop tumbled through the gap and sprinted after his partner through the next-door lot, around the side of the house and down the street toward the unmarked car they had left in the shade of a tree. A dozen men came running after them, and a shot rang out.

Magic fumbled for the revolver in his ankle holster.

"Shit," he swore softly as he wrenched open the door of the unmarked car—a ten-year-old Chevy with no hubcaps and one fender missing. The .38 was gone.

Magic threw himself into the driver's seat and tried to start the engine. It rattled into life, then stalled.

He ducked his head just in time, as bullets ripped across the back window.

"Jesus," his partner said. "You better get this thing started."

The burst of fire had come from an automatic rifle.

The crowd was nearly upon them by the time Magic got the car into first gear. Several youths ran along beside the Chevy as it pulled out from the curb, beating against the doors and the hood.

As they gathered speed, Magic's partner leaned out his window, firing carefully aimed shots over the heads of the men in the street.

Magic heard someone ordering their pursuers to stop shooting. He glanced in the rearview mirror and saw the Jamaican standing in the middle of the road, one hand on his hip, the other clutching a gun that looked suspiciously like his missing .38.

On the far side of Third Avenue, Mary Charlene Brown, the unmarried mother of five small children, was waiting to cross the street. Her nine-year-old daughter, Elsie, was helping to carry the bread and cereal she had bought for the family with the remains of her welfare check. Mary Brown paused to watch the mob chasing the old maroon Chevy as it swung right. Then she took Elsie's hand and started to cross Third Avenue.

"Asshole," Magic muttered. The road ahead of him was blocked by a Coca-Cola truck, whose driver was backing and filling as he tried to make a U-turn. Magic slammed the gear-shift into reverse and zigzagged back, trying to dodge the men who were clustered around the Jamaican at the intersection of Sixty-first and Third. Swerving violently to the left, he missed one of his pursuers by inches.

Infuriated, the man started shooting at the Chevy.

"Elsie!" Mary Brown screamed.

In his rearview mirror, Magic saw the child running forward, across the path of the lurching, rapidly reversing car. He wrestled the wheel back to the right, narrowly missing the girl.

Several of the Black Fedayeen kept firing at the car as it backed away along Sixty-first Street. Magic's partner fired off two more warning rounds.

Thinking only of her child's safety, Mary Brown, still clutch-ing her groceries, ran out into the street, across the line of fire.

Magic saw Elsie, her hair tied up in braids, rushing back to-ward her mother. He saw the child fling her arms around Mary Brown's knees. And he saw the mother's body arc backward, like a leaf blown by the wind, as the bullet entered the side of her head.

Magic stopped the car, looking at the woman's body crum-pled up in the roadway, the spilled groceries, the child's des-perate, uncomprehending face. And the Jamaican, who was staring calmly at *him* as he lowered his revolver to his side.

Magic glanced at his partner.

"It wasn't *me*," the cop said, as if he felt a silent accusation. He held up his gun as if he wanted to throw it out the window. "I swear it wasn't me."

Magic nodded. "I believe you," he said.

But they could already hear the angry roar from the crowd,

which had grown until it filled the whole width of the street.

"Murderers!" the Jamaican's voice rose above the rest. "Cop murderers!"

Magic sat there with the engine idling. The roar grew louder still.

"If we stay here, we're dead," his partner said with unanswerable simplicity.

"I believe you."

With reflex, automatic motions, Magic gunned the engine and drove straight toward the crowd, which fell back as he approached. For an instant, Commander Ali's followers seemed strangely passive. Then they started running after the police car. As they passed the grocery store where Mary Brown had done her shopping, someone threw a brick through the window.

At the corner of Sixty-first and Third, a small girl with braids stood over her mother's body, sobbing and begging her to wake up. Nobody paid them any heed.

WASHINGTON, D.C.

Sunlight filtered through the shutters of the kitchen windows and gave the room a mellow, lion-colored warmth. Julia was sitting, very calmly, at the breakfast table with the big buff envelope in front of her. Hockney prowled the room, back and forth, back and forth, as if it were a prison cell. He would pick things off the counter at random, turn them around in his hands and put them down again, then pause to refill his glass from the uncapped liter of bardolino next to the coffeepot.

"Come and sit next to me," Julia said gently.

"I can't sit still," Hockney said. "I feel so *trapped*."

They had gone over it all the night before. He had called her from Mexico City to explain what had happened, and to warn her about the photographs the Cubans had threatened to send. By the time the taxi from Dulles Airport dropped him off at their Dupont Circle apartment, just after 8 P.M., the envelope

195

had already arrived, hand-delivered by a commercial messenger service.

Julia had obviously looked at the pictures from Cuba. The envelope had been opened, and she had left it in plain view, there on the table. He had felt a slight reserve in her welcoming embrace, but she had asked no questions and made no recriminations, waiting quietly for him to tell his own story. When he had finished, she had said merely, "She's sexy. But not quite your type." They had not made love that evening. But it wasn't that Julia was holding back. It was because he was too agitated, too preoccupied with going over and over what had happened, trying to make some sense of it. And his own stupidity.

The paper had been less understanding than Julia.

He had called Len Rourke in New York an hour after he got home.

"I know all about it, Bob," the Executive Editor had interrupted him before he finished his first couple of sentences. "The Cubans have already put out a statement. It's what you'd expect. They claim you're involved with the CIA."

"Are you going to report it?"

"We have to say *something*, Bob. Everybody else is going to pick it up. It'll just be a paragraph or two. Naturally, we'll deny everything."

"I hope I'll get a chance to present my own version."

"We'll talk that over tomorrow. Ed Finkel's in Washington. You can meet him at the bureau and we'll set up a conference call."

Then the phone in the apartment had started ringing. It seemed as if every newspaper and TV network in the country wanted to do a story on Hockney's experiences in Cuba. He had fielded the calls cautiously, issuing blanket denials, waiting to see what would happen at the office in the morning. He had finally taken the phone off the hook at I A.M., after someone called from L.A. and tried to put him on a live radio show.

What awaited him at the *World* bureau was about as bad as he could expect.

"Nobody's accusing you of anything," Ed Finkel said. "But

this kind of stuff"—he waved his hand over the pile of morning papers, most of which had run items on the Cuban allegations—"is embarrassing for all of us. This is what comes of trespassing."

"Trespassing?"

"Going outside your job. You're supposed to be a newsman. But here you go fucking around inside some secret location in Cuba, dealing with some Intelligence type."

"I was chasing a story. If I'd been caught doing the same thing inside a CIA facility, you'd give me a prize."

"I'm not going to argue about this, Bob. You're accident-prone. We all know that this kind of high profile isn't doing the paper any good. Now, Len and I have talked this over, and we think the time has come for you to do what you discussed with him when you were up in New York. Jack Lancer will take over the Washington bureau, and you'll have a roving brief."

"Subject to whom?"

"Subject to me—That's what we agreed, isn't it, Len?" Finkel interrogated the squawk box. Len Rourke was listening in at the other end of the line, in New York.

"That's it," the Executive Editor confirmed.

"Well," Hockney said. "There doesn't seem to be anything left to discuss. I'll start cleaning out my desk."

"They did most of the packing for you already," Finkel told him with evident pleasure.

"You didn't waste a minute, did you, Ed?"

Hockney and Julia agreed afterward that what had happened was for the best. What Hockney bridled at was the way Finkel had broken it to him, stopping just one step short of bouncing him out on his neck. But as Julia had pointed out, nothing was going to be accomplished by his stewing over it.

He had learned two things in Cuba: that Parodi was an occasional guest at a villa outside Havana, and that the Cubans were sufficiently worried about his own investigations to set out to frame him in order to ruin his credibility and smash up his personal and professional life.

"You remember who got me into this?" Hockney remarked

to Julia. "That police sergeant in Miami. Jay Maguire."

The mention of the name jogged Julia's memory. "He called while you were away," she said. "He seemed excited about something."

"I'm going back down to Miami," Hockney announced. It had been the cop who had produced the address of the villa in Cuba. Maguire would now have to be persuaded to share his source. That was the best way Hockney could see to get off the mud slide he found himself on.

"I want to come too," Julia said, and his gratitude showed in his eyes. He had started to feel pretty lonely since he had gone to his office and found his files in packing cartons.

He picked up the envelope containing the photographs. "What about those?"

"Not a patch on the real thing," she said, smiling for the first time. "I'm going to burn them."

MIAMI

The decision taken, Hockney and Julia threw a few things into a suitcase and made the next flight to Miami. It was a Thursday, and it was easy enough for Julia to call the Committee to announce she was taking a long weekend.

Since Senator Fairchild's death, the Internal Security Committee had been dormant anyway. The new Chairman had conducted only one hearing, on the relationship between urban violence and social deprivation. Most of the witnesses were liberal academicians more familiar with statistical yearbooks than with the streets. The one witness who had impressed her was a black minister, the Reverend Wright Washington, who had risen to national prominence as one of the leaders of the NAACP. He had some sharp things to say about the effects of the Newgate Administration's economic program, but he did not reduce crime or rioting to an abstraction.

She thought of the tall, stooped black minister with his gravelly voice and his mass of white hair when they boarded a cab at Miami Airport and the driver greeted them by saying, "You sure picked the right day to come down. Looks like we got another riot brewing."

When they got to their hotel room, Julia turned on the TV while Hockney tried to call Jay Maguire. To Hockney's surprise, he got through to the Sergeant at the Police Department number straightaway.

"You should have told me you were coming," Maguire reproached him.

"I left a message on your answering machine."

"Yeah. Well, I had plenty else to think about. The shit's really hitting the fan down here."

"Can we get together?"

"Tonight? No way." But the cop paused and said, "They really roughed you up in Cuba, huh?"

"It wasn't my idea of a vacation."

"Did that address I gave you check out?"

"Yes. But I need more help. I need it badly, Jay."

"You and me, brother. Listen, I gotta run. You be at the Marina about ten. If I can make it, I'll see you there."

As soon as Hockney had hung up, Julia called him over to the TV set. They watched a jerky newsreel of a squad of Black Fedayeen marching through Liberty City shouting slogans. The camera switched to a crowd of youths who had rigged up a chain to the back of their car. They hitched the other end of the chain to the metal gate that guarded the window of a liquor store, then drove the car forward, ripping out the gate behind them. In plain view of the TV camera, the youths proceeded to smash the store window, and several of them started running in and out, ferrying armfuls of bottles. Then somebody rushed at the cameraman, and the videotape was cut off.

"While full-scale looting is evidently beginning in and around Liberty City," the commentator's voice came over an aerial view of the ghetto, apparently filmed from a helicopter, "the police have been ordered to hold back. A spokesman for the

Mayor's office says there is concern not to further inflame the situation that arose from the shooting of a black woman in Liberty City earlier today. A black patrolman has been suspended from duty pending investigation of the shooting. David Priest, the Black Fedayeen leader who calls himself Commander Ali, is also wanted for questioning in connection with the shooting, but his present whereabouts are unknown."

"I can see why Maguire sounded pissed off," Hockney commented when they had turned off the program. "It looks like the looters are having a Roman holiday in there."

Julia refused to be left to her own devices in the hotel room, so the two of them were sitting together in the dockside restaurant when Maguire showed up, more than half an hour late. The cop was polite to Julia, but was obviously burning on a short fuse. He told the waitress to bring him neat bourbon in a coffee cup.

"The black cop they suspended was in my detail," Maguire explained. "Andy Riggs. We call him Magic. He's one of the best cops in Patrol."

"Tell us what happened," Julia prodded him.

Maguire described the course of events in Liberty City up to the death of Mary Brown.

"The Ballistics people say she was killed with a thirty-eight. They checked the records, and they say the bullet that killed her could have come from Magic's gun. The trouble is, Magic claims he never had his gun when the shooting started. He says he lost it getting out of that yard. He figures one of those Moslem crazies could have used the gun to kill that black woman. He talks a lot about Commander Ali. Says *he* could have done it."

"Did they find the gun?" Hockney asked.

"Nope. And there are twenty fucking witnesses down there who are ready to swear blind that they saw Magic gun this lady down. Uh, pardon my French," he interjected for Julia's benefit.

"It's okay. Bob's been known to use it too."

"All right," the cop resumed. "We oughta be able to prove

something from the angle of the shot, right? But by the time the crime-scene investigators got down there, Commander Ali's goons were stirring up a full-scale riot, and the body had been moved around so nobody could tell how it fell or where the bullet might have come from. The Black Fedayeen are screaming that the police are trying to stage a cover-up, and there are plenty of people in Liberty City who are going to believe them."

"What do *you* believe, Jay?"

"I believe they set Magic up. Just the way you were set up in Havana. Maybe this woman—this Mary Brown—was killed on purpose, to create a martyr or something. The Jamaican has been down here, on and off, for a couple of weeks now, and he hasn't exactly set the town on fire. Maybe that's what he's aiming to do. Literally. These Black Fedayeen are crazies. I wouldn't put anything past them. But we'll never get your media comrades to believe that. I can see the headlines now. More Police Brutality. Shit."

Maguire drained the remains of his illicit bourbon in a single gulp.

"Maybe I can do something," Hockney suggested. "I could go look for the Jamaican and see what I can find out. I could use my press card."

"You don't know shit from Shanghai," Maguire said. "You couldn't get into Liberty City tonight with a papal dispensation underwritten by *Good Housekeeping*. There's a riot going on. Even *we* aren't allowed into Liberty City tonight. Down here, our blacks don't like white boys around when they get together an' have them a riot"—his voice shifted into a parody of a redneck from upstate—"not even if you was the National Lawyers Guild and the ACLU an' Mr. Hot Dog TV Celebrity all rolled in one."

"I'd still like to see it," Hockney said quietly.

"You want to see it? Okay. You can see it."

Maguire sprang up from the table so fast that Hockney and Julia were taken by surprise and had to run to catch up to him as he hurried along the deserted waterfront toward his patrol car.

"I'm sorry," the cop said to Julia when she reached the cruiser. "This isn't a sight for ladies."

Julia began to protest, but the Sergeant was firm. "Either you go home," he insisted, "or nobody goes."

They found a taxi and bundled her off to the hotel.

Fifteen minutes later, the two men were prowling the outskirts of Liberty City. Hockney saw open fire hydrants spilling water. A crowd of black youths was piling up old tires across a street in a makeshift barricade. As he watched, they doused the tires with kerosene and set them alight. Soon an acrid column of black smoke was rising above the housetops.

"See that?" said Maguire. "At the start of the '80 riots, they set fire to a tire factory. Some of these people are using their brains. They know that rubber makes a terrific stink. But they're just warming up."

Farther on, Maguire slowed his patrol car as they neared a supermarket. Some vandals were tossing bricks through the windows. When they saw the police cruiser, they hesitated, ready to run. Maguire stopped the car, but made no move to get out. After a couple of minutes, one of the youths shouldered his way through the broken glass and dashed into the store, snatching goods at random from the shelves. He came running out again, clasping his loot with both hands.

"Aren't you going to do something?" Hockney asked the Sergeant.

"I told you. We've been told to keep away. It's not my decision," Maguire added. "Listen to this."

The Sergeant called his dispatcher to report a robbery in progress. As soon as he gave the location, the answer came back: "Pull out."

"See? At this rate, we could lose the whole fucking city by sunup."

Both men watched in fascination as the crowd of youths around the supermarket, now confident of their ground, loaded up shopping carts with stolen goods and wheeled them away down the sidewalk. An older couple joined in.

Maguire nosed the cruiser toward them as they headed home with their loot. The man glanced nervously at the patrol car.

"Is it okay?" he asked the Sergeant.

Maguire shrugged. "Hope you choke on it," he said as he put his foot down on the gas pedal.

A few blocks later, they saw a gang of young blacks pouring oil onto the street to make it slippery, so that police cars would skid. A nearby warehouse was ablaze.

"Look at that one!" Hockney pointed at a man with a Molotov cocktail in his fist who was running toward a factory building.

Maguire accelerated and drove straight toward the arsonist. "The Chief didn't say we had to sit back and watch the city burn," he muttered between his teeth.

The arsonist turned and threw his firebomb at the police car. It missed by a foot and exploded in a sheet of flame on the left side of the car.

"Stay put," Maguire growled at Hockney as he leaped from the cruiser and raced after the boy. He was stopped by the crack of sniper fire from somewhere among the rooftops.

Maguire darted back to the car and radioed a description of what was happening to Headquarters.

"Three-fifty," the dispatcher's voice came back, "your order is to pull out."

Maguire banged his fist in frustration on top of the wheel.

"You see what's going on now?" he said to Hockney.

"It's getting to remind me of Cholon during the Tet Offensive."

"You ain't seen nothing yet. Unless the Chief lets us off the leash, it could be worse than last time around. You still think you can walk into the Jamaican's hangout tonight?"

"I guess not," Hockney conceded. "Maybe tomorrow."

"If there's anything left of Liberty City by then."

The sky above the housetops had turned a hellish pink from the fires that had already been set.

They stopped for a drink on the way back to the hotel. The restaurant Maguire picked was hard to miss. El Cid rose out of a wilderness of gas stations and auto dealerships, a floodlit gingerbread castle, complete with mock battlements, moat and drawbridge.

"Disneyland on the outside, Old Havana on the inside," Maguire remarked as they crossed the drawbridge.

The decor inside—Spanish coats of arms, tall straight-backed chairs, wrought-iron chandeliers—and the proximity of the restaurant to Calle Ocho made Hockney think of Maguire's partner, the Cuban cop.

"What happened to Martinez?" he asked.

"He's double-teaming it with a rookie," Maguire replied. "We're way under strength. Before this thing runs its course, we're going to need every body we can get. And if the Chief waits too long before he lets us make a move, we'll be getting some help we can do without."

"What does that mean?"

"Some of your pals from the Brigada Azul were out blowing off steam this afternoon. They were saying that if the riots spread, they're going to take care of their own community. That's all we need. A shooting war between blacks and Hispanics."

"You think that could happen?"

"Sure it could happen. All it takes is a few bullets. Then you'd get something a damn sight more colorful than the Hatfields and the McCoys."

They ordered drinks, and Hockney considered a moment before asking, "What's happened to Parodi?"

"You took your fucking time getting round to that. Now you shoot first. What did you find out in Cuba?"

Hockney described what had happened at the Villa Ya-gruma.

When he had finished, Maguire ordered an Irish coffee and said, "So I didn't give you a bum steer."

Hockney leaned across the table. "We both know Parodi has

to be very big if both the Cubans *and* the CIA are protecting him. There has to be a major intelligence operation involved. This obviously goes far beyond drugs. Now, I can get to Blair Collins—"

Maguire snorted at the mention of the CIA Director.

"No, this is serious, Jay," Hockney went on impatiently. "I can get Collins to level with me, as long as I know what the hell I'm talking about."

"What are you saying?"

"I'm saying I need to talk to your source, your CI."

Maguire slurped his Irish coffee in silence for a while, and it struck Hockney that every cop he had ever gotten to know had shared this same proclivity for coffee well laced with booze and with heaped cream on top. Maybe because it was more discreet to drink liquor out of a china cup.

Maguire said, "I'll ask her. It'll have to be up to her." He was remembering what Gloria had let drop at their last rendezvous. She had mentioned Parodi's foreign trip, and also that the Cuban was planning another journey soon. And that she had been summoned for a party Parodi was throwing out at Key Biscayne that same night. Maybe Gloria would know a lot more by tomorrow.

"Now, listen," Maguire went on. "We've got to think about how to do this. *If* she agrees. With all this shit going down, I may be on duty all day and all night, like in '80. This CI is a working girl. That means the best time for her is late afternoon, early evening. So she can get back on the job at the big hotels and catch the johns after dinner before they all go upstairs to watch Johnny Carson or fantasize over *Penthouse.*"

"Seven o'clock?" Hockney suggested. "Eight o'clock?"

"Split the difference. Seven-thirty. We'll use your hotel room."

"Are you sure they'll let her in?" Hockney asked doubtfully, wondering to what extent this "working girl" looked the part.

"Sure they'll let her in," Maguire said. "She's got class. You trust your wife, right?"

"Right."

"Okay. You tell anybody else about this, though, and I'll cut your tongue out."

The Chief of Police called the Mayor at about breakfast time to resume the heated discussion they had broken off at 2 A.M. From his office at Police Headquarters, Chief Murchison could contemplate the sooty, reddish pall that had spread from the area north of Manor Park to cover most of the city. The weatherman had predicted uninterrupted sunshine, a perfect day for the beach.

"We'll wait until morning," the Mayor had said. "Maybe the riots will have burned themselves out by then."

Chief Murchison remembered the phrase as he sipped thin, sediment-laden coffee from his mug. From his window, it looked as if the city, not the riot, were being burned out.

He said as much to the Mayor.

"I don't think we ought to panic," the Mayor responded. "The trouble hasn't spread outside the black neighborhoods."

"That's because we set up roadblocks," Chief Murchison pointed out. The Mayor had finally agreed to his plan to throw a cordon around Liberty City and Overtown. In the course of the night, police roadblocks had been set up to block traffic moving east and west across Northwest Seventh Avenue at Fifty-fourth, Sixty-second and Seventy-first, and to stop north–south traffic between those streets at Seventh, Twelfth and Seventeenth Avenues. This had placed Liberty City in a state of partial quarantine. A similar cordon had been thrown around Overtown. The police had stopped at least one group of rioters from moving out into the business center. As a result, the looting and arson reported so far had affected only ghetto property, especially stores selling food and liquor and furniture and electrical appliances, and the few factories and warehouses that had survived the 1980 troubles. But both the Mayor and the Police Chief knew it was impossible to stop all movement into and out of the black ghettos, and that establishing no-go areas along ethnic lines was political dynamite. It also meant, as Chief

206

Murchison argued again, that the police had given up the streets, creating a vacuum of authority that the Black Fedayeen and neighborhood gangs had not been slow to fill.

"We're not in an emergency situation yet," the Mayor said. "There have been no reported fatalities. Except that black woman that *your* people are blamed for killing."

"There'll be killings, all right," Chief Murchison responded grimly. "What we need to do is go in there and arrest this Commander Asshole and the other ringleaders and take back possession of the streets. I won't be held responsible for what could happen by the end of the day if we fail to do that."

"We're in touch with community leaders," the Mayor said wearily. "They're trying to dampen things down. They're every bit as worried about this as we are. I talked to Wright Washington at the N-double-A-CP. He carries a lot of influence with some of these people. He says he's going to fly down today and try to help cool things down. We've got to recognize there is a real mood of public concern," the Mayor said. "It would help if we could announce that we're going to press charges against that undercover cop who shot Mary Brown."

"Police Officer Riggs is not going to be any kind of scapegoat for anybody looking to save their political ass," the Police Chief erupted. "Morale in this Department is bad enough anyway. If you want the guy who shot that woman, then you let me send our special units into Liberty City and pick up that big-assed Jamaican who started all this."

"We'll wait," the Mayor said.

Chief Murchison hung up. Through his window he could now see a column of dense black smoke rising above Liberty City. He picked up the phone again and called the Governor.

"I guess you better get set to lend us the National Guard," the Chief told him.

It was a bewildering, frightening day for people all over South Florida.

In broad daylight, not long after opening time, a couple of black youths wandered into a liquor store a few blocks off Calle

Ocho. The store was owned by a Cuban-American, Carlos Tamayo, who had come to Miami in 1959. He had just sold a quart of rum to one of his regulars when the newcomers sauntered in. Tamayo could tell they had been drinking or—more likely—were high on drugs. The bigger of the two blacks swayed as he made his way between the racks, clicking his fingers. Tamayo's customer hastily took his leave and headed for the door. The storekeeper reached for the gun he kept handy in a drawer behind the counter, under the cash register. The second black, he noted, had stayed close to the door, pretending to inspect some bottles of chenin blanc. If these two tried to pull anything, Tamayo thought, he could take them. They were obviously inexperienced. Practiced robbers would come near the end of the day, when there would be a lot more cash in the till and the chance of a getaway would be vastly improved.

"Yeah?" Tamayo said to the bigger of the two men.

"Just gimme the money, man." The man grinned as he displayed his Saturday Night Special. "An' maybe a coupla bottles of Scotch for me and my friend."

At that, Tamayo brought up his revolver, but the robber moved faster than he would have believed possible, and shot him in the throat before he could squeeze off a single round. Blood spurted like a geyser from his neck, and Tamayo collapsed across the counter with a sound like water rushing down a drain.

The regular, clutching his rum in its paper sack, took one horrified look over his shoulder and fled from the store.

He heard whoops and padding feet behind him as he ran.

The robbers caught up with him before he reached the corner.

"I didn't see nothing!" he protested as they beat him to the pavement. His bottle went crashing into the gutter.

There was a *Miami Bugle* vending machine on the corner. The big man picked it up as if it were a paperweight, laughing uncontrollably at some private joke, and rammed the concrete base of the machine down on his victim's face.

The most remarkable thing about the incident, people agreed

later, was that the two men got clean away. Given the number of guns in private hands in Little Havana, it would have been less surprising if they had been mown down in a hail of bullets. Under different circumstances, the killing of Carlos Tamayo and his customer, a father of five named Hernán Madero, might have been just one more gruesome entry in the city's chronicles of crime. But against the backdrop of what had been going on in Liberty City the night before, the bloody liquor-store holdup helped to spread panic and the spirit of vendetta.

It was reported on the midday TV news, and not long after that the Brigada Azul held a meeting in its bungalow head-quarters. Julio Parodi was absent from this meeting, but it was understood by those present that the proposals put forward by the Brigade's *jefe militar*, Andres Fortin, had his blessing.

"*Los animales* are killing our people," Fortin announced to the men in the room. "The police have abdicated control of the city. It is up to us to defend ourselves, gun against gun." There was little discussion after he finished his speech. The men drew lots to decide which of their number would take part in a re-prisal raid into Liberty City.

A few hours later, just west of Miami Airport, a blue Toyota van was speeding along Highway 41, parallel to the Tamiami Canal, one of the city's principal sources of water. For ninety miles more, the road and the canal ran side by side across the flat horizon of the Everglades, the shifting swamplands the Miccosukee Indians called the River of Grass. Every other mile along Route 41, there was a blue sign with white lettering that read, "SOUTH FLORIDA WATER MANAGEMENT DISTRICT."

Through gaps in the scrub, the man in the passenger seat of the van—a man with straw-colored hair and very pale green eyes—could see alligators lazing beside the muddy waters of the canal. The air was heavy with the stench of rotting man-groves, but Beacher kept his window rolled all the way down for the breeze.

"It's coming up now," he muttered to his companion.

From a distance, their objective looked like a huge concrete-framed guillotine. The "blade" was a sluice gate that rose and fell to control the flow of water dammed upstream. The levee, and a section of the canal and its green-brown embankments, were enclosed by a tall fence topped with a triple strand of barbed wire. On the far side of the canal was a small concrete blockhouse, protected by another security fence and a sign that read "DANGER. NO TRESPASSING. VIOLATORS WILL BE PROSE-CUTED UNDER STATUTE NO. 82104."

The barbed wire was more likely to deter campers than sabo-teurs. Next to the sluice gate, a bridge wide enough for cars had been built over the canal, to allow picnickers and fishermen to reach a recreation area on the far side. It made a homey scene: a scattering of stone benches and tables, the charred remains of a barbecue, a shelter propped up on rectangular poles.

"Go over the bridge," Beacher instructed the man behind the wheel. The van made the crossing and circled the picnic area. Beacher noted a lone trailer parked under the trees. An elderly couple in straw hats were sitting beside the canal on folding chairs forty yards downstream, angling for catfish.

"It's okay," Beacher announced. They headed back across the bridge and parked the van beside the canal, out of sight of the anglers. East and west of them, Route 41 was a straight, narrowing ribbon, deserted of cars for as far as Beacher could see.

Without haste, he opened the back of the van, pushed aside an old mattress and removed a bazooka and four armor-piercing shells. Then he knelt down, squinted into the sight and fired the first round at the sluice gate. The noise of the explo-sion knocked the elderly couple on the other side of the canal out of their chairs. Beacher fired his second shell at the side of the massive concrete structure that framed the sluice gate. Re-loading with smooth, methodical motions, he squeezed off his third round and saw the whole structure begin to collapse. He used his last shot on the bridge, and blew a gaping hole. The bridge began to crumble into the canal.

Before Beacher had finished concealing his weapon in the back of the van, the pressure of banked-up water above the gate brought the whole thing tumbling down. The canal burst its banks, drenched the terrified anglers and sent them splashing and floundering back to their trailer, already up to its hubcaps in water.

Beacher jumped into the van, and the driver headed west, deeper into the Everglades. Beacher was annoyed about the fishermen. They had seen nobody when they hit a levee on the Miami Canal—the vital feeder between the city and Lake Okeechobee—in Broward County earlier in the afternoon. The elderly couple could probably give the police a description of the van, if not of the two men in it. Blowing the bridge would probably allow the terrorists all the time they needed for a get-away. But if an alert went out, it would be very easy for the cops to trap them by blocking both ends of Route 41. It was the only road through the Everglades within reach.

Beacher had prepared for this contingency.

"We'll hit the Safari Club," he instructed the driver. One of the useful facts he had discovered in planning this operation was that a tourist center with a reptile house and a marina for the airboats that were used to take visitors for a spin across the Everglades was an easy drive away from the levee. The Safari Club closed down before sunset. The only man who might still be on the premises was the pilot of a small Cessna seaplane that was hired out by day to sight-seers.

When the blue van pulled up outside the office at the Safari Club, the pilot, a choleric, red-bearded Scot who flaunted four stripes on his epaulettes, was stretched out on his cot watching the TV news about the hell that seemed to be breaking loose in Miami. The police had been sent into Liberty City to pull out some bodies and make some arrests after a couple of white kids—defying the official warnings—had gone in to look for the pusher who usually sold them their dope. They had been set on by an angry mob, and some madman had hacked them to death with a butcher's cleaver. The TV reporter was asking one of the cops what it was like "in there."

"What's it like?" the patrolman echoed the interviewer. "Take a look at me. I got blood all over. On my clothes. On my face." The camera panned to show the smears of red. "I got blood in my hair. I even got blood under my fingernails. That's what it's like. It's like a slaughterhouse."

The Safari Club pilot swore copiously under his breath as he watched the scene unfold. The keys to the six airboats in the marina were hanging, as usual, from a rack on the wall of the office next door. Absorbed in the images of arson and pillage that flickered across his TV screen, the pilot did not hear the van pull up, or the faint scuffle from along the corridor as the intruders crept into the office, removed one set of keys and carefully latched the door behind them.

But he jumped off the bed when he heard the roar of an airboat engine. The skimmers were powered by old 472 Cadillac motors, with no cowling and a paddle-sized wooden propeller at the back. The noise from those things sounded more like a Tiger Moth than anything aquatic.

The pilot got to the landing in time to see two men skimming away into the Everglades on one of the flat-bottomed boats. It had three rows of seats, sheathed in plastic that was supposed to look like leopard skin. A tall man with fair hair sat up on a raised seat at the back of the airboat, working the twin rudders with a joystick.

"Come back, you shitheads!" the pilot yelled uselessly after the airboat. His words were swallowed up in the din of the engine.

"A riot is a way of getting attention," Wright Washington had told the Mayor after he flew in that morning. "And the people of Liberty City could sure use some attention."

Wright Washington had made no secret of his anger. He was angry with the politicians who refused to understand that if you turn your back on a community, then the people of that community are going to feel compelled to do something to remind you of their needs. He was angry because once again that reminder had come in the form of destruction. He was angry with outsiders like Commander Ali, who fed on violence, stoked it and stirred it, calling for more. He was angry because this was one of the times when he felt impotent to accomplish what needed to be done.

The black leader had grown up under the spell of Martin Luther King, and King's commitment to nonviolence remained for him a living cause. He opposed violence as a manifestation of the evil in man. As a Christian, Wright Washington believed that there was evil in men, not merely in social and political institutions. This simple belief was not shared by radicals or the fashionable liberation theologians, and some of them distrusted Wright Washington as a potential Uncle Tom, even a closet reactionary, because he insisted that individuals must be held accountable for their actions, that each man had to come to terms with the potential for evil that he contained. In his darker moments, when he contemplated the power of evil that he saw unleashed in men, Washington came close to subscribing to the Gnostic heresy that the world is ruled not by a just and knowing God, but by the demiurge—a lesser, morally ambiguous deity. In that somber vision, the duty of the believer is not to succumb to the ruler of this world, but to go on striving toward a more distant God, the true God, whose face and purposes remain concealed.

It was faith that allowed Washington to walk through the police lines, past a gutted gas station, its pumps grotesquely twisted and mutilated by ax blows, toward the house that Commander Ali had made his fortress.

Hockney stood with Jay Maguire at the roadblock, watching the erect, heavyset figure of the black minister retreating into the distance.

"I'll say this," Maguire remarked. "He's got balls."

Hockney's gaze did not shift from Wright Washington. The minister looked neither right nor left as he passed a gang of youths engaged in stripping a car and a larger group that was holding a street party around a couple of cases of stolen liquor.

He had gone with Julia to the press conference that Washington held after his meeting with the Mayor. The minister had appealed for calm, promising that whoever was responsible for the death of Mary Brown in Liberty City the day before was going to be punished. He had implored the Black Fedayeen to put down their guns, and had announced that he would seek a face-to-face dialogue with Commander Ali. Hockney had been impressed by Washington's natural authority. He was still more impressed by the courage the man was displaying now, as he walked alone through the smoldering streets.

In the course of the afternoon, Hockney had watched the situation turn from bad to potentially disastrous. The news of the killings had spread—the killings of the Cubans at a liquor store in Little Havana, and of a couple of white middle-class junkies who had picked the wrong moment to go looking for their supplier. There were rumors of self-appointed vigilantes, and of strange, possibly unconnected incidents outside the city. There was a story going the rounds that somebody was trying to cut off the water supply. Everyone knew it had been a dry season in South Florida, and the water level in Lake Okeechobee, the main catchment area, was supposed to have dropped nine feet over two months. Now someone in the Mayor's office had let it drop that there had been a series of bombings, or rocket attacks, on the most important canals and pipelines. Sluice gates had been blown up in Dade, Broward and Palm Beach counties. Maguire had added another detail. He had heard from a highway patrolman that someone had dynamited the main pipeline that supplied the Florida Keys. It was not yet clear to Hockney what, if anything, all of this had to do with the riots, but the sabotage attacks had fed the mood of panic that you could sense growing around the city.

"Dry tinder," Hockney said aloud.

"What?" Maguire turned to him.

"Dry tinder," the reporter repeated. "It's all set to burn."

"A lot of it's burning already," Maguire commented, pointing at the sheet of flame that had unfurled from an old warehouse section over to the right.

"Is he safe in there?" Hockney asked, still watching Washington as he marched forward, at the same steady pace, toward a shopfront with a sign that said "POOL" and a cluster of young blacks with berets and guns outside.

"No safer than you or me," Maguire replied. "Maybe less so.

The Jamaican's got more reason to be scared of Wright Washington than of the cops. If I was Mr. Ali, I'd stick a bullet in that preacher's guts."

This observation chilled Hockney. And he was not inclined to dispute it, especially because they both knew that Washington had already tried once that day to hold a meeting with the leader of the Black Fedayeen. Commander Ali had failed to show up. When Washington arrived at the address he had been given, he had found firemen trying to combat an inferno in a derelict apartment house. Someone had thoughtfully sawed through the joists on the fourth floor, so that one of the firemen, unsuspecting, fell through and was lucky to avoid breaking his neck.

Hockney had packed Julia off to the hotel again, and this time she had not gone without a fight. Fortunately, he had had a winning argument, to do with something other than her safety. They were supposed to meet Maguire's undercover informer at seven-thirty. Given the situation in the streets, it was impossible to guarantee what time they would get back from the perimeter of Liberty City, where Hockney was now standing with Maguire. It was vital that one of them be waiting at the hotel when the girl arrived. After all, this was the main object of their visit to Miami; the riots were an unexpected, and unwelcome, bonus. And—who knew?—maybe, as a woman, Julia would establish a rapport with Maguire's hooker faster than Hockney. This was a practical argument that led somewhere, and Julia finally bought it.

Hockney looked at his watch. It was almost seven. It would take all of half an hour to get back to the hotel through the chaos in the streets.

He turned to Maguire and said, "Are you sure Gloria's going to show up?" He was torn between not wanting to be late for the meeting and the desire to see how Wright Washington would fare in Liberty City.

"She'll show," Maguire replied. "She never let me down yet. Whether she'll talk is another matter. That's up to you."

The policeman recalled the phone conversation he had had with Gloria that morning. It sounded as if the orgy at Parodi's place the night before had been wilder than usual. Gloria said she had got the feeling it was a farewell party. Cautious, as usual, on the telephone, she had mentioned only one thing specific. Maguire repeated it to Hockney.

"Monimbo," Maguire said, putting the stress on the penultimate syllable, instead of the final one, where it belonged.

"What?"

"Monimbo," the cop repeated. "Mean anything to you?"

"Don't think so. It sounds African. Maybe somewhere in Africa?"

"Beats me," Maguire said.

Julia was in the hotel room, listening to the announcer explain the regulations on water rationing that were supposed to take effect immediately, when the lights went out. She stumbled over to the window and looked out along Biscayne Boulevard. For as far as she could see, in the direction of the business center, the apartment houses and office buildings were in darkness, as if somebody had thrown a master switch. This accentuated the angry red glow in the sky, reflecting the fires that were raging in Liberty City.

She picked up the phone and called the desk. She got a continuous busy signal. She tried another couple of hotel numbers, and finally the assistant manager came onto the line.

"We're doing what we can, ma'am," his harassed voice explained to her. "The main transmission lines from Turkey Point are down."

"Turkey Point?"

"That's the big nuclear power plant near Homestead. It supplies half the city's power. They say it was sabotage. Somebody blew up a couple of pylons. We should be able to get the lights back on in fifteen or twenty minutes. The company's trying to redistribute the flow."

"Can I get candles or something?"

"Yes, ma'am. I'll send one of the bellmen."

Julia hung up and pulled the draperies all the way back. It was past seven-thirty, she saw, peering at her watch. But it

216

seemed doubtful whether Gloria would come now, in the midst of a blackout. What a perfect night for a power failure, she thought, remembering the looting in New York during the outage in 1977, when all those stores with plate-glass windows high up along Third Avenue had been ransacked. She was glad she had come back to the hotel no later; otherwise, she might be stuck in an elevator.

The knock at the door came sooner than she expected.

"Who is it?" she called out.

"Hockney?" she heard a woman's muffled voice call back.

Through the peephole, Julia could see only a tangle of hair—possibly reddish in color—in the darkened corridor.

She opened the door, and a short, quite pretty girl in a satin dress that exposed a generous amount of cleavage tripped into the room. There was no need to ask whether this was Gloria.

"Shit," the hooker said as she plumped herself down on the edge of the bed and lit up a cigarillo. "I got stuck in the elevator. We had to force the door open. I think I broke a couple of fingernails." She began to examine her lacquered nails. "You should have seen one of the guys in there," she chuckled, starting to feel more at ease. "I thought he was going to have a heart attack. He was screaming and sweating like a pig. You must have heard it."

"No," Julia said. "I'm glad you got out of there safely."

"Do you have anything to drink?"

"I think Bob has something." Julia started fishing around in his briefcase for the brandy flask he usually carried on trips. "I doubt whether we can get room service in the middle of all this. Bob and Sergeant Maguire should be here any minute." She found the brandy and sloshed some of it into a bathroom tumbler, conscious of how Gloria had started to appraise her—or as much of her as she could make out in the half-light.

"You know, I met your husband once," she said to Julia. "Me and another girl. At the Mutiny. He was with Julio Parodi. I told him I didn't like reporters. I guess he didn't know that I was—you know—the one he was looking for. He didn't ask me for nothing."

217

"You must meet a lot of interesting people," Julia said gauchely. It was the first time she had ever talked to a prostitute.

"I meet all kinds," Gloria replied. She started talking about a banker prominent in political circles who liked to be tied up and given a golden shower. Julia was naive enough to have to ask what a golden shower was. When Gloria explained, she was glad of the darkness—it made it easier to conceal the fact that she was blushing.

"Now, Julio," Gloria continued. "He likes to give it to you in the ass. I don't like that too much. I told him once he should go make it with little boys, and he nearly broke my jaw. Cubans don't like to be called fags. It's not *macho*."

Before she went into any further detail, there was a rap on the door.

"Bob?" Julia called out.

"Room Service," a Spanish-accented voice called back.

"That'll be the candles," Julia said to Gloria as she unchained the door. "They certainly took their time."

She had just begun to open the door when it was rammed all the way open. A stocky man in a red T-shirt brushed past her, toward the bed. The second man slammed the door shut and double-locked it.

Julia saw the hooker crouched catlike on the far side of the bed, with a knife in her hand. She heard the big man in the red shirt laugh as he lunged out at her. She began to scream, but the sound died in her throat as a viselike grip tightened around her neck. The sky was streaked the color of blood oranges.

The men in black berets frisked Wright Washington twice before they let him into the poolroom with boarded-up windows where Commander Ali had set up his new base camp. The frisking was more than thorough; it was a deliberate intrusion on the minister's body space.

Commander Ali had changed back from his Moslem robes into paramilitary gear. He had two pistols in his belt, and there were a shotgun and a couple of AR-15s on the stained green baize of the table. The Jamaican was getting ready for war.

"How you doing, David?" Washington addressed him.

The Jamaican's face became a mask of cold hate. No one had called him by his given name for a very long time.

"You got your meeting," Commander Ali said. "Get talkin'. And don't start tryin' to soup me up."

"Who killed the woman?" the minister said.

"You heard what the brothers are saying. That pig killed her. That big motherfucker called Magic."

"The cops want to talk to you about it."

"Yeah. The cops want to frame me. Well, you go tell them where to find me. I ain't movin'."

"Listen to me, David. You don't belong here. Have you looked—I mean, really looked—at that shit that's going down outside? The brothers and the sisters are tearing up their own neighborhood again. That doesn't help anybody. Where are all these folks going to live when the fires die down? Liberty City doesn't need this. It doesn't need *you*, David."

The Jamaican jumped off the pool table and stood belligerently, his hands brushing his hips, in front of the minister.

"You still don't get it, do you?" he challenged Washington. "Well, *you* better listen up. You ain't seen nothing yet. We be settin' a fire. We be lightin' a fire all over this country. The spark is lit right here in Liberty City. All you've been doin' is helping Whitey dig our grave for us. Shit. We got a better idea. We got this."

He pulled one of the automatic rifles off the table and shook it in the minister's face.

"You're full of shit," Washington said, adopting the same language. "So you've got that gun and maybe a couple of hundred more—"

"We got all the guns we want," the Jamaican said triumphantly.

"Okay. So how many guns do you figure *they've* got? You go on with this, and you'll be facing the Army and the National Guard and the police and every scared Anglo who can lay hands on a gun and maybe, if you're lucky, you'll have the Klan and the Cuban crazies coming down here to blow your heads off too.

Nobody around here is going to give thanks to Mecca if you turn Liberty City into a war zone. If you're so full of holy shit you want to play kamikaze, that's real cool, you go do that. But go do it on your own, someplace where you don't take the whole community down with you."

Commander Ali was playing with his AR-15, snapping the safety catch off and on.

"You know what really pisses me off?" Washington pursued his attack. "You're the best thing that ever happened for the racists. They'd just love to shoot their way out of a problem like this. You know the Mayor has been keeping the cops on a leash, waiting to see whether we can calm things down by ourselves. He knows there are things that need to be put right. If you leave off, maybe we'll be able to make him keep his word. Maybe we can actually do something for this neighborhood, instead of burning it to the ground."

"You're a fuckin' dinosaur," the Jamaican said. "That shit is *old*, man. We tried that before. Where did it get us? I'll tell you where it got us. We got a man in the White House now who is cuttin' up the poor, and he don't even give us chloroform. He's cuttin' our throats, and all we get is Band-Aids. If we're goin' to go down bleeding, we might as well fight. We got nothing to lose."

"I'm talking about Liberty City," Washington reminded him.

"And I'm telling you, we're not just talking Miami. We're talking about the whole U.S.A. What happens here is goin' to start a movement all over this country."

"You're crazy. I'm telling you, you've picked the wrong time and the wrong place. And you're not going to win this with guns. The black man can never win with guns."

Commander Ali put the rifle to his shoulder and swung the barrel around the room, making a rat-tat-tat sound between his teeth as he shot at imagined enemies.

"You just run along back to your church, preacher man. You run along up to your friend the Mayor. You go lick some white ass."

"You must have a death wish," Washington said in despair.

"Death, he be a brother of mine."

The Jamaican stood at the door of the poolroom and watched the minister walk back along the cratered pavement, past the corner where some kids were piling rubble, old mattresses and tires around two burned-out cars to form a barricade. Washington glanced down and saw a lizard scuttle out from behind a rock. It stopped just beside his foot, flicking its tongue in and out.

A boy who looked about twelve came along, affecting a springy, bowlegged walk like the hip dudes on the block. When he became aware of Washington peering at him through the dark, he started twirling a gun around his finger. Closer up, Washington could see that it was a revolver, the kind the police used.

"Hey, where'd you get that thing?" he asked the boy.

"Mind your business, motherfucker," the kid spat at him, cocking the revolver too professionally for the minister to need to be told twice.

Wright Washington trudged back toward the police lines, his broad shoulders slumped a little now, feeling drained and defeated.

Then there were headlights, the scrape of metal and the smell of singed rubber as a big car raced toward him from a side street. It skidded left, jolting over the debris in the road, and sped on toward the poolroom. Washington could make out four or five men huddled together inside the car. The windows on the near side were rolled down.

The Black Fedayeen who were lounging about in front of the poolroom scattered as the car hurtled on toward them. A man leaned out from the back seat and sprayed them with automatic fire. Washington heard the sound of a stray bullet, passing close to his head, like the buzz of a fat insect. As the Black Fedayeen started shooting back, bullets struck the side and back of the car with the noise of hammer blows, and Washington heard a man screaming in Spanish. The gun muzzles flamed bright orange in the dark. Only a few yards away, the twelve-year-old kid was shooting too.

Washington watched the car ram into the barricade on the far side of the poolroom, reverse fast and make a jerky U-turn before accelerating back along the street. People were now shooting at it from all sides. He had seen one, maybe two of the Jamaican's guards fall. There was another spurt of machine-gun fire from the rear seat, and the kid let out a high, falsetto shriek and clutched at his belly.

Washington, crouched down, began running back toward the boy. At the same instant, he saw Commander Ali go zig-zagging along the street, behind the car. He saw the Jamaican whirl his arm like a pitcher. The grenade clattered against the hood of the car and erupted just as it was turning back into the side street. The nose of the car plowed into the falling tenement opposite as it turned into a fireball.

Washington was bending over the boy, who was still clutch-ing at his intestines, spilling out from the ragged gash across his belly like eels. The minister could see it was hopeless. He put his hand over the boy's eyes and began to intone a prayer.

He became conscious of someone standing over them. But he waited until he had finished and the boy's groans had stopped before he looked up.

It seemed to him that the Jamaican's face was flushed with a sort of triumph.

"Cubans," Commander Ali said, apparently indifferent to the plight of the boy who had spewed his guts over the pave-ment. "We got four of them. I told you," he added. "I told you this was the only way."

CRAWL KEY

Arnold Whitman liked to shave twice a day. He had sensitive skin, and the friction of his collar against the stubble of his neck, come early evening, was irritating. He was standing in front of the washbasin in an anonymous, flat-roofed concrete building in Crawl Key. The building stood on a secluded promontory, surrounded by water on all sides except for a narrow spit of land with a dirt track leading from the causeway that connected the Florida Keys.

Back in the sixties, in the heyday of the CIA's secret war against Castro, Crawl Key had been one of the main bases for the Formula One and Formula Two powerboats in which the paramilitary types set off on probes into Cuba, aiming for lonely beaches along the coasts of Oriente and Camagüey. It was an ideal location, screened from the Atlantic gales by a necklace of lesser islands and promontories; only a single, narrow channel led out from the sheltered cove to open sea. Even now, Crawl Key was much as Arnold Whitman remembered it from those wilder, less inhibited times. From his window, Whitman could see a semicircle of white sand, ringed with palm trees. The boats were kept under cover on the other side of the promontory. The powerful radio transmitter, used to maintain contact with operatives in Cuba, was in the second concrete blockhouse, out of view from the window.

Whitman squirted shaving cream into the palm of his hand from an aerosol can and smeared it over his cheeks. He shaved rapidly, without care, with a disposable plastic razor, and succeeded in nicking his chin. He turned on the hot-water tap to wash away the blood and shaving foam, but only the croak of the plumbing emerged. He tried the cold-water faucet. There was a wan dribble of rust-brown sludge, then nothing.

"José!" Whitman yelled. "What the fuck has happened to the water?"

A plump, pock-faced Cuban came running in.

"Didn't you hear?" he asked Whitman. "Some guys blew the pipeline from the mainland. But we're okay. We got the rain-water tank."

"Well, do something about *this*." Whitman glowered at the Cuban, an old-time contract employee who had been put back on the payroll to help out in the radio room. The Station Chief was pointing at his lathered face.

José rushed out again to fetch some water.

Before he returned, the alarm bell went off.

In disgust, Whitman wiped away the remains of the foam with a hand towel, and padded down the corridor, still dripping blood from his chin, to find out what was happening.

José and another Cuban from the radio room were loading their guns.

"Well?" the Station Chief demanded.

"Infiltrators," José gabbled. "We got infiltrators."

"Probably just a couple of Cubans who got lost."

"No, they're coming in boats."

At that, Whitman snatched up a rifle from the gun rack and dashed outside, with an agility surprising in such a heavy man.

He was in time to see the first boat rounding the neck of the heavily wooded island that barred the entrance to this side of the cove. It was a mottled brown fishing boat, dangerously low in the water. It was hard to imagine how it could have survived a sea passage, because even in these calm waters Whitman could see waves lapping over the decks, which were crammed with people, row upon row, a straining mass of humanity that began to raise a ragged cheer at the sight of the CIA men on the shore.

"I don't believe it," Whitman muttered. "Boat people. We got fucking boat people."

In their eagerness to set foot in the United States, the Cuban refugees started jumping and rolling and pushing one another off the boat. One of them came thrashing through the water, collapsed face down on the sand, picked himself up and flung himself upon Arnold Whitman, sobbing against his chest.

"God in heaven," Whitman breathed as he extricated himself and headed back inside to radio for instructions.

"Get them out of there," he was told.

"How? Their boat's about ready to sink." As he spoke, he could see a second boat, in no better condition than the first, chugging into the cove.

"Get onto the cops and the INS."

When Whitman finally reached his liaison in the South Florida Law Enforcement Department, the man laughed outright.

"You think *you've* got a problem?" he said shrilly. "Get out of your bunker and take a look at what's going on in this part of the state. We got traffic jammed bumper to bumper all across the Ten-Mile Bridge. Everyone's trying to get off the Keys because of this panic about the water supply. We got Cuban boat people arriving at every beach between Lauderdale and Key West. And Miami is blowing itself up, with a lot of help from your Cubans."

"What do you mean, *my* Cubans?" Whitman asked defensively.

"Sometimes I think you people live in a different country," the cop responded. "Those bastards in the Brigada Azul just went into Liberty City to shoot them some niggers. We're set for a race war up here. You better look out for your own ass."

MIAMI

Maguire stayed close to his car radio as they waited at the roadblock for Wright Washington to come back. Just before the shooting started, he said to Hockney, "You better get back to your wife. I just heard half the city is blacked out."

It had not struck Hockney as odd, until now, that none of the streetlights had come on, in the fading dusk, in this section of the ghetto. In the face of the devastation that confronted them, you stopped looking for signs of normality.

"I'll call her," Hockney said, not wanting to leave before Washington returned.

"From here?" Maguire cocked an eyebrow at him. "Tell you what," the cop went on. "I'll get one of the girls to call and say you're on your way."

He talked rapidly into his Motorola. After a couple of minutes, the dispatcher's voice came crackling over.

Hockney saw the Sergeant frown as he listened.

"What is it?" Hockney asked, as a fear he had not felt for himself, in this ruined street, gripped him like a fist in the pit of his stomach. "Is something wrong?"

"What was your room number again?"

Hockney repeated it.

"Yeah," Maguire said. "I thought I got it right. There's no answer."

"No answer? But . . ." Hockney thought fast. Maybe Julia

225

had gone off somewhere with Gloria. Maybe the hooker hadn't shown up, and she'd got bored with waiting and gone downstairs to get some coffee. But that didn't make sense. Either way, she would have stayed close to the phone. Maybe, with the blackout, she was trapped in an elevator.

"How do I get back?" he asked Maguire.

The Sergeant looked at the crowd of cops around them and spotted a chunky woman patrolman running toward one of the cruisers.

"Hey, Linda!" he yelled. "Where ya going?"

"We got looting in the Omni complex."

"Okay. Take this guy with you," Maguire ordered. "You should be able to get a cab around there," he added to Hockney. "I'll try and check in with you later."

So Hockney missed the scene around the poolroom when a gang of Brigada Azul toughs came looking for trouble and found more of it than they had reckoned on, and the scene that ensued afterward, when the cops were ordered in to try to clean up the mess and came under heavy automatic fire from the rooftops. It was that episode which inspired the Governor to send in the National Guard and ask Washington for Army backup. Instead, Hockney got a glimpse of the first looters who had broken out of the ghetto and headed downtown—a gang of youths from Overtown who made for the arcades of luxury shops around the Omni Hotel, a symbol of high living with inviting plate-glass windows. He witnessed an elderly security man fleeing under the covering fire of the police, dragging a bloodied leg behind him. He did not stay for the denouement. That fist inside his stomach kept tightening.

There were no taxis to be found at the hotel, but he ran out into the street and waved a twenty-dollar bill at a couple of kids in a pickup truck.

"You don't oughta flash money around like that, mister," they said when he had explained where he needed to go and they let him into the truck. "There's people who'd kill you for less than that."

They were rednecks from upstate, and they were packing

226

heavy artillery. Hockney thought he might have made the wrong move when he saw the shotgun and the hunting rifle. But they were hunting different game.

"Figure we might git us a couple of jungle bunnies tonight," the driver said as he stopped to let Hockney off outside the hotel.

He leered and said, "Akia."

"That's code," he bragged, seeing Hockney's blank expression. "A Klansman I am. That's right, eh, Jesse?"

"Akia," the other repeated solemnly.

As he hurried into the hotel lobby, Hockney was thinking that social breakdown brings out the crazies just as hot weather seems to bring out the roaches.

There were armed guards in the lobby, and they made him show his room key. Some lights were on—he guessed that they must have rigged up an emergency generator—but the elevators were still not working. He panted up the stairs, taking them two at a time.

When he got to their floor, he was surprised to find a uniformed cop standing in the corridor. With the mayhem that was breaking loose outside, it seemed unlikely that the Police Department could spare the men to provide this much security for one hotel. As he got nearer, he realized that the policeman was standing outside the door of his own room.

"What is it?" he asked, breathing hard, feeling on the edge of panic.

"Who are you?" the cop relied curtly.

"This is my room."

The patrolman squinted at his notebook. "Are you Hockney?"

"Yes."

"Just a second, please, sir," the cop added, more gently.

Hockney felt the rising terror start to engulf him as he watched the cop open the door. His door.

"Wait . . ." he faltered. "My wife . . ."

But the cop closed the door behind him.

Then a pink-faced man of middle years, with a comfortable

227

paunch and a full head of gray hair, came out of the room.

"Mr. Hockney? I'm Lieutenant Callahan," he introduced himself. "Homicide. I'm afraid I have very bad news for you." He spoke in a monotone, sympathetic but impersonal. The tone reminded Hockney of the officers whose full-time duty during the Vietnam War had been to inform the next of kin about men who had been killed in action. It told him part of what was to follow.

"Two women were murdered here tonight," Callahan said. "One of them may have been your wife."

"Where are they?"

"The bodies were taken to the morgue at JMH. Jackson Memorial Hospital. I'm afraid we'll have to ask you to try to make some identifications."

Hockney did not grasp the import of the words "try to," but they had a bad taste, like ashes on the tongue.

He moved jerkily, like a drunk attempting to walk a straight line, toward the door of his room.

"I think it's better you don't go inside," Callahan said, moving to stop him.

"I have to."

Callahan stepped back. "I guess it's your right," he said. "But don't touch anything."

The room was in darkness, but there were men inside peering around with flashlights. Entering, Hockney felt that he had departed the real world. He felt as if he were under heavy sedation, watching an old black-and-white horror movie on TV.

With the shifting lights, the shadows, this sudden sense of detachment, he could not take in the whole scene, only disjointed pieces. There were the men with the flashlights, to begin with. One of them was crawling around on hands and knees between the two queen-sized beds, only one of them slept in. Another was going over the floor with what looked like a miniature vacuum cleaner.

"Here." Callahan handed him his own flashlight, tiny but surprisingly powerful, shaped like a pen you could clip onto an inside pocket.

Under its beam, Hockney saw blood. At first, just a thumb-print, the whorls clearly defined, on the wall next to the bath-room. Then, lower down, the impress of an entire hand, the fingers elongated as if a child had smeared paint from as high up as it could reach, drawing its arm down until it brought the palm of its hand to rest at the level of Hockney's knee. Then the same shape was repeated lower down, just above the base-board. On the wall above the bed—the bed he and Julia had lain in the night before—blood traced a more abstract design, forming great loops and blotches and ragged lines like a Jack-son Pollock he had seen in a New York gallery. There were deep, dark stains in the pale carpet. Blood had even spattered around the light fixture in the middle of the ceiling, too high for Hockney to reach from the floor, even standing on tiptoe. With that same eerie sense of detachment, he wondered, as if it were some problem in an IQ test, how it was possible for blood to be *there*.

He followed the thin, bright beam of the flashlight round the corner, into the bathroom. There was no blood there, but the shower curtain was torn. And there was something on the mirror above the washbasin. He stared at it under the finger of light. He saw a tracery of pink lipstick—Julia's color, a warm, vibrant shade of pink. It formed the shape of a heart. Inside the heart, the word *"Madre"* was scrawled. The heart was pierced, not by a Cupid's arrow but by something ugly and pronged, like a pitchfork.

It was the juxtaposition of the Spanish word for Mother, in-side the heart, with the rumpled clothing he found strewn about on the tiled floor that brought Hockney out of his daze. He looked at the tangle of underwear, the ripped lilac dress, and staggered across to the washbasin, gripped the porcelain with both hands and began throwing up.

Callahan waited until the retching had stopped before ask-ing, "Do you recognize the clothes?"

"My wife," Hockney gasped. It seemed his chest would not stop heaving. When he tried to breathe, he felt as if someone were squeezing his lungs.

"I'm sorry I have to ask you this now. Where have you been since six o'clock?"

"With Jay—Jay Maguire."

"Sergeant Maguire in Patrol?"

"Yes."

Hockney was dimly aware of Callahan instructing one of his men to call Maguire, and of the other detective saying, "Tonight?" as if he had been asked to jump out the window, and then of the police Lieutenant guiding him along the corridor and down the stairs.

The view from the emergency entrance of Jackson Memorial Hospital was no more pleasing than the scene Hockney had witnessed in Liberty City earlier that evening. Across the road was a parking lot crammed full of burned-out police cars. There were more ruined Plymouths in the lot, on an average day, than the Police Department had available for patrol. There would be more before the night was out.

The lobby was jammed with patients on stretchers. One of them, pleading for attention, held up his hand, and Hockney winced away from the sight. What was left of his fingers looked like a chicken wing with the skin and the flesh peeled back to the bone. Callahan hustled Hockney past the rows of frightened, desperate faces.

They came out a back exit, and Hockney glimpsed a sign across a covered passage that read, "WARD D. RAPE TREATMENT CENTER." Callahan steered him the other way, through a door that opened into a bright, cheerful reception room that was indistinguishable, in most respects, from the one used by the family doctor Hockney had been taken to visit as a boy.

Hockney's eyes met a familiar tourist poster, one he had often seen on the billboard en route to various airports. The slogan read, "MIAMI. SEE IT LIKE A NATIVE."

Callahan cleared his throat. "Rona, this is Mr. Hockney." He cleared his throat again. "The two ladies from the hotel?"

Hockney did not wait for the conversation to go any further.

He went running through the swinging door, past Rona, down a white, neon-lit corridor with the hospital stench of disinfectants, then through heavy metal doors. Beyond, he was greeted by a blast of cold air and a different smell, the sickly-sweet odor of decomposing human flesh.

A tired black nurse was working among the trolleys.

Hockney ignored her. He could see Julia—or rather, her sweep of auburn hair, spilling over the sheet that covered a lifeless form on a trolley at the far end of the morgue.

He ran to the trolley and jerked back the sheet. And saw that it was not Julia after all, but a younger girl, with a round face and a snub nose. With no visible signs of tragedy, and her eyes wide open, the girl looked as if she were resting and might sit up at any instant. Hockney's eyes dropped to the blue Snoopy T-shirt and its inscription: "DON'T WAKE ME TILL THE WEEK-END IS OVER."

Then Callahan was tugging at his arm. "Come away," the police Lieutenant said, in a not unkindly way. "She's not here." He followed Hockney's gaze to the girl in the Snoopy T-shirt. "Some poor kid who OD'ed," he said. He rubbed his chin, thinking of his own adolescent daughter. "I just don't believe that T-shirt," he muttered as he led Hockney back along the corridor.

"Where is she?" Hockney asked in a hoarse voice when they were back in Reception.

"It's a crazy night," Rona said to nobody in particular. "It's a crazy city. We had to put her in the emergency facility."

Callahan knew what that meant. He took Hockney outside, to a big refrigerated trailer parked a few yards away from the back door. The hospital had bought it, secondhand, from one of the fast-food chains. The Lieutenant was thankful, for Hockney's sake, that the staff of the morgue had finally got around to spraying over the sign that had read, "HOME OF THE WHOPPER."

Inside the truck, the corpses were stacked, three tiers high, against both walls. In the confined space, the stench was

231

stronger than in the morgue. As Callahan threw open the door, it made Hockney reel back from the steps as if he had been kicked in the stomach.

The Lieutenant, inured to such things, was blocking his nostrils with a handkerchief.

"Can you make it?" he called down to Hockney.

"Yes." Hockney knew he had to.

Stooped, he followed Callahan along the whole length of the trailer. He leaned over to one side to avoid a protruding foot, and a dead hand brushed his face.

Callahan bent down to inspect a tag that was tied around the ankle of one of the corpses. Then he pulled back the sheet. Hockney leaned over his shoulder to see.

It was not Julia. He could tell that from the frizz of red hair. There was not much left of the face. The mouth was a ragged hole; someone must have hacked off the lips. The remaining features had been battered into a raw pulp.

Callahan was waiting for him to say something. The cop had the decency not to look him in the eye. He just crouched there, holding up the sheet, waiting.

Hockney swallowed and said, "It's not my wife. It may be a woman called Gloria."

The Lieutenant replaced the sheet.

He uncovered the face of the body on the rack above. He raised the sheet a little higher, then dropped it and held it rigid below the chin. "Savages," Hockney heard him say under his breath. "No animal descends to this."

It can't be Julia, Hockney insisted to himself. *There's no reason for it. It's a mistake.*

Then he steeled himself and looked.

A deep furrow ran from the hairline, across the left eye socket and the nose, all the way down to the jawline. The morgue attendants had swabbed away the blood, so the gash looked purplish-blue, white at the edges. It had altered the planes of the face, lifting a corner of the mouth so that it seemed to be curled in a snicker. But the eye that remained intact was opened wide in horror.

Again, Callahan did not ask his question. Hockney's sudden intake of breath gave him his answer.

He moved to replace the sheet, but Hockney reached over him and pulled it back. Callahan started to caution him to leave off, but thought better of it. The cop backed up against the end of the trailer, leaving Hockney as much space—as much intimacy—as the circumstances allowed.

There was another furrow, a gouge mark, around Julia's throat, as if someone had tried to throttle her with wire or a fishing line.

The knife marks on her chest were worse than the gash across her face. The killer, or killers, must have stabbed her repeatedly. Her left breast was almost severed, hanging by a narrow flap of skin.

Hockney forced himself to look lower. What he saw made him faint. He slipped and struck his forehead against the cold metal of the rack above.

Swiftly, Callahan took the sheet and pulled it back up over Julia's head.

But what Hockney had seen was seared into his mind, indelible. The butcher had gone berserk. He had chopped and slashed and gouged at Julia's belly—perhaps in the knowledge that she was pregnant—laying it open. When Hockney closed his eyes, he could see the knife going in, the wounds spouting blood, his unborn child dying under the monster's fury.

Callahan slipped his hands under Hockney's armpits to help support him as he stumbled to the door of the trailer.

A man in blue was there to steady him as he tripped and nearly fell down the steps. Hockney's eyes did not focus on Jay Maguire to begin with.

He spun around in a slow circle, arms outspread, like a child playing at being an airplane.

"Why?" he asked Callahan, Maguire and the night sky.

"In God's name, why?"

Chapter

8

MIAMI

The Confession Room at Miami Police Headquarters looked
more like the set for a TV talk show than an interrogation cell.
It was casually furnished with a couple of chairs and sofas with
brown-and-white upholstery. The walls were bare except for a
large clock that supplied the time and date for the hidden video
cameras that were used to record important interviews. The
room was on the same floor as the Emergency Control Center
from which Chief Murchison was trying to coordinate police
and National Guard operations against the rioters in Liberty
City.

"I'm sorry I have to put you through this," Lieutenant Callahan said to Hockney, motioning for him to sit in one of the arm-
chairs. The Confession Room was normally reserved for the
most serious criminal investigations. That night, it was the only
oasis of calm in the police building. As they had come in the
back way, Hockney had seen the SWAT teams—in their dis-
tinctive military-style khaki uniforms—piling into their trucks.

In the downstairs area, dozens of looters, yelling and jeering, were being booked.

"Is it okay if I stay, Lieutenant?" Maguire asked.

"Yeah. I guess you'd better."

Hockney responded mechanically as Callahan questioned him about the events of the day. When he explained that he had gone into Liberty City with Maguire, Callahan looked at the Sergeant sharply and said, "I hope you got a signed release."

"Oh, sure," Maguire lied. In the day's confusion, he had forgotten all about it. Standing regulations required that a civilian who went on patrol with the cops had to sign an undertaking that the Department would not be held liable for the loss of life or limb.

Callahan finally got round to the critical question. "Who was the woman who was with your wife?"

"Her name was Gloria." Hockney glanced over at Maguire, who nodded his head to reassure him. There was not much point in holding back now. "She was a prostitute."

"A prostitute?" Discreetly, Callahan looked under the desk to make sure that the tape recorder was on. "What was a hooker doing with your wife?" His tone implied that he thought reporters from up North might be capable of any kind of sexual aberration.

"She agreed to give us information. For a story I was writing."

"On hookers in Miami?"

"On Julio Parodi."

Maguire watched Lieutenant Callahan's reactions closely. The Homicide detective stared at his hairy knuckles for a long moment before he asked his next question.

"What's the connection?"

"She was part of Parodi's stable. She knew something about his dope involvement."

"Why did she agree to talk to you?"

Hockney avoided looking at Maguire this time. He made the gesture of rubbing his thumb and his forefinger together.

Whether or not Callahan was satisfied with this explanation, he let it pass.

"You think Parodi could have had them knocked off?" he asked.

Hockney's mind went back to the scene at the paramilitary camp in the Everglades, when the Cuban had shown off his arsenal of automatic weapons.

"I think he's capable of it," Hockney said. It began to make sense to him now. Parodi had found out somehow that Gloria was a snitch for Maguire, and had sent his executioners to silence her. You read all the time about killings in Miami's dope wars, the bodies of informers or rivals being dumped along canals and waterways. Maguire had told him what had happened to another CI who had been spying on Parodi. Yes, that had to be the reason. Parodi's men had gone hunting Gloria, and had caught up with her at the hotel—or more likely, trailed her there, to make sure about their suspicions. Unknowingly, she had led them straight to Julia. His reasoning collapsed into a bitter chaos of ifs and mights. If only he had gone back to the hotel earlier, instead of hanging around watching a riot. If only the riots had started some other day. If only he had left Julia out of this in the first place, instead of leaning on her like a crutch.

This is my doing, he said to himself. *I'm as guilty as those butchers in the hotel room.*

That realization snapped the frail bands of self-control, and he broke down, weeping for his own guilt and what he could not undo. The sobbing racked his whole body.

"We'll get him, Bob," Maguire said softly. "I promise you that. Even if it costs me my badge," he added defiantly.

Callahan's slow, watery eyes turned to the source of this outburst, and Maguire was left in no doubt that the Lieutenant had guessed that *he* was the link between the Hockneys and Gloria.

"*If* you're right," Callahan said to Hockney, "you could be in danger yourself." He shrugged off his jacket and let it fall over the back of his chair, exposing his gun in its shoulder holster.

"But I don't think we want to jump to conclusions. These killings don't look like a professional execution. Professional hit men wouldn't waste time carving up the bodies in a hotel room. Dozens of people could have heard what was going on."

Of course, Hockney thought. He could imagine what the screams must have been like.

"Somebody *must* have heard," he said. "Why didn't anybody do anything?"

"I dunno," Callahan admitted. "Maybe everybody was watching the riots on TV. There must have been a lot of disruption in the hotel, what with the blackout and all."

"Who called you?"

"We got the call after a bellman checked the room. Seems your wife had asked for candles. Anyway, like I say, a professional would have done the job with a bullet in the back of the neck. Through a silencer."

"So what's your theory?"

"You saw that daub on the bathroom mirror?"

Hockney remembered the pierced heart and the word *"Madre."* "Yes," he said. "What does it mean?"

Callahan passed him a sheet of paper, a circular from the police Intelligence unit. It contained a sketch of a hand with the thumb and forefinger extended. On the web between was a small tattoo. Along the top of the page were drawings of seven or eight different tattoos.

"Now, you see"—the Lieutenant got up from his seat and came over to point things out to Hockney—"these are signs that a lot of Mariels had carved on themselves, probably while they were in the slammer back home in Cuba. This one"—he put his finger under a sign consisting of three vertical slashes with two horizontal lines underneath—"means that the guy's specialty is running dope. And this"—he pointed to a tattoo with the same vertical stripes but a star beneath—"this one is used by professional kidnappers. I guess you saw *this* one before, right?"

Hockney looked at the tattoo on the extreme right of the

page. It was the image of the crude scrawl in Julia's lipstick that he had seen on the bathroom mirror.

"That is the mark of the executioner," Callahan explained. "A lot of the guys who sport these tattoos are just punks. They have themselves decorated for status, so they can show off. A professional hit man doesn't go around wearing his trademark on his fist. And he sure doesn't go leaving his calling card in the bathroom when he finishes a job. Right, Jay?"

Maguire did not respond. He was thinking back to a raid he had led on a seedy Mariel bar a couple of weeks before, and to a sturdy young tough he had found there who had a heart tattooed on the web of his hand.

"There's something more," Callahan went on. "A professional hit man doesn't mess around with a lady before he offs her."

There was a pause before Hockney reacted. "You mean my wife was raped?" he said, once the full reality had sunk in. "Oh, my God."

"We have something to go on," Callahan proceeded, brisk and matter-of-fact now that the worst had been told. "We didn't find any fingerprints, but we got the impression of a glove, and some traces of a shoe, and a few strands of fiber from a Dacron shirt. And some other things," he wound up. It was kinder not to mention that the most important physical evidence consisted of traces of semen and pubic hairs.

"I want to be sure I understand," Hockney said. "Are you telling me you think my wife—and Gloria—were killed by some kind of nut? A sex killer?"

"It's a theory," Callahan confirmed. "With these riots, there are all kinds of crazies running amok. They know the cops can't be everywhere at once."

"Why would these—crazies—pick my hotel room?"

"They might have followed the hooker up. There are psychotics who go after hookers. Like Jack the Ripper."

Hockney shuddered and pictured Julia with her arms outstretched, trying to ward off the knife that kept rising and falling. "I can't accept it was so—random." He had nearly said,

238

meaningless. "What are you going to do?"

"I figure we're looking for Mariels. Two of them," Callahan said. "It won't be easy. We got more of these Mariels coming in right now. I don't want to give you any false hopes, Mr. Hockney."

For Chrissake, give me something, Hockney thought.

It was Maguire who spoke up, as if he had heard him say it out loud.

"I think I know where to start looking."

"Sergeant Maguire." The Lieutenant spoke to him with sudden formality. "You're not in Homicide. They need your ass out there in the street."

"Screw that," said Maguire. "This guy's a friend of mine."

"Okay," Callahan sighed. "I'll try to cover your back."

On their way out of the building, Hockney and Maguire ran into Wilson Martinez. He was frog-marching a black man twice his size into the already crowded lockup.

"Jay!" the Cuban cop called out happily. "Guess what this jive brother was up to."

Maguire took a look at the prisoner and recognized Blue, the neighborhood enforcer who usually hung out at The Hole in Overtown.

"Trying to get a little warm pussy, Blue?"

The prisoner opened his mouth wide in an expression between a snarl and a smile and displayed the gap in his front teeth.

"This little mother was trying to break into the National Guard Armory," Martinez explained. "Him and another guy. Guess they hadn't heard the news that the National Guard had been called out. He ran into about a hundred rednecks who were ready to cut his balls off."

"Who put you up to it, Blue?" Maguire asked. "You didn't dream that up all by yourself."

Blue threw back his shoulders and bellowed, *"Allah-u-Akbar!"*

"Jeeze," Maguire said, "he's joined the Black Fedayeen. Has

this whole town gone crazy?" He turned away from the prisoner in disgust, then stopped himself. "Hey, Wilson," he said to his partner. "Will you do me a favor? Unload this guy and get your ass into my car. I need somebody who talks Spaneesh."

Any street cop knows the only person you can count on is your partner. The fact that Maguire needed him was enough for Martinez. He let another cop take the collar for Blue, and came tearing into the police car park after them.

"What's the scene in Little Havana?" Maguire asked as they drove off, Hockney in the back seat, Martinez in the front.

"Pretty wild," the Cuban cop reported. "Everybody's got his gun out since those Brigada Azul crazies got themselves blown up. Andres Fortin is stomping around promising revenge."

"Andres Fortin?" Hockney was not sure of the man's position in the Brigade.

"He's the *jefe militar*—he runs the bang-bang stuff. He's far out. But he knows his business. He went on a raid into Cuba a few years back. They blew up some buildings in Sagua la Grande."

"What's the news on Mr. Big?" Maguire said quietly.

"I haven't heard anything," Martinez reported. "Parodi must be laying low. They've got private guards on the Rickenbacker Causeway in case any rioters try to go out to Key Biscayne. Same thing with the bridges going to Miami Beach. The people in those tourist hotels are really shitting themselves."

Little Havana was quieter than Liberty City. But there were a lot of people on the streets—mostly nervous, excited men openly toting guns—and unofficial roadblocks had been set up around Calle Ocho. Martinez tugged at Maguire's sleeve, and he slowed the cruiser down as they passed one of them.

"Hola, Miguel," Martinez called out to a middle-aged, solidly built Cuban. *"¿Qué dices?"*

The Cuban strolled over to the police car and they had a hasty conversation in Spanish.

"Miguel says they're not expecting any more trouble around here tonight," Martinez translated afterward for the benefit of the other men in the car. "The vets—Brigade Twenty-five-oh-six, the Bay of Pigs veterans, not Parodi's Brigade—have taken over. They've organized community-defense groups."

"You mean vigilantes," Hockney chipped in.

"No, these guys aren't going to go around town shooting up blacks," Martinez rejoined. "But they'll sure give the Black Fedayeen a warm reception if they come looking for trouble in Little Havana. Miguel says a gang of black kids trashed his brother's store. They went right through the stock."

"What kind of store?"

"Cameras, TVs, that kind of crap. They're a good family. They were friends with my father in Cuba. Coño. By the time this is all over, you won't be able to recognize people in this city. I bet Castro's having a big fat belly laugh. You should have seen those National Guardsmen, Jay. They went charging off into Liberty City letting out Rebel yells, just like they were going into battle with Stonewall Jackson. I don't know what they'll do to Mr. Ali, but they sure scared the shit out of me!"

"Yeah," Maguire said, pushing the car to sixty-five as they cruised west toward the string of Mariel bars. He was thinking that things would never have deteriorated to this point had the cops been allowed to go in and do their job at the very beginning. He could picture what might happen when the excited troopers from upstate—kids unfamiliar with the city, as alien to the black ghetto as to a Vietnamese hamlet—started hitting the streets, and wondered how many more corpses would be dumped on the doorstep of Jackson Memorial Hospital before the night was through.

"What you guys been doing tonight, anyway?" Martinez was asking.

Maguire told him in two short sentences.

That silenced the Cuban cop for a time. When he spoke again, he said merely, "I'm sorry. I got family myself."

The riots and the blackout did not seem to have interfered with the customary festivities at the Sugar Shack, at Southwest Eighth and Fifty-seventh. The throbbing pink neon sign above the door was out, but the place was lit by hurricane lamps. From the outside, the saloon looked no better and no worse to Hockney than the tawdry dockside bars of Hamburg or Rotterdam.

"Take the back," Maguire instructed his partner.

He allowed Martinez a couple of minutes to slip around the side of the building.

Then he pushed through the front door, with Hockney bringing up the rear. The jukebox was out too, but someone was providing musical accompaniment on a harmonica for the go-go dancer on the stage. The tinny version of "Guantanamera" stopped abruptly as the cops worked their way into the room.

Hockney stared at the woman on the stage. She looked well into her fifties, and the flickering light from the hurricane lamps did not conceal her varicose veins or the dank hair in her armpits. She was completely nude, and the obscenity of the spectacle was increased by the fact that her private parts were meticulously shaved. Her cheap blond wig had slipped, so that it hung over her eyes.

Apart from a man at the bar with his head on his arms, apparently unconscious, the customers of the Sugar Shack were in a huddle around the stage. They began to scatter as they became aware of the cops. The odd thing was that their attention had not been focused on the dancer, but on something happening inside their own circle.

Maguire grabbed one of them and pushed him roughly over against the bar.

"You scumbags!" the Sergeant roared.

"What is it?" Hockney asked.

"Fucking animals," Maguire swore. "It's a Mariel cockfight. You wouldn't want to look."

Hockney looked anyway. He recoiled immediately, spun around and found himself confronted with a garishly painted plastic statue of the Virgin, projecting from the wall. Two men, crouched on chairs in front of the stage, had been trying to jerk off while the other customers laid bets on which of them would come first. Hockney's disgust was shaping itself into a murderous rage. He felt he had descended into the sewer that had claimed Julia's life, and at that instant he felt capable of doing *anything* to the men in that room, as if all of them were guilty.

"Nobody collects tonight," Maguire growled, hammering his metal-cased flashlight against the bar. Its butt nicked the wooden surface and set glasses and bottles chinking.

The go-go dancer wobbled away toward the back room, the image of wounded dignity.

The contestants in the Mariel cockfight hurriedly hitched up their jeans.

Martinez snapped at the heels of the other men—fourteen or fifteen of them—like a sheep dog, lining them up against the bar, making them spread their legs and raise their arms.

"Watch our backs," Maguire said to Hockney. The reporter stationed himself at the end of the bar near the door.

Maguire walked along the row of men. He picked out two or three who were wearing new jeans. One of them had been in the cockfight.

Maguire jabbed his thumb at him. "Ask this prick when he got here," he told Martinez.

The man was reluctant to answer.

Martinez turned away, as if he had lost interest, then stabbed viciously between the man's legs with his nightstick. The *marielito* yelped in pain, and started gabbling furiously.

"He got here yesterday," Martinez interpreted. "He's one of the new ones."

"Has he got anything on him?"

Martinez frisked the man. "Nope. He's clean."

"Tell him he's got to report to INS—La Migra, huh?—tomorrow, or else I'm gonna come back and stuff his balls down his ears." Maguire knew the threat was unlikely to have any effect, but he had more important things to do tonight than lock up illegal immigrants.

He walked on, along the bar.

He stopped behind a dark, deep-chested man in a red T-shirt.

"This one," he said to his partner. "Tell him to show me his hands."

Before Martinez began to translate, the *marielito* let out a

243

wordless yell and struck out with both fists. The blow that caught Maguire on the chest was so powerful that he reeled backward, winded, and tripped over a chair. The Cuban cop had his revolver out, threatening to shoot, but the man in the red T-shirt was running for the door.

Martinez' finger had started to tighten on the trigger when he saw Hockney hurl himself onto the *marielito*. He grabbed him around the thighs, in a sort of football tackle, and both men went crashing heavily to the floor. Then Hockney was sitting on the man's chest, pounding at his face and throat with both fists.

"Stop it, Bob," Maguire said as he came panting up. "That's *enough*, goddammit." He seized Hockney's shoulders and wrestled him back. "You want to *kill* the cocksucker?"

Blood was streaming from the Mariel's nose and mouth, and one of his eyes was battered half-shut.

"For the record," Maguire said to Martinez, "this happened in a barroom fight before we made the arrest."

Hockney leaned back against the wall, recovering his breath, and that strange sense of remoteness came over him again as he contemplated what he had just done. He heard part of himself saying, *Let him be the one. Let there be an end of it tonight.* But the voice, and the scene in front of him, seemed to be far away.

"Carajo," Martinez said when he looked closer. "This chicken is really out to lunch."

The *marielito*'s eyes rolled until only the whites were showing.

Maguire grabbed his arm. He found the telltale scars inside the elbow. "He's a user, okay."

But he was looking for something else. He prised apart the man's fist. There, between thumb and index finger, was the small, blue-black tattoo: the pierced heart inscribed, *"Madre."*

"Yeah," Maguire breathed. "You could just be the one."

They propped him up on a chair and went through his pockets. Inside his jeans, he had a small plastic sack of white powder. Then another inside his sock. Maguire sniffed and licked.

"What is it? Heroin?" Hockney asked.

"Heroin *and* snow. He was fireballing—shooting up a mixture of both. That's a pretty expensive habit for a Mariel. Let's get him outside."

The men at the bar, relieved that the police had lost interest in them, moved into more comfortable positions and resumed their drinking.

They got the cuffs on the *marielito* out on the pavement. Maguire's glance returned to the track marks on his arms.

"Wilson, ask him where he lives and where he got that shit he was carrying."

Martinez asked a few questions in Spanish. The prisoner seemed to have regained consciousness, but remained silent. "Guess he don't want to talk."

"Okay, you better read him his rights, Wilson."

Martinez gabbled through the formula.

"Good. Now we're going to explain to him why he should talk."

They drove to a deserted lot next to the Orange Bowl.

Maguire looked at Hockney. "You want some?" he asked.

Hockney shook his head, sickened by the degree of savagery he had found in himself before. If Maguire hadn't stopped him, he might have killed this anonymous Cuban, without even knowing if he was Julia's murderer.

"Try not to mark him any more," Maguire said to his partner. "Our friend's done enough of that already."

The Mariel was remarkably stubborn. By the time they were through, he had parted with only one scrap of information: an address a few blocks away from the Sugar Shack.

The cops knew the building. They had checked out a report of a sexual assault on a small boy there a few weeks before.

The *marielito* denied all knowledge of the women at the hotel. He claimed he had got his dope from a black street pusher whose name he didn't know, and that he had got the cash by gambling on jai alai. It was true that frenzied betting went on at the jai alai fronton, but the Mariel didn't strike Maguire as a man with a winning streak.

"Is he the one?" Hockney was asking. The reporter's face was drawn and pale.

"He could be," Maguire said. "We'll hold him on the possession charge. Then we'll check out his place." He did not feel obligated to mention the most urgent part of the investigation— a physical examination of the Cuban to compare his secreta and pubic hairs with the specimens removed from the corpses of the two women.

"You better stay here," Maguire told Hockney back at Police Headquarters.

"No way."

"All right. If I was in your shoes, I'd say the same."

So while Callahan called in the police pathologist, they drove back into Little Havana.

"He could have a roommate," Maguire said as he braked two houses away from the clapped-out boardinghouse where the Mariel lived. "Callahan says there were two of them at the hotel. Let's ask that queen on the second floor."

They hurried up a rickety flight of stairs to a half-open door. Inside, a swarthy man in his fifties was slouched, shirtless, in a broken wicker chair. His pendulous gut overhung his soiled jockey shorts. Roaches scurried around a heap of unwashed dishes in a sink that smelled as if it did double duty as a urinal. It was obvious that the man had not washed or shaved in several days. Hockney stared at him over Maguire's shoulder. The man sat up, startled, then slumped back into his chair as if no one were there.

"Ask him about the Mariel," Maguire instructed Martinez.

The man's first response to the question was a copious belch. Hockney noticed a pile of beer cans on the other side of his chair.

"Remind him he was supposed to report to Headquarters last week," Maguire said to his partner. For Hockney's benefit, he explained that a woman in the house behind had complained that the old man had been molesting her five-year-old son. The child's account of the incident, unfortunately, had been too incoherent to stand up in court.

246

Hockney pointed to the light switch in the hallway, outside the door. It was surrounded by a metal plate, carved and painted to look like a fat man with his trousers down around his ankles. The switch itself jutted out from between the fat man's thighs.

"Yeah," Maguire said. "This is the right guy, all right. Wilson, tell him unless he cooperates, we'll take him down and book him tonight." It was a hollow threat, but there was no reason why the fat Cuban—another of the boat people of 1980—should know that.

The man became noticeably more accommodating. "One of them arrived just a few days ago," Martinez reported. "He's up there now."

"Name?"

"He says the one upstairs is called Coco Marín," Martinez interpreted.

"Come on, then," said Maguire, stepping back out onto the landing. "Let's take him."

"Wait," Hockney intervened as the Sergeant started running up the stairs.

"What's the problem?" Maguire had his gun out. He crooked his head, listening for any sound of movement from upstairs.

"Well," Hockney said, thinking fast. "Suppose Callahan is wrong. Suppose it was a hit. If we arrest the other one now, we may never be able to prove anything."

"If the scumbag knows something, I'll get it out of him," Maguire promised.

"We didn't get far with the other one," Hockney reminded him.

"Aw, he didn't know shit." All the same, the Sergeant remained where he was, halfway up the stairs. Then he crept back down to the landing. "You stay here, Wilson," he instructed his partner. "I'm going to call Callahan and see if he'll buy a stakeout."

Hockney followed him out to the car.

When Lieutenant Callahan came onto the radio, he made it plain he was not impressed by the idea of a stakeout.

"How many spare detectives do you figure we got?" Callahan demanded. "Pull that greaser in now. I wouldn't care if he got himself shot resisting arrest. He's the one we want, all right. We got his partner nailed."

"I think we ought to wait until morning," Maguire insisted. "If this was a contract job, the one we got here—Coco—may get scared when his friend doesn't show up and try to contact whoever hired them."

"Contract job?" Callahan echoed him derisively. "These are a couple of mad dogs. Fucking junkie sex perverts. You know what we found on the other one?" He explained that the pathologist had detected a minute clump of mucus under the *marielito*'s foreskin. It contained traces of brightly colored fiber. Under the microscope, they had established that it matched the bedspread in the Hockneys' hotel room.

Listening to this exchange, Hockney began to shake. He folded his arms tightly across his chest and squeezed his knees together, but his body went on vibrating. His lungs felt constricted, as if his ribs were caving in; he could barely breathe. He could picture every last detail of what had happened at the hotel, but it was all mixed up with the sordid spectacle at the *marielito* bar.

Maguire put his hand on Hockney's shoulder and pressed it gently.

"We're gonna bring Coco in," he said. "We ought to have enough to put both these sons-of-bitches away for life. I wish to hell that wasn't all."

They had the car doors open when they heard the shot.

They found Martinez squatting on the second-floor landing, hugging his leg.

"The fire escape," he gasped.

Maguire hesitated for a moment. "Are you okay?"

"Yeah. I heard a noise—feels like the bastard blew off my kneecap. I can't walk."

Maguire raced up the stairs. The window on the landing was open. He peered down the fire escape and saw a shadowy figure running along the back of the building. He squeezed off a couple of rounds, but the man ran out of his line of sight, around the corner of the boardinghouse.

Maguire bowled past Hockney, back down to the front entrance and out into the street. All he could see was the cars at an intersection a couple of blocks north. Coco could have ducked into any of the buildings along the street.

"Shit," Maguire cursed as Hockney came up behind him. "We lost him. You go back to Wilson and try to get a description of this Coco from that jerk on the second floor. I gotta call up an ambulance."

They stayed with Martinez until the paramedics came. Then Hockney drove back to Headquarters with Maguire and waited while he put in his report. The description of Coco could have fitted thousands of Hispanics in the city. He was young and slight, with a mustache and short black hair.

One out of two, Maguire was thinking as they drove along the South Dixie Highway, past the wooded park around the Vizcaya Palace. It was *something*. Only a fraction of the homicides in Dade County ever got solved.

Hockney was sitting in the front seat of the cruiser, scanning the side of the road on the impossible chance that the second *marielito* might suddenly materialize. He coughed slightly as he taxed his throat with one cigarette after another.

"Where are we going?" he finally said to Maguire.

"We're going to my place. In the Grove. I think you better hole up with me for tonight. If that's okay with you."

"That's fine. Thank you."

The shared frustration, and the understanding that had grown between them, was a rope that each could hold on to. Hockney had begun to experience a dizzy sensation of falling, as if he were in an elevator car that had shot up to the top of a tall skyscraper and then come hurtling down, to stop with a jolt between floors halfway down the shaft, where it now swung, unsteadily suspended by a cable that threatened to give way at any moment.

When they reached Maguire's littered apartment, the cop popped open a couple of beers and pulled down the sofa bed in the living room.

"Is Callahan right?" Hockney asked.

"I don't know."

"It seems so—incredible," Hockney persisted. He still found it impossible to believe that Julia had been swallowed up by this horror because the man from the Sugar Shack, crazed with dope, had picked their hotel room at random. Yet Callahan was right about one thing: the man bore no resemblance to a professional killer.

Maguire, who had seen even worse things happen for less reason, was no longer certain about anything. The frenzy of the chase had dulled his personal sense of loss until now, past three in the morning, when he realized that the little hooker from Okeechobee had meant more to him than he had ever cared to admit while she was alive. She had also been the only weapon he could use against Julio Parodi. Coincidence or not, Parodi was the one person who had gained from the double tragedy.

"I'm not going to let him get away," Hockney promised. "He's going to pay."

Maguire knew whom he meant. The cop said, "You mean you're going to walk into his penthouse and ask him to 'fess up he paid a couple of Mariels to kill your wife?"

"No." Hockney did not have a plan, but one began to shape itself as he spoke. "I'll try to find out what it was so important to Parodi to keep secret."

"And how are you going to do that?"

"I'll follow him. Spy on him."

"Gloria said he was about to leave town," Maguire reminded him.

"Well, I'll spy on his people. I'll force Arnold Whitman to talk. Will you help?"

"Do you need to ask?" Maguire put his gun on the coffee table. "Do you know how to use one of these?" he asked, patting the butt of his .38.

"Sort of."

"You better get one."

For half an hour, Hockney questioned the cop about everyone in the Miami area who was a known associate of Parodi's, jotting down names and addresses on a piece of scrap paper. He put big black crosses next to some of them: Mama Benitez, Parodi's chauffeur-cum-bodyguard; Felix Rey, the manager of his arms business, and Andres Fortin, the *jefe militar* of the Brigada Azul. He also scribbled the names of a couple of Cubans who were known enemies of Parodi's—a rival cocaine dealer who believed he had been jailed because Parodi had informed on him, and a businessman prominent in rightist circles who had attacked the Brigada Azul for its rabid policies and open avowal of terrorism, which he believed did damage to the image of the community as a whole. It was enough to start with.

Maguire showed no signs of retiring to bed, so they sat there for a long time in silence. Hockney's mind turned to other practical matters: contacting Julia's family, making arrangements for the funeral, calling the paper to explain that he would be going on leave indefinitely. He tried to focus his thoughts on anything other than the scene in the hotel room. But it kept coming back, and he saw Julia's face as vividly as if she were sitting in Maguire's place, so real that he felt he could reach out and touch her. It scared him, being able to see her so clearly. He could not face her, and her mute accusation that he was to blame.

NEW YORK

The whir of the traffic over the narrow span of the Brooklyn Bridge reminded Frank Parra of the sound of an old propeller plane. There was a fancy restaurant under the bridge in the warehouse district on the Brooklyn side, but Parra's friend preferred a two-fisted drinking establishment on Front Street nearby.

Captain Joe Fischer, the chief of the Emergency Services

Unit, was waiting for Parra in the tiny back room, behind the bar with its hanging lanterns and tin-lined walls.

"How are you, you Hump?" Parra greeted him. Frank Parra had been in New York long enough to pick up a few bits of useful slang. HUMP—the acronym for Higher-Up Management Personnel—was a private code used by some of the cops as a form of identification or a friendly insult.

The lively Puerto Rican waitress came skipping up to Joe Fischer, planted another Rob Roy in front of him and kissed the top of his head, smearing lipstick over his shiny bald pate.

"Old Puerto Rican custom." She grinned at Parra. "Bald men bring good luck."

"I'm sorry I've got too much hair," the FBI man joked.

In the few weeks he had been working out of his new office on Fifty-sixth Street—an unmarked red brick building with smoked-glass windows, next door to the Castilian Restaurant— Parra had learned that there was no love lost between his FBI colleagues and the New York Police Department. It had been the same in San Juan. It was probably the same in any town. Rival agencies were always jealous of sharing sources, or credit. But Parra did not believe in sitting back in an office waiting for information to come to him through established channels. To get information, you needed to have friends. Joe Fischer was one of the men at Police Headquarters he had set out to make his friend, and he had picked him because the German-American cop knew his city as well as anybody.

"What the fuck is going on in Miami?" Fischer was asking.

"I think it's organized," Parra replied. He had spent much of the morning in a briefing session on the riots at the FBI building. "There's a new pattern showing up. Number one, there are at least two radical organizations that are getting people out into the street. The Black Fedayeen and those Cuban crazies, the Brigada Azul."

"Yeah," Fischer drawled over his drink. "Those Black Islamics were out demonstrating on a Hundred and Twenty-fifth in Harlem last night. They tried to shoot up a patrol car. What's with these Cubans? Are they the same group that tried to kill that Cuban diplomat at the U.N. a couple of years back?"

"Different outfit," Parra commented. "These guys are either nuts, or they're working for Castro."

"What makes you say that?"

"Well, they've turned what could have been just another ghetto riot into a racial confrontation. They got the blacks and the Cuban community at each other's throats. That's never happened before, and I don't believe the mainstream Hispanic community is going to thank them for it."

Fischer grunted. "Well, it looks like those good ol' boys down there in Florida are gonna put a stop to it," he said. "They've just about built a wall around Liberty City." He chortled at the memory of the TV newsreel, showing National Guardsmen moving in, escorted by tanks and armored cars. "It'd never happen here," he went on. "We've got a couple of APCs, but we've been ordered to keep them well out of sight no matter what happens. Too provocative, the politicians say. Fuck 'em if they can't take a joke. To New York, God bless her." He raised his glass.

Fischer called for a refill, then said, "What about the saboteurs?"

"That's the most worrying thing of all," said Parra. "And it's another new element in what's happening in South Florida. They set out to sabotage the entire power and water supply, and they just about succeeded. But nobody's claimed responsibility, and the police and our field office have come up with exactly zilch. Except for one thing. You know that reactor at Turkey Point?"

"Yeah. They cut the transmission lines or something, didn't they?"

"That's what caused the Miami blackout," Parra confirmed. "Somebody also tried to fix the cooling system at the power plant so that there'd be a serious leak. The whole thing looks like an inside job. We checked into it, and discovered that one of the technicians disappeared about the same time. He'd been living out in some trailer camp, called Southern Comfort or some hick name like that. He just went missing."

"American?"

"No, Cuban."

Fischer considered this information. "Do you think they're the ones doing this?" he asked. "The Cubans?"

"It's possible," Parra said. One aspect of what was taking place in Miami reminded him of the kidnapping of Senator Fairchild in Puerto Rico. On both occasions, he had formed the clear impression that there was a group involved that was operating completely outside the known radical networks inside the United States. Even when the police and the FBI were able to plant undercover agents inside the identified revolutionary groups, the information they came up with could not help to deal with an independent outfit like this. That might explain why neither the kidnappers nor the Miami saboteurs had been caught.

"When I went down to that course your people run in Quantico," Fischer remarked, "I learned one thing apart from wearing dark glasses in class so the instructor can't tell whether you're asleep. We were given some choice little brochures by Robert Williams. You remember Robert Williams?"

"Sure. The Black Power militant in the sixties. Called himself a Maoist or something."

"Yeah. And he wound up in Cuba. Williams' kick was that you could destroy the United States in about ninety days—I remember he said it would take ninety days—with a mixture of organized terrorism, sabotage and massive fire storms. He wanted black radicals to seize Northern cities, drive people out of the ghettos into the white neighborhoods by setting fires and hold the white suburbs hostage while they set up some kind of separate republic in the South. Black moderates who opposed this were supposed to be bumped off. You think we could be up against something like that?"

"I wouldn't rule *anything* out," Parra responded. "But this thing doesn't seem to be spreading yet. And I don't think Robert Williams has many followers in the black community today."

"As I recall"—Joe Fischer frowned—"Williams also said

254

something about how his terrorist squads would get help from infiltrators inside the police and the armed forces. Now, that hasn't happened yet. But some of these black Fedayeens were in Vietnam."

"Yes."

"And—well, maybe this is way off base, but I was thinking about that burglary a few nights ago in Queens."

"What burglary?"

"There's a clothing store in Queens that supplies a lot of our uniforms," Fischer explained. "Some guys broke in there and just about cleaned them out—uniforms, all sizes, even hats and bats. Now, why would anybody want all those cop clothes? For a fancy-dress party?"

Frank Parra thought about it. Any kind of criminal might be able to make use of a police uniform. There had been plenty of robberies committed by fake cops. There was no reason this should be connected with any riot conspiracy.

Still, Fischer jolted him a little by adding, "There are eight patrol cars reported missing in the city. The number went up as of this morning. Somebody borrowed a car from the Nineteenth Precinct."

That made it considerably more disturbing. Parra had met a smart young crime reporter with one of the local TV stations who managed to go just about anywhere he liked within the city limits, at any speed, by sticking a red light on top of his car and switching on a siren. You could go a damn sight farther in a police car, dressed as one of New York's Finest.

MIAMI

The player in red lunged over to the right, caught the *pelota* in his scoop and fired it back at the far wall. It ricocheted off the hard surface, fast and lethal as a cannonball. The player in blue skipped sidewise, trying to field it, but was not swift enough.

The *pelota* caught him on the forearm. He howled in pain and tumbled onto the floor of the court. There were more hisses than murmurs of sympathy from the sprinkling of spectators on the raised bleachers in front of the court. In the larger area over to the right, beyond the netting, some of the fans who had been watching the game on a huge closed-circuit TV screen started drifting back to the betting counters.

There were more security guards than normal, dotted around the jai alai stadium, to supervise the tens of thousands of dollars changing hands at the betting booths. That was the only sign that the nightly routine had been affected by the events that were convulsing other parts of the city. If anything, the gambling seemed even more frenetic than usual. A little old widow, dressed all in black with an antiquated pillbox hat, plumped down eight hundred dollars on the *quiniela* wheel, playing her favorite number—the day of her wedding—together with all possible combinations. With so much at risk in the city, it seemed reasonable to hazard everything *here*.

There was one man in the crowd who was paying no attention to either the flight of the *pelota* or the numbers that were being called. He paced the netting along the side of the court, or stood seesawing on his heels, looking repeatedly at his watch. The man he was waiting for was late, and Coco Marín felt isolated and exposed.

He had spent a sleepless night, roaming the streets and avoiding the cops, since the raid on his apartment house. He was not sure whether the cops had evidence to link him to the murder of the two women at the hotel, but he was not taking any chances. He wanted to collect his money and get out of town. When he finally made out the familiar, obese figure of Mama Benitez, Parodi's chauffeur, it was all he could do not to go running up to him.

Without giving any sign of recognition, Mama shouldered his way through the spectators and took his stand next to Coco, against the netting, his eyes fixed on the game.

"Do you have the money?" Coco whispered.

"Later," Benitez forcibly whispered back.

"But you promised—"

"Later," Benitez repeated. "The cops have got your partner."

This confirmed Coco's worst fears. He was also astonished that Benitez knew the identity of his partner. "How did you find out?" he murmured, keeping his face turned away from Benitez.

"That doesn't concern you. How much does he know?"

"He knows nothing."

"How did you explain the money?"

"I said it was a contract. That's all. I swear it."

"You'd better not be lying. Did you tell him about me?"

"No. I told you, Vasco knows nothing."

There was scattered applause from the jai alai fans for a good rally between two fresh players on the court. Mama Benitez noticed that the player who finally missed the ball was wearing his own special number, four.

He seized Coco's wrist and squeezed it so tightly that the *marielito* could feel the circulation cut off.

"On your mother's life."

"On my mother's life," Coco dutifully repeated. When the grip on his wrist relaxed, he said, "What about the money?"

"Outside."

From his stool at the snack bar, thirty yards away, Hockney had an unimpeded view of this exchange. He had rented a car in the morning—an old LTD with a souped-up engine that belonged to an auto fanatic who was a friend of Jay Maguire's—and had started making the rounds of Parodi's hangouts. In the afternoon, he had caught sight of the chauffeur leaving the gun shop on Flagler Street. Hockney had decided to tail him, in the hope that he would lead him to Parodi. Instead, Benitez had made what looked like a mail run, dropping in at a bank and at the bungalow headquarters of the Brigada Azul, near the Orange Bowl. Hockney had spent most of the afternoon sitting in the stifling heat, waiting. He was ready to abandon his amateur surveillance when Mama Benitez started out on the road to the airport. Then the chauffeur had pulled off the expressway and left the Dodge in a parking lot on Northwest Thirty-sixth Street, opposite the stadium with its coral-red sign.

Benitez had stopped to place a bet on his way to the court, and for a moment Hockney had been convinced he was wasting his time. The chauffeur was just spending an evening watching jai alai, which was more popular with Cuban betting men than the racetrack or the dogs. It was not until Hockney saw Benitez squeeze the arm of the slightly built young man standing next to him that he realized he was witnessing a meet.

"*¿Teléfono?*" Hockney asked the girl behind the snack bar.

She pointed to a row of pay phones along the passageway.

The receptionist at Police Headquarters had just picked up when Hockney saw Benitez and the younger Cuban walk past him, toward the doors.

"Lieutenant Callahan in Homicide," he gabbled. "It's an emergency."

He was still waiting for Callahan to answer his extension when Benitez pushed through the doors. He dropped the phone and threaded his way through the crowd after them.

He was in time to see Benitez and the other man engaged in some kind of argument beside the Dodge. Benitez pulled a gun, and the younger Cuban stopped protesting and climbed into the car. Hockney, without a weapon of his own, felt naked and helpless. But he got into the LTD and followed the blue Dodge as it cruised along the road and turned left down LeJeune Avenue, trying to keep two or three cars between them.

It had come to him that the Cuban whom Benitez was holding at gunpoint could be only one man: the second killer, Coco Marín.

Mama Benitez headed south along LeJeune Avenue, one hand on the wheel, the other holding the snub-nosed automatic against his well-padded thigh, where Coco Marín could see it.

"Forget the money," the *marielito* was pleading. "Just let me go. I swear I'll never talk to anyone."

"You're right," Benitez said with an unpleasant smile.

He had heard about the arrest of Coco's partner from a con-

"Now, listen, Bob. You're entitled to have any theory you want, but we haven't got one scrap of evidence to tie these killings to Parodi or this fat slob Benitez. You don't *know* that the guy you saw at the jai alai was Coco Marín. You just *want* it to be him. We can't go busting down Mr. Parodi's door on the strength of *that*. The other Mariel has made a confession. He says he and his friend Coco did it, and it was all their own idea. They followed the hooker in off the street, did their stuff and grabbed the money and the jewels."

Hockney did not listen to the end of it. He slammed out the door in disgust. He rode down in the elevator and hurried around the reception desk on the ground floor into the warren of glass-walled cubicles that belonged to the Patrol Unit. The cop manning the reception desk waved at him as he ran past; most people around Headquarters had got to know his face.

He nearly crashed headlong into Wilson Martinez. The Cuban cop thrust out one of his arms to hold them apart. The Cuban's other arm gripped a crutch.

"Sorry," Hockney mumbled. "I have to find Jay."

"You're in luck," Martinez said. "We were just on our way to hit the streets again."

He led Hockney, at a one-legged run, out to the car park where Maguire was waiting with his engine idling. In telegraphese, Hockney told him what he had seen.

"Shit," Maguire said. "We can go get Benitez for dangerous driving. I've always wanted to take a peek inside Parodi's pad. Are you in on this, Wilson?"

"Sure," his partner replied.

"Jeez, you're as crazy as I am. Callahan could try to take away our badges for this."

The excited men with guns who were standing guard over the unofficial roadblock on the Rickenbacker Causeway stepped aside to let the police cruiser pass.

"Look at those assholes," Maguire muttered. "You'd think there was a revolution."

The guards at the checkpoint on the private road leading to

Parodi's apartment complex were less accommodating. They wanted to call up to the penthouse before letting the patrol car through.

"You get that thing up," Maguire said, pointing to the barrier, "or I'll put your ass in a cell."

A young girl in a maid's uniform came to the door of the penthouse. She explained in broken English that Parodi had left that morning and would be abroad for a long time.

"What about Mr. Benitez?" Maguire asked her.

Hockney saw the look of revulsion that went fleeting across her face, and wondered what liberties Mama Benitez was allowed with the household staff.

She said that Benitez had gone too.

Without asking, Maguire walked past the girl and started a room-by-room inspection of the apartment. He whistled at the batteries of electronic equipment and the broad terraces, facing the city and the Atlantic Ocean. He sat down on the circular bed in the master suite and played with the console built into the wall above it. There were a dimmer switch, a button that produced soft music, another that turned on a movie projector. Scenes of a complicated sex act involving two girls, a man and a German shepherd appeared on a screen, reflected in the mirrors that covered the ceiling and most of the walls.

"Nice," Maguire commented, turning off the projector.

Hockney had already gone into the room that most resembled a den. There were modern paintings on the walls, the sort that a man like Parodi might buy by the dozen, sight unseen, with the guarantee that an absurd price tag made them worth something. He had no idea what he was looking for, just the feeling that there had to be something which, inspected properly, would offer some clue.

There were a few scraps of paper scattered on the desk, the kind of things that a man in a hurry might dump on his way to catch a plane—old credit-card receipts, a used airline coupon, a betting slip, a couple of ticket stubs, the business cards of a lawyer and a real estate broker, a bank statement. It all looked innocuous enough. It was not likely, after all, that Parodi would take off leaving compromising evidence conveniently lying about on his desk. Then Hockney examined one of the tickets again. It was a season ticket to Yankee Stadium.

So Parodi likes baseball, he thought. But a season ticket to Yankee Stadium in *New York*? From what he knew of the Cuban's lifestyle, that didn't make sense at all. He tucked the ticket into the breast pocket of his coat.

On a night on which arsonists destroyed the equivalent of five or six city blocks, nobody at Police Headquarters thought much of yet another report from the Fire Department of a DOA— Dead on Arrival. The report was referred to Lieutenant Callahan's unit because of the skull fractures, which could have been inflicted before the boat shed on Northwest Sixteenth Street— a relatively quiet neighborhood near the river—had burned down. The body lay in the posture of a boxer making his last stand, arms outstretched, fists forward, legs bent outward at the knees. This pugilistic stance was characteristic, Callahan knew, of corpses found in fires. The heat of the blaze caused the muscles to contract, just as it slowly cracked skin and soft tissue and caused bones to become brittle, until they splintered. There was not enough left of this corpse to attempt an identification, and no personal effects apart from a few charred fragments of clothing. When they got around to the autopsy the following day, the most that could be established was that the man had almost certainly expired before his body was exposed to the fire. There were no traces of soot or inhaled smoke in his respiratory organs. That pointed to murder, whether or not the fire had been accidental. The case was logged along with the dozens of other cases of unidentified victims on the books of the Crimes Against Persons Unit, to be checked against reports of missing persons. There was no reason, as far as Lieutenant Callahan was concerned, to connect it to the ongoing investigation into the murder of Julia Hockney and her companion.

"I'll find another hotel today," Hockney said to Maguire over breakfast. "I must be getting under your feet."

263

"Shuddup and drink your coffee," Maguire told him. "We're stuck with each other now."

"I'd better at least get my stuff," Hockney said. "I'm wearing out your wardrobe." He looked at the sleeves of the light blue shirt he had borrowed from the cop. The cuffs stopped about two inches short of his wrists.

"Take what you need." Maguire went padding out to the narrow, lightless kitchen. It smelled of old cooking oil and vegetable mold. "I'm hungry," the cop announced. "I got eggs," he added, inspecting the almost empty racks inside the refrigerator.

"That's fine," Hockney called back. He got up and went out to watch Maguire scrambling the eggs with a dab of margarine.

"Jay," he said, "is there some way you could find me Arnold Whitman's home address?"

"Our friendly local spook, huh?" Maguire said without relish. "Yeah, it's about time one of us asked him what kind of deal he's been cutting with Parodi. I can get it," he went on. "That is, if a CIA Station Chief rates a home phone. I've got a friend at the phone company who can get any unlisted number you want."

Maguire stirred the eggs with a spoon to keep them from sticking to the bottom of his blackened saucepan. They came out more gray than yellow.

There was one call that Hockney had decided to make that he did not mention, even though it was Jay Maguire who had first raised the subject with him. He had never owned a gun, never thought of owning one. After the night before, and the bitter frustration of coming so close to two of the men who—he knew in his gut—were responsible for Julia's savage death without being able to touch them, he realized he had to be armed. As Jay might put it, he was not a civilian anymore. He was at war, and would remain at war until he had exacted justice.

Later, when he had been to the gun shop off Flagler Street and paid three hundred dollars for a 9mm Walther P-38—no questions asked—he derived some meager satisfaction from the irony that Julio Parodi, without knowing the fact, had put a gun in his hand.

There were a small, but lovingly tended, garden at the back of Arnold Whitman's house in Miami Beach and a pool, and a pier that jutted out into the Bay. He liked to sit out there when the heat of the day began to fade, with a bottle of Scotch and no light except for the blue glow of the device that his wife, Betsy, had bought to attract and incinerate mosquitoes and other flying bugs. Whitman was stretched out on a La-Z-Boy, half-dozing, remembering how they had had to tie the boat people who had arrived at Crawl Key to the masts and the railings of their fishing vessels to keep them from swarming all over the secret CIA base. In the face of everything, Washington's diktat was still: Send them back. He wondered how many of those who had tried to land on Crawl Key could have survived the outward journey, escorted by a Navy minesweeper that had been called in to relieve the overworked Coast Guard.

He had flown back from the Keys by helicopter that afternoon, and had got a bird's-eye view of the stream of scared residents and tourists that had clogged the Ten-Mile Bridge in their cars. Funny how little it took to cause a panic, he thought. Between the faucets' drying up, and the new wave of boat people, and the rumors of what was going on in Miami, a lot of people in the Keys seemed to believe that their world was coming to an end, and had set off from their homes in their boats or cars. Others had bolted their doors and pulled down their hurricane shutters and were standing guard with shotguns and hunting rifles over their rainwater tanks and their freezers.

At least the new radio link seemed to work. They had tested it in the middle of the night, and got a clear signal from the other end, lasting less than a second: a burst transmission, relayed by satellite, that it would be next to impossible for the Cubans to intercept—or, in the unlikely event it was picked up, to decode. The operator on the Havana side was a sleeper agent whom the CIA had been holding in reserve for more than five years. He would now provide the communications channel between Arnold Whitman and Julio Parodi. It had come together beautifully, Whitman thought. There had been moments when he had doubted Parodi's value, as well as his loyalty, which he had never taken for granted. The latest performance of his comic-opera Brigada Azul in the Miami riots would have made the dullest spectator wonder whose interests its boss was actually serving. But it now looked as if the investment in Parodi were going to pay off handsomely.

He heard the sound of the doorbell, and Betsy's voice from the kitchen.

"I'll get it," she called. He had urged her to go up to her family in Maine and stay there until the riots burned themselves out. But Betsy was a tough Agency wife who had kept her head through coups and insurrections in several Third World countries where they had been posted. She could have taught Quayle, the head of the Agency's Cuba Operations Group, a thing or two.

Whitman guessed that the night caller must be a messenger from the station, no doubt bearing yet another missive from Quayle. But Betsy seemed to be spending a long time in the front room.

"Who is it?" he called through.

Getting no reply, he hauled himself reluctantly out of his lounger and went inside the house. He found Betsy arguing with a tall, youngish man with thick, tousled hair who looked as if he hadn't slept for a couple of nights.

"Who are you?" Whitman challenged him.

"He's a reporter," Betsy said. "I told him you couldn't see him."

"Robert Hockney," he introduced himself.

"It's all right," Whitman said to his wife. Then, to Hockney, "You'd better come with me."

They went into Whitman's den, a stuffy little room that smelled like an ashtray. There were a few plaques on the wall, testimonials from various foreign governments. Whitman extracted a bottle of Famous Grouse from his private hoard and poured each of them a slug.

"It's taken me a long time to find you," Hockney said.

"I guess it has," the Station Chief agreed. "Look. I heard about what happened to your wife. It's a goddamn horrible business. I'm sorry."

"I suppose you also heard about the killers."

"I heard the cops arrested a *marielito*."

"There were two men involved. The second was working for Julio Parodi."

"That's not possible." Whitman retrieved a half-smoked cigar from a big brass ashtray on his desk and tried to relight it. He struck the match awkwardly, and a phosphorus spark flew off, burning a hole in his shirt below the breast pocket.

Hockney began talking fast, and had to slow himself down to avoid tripping over his words. "The second killer was a man called Coco Marín," he explained. "I saw him with Parodi's chauffeur at the Miami Jai Alai last night. Mama Benitez took him away at gunpoint. I lost them, but I know what happened. Benitez murdered him to keep him from talking."

"Bob, I know you're terribly upset—"

"It's not a question of whether I'm upset," Hockney went on, furious now. "I'm telling you what happened. I'm here because I want you to explain *why*."

"I'm afraid you've lost me."

"Have I?" There was suspicion, as well as anger, in Hockney's face. He could not rule out the possibility that Whitman and the CIA were accomplices to the murders and the cover-up. To avoid his eyes, Whitman returned to lighting his cigar. "I want to know what Parodi is trying to hide," Hockney said. "I think you know the answer. My wife was killed because she was meeting another woman—a woman called Gloria—who knew something about Parodi that was so explosive that they had to be murdered so it could remain secret. I know that Parodi was involved with Cuba. That's why the Cubans had me arrested in Havana and tried to blackmail me. I'm sure you know all about *that*."

"Go on."

"I also know that Parodi was working for you."

267

"You don't seriously expect me to comment on that, do you?"

"*Someone* had better start telling me the truth," Hockney yelled at him. He felt the weight of the gun against his ribs, under his jacket, and for a crazy moment he was on the point of pulling it out and brandishing it in Whitman's face. He calmed down enough to add, "The police went around to Parodi's apartment last night. It seems that he's skipped the country. So has Benitez. If you don't level with me, I'm going to put your face on the front page of every newspaper in this country." It was not much of a threat, but it was better than waving the gun.

Whitman considered it in silence for a while, dusting down the front of his shirt.

"You've made some very serious allegations," the Station Chief observed. "Can you prove any of them?"

"I've just told you. I saw Parodi's chauffeur and Coco Marín with my own eyes."

"Can you prove that Benitez killed him? Can you prove that this Coco character was involved in your wife's murder? Are you even sure that the man you saw was Coco Marín?"

Hockney hesitated. The questions were almost identical to the ones Lieutenant Callahan had posed. They penned him in like bars around a cage.

He countered with another question. "What about the fact that Parodi ran away? That proves he's guilty."

"Parodi did not run away." The simple, flat assertion marked a turning point in the conversation. For the first time, Whitman had admitted his relationship with the drug-runner.

"Then where is he?" Hockney asked.

"I can't disclose that."

"Is he in Cuba?"

Whitman scratched the side of his dish-round face and said, "I'm human, Bob. I understand what you're going through. I'm prepared to tell you something as long as it doesn't go outside this room." Hockney saw the old trap opening up in front of him—the snare of supposed confidences, nonattributable lies, or half-lies, whispered behind the hand of someone who could never be held accountable—and was resolved that he would not fall into that trap again. Whatever Whitman told him he was ready to *use*.

"Julio Parodi is a prize bastard," Whitman continued. "But it also happens that at this time he is performing an important mission for this country."

"You mean letting those thugs from the Brigada Azul start a race war in this city?"

"That was unfortunate," Whitman said. "Things got out of hand. I don't believe that Parodi is personally responsible. But frankly, that's secondary."

"Secondary?" Hockney choked on the word. "Have you *seen* what's been happening in this city?"

"I've seen it," Whitman said. "We both know it's a dirty world out there. It's sometimes necessary to make use of people who are less than saints. That's all I'm prepared to say."

"I think you are unbelievable," Hockney said with feeling. Then he fired the question he had waited to ask. "Tell me about Monimbo."

"Monim*bó*?" Whitman corrected his pronunciation. "It's an Indian village in Nicaragua." He seemed only moderately surprised by the mention of the name. Hockney had hoped for a stronger reaction.

Groping in the dark, he said, "What's the connection between Parodi and Monimbó?"

This time he was rewarded. Whitman looked genuinely shaken. "I don't understand," the CIA man said, fumbling with his glass.

"Gloria—the girl who was murdered with my wife—found out something about Monimbó. That's why Parodi had her killed."

"Oh, Jesus," Whitman groaned, and Hockney knew he had found his target. But he still did not know what Monimbó meant.

"I'm going to go public with this unless you give me the whole story." This time, the threat was more effective.

"Off the record," Whitman began. "We got a defector from Nicaragua. This is recent. Within the last week. He was picked up on the Honduran border and asked to be taken to the U.S. Embassy in Tegucigalpa. He's an army lieutenant, just a kid, maybe twenty years old."

"Does he have a name?"

"Díaz. Jesús Díaz." Whitman remembered all the details, because he had glanced through a summary of the debriefing that Quayle had sent down when he got back to the office that morning. "According to Díaz," he resumed, "a secret meeting was held in Monimbó in the summer of 1980. A number of revolutionary leaders from Central America and the United States were present. Fidel Castro made a speech in which he said that the Cubans have a plan to destroy the United States through coordinated acts of sabotage and terrorism and the incitement of race riots in the major cities."

"The Monimbó Plan," Hockney murmured. "What have you done with this Nicaraguan defector?"

"They kept him on ice down there in Honduras."

"In God's name, why?"

"The debriefer rated him a source of doubtful reliability," Whitman reported, looking more than slightly embarrassed. "You remember that other defector from Managua the State Department put on TV a couple of years back? The one that turned around and told the media that he was being forced to tell lies and left the people at State with egg all over their faces?"

"I remember."

"Well, the debriefer got the feeling this guy Díaz was another plant. His story sounded pretty off-base. I mean, he was about seventeen when Castro is supposed to have unveiled this Monimbó Plan. How does a teenager get access to a Top Secret briefing session being stage-managed by the DGI? Our man's instinct was that the Díaz story was a plant and that if the kid was shown to the media, he'd start denying everything and making out that we'd rehearsed him under torture. Or worse, that the Administration might buy the whole package and get so psyched by it that we would end up taking some kind of precipitate action against Castro that would have the whole

270

country rising up in protest. I don't need to remind you what happened when your paper published that piece of disinformation on how we were supposedly planning to invade Nicaragua."

"No."

"And I guess there was another factor in the assessment—what you might want to call a political factor."

"What was that?"

"Well, the FBI Director has gone on record more than once as saying that there's no hard evidence of Cuban involvement in terrorist violence in the United States, if you discount some of the Puerto Rican stuff—and in fact, he hasn't always bothered to make even that qualification. Now, the Agency is not supposed to get involved on the domestic front, right? How is it going to look if we suddenly produce a report that Castro has a plan to blow up our cities, without any supporting evidence except the word of some Nicaraguan kid who may or may not stick by his original version if we stand him up in front of the TV cameras? Do you follow? I mean, what would your editors say if you walked in on them and declared that Fidel was planning a race war in the United States, and you had nothing more to go on than that?"

"They'd probably think I'd joined the John Birch Society." Hockney could picture Ed Finkel's face, puckered with disdainful incredulity. "But it's not much of a comparison," he continued. "I don't have Julio Parodi on my payroll."

Whitman was weighing the implications of what Hockney had told him. In all his meetings with Parodi, the Cuban had never revealed his knowledge of any Monimbó Plan. Yet the fact that the call girl knew something about it suggested that Parodi had been directly involved, and that all the time he had been keeping Langley happy with tidbits of information—leads that had resulted in the arrest of a couple of low-level DGI agents and the capture of several arms shipments to guerrillas in Central America—his primary loyalty had been to Havana. It meant that the dangerous operation on which the CIA was now embarked inside Cuba could be a DGI ruse, a time bomb set to blow up in the Agency's face in such a way that it would provoke—and justify—the next phase of the Monimbó Plan. What better way to set the scene for a nationwide wave of demonstrations and riots than to implicate the CIA in another assassination attempt against Fidel Castro?

Hockney was thinking about a related question. If there really was a Monimbó Plan, what was the next step? The Miami riots were spectacular fireworks, but no more than fireworks as far as most of the country was concerned. They had left the other cities untouched. Where, and how, would the Cubans strike next?

Chapter

9

NEW YORK

Crossing the Triborough Bridge, the man in the back seat of the big car watched the East River skyline draw together like a concertina until the gaunt housing projects of Harlem, in colors of rust and dung, screened out the cathedrals of capitalism downtown. The whole scene folded back like a pop-up diorama in a children's book, and then the car was making the loop down to the FDR Drive along the river. It was a fancy car, a gray stretch limousine which made the bumps and dips in the road feel like deep-pile carpet, and the driver up front was wearing a chauffeur's cap and a little bow tie and a suit that was black enough for a pallbearer. It was not so fancy that anyone would crick his neck to look at it, not in Manhattan, where stretch limos are less unusual than air-conditioned subway cars or a biker who stops for a red light. The limousine had smoked-glass windows, the kind that are supposed to deter people from coming up and peering in and asking, "Are you anybody?"

The man in the back had an old-fashioned whitewall haircut

that made him look as if he had just stepped out of the frame of a Norman Rockwell barbershop. He wore a club tie and a starched white shirt with a natty gold pin through the collar and tinted lenses that changed with the light. He did not look much like the man Hockney had seen on the deck of the *Duchess,* staring wildly across the choppy waters to San Juan. You would guess that his destination was Wall Street, or maybe Madison Avenue.

But as they glided through the U.N. underpass, the driver called back, "Coming up now."

The limousine pulled into the right lane, slowing from thirty-five to fifteen.

Beacher fiddled with a watch that would not have looked out of place on the control deck of the space shuttle, then hit a button on the right-side door, so that the window came sliding smoothly down.

On the block between Thirty-ninth and Thirty-eighth Streets, clearly visible over a brick wall topped with razor wire, was a big raspberry-colored transformer, surrounded by a jumble of coils and pipes and porcelain bells.

The chauffeur accelerated as the transformer passed out of view.

He said, "You got it?"

"Easy," Beacher replied.

There had been time enough to fire one, possibly two rifle bullets into the oil-coolant tank attached to the high-voltage transformer, without having to stop the car. Beacher glanced back at the ugly smokestacks of the Waterside generating plant the transformer served.

The big car cruised on, past Bellevue Hospital and the barrackslike low-rent apartment houses of Stuyvesant Town, their bleakness relieved a little by elms and birches. The green sign overhead read, "EXIT 6—E. 15 ST."

The driver pointed and said, "There."

Sandwiched between two huge Con Edison buildings Beacher saw the second transformer, as easy a target as the first.

"It belongs to *that*," the driver said, nodding toward another collection of smokestacks. "The East River power plant. Something blew up in there by accident a couple of years back. The lights went out in the Village, SoHo, Little Italy, the Lower East Side, Wall Street, the whole shebang. You want to take another look? We can get off at Houston and swing back the other way."

"No," Beacher responded. "Let's go down to the World Trade Center."

"You're the boss."

The skin at the back of the driver's neck had the smooth creaminess of milk chocolate. Beacher was pleased with his guide. He knew the city well; he was efficient and not talkative. He moved with a quiet sense of purpose, and did not ask about things he did not need to know. In Cuba, he had acquired the nickname Bujía—Spark Plug—because of his keen interest in cars and their insides. The tag Plug had stuck to him. Born in Brooklyn, brought up in a single-parent family, Plug had taken no real interest in politics until he received his draft card during the Vietnam War. Then he had attended an antiwar teach-in at a community center on the Lower East Side. One of the side-shows had been an enthusiastic account of life in Cuba by a young activist who had just returned from Havana. He urged anyone who wanted to help the cause of liberation in the Western Hemisphere to join the Venceremos Brigades. He didn't talk about the pleasures of sailing to Havana on a converted cattle boat from the frozen port of St. John in Canada, or the backbreaking, monotonous drudgery of harvesting sugar cane, which seems, after a few hours, like cutting steel spaghetti, or the other experiences of the first recruits for the Venceremos Brigades. He made his season in Cuba sound magical. He was looking at Plug when he declared that in Cuba there was only one race, the human race.

Plug was proud to think of himself as a member of an elite force. He was having a grand time play-acting up in front of the stretch limousine with the man in the back seat who looked like a preppy broker from Connecticut with two-point-one kids but had ice in his veins and knew everything about plastic there was to know.

"Pick me up in twenty minutes," Beacher said when the car pulled up on West Street outside One World Trade Center.

There was no romance about the World Trade Center. Its twin towers soared for a hundred and ten stories, and then stopped abruptly, as if the builders had been told, "That's enough. We're bigger than anyone else in New York." They were a solid assertion of size and commercial power: no place here for the Art Deco excesses of the Chrysler Building, or the rakish slant of the Citicorp complex, for dash or flourish or filigree. But fifty thousand people went to work every day in the twin towers and the other buildings on its sixteen-acre site.

Atop the giant tower Beacher was now entering was a three-hundred-sixty foot mast supporting a cluster of TV and radio antennas which sent out the signals of all the commercial broadcast stations in the metropolitan area, while the Cable News Network had its studios on the ground floor.

The Center was patrolled by only thirty Port Authority cops, whose headquarters was hidden away on the same subbasement level as the PATH train terminal. Beacher had taken note that the Center had five emergency generators which were supposed to keep the lights on and the elevators moving for a few hours in the event the normal flow of seven hundred thousand kilo-watt-hours of electricity a day from the Con Ed grid should be cut off.

Beacher crossed the immense lobby of One World Trade Center, and its sea of wall-to-wall purple carpet, carrying two nondescript Samsonite suitcases. He set them down by the first desk on the right—the Federal Express desk—as he surveyed the airline counters farther along and then, directly in front of him, the core of the great building: two gigantic elevator shafts, encased in white marble, containing dozens and dozens of moving cars. Some of the elevators traveled nonstop to the seventy-seventh floor, or the Skylobby on the forty-fourth, where you could switch to another car to ride up to the plush Windows on the World restaurant or the rooftop promenade. Beacher watched hundreds of people hurrying in and out of the banks of elevators, and their milling patterns made him think of a beehive.

There was no sign of a guard, only an elderly man at the information desk reading the baseball page of the afternoon paper.

Beacher picked up his suitcases and strode briskly toward the bank of elevators that serviced floors 33 to 40. Scores of people waiting for the next car paid no attention to him as he positioned himself against the wall at the end of the aisle and set down his bags. He waited until an elevator arrived and the people started pushing forward to get in before glancing at his watch with an expression that suggested he had just remembered something. Then he walked off at the same brisk pace, the image of a responsible, even severe man of affairs who knew exactly what he was doing. He swung through the revolving glass doors that led to the underground concourse, with its shops and restaurants. He waited a full twelve minutes before he returned upstairs to pick up his bags. Nobody had interfered with them. Nobody paid him any attention when he collected them.

It would be just as simple as Plug had told him, Beacher thought as he walked out through the West Street entrance. He had been a little skeptical before making his dry run, and had even rehearsed the explanation he had intended to give if anyone challenged him about the suitcases—a banal story about how he wanted to make some purchases in the shopping mall and needed the bags to take them home. But there was still no guard to be seen anywhere as he left the building.

Plug took the suitcases and put them back into the trunk of the limousine.

The black driver raised a questioning eyebrow as they drove off, and Beacher gave a thumbs-up sign.

When he revisited the World Trade Center, the suitcases would contain a hundred and fifty pounds of PETN plastic explosive—enough to gut the core of the tower with the TV mast on top, and set the police and emergency services of the entire city to flapping about like a chicken without a head.

WASHINGTON, D.C.

"How long has Julio Parodi been on the Company payroll?"

The CIA Director looked at Quayle, who looked at Whitman.

It was Arnold Whitman who replied: "Since 1960, on and off."

"How many times has he been polygraphed?"

"Five, maybe six times. But you can't trust those things to tell you more than whether the subject's sweat glands are working."

They were sitting in the Director's office on the top floor of the CIA headquarters in Langley, Virginia, a building with as much personality as a refrigerator. But Blair Collins had had his office redecorated with a few good pieces of furniture and some paintings from his private collection. An Escher lithograph on the wall had caught Whitman's eye, one of those curious geometric compositions in which vaguely sinister, medieval figures toiled up and down staircases. All rules of perspective had been suspended; the way up was also the way down. The picture seemed the right choice for this room.

Blair Collins said, "You're telling me we can't trust Parodi anymore because a whore he used had heard of Monimbó."

"That's what I'm saying," Whitman agreed.

"In other words, we've been taken."

"That's how it looks to me."

Quayle was trying to catch his eye. Quayle liked to come right up to you and look you straight in the eye. He thought he could catch people off balance that way. Whitman stared out the window, toward the woods beyond the Company car park.

Quayle said, "I don't think we ought to rush to conclusions. Sure, Parodi may have held out on us. He's that type. He'll cheat anytime he thinks he can get away with it. But he's given us some good stuff. We oughtn't to scrap this whole operation because he didn't tell us about something in Nicaragua. That's assuming the whore heard about Monimbó from him, and wasn't fed the story by somebody else in order to confuse us."

"Confuse us?" Whitman echoed in disbelief. "The whore—and Robert Hockney's wife—were murdered so none of this would get out."

"That's purely speculative," Quayle objected. "Miami Homicide thinks it was a random sex killing."

"Miami cops aren't infallible."

"Does it actually matter?" Quayle sniffed. "Suppose you're right. Suppose Parodi had the women terminated because he thought the hooker was an informer. What's it mean? Maybe all it means is he was scared he would have to face another drug rap."

The sound that escaped from Whitman's mouth was like wind rushing out of a bellows.

He said, "You can believe whatever you want to believe. I'm saying that there is a Monimbó Plan, and that Parodi knew about it, and that he's been ready to kill more than once to keep anyone outside the DGI from figuring out his real game."

"That's a hell of an accusation to bring against someone you've been running for years," Blair Collins observed. "I remember when I took over this office, I was given to understand that Daiquiri was about the best thing we had going in Cuba. I sent several reports based on his information to the President. And now . . . Jesus, I don't even want to think about it. What's our next move?"

"We have to cut our losses," Whitman said. "We have to roll up the Cuban operation—or at any rate, postpone it—until we can get hold of Parodi and put him through the wringer. The whole network he's involved with inside Cuba must be regarded as compromised, and treated accordingly. We must assume that radio signals coming out of the Havana transmitter are monitored by the DGI, if not actually dictated by them. And we'd better get ready for the publicity fallout if the Cubans decide to do an Otto John stunt with him." The name of Otto John was legendary in intelligence circles: the former West German security chief had been lured to East Berlin—or else had defected, but no one was ever quite sure—and put in front of TV cameras to denounce the crimes of his own service. Blair

Collins winced at the thought of Julio Parodi holding a press conference in Havana to disclose the details of the CIA operation in which he was involved.

"We have another option," Quayle rapped, and the CIA Director transferred his attention to the little man with a glimmer of hope in his pale, bulging eyes. "Aggressive CI," Quayle went on. The chief of the Cuba Operations Group could never resist a buzzword. "Now, I'm not saying Arnie is wrong. We've played Parodi—Daiquiri—as a double, and it's certainly possible that somewhere along the line the Cubans put the thumbscrews on and turned him. It might have happened last week, or it might have happened in the early sixties."

"I would bet it happened in the early seventies," Whitman chipped in, "when we gave him and a lot of the other contract paramilitaries the pink slip."

"That's as may be." Quayle pursued his theme. "Right now, the question is pretty theoretical. We have Parodi in place in Havana, in touch with an underground group that represents the most dangerous opposition that Fidel has had to square up to in a couple of decades."

"Or so he claims," said Whitman.

Quayle refused to be derailed. "Look, I won't argue with you, Arnie. It could all be a lot of cigar smoke. What we know—at any rate, what we've been told—is that there are some top military and intelligence people in Havana who want to dump Castro. They're resentful of the way their Soviet big brothers go throwing their weight around, and they'd like to open up trade with the United States and get some hard currency to start rebuilding the economy. And they're not averse to private gain. *That* much we're sure of, right? We know that Parodi's been making some big payoffs to generals in the DGI and admirals in the Cuban Navy who've been helping him smuggle his dope into this country. We know about the transfers he's made to banks in Panama and Mexico and to numbered accounts in Switzerland. I'm sure the distinguished Cuban socialists who've been on the take from Parodi don't appreciate the prospect of being sent to jail for accepting graft. That means we have some control over them."

"Have we?" Whitman said mockingly. He had done some brainstorming since his session with Hockney, and nothing looked quite the same to him as it had the day before. "I suspect that all we've been doing was helping ensure a flow of operational funds for the DGI. Okay, Calixto Valdés or General Abrahantes could have been skimming some cream off the top, but I'm beginning to doubt that. I think the whole arrangement has been controlled by the DGI all along."

"Suppose you're wrong?" Quayle challenged him. "We'd be abandoning a unique opportunity. If there's even a twenty-percent chance that Parodi has been on the level with us, I think we ought to follow through. That way, we'll find out soon enough if we've been had. Now, we've been told there's a group in Havana that is ready to attempt an anti-Soviet coup that would solve most of our problems around Central America. All they're asking from us is a guarantee that we'll back them up if they succeed and the Russians try to intervene."

"You haven't mentioned the best part," Whitman remarked. "They also asked us to supply the special weapon that is supposed to be used to knock off Castro, and a radio link from Havana. That means we're in it up to our eyeballs."

"So what have we got to lose?" Quayle parried. "If we let the plot go ahead, we'll find out soon enough if Parodi belonged to us or the DGI. At the worst, we'll be accused of cloak-and-dagger meddling. At best, we'll be rid of Castro."

"I think you're crazy," Whitman protested. When the plan to kill Castro had first been raised by Parodi, he had reported it to Langley with profound misgivings. He had a clear enough recollection of the ludicrous conspiracies that were hatched in the heyday of the Kennedys, plots involving poisoned cigars and wet suits and Mafia hit men, to have a healthy skepticism about any new proposals to remove Fidel. He suspected that the death of Fidel would result in a takeover, teleguided from Moscow, by the most unconditionally pro-Soviet elements in the Cuban regime, for all Parodi's talk about the growing strength of a secret resistance organization. Now he was inclined to believe that the assassination plan had been cooked up in the twelve-story building at the corner of Linea and A Street in Vedado that housed the headquarters of the DGI.

What surprised him was the enthusiasm with which the higher-ups had seized on Parodi's tale of a clandestine plot against Castro. He knew this enthusiasm extended as high as the White House. Reluctantly, he had carried out the order to present Parodi with a ball-point pen with the name of an East German manufacturer on the clip. The plastic shell of the pen concealed a small vial of inert gas, capable of ejecting a stream of minuscule cyanide crystals over a distance of three feet. A victim would appear to have died of a heart attack. Only a microscopic examination of the victim's face would reveal traces of the cyanide crystals—and such an inspection was unlikely to be carried out until hours after the pen had been used. The weapon had been supplied from the CIA's arsenal of exotic killing devices. In Parodi's hands, it might now constitute physical proof of the Agency's complicity in a plot to kill Fidel. So there was some merit in Quayle's argument. If Parodi was an *agent provocateur* for the Cubans, the CIA was going to be embarrassed anyway. Why tear up the betting slip before the race began?

But Whitman continued: "If we abort the operation and order Parodi to attend a meet outside Cuba, we'll force him to show his hand. At the least, we'll be able to prove that we never went ahead with the plot against Castro. Can you imagine what the political fallout is going to be like if all this is made public? It could make the nuclear-freeze rallies and the vigil over Nicaragua look like garden parties. It's certainly the last thing the President needs for his election campaign."

Blair Collins, a Newgate appointee and one of the President's closest friends, was impressed by this argument.

"Whitman's right," he told Quayle. "We have to abort. Can you get the signal through right away?"

"We'll have to check the frequencies," Quayle said.

"Do it now," the CIA Director ordered. "Here, use my phone."

Quayle perched on the edge of the Director's desk and called down to his assistant. His expression changed as he listened to the man on the other end of the line. When he put down the receiver, his mouth was creased in a confident smirk, and his flat brown eyes shone brightly.

"No go," Quayle said.

"Whaddya mean, no go?" Collins snapped. His patience, never unlimited, was beginning to wear thin, and he was having trouble working out how he would relay what had happened to the President.

"Crawl Key picked up a signal from Havana," Quayle explained. "They just got through rerecording and decoding. Daiquiri says the operation is all set for Thursday. They're following Plan E. He said they're suspending the radio link because they think state security has picked up the traffic."

"You mean we've got no way of communicating with Parodi?"

Quayle shook his head. He looked as if he had just won a small prize in a lottery.

"We could send a man in," Whitman contributed. "It wouldn't be hard with all these boat people being sent back. Or we could call in a favor from our friends at one of the European embassies in Havana. The Brits and the Italians both owe us one."

"Very risky," said Quayle. "If Parodi is still our man, we might blow him sky-high. And if he isn't, we'd blow yet another asset."

Collins massaged the loose flesh under his chin.

"You could be right," Blair Collins conceded. "What's Plan E?"

"The boat people we're sending back to Cuba," Quayle began. "Fidel's putting them in a holding area—a concentration camp, by the sound of it—not far from our base in Guantánamo. He wants to make a big spectacle of the fact that Uncle

Sam is no longer willing to play host to Cubans who want to bail out of the socialist paradise. We knew he was going to make a big speech there. I guess it's set for Thursday."

The CIA Director's hand moved up to his earlobe. He started kneading it. "Guantánamo, huh?" he repeated.

"Yes, sir."

"That doesn't mean the assassin might try and make a run for it into U.S. territory, does it?"

"I'm not aware that there was any provision for that in the plan," Quayle responded in correct bureaucratese, but his confidence had begun to slip a bit.

Whitman said, "We're being set up."

Blair Collins got up from his desk so fast that he set his swivel chair spinning and created a blur of papers over the vast expanse of his mahogany desk. "I gotta go to the White House," he said. "You better see if you can get that radio to work. If we can't reach Daiquiri"—he glared at Quayle—"you better get your ass out to Guantánamo and practice some damage limitation. Do you read me?"

"Yes, sir," Quayle replied, chastened. "I'll talk to the Pentagon."

"Mr. Director," Whitman called to him as he scooped up an attaché case the size of a carpetbag and reached for the soft felt hat on the stand. "There's one thing more."

"Yes?"

"The Monimbó Plan. We've been sitting on the debriefing reports from that Nicaraguan defector."

"I saw that. How was he graded?"

"Unknown reliability, sir."

"Change it to usually reliable and get those reports out to the Bureau and the other agencies. And Whitman—how much does Robert Hockney know about all of this?"

"He's got Parodi's number. He doesn't know what Parodi's doing in Cuba. I think he's trying to check out Parodi's connections inside this country."

"Okay. What's the name of his editor?"

"Leonard Rourke," Quayle responded.

"I know Rourke. Haven't we got something on him?"

"He worked for us on contract in the early fifties," Quayle said helpfully.

"He hasn't done much for us lately," Director Collins commented, bristling at the memory of the Nicaragua "leak."

Quayle said, "Maybe you ought to talk to him."

"I might just do that."

NEW YORK

Glacken's, on the Grand Concourse in the Bronx, was a serious drinking establishment. There were no stools along the bar; you stood up until you were ready to fall down. They sold two-ounce shots of neat liquor for a buck forty, or mixed drinks in glasses big enough to bail out a yacht. There was an old black-and-white TV for the patrons. Across the street was a ritzy old bingo parlor, lit up like Radio City. By night, the sky above Glacken's was a shimmering electric blue, the reflected glare of the lights at Yankee Stadium.

Frank Parra was drinking bonded bourbon without the trimmings. Above his shoulder hung a picture of a green nude, her torso the color of seaweed, and a poster advertising some benefit for the Guardians, the housing cops' association. It was a good place to get tight, or to drink yourself sober. Hockney was approaching the far side of that bridge. He was starting to feel wonderfully in command of himself, and his world. He knew he could explain everything to Frank Parra, if only his swollen tongue would go back to its normal size and let the words come out right.

Parra offered him a Camel. He took it, but the taste wasn't right, and the paper stuck to his chapped lower lip like adhesive tape.

"Are you feeling okay?" the FBI man said.

Hockney said, "Never better." But his legs buckled as if someone had unscrewed the joints.

"We better sit down."

There were a couple of tables over by the TV, and Hockney bumped into only one of them before he got to a chair. His body was an embarrassment, but he experienced a marvelous sense of clarity, as if he had finally broken through dense undergrowth into a clearing on high ground. He might pay for it in the morning, but he was ready to go on all night.

"Ever been to Yankee Stadium?" Parra was asking.

"Oh, yeah. I went last season. The Yankees were playing the Rangers and Dave Winfield hit a home run." The words came more easily now. He was thinking about Parodi's season ticket. It was hard to picture the Cuban sitting up there on the bleachers eating hot dogs and yelling, "Charge!" when the organist drummed out the Yankees' call to battle. He told the FBI man about the season ticket he had seen in Parodi's apartment on Key Biscayne.

Parra wiped his mouth and said, "I know another Cuban who's a Yankee fan. From where I sit, he's the most interesting Cuban in the state of New York. Ever hear of Teófilo Gómez?"

The name set off a peal of bells. Gómez was a minister at the Cuban Mission to the U.N., and the DGI Station Chief in New York, and the man who had arranged the trip to Havana during which Hockney had been neatly fitted for a frame. And—Hockney was pretty sure of it—Gómez was Angela Seabury's sometime lover.

He said to Parra, "Do you figure Gómez was the reason Parodi was going to Yankee Stadium?"

"You call," the FBI man suggested. "Listen, we have a couple of Agents on this Cuban's tail all the time. He gets around. We've tracked him to Coney Island, to a Chinese restaurant in Queens, to the bear cage in the Bronx Zoo, to the Godbox."

"The Godbox?"

"That church center in Riverdale. We've tagged him to a millionaire's mansion in Southampton and a gay bar on Christopher Street. We've never yet been able to sit in on a clandestine meet. We'd need a dozen guys for that, and we just don't have them. Gómez is a pro. He likes to play subway tag. But his favorite place for losing a tail is Bloomingdale's."

"Anyone can get lost in Bloomie's," Hockney observed. "I get lost there myself."

"I tell you," said Parra, "this city is paradise for a spy. You can talk with any foreign accent and still pass for a native New Yorker."

"Unless you speak English," Hockney commented. "I mean, unless you talk like a Limey."

"I can't think of a better city in the world to arrange a dead drop or fix a clandestine meet," Parra pursued. "And communications are a dream. Just about anywhere you go, there's a kiosk where you can make a phone call for a dime. Then you've got the biggest safe house for spies in the world—the U.N. building—and all those church centers, like the Godbox, that we're not supposed to touch because they're religious institutions. The main risk for a spy in New York is of getting mugged."

"I can see you're in love with the place."

Frank Parra contemplated their empty glasses. He said, "Reporters drink too much."

"You're right," said Hockney. "Almost as much as cops and Bureau people. I'll buy."

This time he made it to the bar and back without spilling a drop. A couple of gnarled old-timers in the corner were talking about how the third Yankee manager of the season had got fired. The door of Glacken's was open, but it seemed as airless outside as in. A still, baked heat rose from the pavement. It was a night like a collapsed lung, a night when husbands and wives went squalling at each other in their still, boxlike rooms for ventilation and tough kids prowled the streets to make a breeze.

Hockney said, "What do you figure Teófilo Gómez wanted with Parodi?"

"You're the one who seems to have all the answers tonight," the FBI man told him. "We know that Parodi peddles dope and guns and doubles in brass for the Cubans and our kissing cousins at Langley. You believe that Parodi was a base hitter in the Miami riots, and that they were just a tryout for something bigger, something called the Monimbó Plan. Well, it could be New York is the next target. In which case, we're looking for something special that your Cuban friend could contribute."

"How about guns?" Hockney proposed. "I visited his arms business in Miami. Camagüey Internacional. They seem to be shipping all over the world."

"Guns for who?" Parra asked him. "There are about a million unlicensed guns in this town already. Anybody who wants a rod can get one, whatever the Mayor says. And suppose Parodi did bring in some hardware. Who gets to use it? The Fedayeen? The Puerto Rican terrorists? Or are they just going to drive a truck around the South Bronx handing out M-Sixteens to anybody who wants one?"

"I don't know." Hockney brushed away a fly that had settled on the lip of his glass.

"We have to ask ourselves what the Cubans want to get out of this. And what the Soviets expect to gain, since I imagine Fidel would need a green light from Moscow to mount an operation on the scale you're talking about."

Hockney thought about it. The Soviets' calculations were not easy to read. They had plenty to keep them busy in their own backyard—Poland, Afghanistan, the mess they had made of their economy. On top of that, it was obvious that the power struggle inside the Kremlin had not ended with the election of Yuri Andropov to succeed Brezhnev. It was anyone's guess how long the former KGB boss would be warming his present seat. Was it really conceivable that the new Soviet leader—a ruthless pragmatist whose highest principle was personal survival—would risk his tenuous grasp on supreme power by licensing Castro to initiate an undeclared war on the United States whose consequences could not be predicted?

"There are two possibilities," Hockney suggested. "Either Fidel has slipped the leash and taken advantage of the confusion in Moscow to pursue his private vendetta against this

288

country. Or else Moscow is giving him secret backing, on the understanding that nothing that takes place will be directly attributable to the Soviets. I'd bet that the second version is nearer the truth," he went on. "After all, the Monimbó Plan wasn't hatched yesterday. Andropov was running the KGB when that meeting in Nicaragua was held in 1980." He was reminded of something the Russian dissident Vladimir Bukovsky had said on an American television show soon after Andropov's elevation to the post of General Secretary had been announced. "You will soon feel Andropov's hand on your throat," Bukovsky had warned, angrily dismissing the opinions of Kremlin-watchers in the State Department and the media who had expressed the hope that the former Secret Police chief might prove himself to be a "closet liberal."

"The Soviets feel vulnerable," Hockney pursued. "So does Castro. They both see themselves losing ground. They see America in the process of rearming. They fear that the Newgate Administration may seize the opportunity to reclaim a little lost real estate—if not in Central America, then somewhere else."

"You're saying what they want to do is give the President so many headaches at home that he won't be able to act abroad," Frank Parra interjected.

"Something like that. And if I'm right—if their objective is to sow urban chaos and race hatred across the United States— then New York matters a lot. It's the biggest showcase in the world. Whatever happens here is theater for the world. If I'm right," he repeated, looking at Parra, whose clouded glass seemed to be stuck to his mouth—"if New York is the next target, would you have any warning? Would you know the signs?"

Parra set down his glass and said, "I'll tell you when it happens."

It had seemed to Hockney that Frank Parra was the right man to turn to after he got through talking to Arnold Whitman in Miami. Whitman had promised to check into Parodi's bank accounts and the affairs of Camagüey Internacional, and to let him know if he found anything that might tie in with Monimbó.

But Hockney did not trust the CIA man. Hockney counted on his cop friend, Maguire, to keep the pressure on Lieutenant Callahan to pursue the homicide investigation; so far, the Mariel they had picked up at the Sugar Shack was sticking to the story Callahan wanted to buy—that he and his crony had picked on the two women at random, because it was a hot night, and the city was being turned inside out, and they were *there*.

As for the riots, the worst of the damage seemed to have been done, and the citizens of South Florida were left to count the cost—in lives, and gutted buildings, and the loss of a sense of community and self-esteem. The opposing black leaders, Commander Ali and Wright Washington, had both left town. Commander Ali was being sought by the FBI on conspiracy charges, and Wright Washington had appeared on Angela's TV show and bitterly condemned the actions of the National Guard in Liberty City, warning that if the authorities failed to recognize that the riots had been a means of getting attention for a community that had been badly neglected, then the riots could be repeated somewhere else.

So Hockney had come up to New York, because of a hunch about a season ticket to Yankee Stadium, because there was a man there he could trust who might be better able to prise information that he needed out of the vaults of the intelligence agencies, and because he wanted to get away from the place where Julia had been killed. When he crawled from Glacken's bar into Parra's car, and he watched the lights along the Harlem River as they crossed the Third Avenue Bridge, a single resolve burned inside his head like a steady flame. He would avenge Julia's death.

Parra said to him in a soft whiskey voice, "Have you got a license for that thing?"

The question caught Hockney off guard. He hadn't mentioned the Walther, and he was wearing a coat. But it was dumb of him not to have realized that Parra would notice.

He mumbled, and Parra went on: "They'll put you away for a year in this city if they catch you packing heat. I've got a friend who can take care of it. You can get a license in Nassau County in about the time it takes to gargle a fifth."

"Thanks."

"Hey, if you start thanking me, I'm going to change my mind. Anyway, I need you to do the legwork on this case."

Hockney still carried a press card that said he was employed by The New York World Company, but he had not had much contact with his colleagues since he had come back from Cuba and found that they had cleaned out his desk for him.

He was now trekking across midtown toward the *World* building on Eighth Avenue, a sooty fortress complete with flying buttresses and gargoyles and a clock that sometimes gave the right time. He had put up at the St. Regis, because the King Cole Bar there was a good place to talk; people didn't crowd you, the martinis came in perfectly chilled glasses with long twisted stems and the waitresses had smiles that didn't look as if they had been frosted on with a cake decorator's cone. The *World* building shared its block with an X-rated movie house, a topless bar and a couple of peep-show arcades. Hockney sidestepped a wino in an ancient tailcoat who was sprawled out across the sidewalk and made his way up the wide, shallow steps into the home of the paper that made the proud boast on its masthead "ALL THE NEWS IN THE WORLD."

The Executive Editor of the *World* said, "You look terrible," and Hockney accepted that, along with another cup of coffee. In fact, it was Len Rourke who looked as if he were on his last legs. His sunken cheeks were hot and flushed, but the rest of his face was parchment white. He looked as if he had been stitched together from spare parts. That worried Hockney, because Rourke was the one man in the *World*'s editorial offices he knew he could count on.

"Is there going to be a memorial service?" Rourke asked.

"It'll be at St. Bart's. Friday after next," Hockney told him, feeling momentarily guilty that he had left all the arrangements to Julia's mother.

"We'll all be there," Rourke said. "She was a helluva nice girl." Rourke himself had been through two divorces, and knew how loss ages a man. "If there's anything I can do . . ." His voice trailed off.

"I came to talk to you about a story," Hockney said.

"Talk to me."

"Have you heard of Monimbó?"

Rourke tasted the awkward word. "We had a piece a while back," he ruminated. "I guess you were away."

"About Monimbó?"

"Yeah. There were some disturbances there. Some priest got himself arrested, and there were antigovernment demonstrations. Some kids took over the Catholic school. The government said it was all part of an American plot."

"That would fit." Hockney started to tell him the story of the defector from Nicaragua, and the plan that Fidel Castro had unveiled in Monimbó. Then he explained why he thought the Cubans had stoked up the racial fires in Miami. Finally he got round to Julio Parodi.

Rourke was fidgeting, shifting his weight from one narrow buttock to the other. But he heard Hockney out.

Then he said, "You recall what I said to you when you started out on this paper? We publish the news. We don't create it. That still holds good, Bob. You spin a damn fine yarn, but you haven't given me one solid fact to hang a story on. You're a good enough reporter to recognize that."

"Suppose I fly down to Honduras and get the defector's story out of the horse's mouth?"

The noise that Rourke's teeth made when he was agitated sounded like the distant chatter of a typewriter. He said, through the teeth, "The trouble with defectors is their memories seem to get better from month to month. Especially when they get a little coaching. We can't take a stand on what some teenager from Nicaragua might say."

"Well, what about David Priest?"

"Who?"

"Commander Ali. The leader of the Black Fedayeen. We

know he was trained in Cuba."

"That doesn't prove that he's taking orders from Havana now."

"And what about the Brigada Azul?" Hockney went on, ignoring his editor's objections.

"They're rightists, for Chrissake."

"Well, who says that rightist groups can't be penetrated and used by the Cubans, or the Soviets? We know there are neo-Nazis in Europe who have ties to the East Germans and the PLO. We know how easy it is for Castro to get agents inside these émigré networks. And we know that Julio Parodi is the Daddy Warbucks of the Brigada Azul."

Rourke was messing around with a battery of medicine bottles. He took one pill from each, and swigged the lot down with a gulp of water. Obviously, his triple bypass had not ended his problems. Hockney watched him with a mixture of anger and compassion.

"I think you're on the weakest ground of all with Parodi," Rourke said when he had finished dosing himself. "You've convinced yourself that he's working for Castro. Now, I'm ready to believe that some officials in Havana are on the take from him and from some of these other dopers. That kind of thing happens in the best-regulated families. But if there's a chance, even an outside chance, that Parodi is our man . . ."

He started coughing, an unpleasant, ratcheting cough, as if the pills had got stuck in his throat, and Hockney parroted, "Our man?"

"I'm saying," Rourke resumed after swallowing some more water, "that if there's just one chance in ten that this Cuban's loyalties are to the United States, we could be putting his life in danger by printing your allegations. Not to mention what our lawyers might say about million-dollar libel suits."

The skewer on the right side of Hockney's head seemed to sink in an inch deeper. He didn't like the sound of what Rourke was saying. The Executive Editor had never raised the same objection to Jack Lancer's stories about CIA operations. Hockney knew that Rourke felt vulnerable on that front because, back in the heyday of the Congress for Cultural Freedom, when the CIA had been uninhibited about using media cover, the Executive Editor of the *World* had had relations with the Agency that extended beyond a cozy buddy-buddy acquaintanceship. That, at any rate, was stale gossip around the corridors of *The New York World*, and Hockney suspected that it was why Len Rourke, by temperament a Cold War liberal, was so supine in his handling of Ed Finkel and Jack Lancer and the steel-rimmed radical who decided what appeared on the Op-Ed page. It had never occurred to him that the Agency might still have a handle on Rourke. It occurred to him now, because Rourke's argument so exactly paralleled Arnold Whitman's.

"I've talked to the CIA man who was Parodi's case handler," Hockney said. "I know that Parodi had the Agency pretty well fooled. Maybe he's *still* got the CIA fooled. But don't you see what that means? I don't know what he's supposed to be doing inside Cuba, but I know one thing—it's going to end in disaster unless Washington wakes up. I think we have a responsibility to print what we know and blow him out of the water. If that means some red faces at Langley, they wouldn't be red for the first time. And I haven't heard anyone around this building say that we ought to spike a good story because it might embarrass the CIA in a fairly long time."

He could see the shaft hit home. It was a funny thing, but if you suggested that a staffer on *The New York World* had been duped or suborned by the Cubans or the KGB, you were contemptuously accused of runaway paranoia. If you hinted at a possible case of CIA manipulation of the news, on the other hand, all the alarm bells were set ringing and people acted as if you had accused them of stealing a blind widow's handbag. Rourke's cheeks were purple, the veins on his nose stood out and his Adam's apple was bobbing like a Yo-Yo. He gnashed, and he spluttered.

"I'm perfectly serious, Len," Hockney persisted. "Look at that." He ran his finger under the motto at the top left-hand corner of the morning edition: "ALL THE NEWS IN THE WORLD." He said, "If we ever had a duty to live up to that, it's now. If we don't, we'll risk more than losing a sensational story. We'll be responsible for what could happen in Cuba and in our own country." He was loud and he was clumsy, and he knew from Rourke's face that it wasn't going to work.

"I'll raise it at the story conference," the editor said.

Hockney knew what that meant. He could picture the way Ed Finkel's nose would wrinkle.

"I can understand how you feel," Rourke was saying. "But I think you're overemotional. You really ought to take that vacation. Then you can come back at all this with more objectivity."

"Thanks a lot, Len."

Hockney picked up his copy of the morning paper and headed for the door.

He turned and said, "Do you mind if I take the story someplace else?"

"You know what your contract says," Rourke reminded him.

"It doesn't say anything about TV appearances."

"Bob, I wish you'd take my advice." He got up and came over, and Hockney was shocked by how much weight he had lost. But for his red-striped suspenders, it looked as if his trousers would slide off his shrunken hips. "You've had a lousy year," Rourke said. "What with that Havana episode, and the Washington problem—and Julia. I really do understand. Listen, my Irish grandmother used to say to me, 'Seeing is believing, but feeling is God's own truth.' The thing is, you still have to make people *see*. And you can't do that in your present state of mind."

"Thanks a lot," Hockney repeated the hollow words. "I have to try."

SANTA MARÍA DEL MAR, CUBA

"A real woman loves the smell of a good cigar. Isn't that right, Gisela?"

The shapely *mulata* set down her tray and came over to the

295

Russian who called himself Favio. She relieved him of the unlit cigar—one of Fidel's private stock—caressed it with her fingertips and started sucking the end. Then she lit it expertly, revolving it over the flame until the tip was evenly aglow. She took a couple of deep drags before planting it in Favio's mouth. The Russian patted her rump appreciatively.

His attention returned to the two other smokers on the shady veranda of the Villa Yagruma.

There was a rustling sound, like that of tissue paper, as Calixto Valdés exhaled through his nose.

Valdés said, "It's set for tomorrow. Fidel will spend the night in Santiago de Cuba, and drive to Guantánamo before noon. He will have the usual escort."

"Who's in charge?"

"Colonel Sanfuentes. He knows what to expect. I briefed him myself."

"Good." The Russian moved his head slowly, as if his neck were in a brace, and fixed Parodi with his heavy-lidded eyes. He said, "The last step is up to you."

Julio Parodi was a man who sweated too easily. He was sweating now.

"All it takes is one phone call," Parodi said. "But the man is serious. He'll be standing right next to Fidel. Wouldn't it be better to arrest him now? I mean, suppose there's a slipup?"

"There won't be," Valdés responded. "Sanfuentes is a good man. He knows how to take care of it."

"The point," Favio interjected, "is that the world must *see* the assassin make his attempt on Fidel's life. That will ensure that no one will believe the Americans' denials." His voice gave a liquid, quicksilver quality to the Spanish words. He could have been reciting García Lorca instead of discussing an assassination plot. There was a residue of something foreign in his voice, but the accent was Castilian rather than Slavic. Favio, with his face like old leather just scrubbed with saddle soap, was probably the last surviving active-duty KGB officer who had personal experience of the Spanish Civil War. His understanding of men and their motivations had ripened over half a century in the field. The Cubans, resentful of the heavy, domineering manner of other Soviet advisers, were in awe of this one, who had lived so long and spoke their language so well.

"Go and make your phone call," Favio instructed Parodi.

When Parodi had disappeared into the living room, the Russian sighed—a wistful sigh, as if something pleasurable had floated to the surface of his memory—and said to Valdés, "Do you read Machiavelli?"

"Not for a long time," the DGI man admitted.

"That's a pity," Favio went on. "Some authors are timeless. There is a passage in Machiavelli in which he says that any injury a prince may do to a man should be of such a kind that there is no fear of revenge. That is excellent counsel, in my estimation. Tomorrow will make it impossible for the Americans to take revenge for anything we do to them."

NEAR GUANTÁNAMO NAVAL BASE, CUBA

From the window of the spartan room where Juan Garrido slept, he could make out the gray blur of buildings inside the security perimeter of the U.S. naval base at Guantánamo, a mile or so down the road. Fidel had personally chosen this setting for the new detention camp that had been thrown together to hold the boat people the Americans were sending back. It was a skillful propaganda ploy. The proximity of the U.S. base mocked the hopes of the refugees who had tried to escape to America, only to be turned away. At the same time, by moving them here Castro could call attention to his long-pressed claim that the Americans should get out of Guantánamo. Meanwhile, the boat people waited, in their limbo behind the barbed wire, for Fidel to decide their ultimate fate.

Juan Garrido was a slight, wiry man with a narrow face, whose features were crowded too close together. He held the rank of captain in the security police. He was one of the officers who had been assigned to screen the thousands of Cubans who were being brought to the detention camp, to identify hard-core political dissidents and possible CIA infiltrators. His orders for the day were to put himself at the disposal of Colonel Sanfuentes, the chief of Castro's personal bodyguard—Unit 49. Fidel was expected, in the early afternoon, to deliver one of his four-hour sermons on the infamy of the United States. There would be reporters, and TV cameras, and at least one American correspondent: Brad Lister, the resident stringer for a number of U.S. news organizations.

The day had hardly begun, but Juan Garrido could see it stretching ahead, a limitless desert expanse. His eyes were sore and red-rimmed from lack of sleep. All of his body functions were disturbed. He had run to the bathroom three times since waking. He had the sensation of flushing all over, rapidly and repeatedly, like a toilet tank out of control. He knew he should not have started drinking the night before, but after the phone call he'd received, it was the only way he could get through the hours of darkness.

There had been times, in the hollow between midnight and dawn, when Garrido had told himself he could not go through with it. But there were risks in pulling out, as well as in executing his plan. Secrets are highly perishable among Cubans. There was the chance that somebody, maybe Parodi, would let something drop. The fact that he had joined in the conspiracy would be enough to send him to a secret firing squad—or worse, a life in a stinking, airless cell. His superiors in state security would not show mercy because he had not had the balls to go through with the plot. So having gone this far, he decided bleakly, there was no possibility of turning back.

Garrido was no kind of kamikaze. He had insisted throughout that he would not carry out the mission unless he had a reasonable chance of escape. When he was transferred to the Guantánamo camp, he had thought at first that he was off the hook. On assignment to a detention center at the back end of the island, there was no way he could take part in an operation to liquidate Fidel. Others would have to do the job. Then Parodi—who seemed to have his ear open to everything that went on in the capital—had come up with the news that Fidel was planning a big publicity stunt at the camp, and that Garrido, as one of the people in charge, should have no problem getting close to him.

"You can go right up and shake his hand," Parodi had said.

The location of the camp was what Garrido was counting on to solve the getaway problem. He had counted out every millimeter of the distance between the camp and the checkpoint at the gates of the U.S. naval base.

"They'll be waiting for you," Parodi had promised him.

"They better be," Garrido had replied. "I may be coming down that road with my ass on fire."

Now, as he finished buttoning the jacket of his uniform fatigues, Garrido patted the ball-point pen in his outside breast pocket. The cyanide pen was the element in the plan that gave him a gambler's chance of fulfilling the mission and living to collect his reward. As long as he could get within three feet of El Líder Máximo.

Cheerleaders whipped the crowd into a frenzy long before Fidel's cavalcade appeared. Tens of thousands of Cubans had been bused in from nearby towns to shake their fists and yell taunts and insults at the detainees on the other side of the wire. Their jibes were the old ones:

"¡Escoria!"

"¡Mariquitas!"

"¡Gusanos!"

From time to time, some of the demonstrators pushed forward to hurl rocks and scraps of refuse at the rejected boat people who hung about sheepishly inside the camp. The guards did not intervene. Some of the detainees moved back, to shelter behind the drab, prefabricated barrack buildings where they slept, crammed shoulder to shoulder, thighbone to thighbone, on thin, evil-smelling pallets. Nobody knew why Fidel was coming. There were rumors in the camp that in order to show up the *yanquis,* he was going to make a magnanimous gesture, maybe even allow the boat people to go back to their homes and their former jobs.

But to most of these people, the President of Cuba was as unpredictable, as unknowable, as a power of nature. They waited, with both anxiety and resignation, as they might wait to see whether the sky turned red at dusk.

"Hola, linda," a thickset government supporter leered at an adolescent girl behind the wire. "I'm going to squeeze your papaya."

A stooped old man who might have been her grandfather shook his fist in impotent rage.

Then a high, reedy voice rose in defiance from somewhere inside the camp. *"¡Mejor Batista con sangre que Fidel con hambre!"* it screeched. Better Batista with blood than Fidel with hunger.

Guards ran, prodding and pushing, through the ranks of the detainees, seeking the source of this outburst.

Some of the government supporters returned to the attack, hurling rocks and bottles. Nobody threw eggs. Eggs were too hard to come by.

The chanting assumed a new pattern as word spread that Castro's convoy was approaching. The cheerleaders started vying with each other, bellowing more and more extravagant slogans.

"Our whole life for Fidel!" one of them roared.

From his position next to the podium, Juan Garrido watched a jeepload of security men flanked by motorcycle outriders approach through a cloud of dust, and his hand strayed again to the pen clipped to his breast pocket.

The podium had been set up the day before, facing the detention camp. A giant-size Cuban flag formed a canvas wall behind the platform. A battery of microphones had been set up, to carry Fidel's statements to the Cuban people and the outside world. There was a press section over to the left, and Garrido recognized the American stringer, Brad Lister, among the reporters. The idea was that Fidel would address the *gusanos* be-

300

hind the wire over the heads of his massed supporters. Following the usual practice, the first rows in front of the platform were occupied by security men, many of them in civilian clothes. The apparent formlessness of the crowd itself was deceptive. Most of the people who had come by bus belonged to local Committees for the Defense of the Revolution. They could be counted on to applaud at the right times.

The armored Zil crawled to a halt near the platform, screened by Unit 49 heavies with Kalashnikovs. As the wide, strong, familiar presence descended from the limousine, preceded by his beard and his cigar, the camp commandant moved forward to greet him, and Captain Juan Garrido stepped up smartly behind.

Fidel was all nods and smiles.

"Compañero Presidente," the commandant addressed him, "the people are waiting for you."

Garrido cleared his throat. On the far side of the Zil he could see Sanfuentes, the head of Fidel's bodyguard, scanning the crowd with eyelids that narrowed like a visor.

The commandant was making introductions. He presented the leader of the local Party cell, his deputy, the camp medical officer. Finally it was Garrido's turn.

Fidel patted the security captain's arm and started to make a joke about the boat people in the camp, who had fallen completely silent since his arrival. One elbow propped on Garrido's shoulder, Fidel gestured expansively with his cigar. He was paler and fatter than the young Cuban had expected, his girth exaggerated by the body armor he was wearing under his Russian-style uniform. When he turned his gaze on Garrido, the captain saw that he suffered from mild astigmatism. He had not expected that either—or the odd look in the Cuban leader's eyes. It was a look of intense recognition, the look of a man who has recognized death and is shaping the incredulous word "You!" in his mouth.

At the instant that Garrido reached for the ball-point in his breast pocket, he saw Colonel Sanfuentes' arm drop like the blade of a guillotine. He heard the snap of safety catches' being released and felt, rather than saw, a couple of the men of Unit 49 moving in on him. There were only two of them, moving at a quick but deliberate stride, trying not to cause a stir.

Fidel swiveled away and began his walk up to the podium. Ahead of him, on the path that had been cleared through the crowd, TV cameramen jostled each other, angling for the best shot. The President was five or six yards away, out of range of the cyanide pen.

Garrido went running after him.

He yelled, "Take shelter! There's an attempt on your life!"

Fidel turned on his heel to look at the security captain, now only a couple of yards away, with a burly soldier from Unit 49 at his heels. The bodyguard dropped to his knee and fired—at the exact moment when another of Fidel's security men thrust himself between the President and Juan Garrido. The captain dodged sidewise and darted around him, and the bullets made a neat line of punctures across the bodyguard's uniform jacket.

"Get down! Get down!" Garrido kept yelling at the President. There were screams from the crowd. Behind them, Colonel Sanfuentes was yelling commands that were intelligible only to the men standing next to him. Fidel was strangely passive. He neither moved nor ducked. He stood there facing Garrido, as if rooted in the ground.

Garrido turned his head abruptly, apparently to study the commotion behind. His right fist went up, pointing the tip of the cyanide pen into the white, unmistakable face that had appeared in millions of photographs.

Then the big man's cigar went spinning earthward, and he crumpled—not all at once, but in stages, like a jointed marionette on wires.

Someone was grabbing at Garrido's jacket.

He pulled free and saw it was one of his own men, one of the security detail at the camp.

"¡Médico!" Garrido screamed. He saw Colonel Sanfuentes trying to clear a path for himself through the mob that had spilled over the path. He saw the American reporter—Lister—

302

trying to get close enough to see what had happened. The American's face looked frozen.

Garrido had been standing so close to Fidel, with the body of the pen concealed in his palm, it was unlikely that anyone had seen him fire the cyanide crystals. In the general confusion that now reigned, the only people he had to fear were Sanfuentes and the bodyguards who were acting under his direct orders. To his surprise, the men of Unit 49 who were now converging around the body from their positions near the podium made no move to arrest him.

He pointed to the American reporter and screamed, "Yankee assassin!"

It created a useful diversion. Government supporters and security guards threw themselves onto Brad Lister, flailing their fists.

Garrido was already edging his way through the crowd, trying to keep his head down. People made room for him because of his uniform. In the press section, he saw one of his colleagues in state security putting his hand over the lens of a TV camera. They would not be able to black out the news for long, he thought.

On the far side of the platform, he paused for long enough to dump the cyanide pen and to give himself a dose of antihistamine from the vial that was in his other pocket.

Then he was running again, running until he could taste blood in his mouth, toward the jeep he had left outside the perimeter fence of the detention camp. He saw a soldier he did not recognize standing next to it, probably one of Sanfuentes' men, but he did not skip a beat.

"Hurry," he shouted. "Colonel Sanfuentes' orders."

The soldier jumped aside, and Garrido clanked away, trying not to push the gas pedal down to the floor of the jeep. He passed a truckload of Unit 49 troops, hurtling past him toward the podium. They made no effort to stop him.

Then he heard shouts, and the blast of a car horn, and warning shots zinged overhead. Garrido paid no heed. As the jeep

303

jolted and bounced along the rough, unfinished road, he could make out the olive-drab figures of the men on guard at the checkpoint on the Cuban side of the security fence around the U.S. naval base. An officer strolled into the middle of the road and waved for him to stop. Garrido waved back, as if in greeting, then gunned the jeep forward so that the Cuban officer had to throw himself sidewise to avoid being flattened.

As he saw the Marine guards at the U.S. checkpoint ahead, Garrido threw back his head and started laughing in high, windy gusts. He had just changed the destiny of Cuba. And what was waiting for him just ahead was five million dollars and a safe passage to the United States to enjoy it.

Beside the flimsy barrier at the U.S. checkpoint, a natty little man in a tailored safari suit stood watching the approaching jeep. Next to him was a young Marine captain built like a defensive lineman for the Pittsburgh Steelers. The Marines positioned around the gate had their M-16s at the ready.

"That him?" Steeler said to Quayle.

"That's him," the CIA man confirmed. Quayle took a second look through his field glasses. The Cuban in the jeep had eyes that were set too close together, like his own. He had a grin smeared all over his face, as if he were going to a picnic.

Without haste, Quayle lowered the binoculars. He said, "Captain, I want you to order your men to shoot the Cuban who is in that jeep."

"Sir," Steeler faltered, "I don't think I can do that, *sir*."

The final word came out snappy as a salute, but he looked as puzzled as if the referee had wrongly ruled he was offside.

Quayle said, "You understand my status."

"Yes, sir. But I have no orders to shoot Cubans, *sir*."

"This is a case of an armed Cuban, in uniform, trespassing on a U.S. military facility. Carry out my orders, Captain."

While the Marine officer hesitated, Quayle pulled his own pistol out of the waistband of his spotless Permapress pants.

Juan Garrido had slowed his jeep until it was crawling along

304

in first gear as it approached the barrier. He called out words of greeting to the guards. Behind him, Colonel Sanfuentes and a platoon of Unit 49 troops had piled out of their trucks and were cautiously advancing, rifles pointing at Garrido's back. Sanfuentes barked at him to turn back.

"I did it!" Garrido shouted at the Marines. "Cuba is free!"

Quayle dropped to a crouch, holding the gun in front of him, his left hand supporting his right wrist.

Juan Garrido was only a few feet away from U.S. territory when Quayle's bullet caught him just below the right eye. As the spent cartridge exited the back of the Cuban's head, it created a puncture like a ragged star. His body collapsed over the wheel, and the jeep veered off the road, hit a rock and flopped over onto its side.

Quayle sniffed the muzzle of his pistol in an abstract fashion and tucked it back into his waistband.

Only then, with the damage limitation attended to, did Quayle permit himself to smile. He did more than smile. He took a little spring into the air.

"Goddammit," he said to the astonished Marine captain, "do you know what we did? We just went and made ourselves a revolution in Cuba."

The Marine's jaw dropped open as he watched the CIA man hopping away, his chest puffed out like a bantam rooster's. His glance returned to the Cuban security men who were busy loading Garrido's body onto a truck.

"¡Asesinos!" one of them shouted, and hawked a yellow gob of spittle onto the road.

Chapter

10

NEW YORK

It was the kind of furnace day in the city when people faint in the subways and kids open the fire hydrants to cool off in the spray and rooms in the ghetto are pressure cookers ready to boil. But it was cool inside the black glass tower that housed Angela Seabury's TV network and the megacorporation that owned it, so cool that people kept their jackets on and still caught summer colds. Angela rated an office to herself, next to the corner suite that was occupied by the head of Programming. She had softened its hi-tech trappings with a collection of bright rugs and artifacts from India, Mexico and Morocco. The effect reminded Hockney of the UNESCO shop he had once visited in Westwood in L.A., near the university campus.

Angela was friendly, supportive, but Hockney could tell that she didn't like what he had been telling her, but couldn't quite bring herself to say so directly. She was wearing a red silk blouse and matching lipstick. It was not her color, Hockney thought. Against it, the whiteness of her long, perfectly curved neck seemed eggshell-frail.

She said, "I'll have to talk to my producer."

He met her soft, gray-blue eyes. She picked up the phone and punched out Simon Green's extension.

A woman's voice answered. "Simon's on long-distance. No, wait."

Then the producer came on. "Angela, you'd better pick up on this. I've got Brad Lister on the line from Cuba."

When Lister's voice came over the squawk box on Angela's desk, it sounded as if he were talking from inside a submarine. There was rippling interference that drowned out parts of his sentences.

"Say that again, Brad," the producer instructed.

"Fidel . . . murdered . . . CIA hit man."

"Brad!" Angela leaned over the box. "Can you hear me? Are you saying Fidel has been assassinated?"

"Assassinated," Lister yelled harder. "At Guantánamo . . . Killer tried to escape . . . U.S. naval base . . . Captain Juan Garrido . . . CIA."

There was something about cyanide and a poison pen, but they couldn't quite catch it.

"Brad," Angela shouted into the squawk box, as if raising her voice would improve the reception from the other end, "is it confirmed that Fidel is dead?"

"I saw . . . was there."

"Can we get a better connection? I want to put this on the air. Brad?"

They listened hard, but all that came back was noise like rolling waves.

"Brad?" Angela repeated.

The producer said, "He's been cut off. What do we do with this?"

"Can we call him back?"

"I don't know. He was calling from some village in eastern Cuba."

"Let's try to raise him. Meanwhile, we'd better get ready to run with this."

She put down the receiver and glared at Hockney fiercely.

"So much for your stories about a Cuban plot," she said. "The CIA finally did it. They've been trying all these years, and they finally did it. Well, they're not going to get away with it. This is going to be the end of the CIA—and maybe the whole Newgate Administration."

"Now, wait, Angela. Are you sure—"

But she slammed out of her office. "I've got to talk to my boss," she called over her shoulder.

Twenty minutes later, Hockney was sitting in the control room, behind Simon Green, watching Angela preparing to interrupt the afternoon soap opera with her news flash. Then the light on Camera I flashed on, and Angela began reading from the monitor.

"We interrupt *Dark Fires*," she said carefully, spacing the words, "to bring you a shattering news exclusive. Our correspondent in Cuba reports that just over one hour ago, President Fidel Castro was shot and killed by an assassin using a cyanide gun. This tragic event took place while President Castro was preparing to deliver a speech to Cuban refugees deported by the U.S. Administration, at a site near the U.S. naval base at Guantánamo. The assassin has been identified as Captain Juan Garrido. He was apparently killed while trying to make his escape to the Guantánamo naval base. A high-level State Department source who does not wish to be identified has confirmed that President Castro is dead, and denies that the U.S. Government was involved. We are still awaiting official comment from Havana and Washington."

Halfway through the announcement, one of the phones in the control room had started to purr. Hockney watched the expression on Simon Green's face switch from astonishment to relief to professional urgency as he listened to the voice at the other end.

Angela was just beginning to repeat the headline when the producer's voice came through her earphone.

"Commercial break," he told her.

Angela looked up at the camera and said, "We will be right

back with the latest developments in the Castro assassination after station identification."

The light on the camera blinked off, and the producer rushed into the studio.

"I've got Brad Lister on the line again," Green told her. "He sounds pretty mixed up. But the latest word is this. Castro's okay. He must have been rushed away for emergency treatment. He's going to appear on live TV in thirty minutes. Lister says he will present irrefutable evidence that the CIA engineered the assassination attempt."

"I don't understand," Angela said. "We got confirmation from the State Department that Fidel had been killed."

They all thought about it. Hockney was hovering beside the open studio door. He recalled how, in the confusion and uncertainty that had followed the shooting of Egypt's President Sadat on the reviewing stand, one of the networks had run an interview with its diplomatic correspondent in which he quoted his "high-level State Department sources" as saying that Sadat had received only minor injuries. An hour later, it was officially announced that the Egyptian leader was dead. Was it just another case of lousy information? A different explanation dawned on Hockney, and it dawned on Simon Green too.

The producer spoke first. "I've got it," he announced. "This proves the CIA was involved. They thought Castro was dead because they arranged the operation. Why else would we get a statement out of Washington before we got anything out of Havana? We can nail them," he added triumphantly. "Hell, we can really go to town on this."

WASHINGTON, D.C.

"I wrote this as soon as we got the news. It's effective as of now."

The CIA Director put his resignation on President Newgate's desk. The prose was suitably opaque.

"Put it away, Blair," President Newgate said wearily. "It wouldn't do either of us any good just now. We can talk about it later, when the dust has settled."

Blair Collins subsided into a chair, all the wind gone out of him.

"I'm going to be very careful about how I express this, Blair," Jerry Newgate went on. "Can Castro prove that we were involved in this? Or that we had prior knowledge?"

They had both watched Fidel's telecast. The Cuban leader had pinned the blame squarely on the CIA. He had produced the cyanide pen, and had laid heavy stress on the fact that the would-be assassin had tried to make his escape to the Guantánamo naval base. But he had not produced Julio Parodi, the double agent who could have made his charges conclusive.

Blair Collins rubbed the loose folds of flesh around his throat and said, "There's a risk."

He waited for the President to ask for the details. Instead, Newgate said, "When I asked you to take charge of the CIA, I promised you a free hand. I simply requested that you avoid getting this Administration dragged down into the mud. Now, I can go on national TV tonight with a perfectly clear conscience and say that I had no knowledge of a conspiracy to kill Castro. I'm ready to do that, Blair. But I'm not going to do it if there is a possibility that Fidel Castro can then get up and cut me off at the knees. You're telling me there is such a possibility."

Director Collins swallowed. "There is," he admitted.

"This poison ball-point, or whatever it was—"

"Has East German markings."

"But you're saying there's something else the Cubans could use."

"There might be."

"All right, Blair. So how do we handle this?"

"I recommend we keep our distance, Mr. President. Have the State Department spokesman issue a routine denial. There's no need for you to get personally involved."

"You know there's bound to be a Senate investigation. How are you planning to handle that?"

"I never regarded Capitol Hill as a confessional," Collins said.

The President nodded. "Just tell me one thing," he went on. "If this hit man—Garrido—was standing closer to Castro than I am to you, and sprayed cyanide in his face, how the hell did Castro survive?"

"He had a double. Our information is, the body was burned. All the TV footage was confiscated."

"A double, huh?" President Newgate said thoughtfully. "I could do with one of those myself."

At the same moment, Wright Washington was sitting in a Congressional conference room in the Rayburn Building. The room had been booked, on short notice, by Coleman North, a liberal Democrat who had been one of the most energetic critics of the Newgate Administration's policies in Central America. There were more than sixty people there—liberal Congressmen, leaders of the Black Caucus, organizers from church groups and the peace lobbies and Latin American solidarity committees that proliferated around Capitol Hill. Wright Washington was a reluctant member of this gathering. He had always held the view that it did not serve the interests of his own community to confound them with foreign-policy debates. Although he had been bitterly opposed to the Vietnam War, he had been one of those who had pleaded with Martin Luther King not to commit himself and his movement to the antiwar campaign. But the shock of the attempt on Castro's life, and an emotional phone call from Willard Holmes, the head of the New York–based Interdenominational Brotherhood for Peace, had persuaded him to attend the meeting. He had promised only that he would listen.

There was no doubt as to who was the moving spirit in that dark, paneled chamber in the Rayburn Building. Willard Holmes, by origin a New England Episcopalian, talked with the raw passion of a Southern Baptist preacher. He was dressed informally, in a plaid shirt and gray slacks, and his eyes were fixed on Wright Washington when he made a great arching gesture with his hands and said, "Dante wrote about a place of howling at the gates of Hell that is reserved for people who

311

neither rebel against God nor are faithful to him, a kind of separate Hell for those who remain neutral in a time of moral crisis. We all know that peace is indivisible. We cannot condemn the violence that takes place in the streets of our cities unless we condemn the violence for which the United States is responsible throughout the Third World. We have no moral right to condemn suffering in our own country and turn our backs on the suffering that our government inflicts on the people of other countries."

There were many others who spoke—excited young men who accused the Administration of pursuing a policy of "starvation and war"; cooler professional militants who discussed sit-ins and numbers and logistics in the way a platoon commander might rehearse a military operation; impresarios who tossed off the names of movie stars and rock singers who could be conscripted—but the words that stayed with Wright Washington were those of Willard Holmes.

When the others had had their say, Holmes turned to him.

Holmes said, "Wright, I know that everybody in this room admires what you did—what you tried to do—in Miami. You stood up against the Black Fedayeen and the National Guard. You tried to make the people in the Metropolitan Club and the Chevy Chase Country Club understand why riots come about. A lot of people in this country—and not just black people—are coming to identify with you. Even the President has had to sit up and pay attention."

"I'm flattered," Washington interjected. "What exactly are you asking me to do?"

"I'm asking you to come off the fence. We're going to mount a nationwide protest over this attempt to kill Castro, starting off with a rally in New York. I want to get as many people turning out in Central Park as we had for the nuclear-freeze campaign. And I want you up there on the platform."

"It seems to me you did pretty well without me last time," Washington observed.

"Listen, Wright. I remember one of the first big meetings we held for the nuclear-freeze campaign was down in San Antonio, among all those retired colonels and Air Force bases and Texans who think gun control means being able to hit a man between the eyes. We held it in a black church, in a black neighborhood, and there was standing room only. And in all that crowd, I saw only three or four black faces, and two of them were from out of town. This is a united struggle, and this time the black community should not be a silent partner. I want you up front. In fact, I want you to lead a delegation from Harlem to the United States Mission to the U.N."

Washington was still hesitating when a sharp-faced young staffer from Coleman North's office spoke up. "Maybe he doesn't want to do it because the Administration has offered him the Civil Rights Commission."

That stung. Wright Washington had in fact been approached by a White House aide who had been putting out feelers. He had already decided to turn down the job, if it was formally offered, because he knew that many of his friends, as well as his critics, would think he had sold out.

"That's nonsense," Washington snapped.

Willard Holmes was waiting, his hands clasped behind his back. He looked like a schoolteacher waiting patiently for a backward pupil to come up with the answer to a simple math problem.

"All right," Wright Washington said, without enthusiasm. "Count me in."

NEW YORK

Running undercover agents, Frank Parra had learned, was like keeping indoor plants. You had to keep checking that they were getting enough water and sunlight. Otherwise, they forgot who they were; their assumed identities—and loyalties—became more real to them than their original ones. He kept appointments with two undercover agents that day, and each of them gave him something to think about.

The first had a nothing job writing press circulars and running errands for the local chapter of the Council for Hemispheric Understanding. Over a meal at a Chinese restaurant on Pell Street, he told Parra that Teófilo Gómez had been in and out of the office several times, checking the arrangements for the protest rally that was supposed to climax in a mass gathering in Central Park the following day. Parra chewed that over, along with his beef in red pepper sauce. The police seemed to be fairly relaxed about the rally. After all, the city had been able to contain a nuclear-freeze rally that had mustered close to a million people without any outbreaks of violence. On the face of it, the fact that the head of the DGI network in New York was taking a close interest in a demonstration to protest U.S. involvement in a plot to kill Castro was less than surprising. But Teófilo Gómez was a link in the chain that connected Julio Parodi, the events in Miami and Monimbó. When the FBI agent got back to his office, he pulled four men off other cases and ordered them not to lose sight of Gómez in Bloomingdale's or anywhere else.

In the afternoon, in a noisy steak house in the Bronx, Parra met a young Puerto Rican built like a longshoreman who flaunted tattoos of naked ladies on both of his muscular forearms. Rico worked at Hunts Point. One of Frank Parra's first outings, after he was assigned to New York, had been to the fruit-and-vegetable market there, the largest in the United States. Four thousand trucks an hour drove through its tollgates. Hunts Point was a natural entrepôt for smugglers. He knew that more and more of the dope-runners, nervous over U.S. Navy operations off the Florida coast and the troubles in Miami, were rerouting shipments direct to New York and other ports on the northeast coast. For some of them, this was also a way of cutting out the middlemen in Miami.

The undercover man started off by talking about that.

"There's gonna be a shooting war," he predicted. "It's gonna be like a Jimmy Cagney movie. Some of the Colombians are selling their stuff direct to New York, and the Cubans don't like it. They want their piece of the action. There's a lot of talk about that on the street."

Parra nodded and sipped his coffee. He didn't much mind the idea of rival gangs of dopers blowing each other's brains out. It could save the Bureau a lot of work.

Then the Puerto Rican said, "We got a boat in from Panama yesterday. Mangoes and bananas. Or so they said."

"Yeah?"

"The funny thing is, some of those crates weighed a ton. I saw a guy drop his end of one. He just about broke his foot."

"Yeah?" The FBI man's interest had been pricked by this detail. He reasoned that if the shipment of fruit was a cover for drugs, the crates would have seemed lighter, not heavier, than normal.

"I hung around for a while," the Puerto Rican went on. "They trucked the stuff to Harry Diva's stall. I didn't see much of it come out again. Maybe half the crates, at top. And they were getting premium prices for mangoes last night."

"Yeah?" Parra found this observation significant. He had watched the bidding that went on at night at Hunts Point, under the spooky yellow light from the tall lampposts around the hundred-and-twenty-five-acre site. Every seller knew he was dealing in perishable commodities; the value of his merchandise would decrease with every passing hour. So every stallholder was anxious to dispose of as much fruit as possible by the time the buyers' trucks rolled in at 3 A.M. If all of the crates from Panama contained mangoes and bananas, they would not be left at the back of Harry Diva's stall to blacken and grow mold.

It was a loose end, and there was no reason it should be connected to any of the other things that were weighing on Frank Parra's mind, but he was just desperate enough to want to grab hold of it.

"You say Harry Diva's stall," he repeated, and the Puerto Rican's face, crosshatched with tiny lines as if he had been sleeping on a burlap sack, twisted into a grin.

"I guess it's worth something, huh?" he suggested.

"I dunno," the FBI man said, honestly enough. But he slipped the Puerto Rican a couple of twenties anyway. You had to water your plants.

As Parra drove the big flatbed truck along Edgewater Road, he had to stop for a light, and a hooker picked that moment to hoist herself up onto the running board. She was wearing a black shiny raincoat, and nothing underneath except a pair of bikini briefs. She let Parra have a good look. The FBI man did not like what he saw, but he showed his teeth in a lopsided smile and said, "Later, sweetheart."

"Come on, big boy," she urged. "Buy one, get one free. Your friend wants a good time too."

Wallace, one of the handful of black FBI Agents who worked out of Parra's building, gave her a friendly flutter of the wrist.

She didn't give up easily. She clung to the side of the truck until it started to pick up speed. As she dropped off, they heard her describe in impressive anatomical detail what they ought to do with themselves.

Wallace said, "That's no way to treat your grandmother, Frank."

Parra paid over seven dollars to the man at the tollgate and called out the number of a stall at random.

"E-Seven."

That was all the identification they needed to get into the Hunts Point market.

The truck lumbered among the rows until they reached Harry Diva's stall. The yellow light made everything look wan and sickly. There was a platform at the rear of Harry Diva's stall, where the railroad track ran, and another at the front, for the trucks, raised five feet above the ground.

A swart, paunchy little man in front was yelling, "Ten-fifty California twenty-sevens."

When Parra pulled up, he said, "Take a look. The cantaloupes are just beautiful. Ready to go."

Parra's eyes were on the station wagon that had just driven off. He made a mental note of the license number.

"How about mangoes?" the FBI man said.

"We're fresh out."

A pungent aroma filled Parra's nostrils as a forklift truck

trundled past, loaded up with crates of garlic.

"Are you Harry Diva?"

"Harry DiVitale," the trader corrected him. "What's it to you?"

"A friend told me you had terrific mangoes."

"That was last night. Tonight, I got California twenty-sevens. You buying, or just wasting my time?"

"Mind if I take a look inside?" Parra was already out of his cab. He walked across the platform into the closed stall.

"Hey!" Harry Diva called after him. "Whaddya think you're doing?"

A tough-looking porter came up and folded his arms and looked at Parra as if he wanted to make an early breakfast of him. There were no mangoes inside the stall.

"Why don't you go do a few push-ups?" Parra said to the porter. The big man grinned and reached for a crowbar.

"Tell him to do it," Parra said to Harry Diva. "We need to talk. Mike Santini isn't happy. He ain't happy at all. You've been free-lancing, Harry."

At the mention of Mike Santini's name, the trader turned as yellow as the lamplight.

"Take a walk, Pete," he told the porter.

You couldn't grow up on Arthur Avenue, like Harry DiVitale, and not know about Mike Santini. His name was as familiar as clam sauce. Harry DiVitale had met Santini only once in his life, but he had bent to kiss the man's ring the way they did in the movies. Mike Santini was the head of one of the most powerful Mafia families on the East Coast. He was also the most efficient garbage collector in New York. When Santini's name was mentioned, there was always something you did. You showed respect.

Frank Parra had done some checking since he had talked to his undercover man from Hunts Point. He had learned from the organized-crime specialists in the New York office that Harry was a very small cog in the Santini machine. He was taking a gamble now—gambling on his hunch that the trader had been doing a little fencing on his own account. From the way the little man had started to splutter and protest, he felt more and more confident that he was on the right track. It was lucky that he spoke Italian with barely a trace of an accent. For a Spanish-speaker, that had not been a difficult gift to acquire.

"I can protect you," he reassured Harry Diva. "But Mike wants to know about these guys who took delivery."

"I thought it was kosher," the trader was saying. "A guy from Miami made the connection. I've dealt with him before."

"Oh, yeah? I'm sure Mike will be interested in that. Who made the pickup?"

"A couple of guys I never seen before."

"It wouldn't be nice if you were putting me on," Parra said. He started polishing his nails.

Harry Diva spluttered some more, and said, "I can prove I'm leveling with you."

"I'm listening."

Frank Parra didn't get many breaks, but he was ready to light a candle for the one he got now.

"There's another pickup tonight," Harry Diva said. "Four o'clock."

Clinton Street, on the Lower East Side, is not a place where sober citizens hang out at any time of day, least of all in the weary hours before dawn. The blocks between Houston and Delancey are void of those cheerful greengroceries the Koreans seem to be running all over the city, with spotless fruit spilling out in great tubs all over the pavement. It is not an area where you would expect to find fresh mangoes from the Caribbean.

As Frank Parra tooled along Clinton Street at 4:45 A.M., driving his own car—a battered old Chrysler that concealed a 440-horsepower engine under the hood—he saw the steerers darting back and forth at the street corners. This was a place for nickel-and-dime drug pushers, offering ten-dollar bags of heroin or "the works"—a syringe to stick the stuff in—for three bucks. He watched out-of-town kids from New Jersey or Pennsylvania wandering the blocks, nervous and shifty, looking to buy ten or fifty bags they could take home to resell for double the starting price.

Parra was following a green van. There had been two of them at Hunts Point, one green, the other off-white. Wallace had tailed the other one. Now Frank Parra watched his van pull up outside a ramshackle building just off Clinton Street. He slowed the Chrysler, wondering if he had been spotted, cursing himself for not having brought more Agents in on the case. One of the steerers—a black kid in a wide-brimmed fedora and cowboy boots—came waltzing bowlegged along the sidewalk and looked at him speculatively.

"Gimme a couple of dime bags," he called out in a low voice, trying to play the part.

The steerer snapped his fingers for the money, and Parra slipped him a portrait of Jackson.

"Hey," the FBI man said, as the black kid started strutting back toward a doorway down the street, "how do I know you're not ripping me off?"

The steerer lounged over the car and said, "Hold these, man" as he handed Parra a plastic bag full of syringes.

Before the kid in the fedora came back, a patrol car came cruising along the street, and Parra decided it was not desirable to get involved in complicated explanations. He drove on for a few blocks, then pulled out the Motorola he kept hidden under the front seat.

"Stakeout," he ordered when he got through to a dozy night-duty man. He gave the address, then lingered until he made sure the new Agents had arrived, and were not dolled up in gray suits and black wing-tips. He was halfway back to his office when he realized that he still had enough syringes for the whole of Clinton Street to shoot up with on the floor of his car.

"Frank Parra says I can trust you," Captain Joe Fischer told Hockney, "and that's good enough for me. But I wouldn't talk too loud around here about being friends with the FBI."

They were on the eighth floor of the honeycomb fortress on Police Plaza. Fischer pushed open a door numbered 803.

"This is where it all happens," he said to Hockney. "Hi, Lew," he said with a wave to the duty officer in the Operations Room.

"We got open lines to the Mayor's office and all the emergency services—Fire, Medical, Port Authority, Traffic Control, even the FBI," Fischer explained. "Those phones behind Lew's desk"—he pointed to a battery of red, black, green and yellow telephones on the wall—"are our direct line to God. Right, Lew? They get you the Commissioner and the top brass. This one"—he tapped a blue phone on the desk—"gets you Con Ed in case there's a blackout. I hope we won't be using many of them today. If we're lucky, our biggest headache will be fighting gridlock."

"Don't be too sure," the duty officer commented. "It's going to be a great day for burglars and bank robbers. We've got five thousand cops tied up with this fucking prayer meeting."

"How many people are you expecting to show up for the rally?" Hockney asked.

The two policemen looked at each other and shrugged. "Maybe a hundred thousand in the park," Fischer suggested. "It won't be anywhere near as big as the nuclear-freeze turnout, but I figure a lot of people will show up to catch a few rays and listen to the music. We're betting that less than ten thousand will march to U.N. Plaza. That's where we're likely to get some trouble. That's where the angries will be wanting to get themselves arrested. But if it's like last time, they'll sound off their slogans and go limp and peaceful so we can cart them away and book them and make them happy. As long as they stick to the prescribed route, we should do okay. We have an understanding with the organizers."

"You mean Willard Holmes?"

"Yeah. We got a bit nervous when we heard about this group coming down from Harlem—we could get the Fedayeen and the Black Panther types—but Holmes swears it's all under control. He says Wright Washington is taking care of the blacks. You know about him?"

"Yes," Hockney said. "I met him in Miami. He's an impressive man. And he's built his whole life on nonviolence."

"Well, fingers crossed, hey, Lew?"

The duty officer made the sign.

"You may as well take a peek at our turret operators while you're in here," Fischer went on.

"Turret operators" turned out to be police jargon for the operators taking 911 calls in the five radio rooms—one for each borough—of the Communications Division. On the way, Fischer showed Hockney the TV monitors that would be providing constant coverage of the march and the rally from cameras in police helicopters.

Hockney followed as the police captain returned to Room 803. They found the duty officer trying to talk on three phones at once.

"Here, you take this one," the duty officer said, handing one of the receivers to Fischer.

Hockney watched the heavy man's face set into an expression of dutiful resignation.

"Yeah, Chief," he said.

Fischer listened for a moment; then his jaw dropped. "The World Trade Center?" he echoed. "Holy Mother. Yeah, I'll get down there right away."

He slammed down the phone and said to the duty man, "Where's the bomb squad?"

"Both trucks are out. We had three bomb alerts in the last five minutes."

"Shit. I'll be at the World Trade Center. We'll need every man we can spare."

"The Chief's already ordered a Ten–Seventy-seven." A 10–77 meant that every off-duty cop in the city was being called in.

Hockney ran to the elevators at Fischer's heels.

"What's going on?" he asked, breathless and confused.

"Somebody set off a couple of bombs in One World Trade Center," Fischer reported. "Sounds like he knew his job. He blew a hole clean through the middle of the thing."

Hockney looked at his watch. It was just after nine-thirty. The march was due to begin about eleven.

Captain Fischer had to wrestle his car through the gridlocked traffic across town to the World Trade Center.

Hockney could hear the screams, through the wailing of sirens, from a couple of blocks away. As they rounded the last corner, he saw a dense cloud of smoke, as thick as gray absorbent cotton, billowing out of the lobby level of one of the tower blocks. The police had already roped off a perimeter around the building, and were shunting cars up onto the sidewalks to clear a path for the emergency vehicles. As Fischer parked his car, Hockney watched a fire truck—Hook and Ladder Company 8—drive straight through the shattered glass into the vast lobby area. As they walked through the police lines, he saw the paramedics scurrying in and out with stretchers, ferrying the bodies of the dead and injured.

A Port Authority cop hurried over to greet Fischer.

Fischer asked, "What's the picture?"

"Two bombs—probably plastic explosives; on either side of the elevator shafts. They blew out the whole core of the building. The elevators are out, ditto the emergency stairways, the power supply—the emergency generators aren't working above street level. We're not sure how far up the blast damage extends. We figure at least six floors. But Jeez, the lobby . . ." the cop shook his wizened head. "It was like a slaughterhouse in there. Hundreds of people got caught around the elevators. There are hundreds more up on the mezzanine. God knows how many are trapped inside the elevators."

"How about the fire?"

"The Fire Chief says it's not too bad. They got an automatic sprinkling system on the floor above the mezzanine, and a smoke-purge setup that's sucking up the worst of the flames." He paused to wipe a cinder from the corner of his chin. "The biggest problem is getting to the people who are trapped. They're starting to panic up there."

Fischer craned his neck to look up to the top of the hundred-and-ten-story tower.

"Maybe we can take some of them out by chopper," he suggested. "Get them to filter up onto the roof. Then we could pick them up and rotor them over to the other tower block, so they can use the elevators in there."

"Yeah," the Port Authority cop said. "We still got to handle people like *him*." He pointed his stubby finger at a window on the tenth floor. A round-faced man had broken the glass and was thrashing his arms about to get attention.

"I gotta get down!" he screamed. "There's a fire on this floor!"

Fischer raised his bullhorn and called back, "Please stay calm. Rescue workers will get to you."

The men of the Emergency Services Unit's Truck A, normally stationed in Brooklyn's 10th Precinct, had just finished inflating a huge air bag and were dragging it closer to the wall of One World Trade Center.

"Stay where you are!" Captain Fischer boomed through his loudhailer. "You're too high up. We'll get to you very soon."

But in his terror, the man on the tenth floor refused to listen. He squeezed his bulk out onto the window ledge, crouched and jumped. He fell like a broken toy, turning a dizzy somersault to land headfirst. From that height, the air bag was not enough to break his fall. As Hockney ran after Fischer toward the air bag, he heard the crack of bones, like a dry stick being snapped across your knee. The man lay inert, his head twisted over to the right at an angle that would have been impossible for someone whose neck had not been broken.

Fischer swore under his breath.

Hockney walked over to where a knot of reporters had formed around one of the Mayor's aides.

"Have we got any idea how many people are trapped in the building?" someone asked.

"That's hard to assess. There could be as many as twenty thousand. The Fire Department has put out a borough call. That's very exceptional. It means that engine and ladder companies from all over the five boroughs will be mobilized. We're trying to bring the injured people from the mezzanine down with ropes and baskets. I'm afraid it's going to take a while to get to the people in the elevators and the people on the upper floors."

"Isn't it true that some of the world's foremost bankers are meeting in the Oval Room on the forty-third floor?" another reporter asked.

"I'm afraid that's true."

"Is there any special plan for getting them out?"

"No special plan. We're studying the possibility of moving some people out by helicopter."

"Is it true that the blast was so powerful that the building is listing over to one side?" someone else asked.

"The World Trade Center was built to withstand an earthquake," the aide said.

"But it *is* tilting," the reporter persisted. "I reached someone on one of the top floors by phone. He has a plumbline in his office. He says the building's leaning over at least twenty feet."

Hockney stared up at the facade of the gigantic, impersonal tower block. It didn't look like the Leaning Tower of Pisa. But if word spread that it had begun to tilt, panic could take over.

He saw an ambulance that had just been loaded up with the bodies of blast and fire victims trying to fight its way through the traffic to Beekman Downtown Hospital on William Street.

He went back to Fischer, who was deep in conference with the Fire Chief and a deputy commander from Emergency Medical Services, a black in olive-drab fatigues with a star on his epaulettes.

"The Coast Guard is going to lend us a couple of Sikorskys," Fischer was saying. "We got plenty of commercial choppers from the WTC and Thirty-fourth Street heliports. We can get some of these people moving out now. The problem's going to be to keep it orderly."

Cops from the ESU's Truck 1 moved past, lugging a Hurst machine—a tool powered by compressed air that was used for cutting through wreckage to rescue trapped victims.

A couple of paramedics were yelling at a cluster of sidewalk ghouls who were trying to get a better look at the twisted body on their stretcher. Policemen rushed forward to push the spectators back, and they got the stretcher into their yellow-roofed black truck.

Fischer's men had brought in a mobile communications van, and the chief of the ESU took a couple of radio calls before he shouted, "Hey, Hockney."

"Yes?"

"Did you ever hear of an outfit called The Liberators?"

"Just that? The Liberators?" It sounded like the title of a World War II movie.

"Yeah. A black radio station in Harlem just got a call. Some joker claiming to speak for The Liberators says this group is going to attack the symbols of U.S. capitalism in revenge for the murder attempt on Castro, the slaughter of the Palestinians in Lebanon and the treatment of blacks and Puerto Ricans in this country."

"Are you sure it was a bona fide call?"

"Pretty sure," Fischer said. "The guy described where the explosives were placed. He knew what he was talking about."

"Well, The Liberators is just a cover name," Hockney went on. "But I was thinking—it wouldn't just be coincidence that this happens on the day of the rally, would it? I mean, suppose you wanted to spark off citywide riots in New York, like Miami but a hundred times worse. What's the best way to start? By getting the police and the emergency services running all over town putting out fires. How many men is this going to tie down?"

"Maybe a thousand. Maybe more. Depends how much help we get. Yeah, I know what you're saying. We got less than twenty-five thousand cops for the whole city."

"And the march is due to begin in forty-three minutes," Hockney reminded the police captain, counting off the minutes on his watch. "I've got a feeling that whoever did *this*"—he gestured toward the buckled core of One World Trade Center, now partly visible through the smoke—"has something planned for uptown that will make this look like a sideshow."

"You mean more bombs? You mean a bust-up between the marchers and the police?"

"I'm not sure." Hockney groped for what he wanted to say, for what he was trying to see more clearly. "The Liberators—whoever they may be—talked about symbols in that call to the radio station. I think that's the key."

"A symbol?"

"A symbolic act of violence that will ignite the entire city, maybe all our cities. An attack on an institution—or a man." As he expressed the last part of his thought, Hockney remembered something that made him anxious to get uptown, to where the marchers would be slowly converging on United Nations Plaza. He saw Wright Washington walking, upright and alone, into the flames and flying bullets of Liberty City. Washington would be leading part of the procession today, and Hockney suddenly feared for him. The assassination of Martin Luther King, Washington's mentor, had created a chain explosion of anger and grief in more than a hundred American cities. It came to Hockney, in a terrible dawn of insight, that if the men who had adopted the cover name The Liberators were bent on fulfilling the design that Castro had laid bare in Monimbó, the ideal target was not President Newgate or a Wall Street billionaire. It was a black leader like Washington, a moderate whose loss would be mourned by a whole nation, who stood in the path of the militants who wanted to lead his community into violent revolt, but whose death—under the right circumstances—could be used by them as a rallying cry.

"I have to get to the rally," he said to Fischer, who looked at him thoughtfully.

"You better hoof it over to Fulton and get the subway," the police captain suggested. "Nothing on rubber tires is going to get you out of this shit in a hurry."

New York loves a parade, and despite the torpid heat, and the fact that it was a weekday, a big crowd turned out to watch the Peace with Cuba marchers making their way down First

326

Avenue, in a column as sinuous and colorful as a Chinese dragon. Costumed volunteers headed the procession, tolling bells and blowing trumpets, providing plenty of visual excitement with huge papier-mâché puppets depicting President Newgate and the CIA and the Pentagon generals as fire-breathing monsters. The placards and banners that followed in their wake advertised every conceivable cause, from the Irish Republican Army to the Lesbian Mothers' Commune. There were the red flags of the Marxists, the black or black-and-red flags of the anarchists, the pastel blue-and-white of the Interdenominational Brotherhood for Peace. There were the flags of Cuba and the PLO, Nicaragua and Vietnam. The initials of the scores of union locals and grass-roots organizations taking part made an alphabet soup. The notables in the front rows were churchmen, actors, a retired admiral, a Congressman or two and a novelist with a whiskey breath who was generally expected to get himself arrested so he could write a book about the proceedings.

You could feel the excitement building as the head of the dragon wound closer to the drab edifice, opposite the formidable glass pile of the United Nations, that housed the United States Mission to the world assembly. But word of the bombing downtown, at the World Trade Center, was beginning to spread, and there was nervous tension in the air. The police were courteous and distant. Still, many of the people on First Avenue sensed that something dramatic was going to happen, if only to ensure that the march was not wiped off the front pages and the TV news by what was going on at the other end of the island.

It was not by intentional segregation that Wright Washington's group was following along at the tail end of the procession. He had made a late start from Marcus Garvey Park, where he had assembled several hundred activists from the mainstream civil rights organizations, because he had been heckled and openly challenged by a band of Black Power militants who denied his right to speak for the community. Some of them wore the skullcaps or paramilitary gear of the Fedayeen, whose leader, Commander Ali, was continuing to broadcast incendiary appeals for a black uprising from his new exile in Grenada.

The trouble began in the Sixties, when the marchers from Harlem were passing a bank and a couple of chichi restaurants, and some of the kids at the back of the column threw rocks and bottles. Washington heard the noise of shattering glass, saw frightened faces in the crowd and cops wading in with their nightsticks. He stopped the march and picked his way back through the ranks.

"This is not the way!" he kept shouting. "We will have no truck with violence!"

"Tell it, Doctor," a few of the older marchers chorused approvingly.

But the Fedayeen and the Black Berets jeered him.

"If the pigs want a fight, we'll give them a fight!" one of them yelled.

There was a skirmish as a couple of the rock throwers were grabbed by the police and manhandled toward a waiting van.

A fellow minister came and plucked at Washington's sleeve and pointed to a bulky man in a police inspector's uniform who was waiting patiently on the curb.

"He wants to talk to you."

"Yes, Inspector?" Washington said to the cop.

"You got some rough characters with you, Reverend. Can you handle them?"

"I'm trying. We want a peaceful demonstration."

"Seems to me they're aiming to start a fight with the police."

"We'll try not to satisfy them." Washington spoke with more confidence than he felt inside himself.

The Inspector looked at him skeptically, but waved them on.

The trouble got worse in the Fifties, when some of the roughnecks tried to break away from the body of the procession and head west toward Fifth Avenue. The police quickly formed a line to head them off. By the time the fighting was over, a dozen more arrests had been made. Nobody at the back of the column wanted to listen to the marshals, or to Wright Washington him-

328

self. He felt he was driving a car whose wheels were about to come off.

Hockney rode uptown on the Lexington Avenue IRT line, in a subway car whose walls and ceiling had been totally covered with illegible graffiti, meaningless initials that writhed like snakes. He got off at Grand Central and raced across town toward United Nations Plaza. With the help of his press card, he worked in and out of the mass of demonstrators, looking for Wright Washington. He glimpsed Willard Holmes, coming out of the U.S. Mission building with a cherubic smile on his face after presenting his petition. He saw a couple of fortyish women whose clothes would have been right for Haight-Ashbury, circa 1965, make the middle-aged hippie gesture of handing one of New York's Finest a big yellow sunflower. He saw college kids, and the famous novelist, lie down in the street, and go limp when the cops moved in to arrest them.

Hockney pushed his way through to the north side of the plaza, where a small group of hard-hats were yelling abuse at the protesters, and heard a different kind of chanting, a rhythmic, full-bodied rendition of an old spiritual. From his new vantage point, he saw Wright Washington, tall, straight-backed, soberly attired in his dark suit and dark tie, setting the pace for his ragged column. Hockney started walking toward him, around the side of a truck with a TV camera mounted on the back. He became aware that the people in the rear guard of Washington's column were not joining in the spiritual. They were bawling out their own slogans.

"What do we want?" one of their leaders boomed.

The response was not the old civil liberties cry: "Freedom!"
The chorus came back: "Black rev-o-lu-*tion*!"

One of the placards read, "CYANIDE FOR NEWGATE."

Behind the protection of the police line, a heckler bellowed, "Go back to Africa!" and then, when this had little effect, "Long live the KKK!"

That got more of a rise. In plain view of the TV camera,

several black youths hurled themselves at the *provocateur,* and succeeded in breaching the police line. More cops rushed to the spot, and were caught up in the melee of whirling fists. A youth in a black beret flung what looked like a rolled-up newspaper at a paunchy patrolman. It caught the side of his head, and he screamed in pain. As he fell, Hockney saw blood streaming from a circular wound above his ear. As the Black Beret reached down to retrieve the iron bar he had concealed inside the paper, another cop brought his nightstick smashing down across his collarbone.

An inspector standing near Hockney gabbled urgently into his walkie-talkie, "Hats and bats. Hats and bats."

Hockney hurried toward Washington, who was trying to make himself heard above the clamor, pleading with the Fedayeen and the Black Berets to stop fighting.

"This isn't what we're here for," Washington protested.

"That's what you think, Granddad," someone spat at him. "I want to kill me some pigs!"

Some of the police had formed a wedge, trying to break up the knot of black demonstrators that had edged onto the pavement.

Then the shooting started. It was not shooting to begin with, but neither Hockney nor most of the increasingly jittery cops on First Avenue knew that. Somebody among the marchers set off a couple of firecrackers—the big M-80 bangers that pack as much power as a fifth of a half-pound stick of dynamite and will blow your hand off if you dally too long before you throw them. The noise they made was more of a boom than a crack. They sounded like shotgun blasts.

The spectators along the sidewalks scattered. Women shrieked, and Hockney saw somebody trip and fall over a baby stroller.

"Get back!" a red-faced patrolman with his gun out yelled at Hockney, but he took no notice. He was running now, running to where he could see Wright Washington's thatch of white hair above the mob.

A lot of the policemen had their guns out, and there were

more advancing in full riot gear—reinforcements who had been held in reserve in a side street. The Inspector was calling on Washington's group to disperse.

He was answered by the crack of a real bullet, fired by someone in the back of the crowd.

Hockney had been only a couple of yards from Wright Washington when he saw a trim, broad-shouldered cop take careful aim with his revolver. There was something familiar about this policeman. Not the hair, which was the wrong color. Not the severe, steel-rimmed glasses. Certainly not the uniform, which looked about a half-size too big. It was the eyes: the pale green of cat's eyes or shallow Caribbean waters.

It took a second, maybe two, before recognition was fully shaped in Hockney's mind—too long to have saved Wright Washington's life. But he had moved before then, guided by instinct, thrusting himself past a couple of Washington's followers, colliding with the black minister and sending him sprawling across the road, so that the bullet from the cop's gun passed through his shoulder instead of his heart.

Hockney bruised his knee badly in the fall, but uncaring, he picked himself up and sprinted after the man with green eyes whom he had first met on a cruise ship steaming to San Juan. He was oblivious to everything but the need to stop this man: to the cries of anger and fear that were raised all around him, to the effect of pulling his own gun—the Walther he had worn ever since he had bought it from Parodi's gun shop in Miami— as he gave chase to a man in police uniform. The man with green eyes twisted away from him, through the crowd. Then, for an instant, Hockney had him in his sights, with an unobstructed line of fire.

But strong hands were laid on him, his wrist was screwed like the top of a jar until the gun fell from his hand and then he was on the ground, with heavy boots hammering at his stomach and his groin.

He heard the words "Kill a cop, would ya?" from a ripe, Irish-American voice. Then someone kicked him in the throat, and everything receded into a purplish dark.

331

At five in the afternoon, in the middle of what would have been the rush hour if traffic had been moving anywhere in Lower Manhattan, a TV reporter intercepted Joe Fischer on the steps of City Hall.

"Captain Fischer, can we get your comments on what the Police Department is doing to bring the situation under control?"

Fischer looked at the microphone as if he were thinking of wrapping it round the young reporter's neck.

He had an odd twinkle in his eye when he said, "We can see the elephant."

"I didn't quite get that."

"Don't they teach you kids American history anymore?" Fischer asked. "That's what Civil War soldiers said after going into battle for the first time. We have seen the elephant."

At five on the dot, a series of explosions knocked out five power substations in Manhattan, Brooklyn and Queens. Later investigations showed they had been caused by limpet mines, detonated by radio control. Consolidated Edison had already been forced to close down several transformers that had been damaged by sniper fire. A few well-aimed shots from a high-powered rifle had punctured their cooling tanks, causing the oil coolant to seep out.

The city had experienced blackouts before. In 1965, the failure of a shoe-box–size relay system at the Sir Adam Beck station in Canada, just north of Niagara Falls, had led to a chain disaster that had turned off lights and stopped subways and elevators all over the five boroughs. Again, in 1977, equipment failures and the effect of lightning on high-voltage transmission lines had produced a blackout in much of the city and triggered widespread looting and street crime. Con Edison and the city and state authorities had since tried to guard against another major power failure by opening up feeder lines from New Jersey and revamping the whole grid. But what the city was not prepared for was the pinpoint sabotage of local transformers and switching stations. As off-duty Con Edison employees tried to get from their homes to the nearest power station, the Mayor was told that for most of the night, all of the city except for Staten Island and a small section of Brooklyn would be in darkness.

Since the explosions that had ripped apart One World Trade Center, many of the offices in the business district—following a public appeal from the Mayor—had closed down early, and people who drove to work from New Jersey and the outlying boroughs had been trying to fight their way through the gridlock to the bridges and tunnels that anchored the island of Manhattan to its dormitory suburbs. Traffic was jammed bumper to bumper all the way up the FDR Drive to the Triborough Bridge. Its great span carried more than one hundred sixty thousand cars on an average day, but only a fraction of that number was getting through. When a truck had jackknifed across the inbound lanes, it had caused a multiple pileup. Then the truck had burst into flame; it seemed that its cargo was liquid paraffin. Deliberate sabotage was suspected, since the driver had vanished, apparently in a waiting car. The police had been reduced to banning all inbound traffic across the bridge.

Then, in midafternoon, there had been an almost identical incident in the Midtown Tunnel. This time, nobody was left in any doubt as to whether it was an accident. Near the Queens exit from the outbound tube, a delivery van skidded to a stop, and the driver was seen to throw himself free just before the two cars behind plowed into the back of the vehicle. Within minutes, four hundred pounds of dynamite turned the delivery truck into a fireball, shattered the walls of the tunnel and blew out the eardrums of some of the survivors who managed to haul themselves out of the wreckage of their cars two hundred yards back.

The third link between Manhattan and Long Island that was hit that afternoon was less important than the others, when measured in the dry statistics of the volume of daily traffic that flowed over it, but it held a special place in the imagination of every New Yorker, and of everyone who had ever dreamed about New York. From a distance, the suspension cables of the Brooklyn Bridge looked fine and gauzy as dragonfly wings.

The strongest were corded steel, eighteen inches thick. In the early hours of the night, it had taken the Puerto Rican in Beacher's group less than three minutes to shinny up to the underside of the bridge on the Brooklyn side, using a handy drainpipe for support. They called him El Gato for a reason; he could climb like a cat, and was completely at home in the dark. He climbed to where four huge suspension cables were secured by a stone anchor the size of a three-story town house, and placed two charges of plastic explosive. The timers were set for 5 P.M. The first part of his job complete, El Gato repeated the operation on the Manhattan side of the bridge. There was another convenient drainpipe that could be approached through the dusty parking lot under the ramp. Nobody noticed the charges during the day; one of the charms of *plastique* is that it looks like putty, or fresh cement. When the twin explosions cut the cables at either end of the bridge, the police had to set up barriers—lines of shiny blue sawhorses—to stop the traffic going both ways.

But the police could not be everywhere, and the same went for the men in all of the city's emergency services. Fire alarms were going off all over the five boroughs, many of them fakes. Throughout most of the city there was an alarm box on every other street corner, advertised by a glowing amber light on the side of a building or a lamppost, twenty feet above the ground. Dozens of these alarms were tripped.

In a room the size of a tennis court in the Maspeth area of Queens, near Mount Zion Cemetery, the commander of the city's Emergency Medical Services, stunned by the number of MCIs—Multi-Casualty Incidents—that his operators were reporting, had to do some fast reordering of priorities. He had just over a hundred municipal ambulances at his disposal. Their normal reaction time was 10.8 minutes. With gridlock squeezing Manhattan like a vise, it was taking more than three times as long to respond to the most urgent calls.

"Normal medical emergencies go to Priority Two," he ruled. "We have to get to the bomb and the riot victims first."

334

"Does that go for CVAs too?" one of his deputies asked. CVA was the abbreviation used on the computer terminals for cardiovascular accidents—heart attacks.

"It goes for CVAs too."

In another building in Queens, near the exit from the Fifty-ninth Street Bridge, the city's traffic controllers were ready to throw in the sponge. A huge semicircular map on the wall showed the five boroughs, and the lights at the intersections. Guided by videocameras, sensors and police reports, the traffic controllers could adjust the speed at which the lights turned from green to amber to red to avoid logjams. What was happening in the city now was beyond their realm.

"We might as well turn off all the traffic lights in Manhattan," suggested a harassed man who had been chain-smoking all afternoon. "Even the fire trucks and the ambulances can't get through. The only way we can get things moving is if the cops start dumping cars in the river."

"It could happen yet," his boss commented. The expression on his face did not suggest he was joking.

Over at the Transit Authority building, on Jay Street in Brooklyn, the trainmaster got down from his raised pink booth and padded across the pea-green carpet to one of the line watchers who was studying the hundred-foot-long wall grid that displayed the city's subway system. One by one, all the lights along Line 4 had flashed red. The same was happening to the other lines.

"How many trains would you say we had running?" the trainmaster asked.

"I guess about five hundred at this time of day."

"Yeah," the trainmaster agreed. As he watched, more red lights were tripped along the route of the Seventh Avenue Express, all the way from Two Hundred Forty-second Street in the Bronx to its Jamaica terminus. "And I figure half those trains are stuck in the tunnels."

The line watcher said, "Ed, my daughter usually takes the subway home about this time. Do you mind . . ."

"Yeah. Go and make the call. The phones are about all that's working in this town."

In some of the trapped subway cars, straphangers inured to long delays were taking things calmly. Strangers even started talking to each other amiably, which is a rare occurrence on the New York subways. On a train that had ground to a halt about a block away from the Bowling Green station, a retired Marine colonel took command—making sure that seats were available for the elderly and for women with small children; issuing brisk instructions about how people would take turns walking to the last car to relieve themselves. There was an emergency exit leading up to the street less than twenty feet away from the train, but nobody thought of looking for that in the dark.

In Tutie's, a watering hole in Richmond Hill under the El, the bar started to fill up with passengers who had climbed off a stopped train, and for the first time in years the amazing array of scrap metal hanging from the ceiling ceased to rattle and bang with the thunder of the "African Queen"—as the owner referred, not altogether fondly, to the J-line express. A girl with nice legs came in, and he was disappointed that he could not play his favorite trick when she went to the ladies' room, now that the power was out. He had rigged up a Heath Robinson device that rang bells and flashed lights and blew up a nice warm gust of air under a girl's skirt as she came out of the rest room. What a pity, the owner thought as he popped open a couple of Budweisers. You didn't get many pairs of legs like those in Tutie's anymore, and if you did, they were safely encased in blue jeans.

At the FBI's emergency command post on the twenty-eighth floor of 26 Federal Plaza, Malone was sitting on open lines to Police Headquarters and the Director's office in Washington. He was getting the same question from both parties.

"No," he repeated for the Director's benefit. "We haven't arrested any saboteurs yet. We still don't know whether these calls from The Liberators are a blind or not. Nobody here has

336

ever heard of them before. . . . Yes, sir, that's in hand. . . . Yes, sir, I'll let you know as soon as anything breaks."

Malone set down the receiver and let his big jaw fall against his chest. He was not an imaginative man, and he could not conceive of how this mayhem had been brought to pass in *his* town. But now it had happened, he knew what to do. You went by the rule book. The rule book said that in the event of civil disorders, one of the primary responsibilities of the FBI was to make sure that nobody broke into the vaults of the New York banks and made off with the bullion and all those fat deposits insured by the FDIC. More than half of the eight hundred sixty Agents in the city were taking care of that, sitting underground in front of those big combination locks strumming the chambers of their revolvers, waiting for Bonnie and Clyde.

"I bet it's those Puerto Ricans," Malone said when an Agent came in with his coffee. "Remember, we caught some of those greasers with plans of the electrical system at Madison Square Garden a couple of years back? Where the fuck is Frank Parra? He's the one who ought to know."

Before Hockney woke, he dreamed that his intestines were being run through a sausage machine whose tube led through his mouth. It was an appallingly graphic dream, and when he came to, he found that his chin was covered with a thin stream of bile. He touched it, then pulled his fingertips away and felt lower. His neck was covered with bandages. The light from the open window hurt his eyes. He blinked away from it.

He knew the face that was leaning over him—the dark, intelligent eyes; the proud beak of a nose; the longish black hair.

Frank Parra said, "Don't try to talk."

It was sound advice. The first words that Hockney tried to utter made gargling sound like polite conversation. And they hurt. He felt as if he had just had his tonsils extracted.

"Count yourself lucky they didn't kill you," Parra went on. "The patrolman who kicked you is named O'Keefe. He grew up in a rough neighborhood. He must have slipped as he went

337

for your throat; otherwise, you wouldn't be here."

"Where . . ." That was better. By sucking in his bottom teeth and sticking out his lips, Hockney got out a sound that resembled human speech.

"You're in Lenox Hill Hospital," Parra said. "Don't thank me. Thank the cop who was smart enough to go through your pockets before letting O'Keefe finish his job. They found your press card. And my phone number."

"Wash-ing-ton." That took a greater effort.

"He's here too. I guess you saved his life. They cut a bullet out of his shoulder. He's weak, but he'll live. Here, let me help you."

Hockney was trying to lift himself into a sitting position. Parra took one of the pillows, doubled it and stuffed it behind his back.

"You two were the life and soul of the party," Parra said. "After that cop shot Washington, we got a full-dress riot. About five hundred arrests, just on U.N. Plaza. Then some of the crazies grabbed the microphone in Central Park and called for war. God knows what's going to break loose tonight. You're in one of the few rooms in this city that's got any lights."

Hockney squinted to look at his watch, but found that someone had removed it.

"You've been out for about five hours," Parra told him.

"The cop . . ." Hockney gasped.

"Rest your voice," the FBI man told him. "The doctor says there's nothing that won't heal if you take it slowly."

"Have—to—talk," Hockney insisted. He made the gesture of scribbling on the palm of his hand, and Parra brought out a notebook and a ball-point.

His hand shook as he wrote. The letters came out feathery and slightly backhand, like the writing of a child who was trying to keep within the lines.

"Cop who shot Washington," he wrote, *"not cop. Mitch Lardner. San Juan."*

He passed the notebook back to Parra, who frowned over it and said, "Are you sure?"

338

Hockney tried to nod his head, but that hurt too. However, the motion was not lost on the FBI man.

"You could be right," Parra said. "We made some inquiries. None of the other cops on the street knew this guy. Including our pal O'Keefe. The man who shot Washington just seems to have faded clean out of the picture. If you're right . . ." He paused, then went on: "Well, they didn't get a martyr today. But the way people are talking about it up in Harlem, you'd think they did. And God knows what Wright Washington's going to say about it when they discharge him. He seems to believe that the cops were out to murder him. Jesus." He thought about the effect the videotape of the near-assassination must be having around the country. Everywhere but in New York—where television was a casualty of the blackout—audiences would be watching a man in police uniform gun down one of the most respected black leaders in the United States.

Hockney motioned impatiently for Parra to return the pad. "*I have to talk to him*," he scrawled.

Parra said, "We'll see. Meantime, I want you to take a look at this."

He reached inside his jacket and pulled out a grainy six-by-four photograph, obviously a blowup. The picture showed two men huddled together in conversation at a restaurant table in the angle of two big windows. One of them had his hand over his mouth, as if afraid of lip-readers. You could just see the tip of a curly mustache, the bushy kind that picks up crumbs. He was a flat-faced, squatty man, but he was a very snappy dresser.

The man he was with was looking straight at the camera. Even in his preppy clothes and his glasses, with his hair dyed a darker shade and cut severely short, he was not someone Hockney would ever mistake. Nothing could disguise the intensity of those pale eyes, which showed up even in this smudgy black-and-white snapshot. He was staring at the same man who had pumped a .38 bullet into Wright Washington that afternoon: the man he had first encountered on the cruise ship *Duchess*, when he had called himself Mitch Lardner and had a ravishing Latin beauty as his companion.

Hockney stabbed his finger at Beacher's face. He croaked, "It's him."

"I thought it might be," Parra said as he pocketed the photograph.

Hockney took a gulp from a tumbler of pinkish liquid that had been left on his bedside table. It tasted like the stuff dentists give you to rinse your mouth with after they have been drilling into your nerves, but it helped. Hockney was able to get out a whole sentence.

"Where'd you get this?" he rasped.

Parra's face set into the enigmatic smile of a Mayan bas-relief.

"For the record," he said, "it came in the mail from an anonymous benefactor. Between you and me, it was taken yesterday afternoon inside the U.N., at that restaurant on the second floor."

Hockney knew the place. One of its caprices was to offer a surprise cocktail—an "unusual"—every day at lunch. Last time he had eaten there, the "unusual" was a blend of gin and Campari and Triple Sec, surprisingly kind to the palate. He could have done with one now.

Of course, the United Nations building was supposed to be consecrated ground, off limits to FBI Agents and New York cops. Hockney waited for Frank Parra to explain how they had happened to catch the man with green eyes in there.

"You didn't recognize the other guy, did you?" Parra asked.

Hockney shook his head.

"Funny," Parra went on. "I would have bet you two knew each other. He's the one we were keeping tabs on. His name is Teófilo Gómez."

He waited for a reaction, and he got one. Hockney was so excited that he almost choked himself trying to talk, and had to down some more of the pink bilge. He had never seen Gómez in the flesh, but he knew that the chief of the Cuban spy network in New York had been a prime mover in the events that had scarred his life over the past months. Teófilo Gómez was the man who had arranged his disastrous trip to Havana. Almost certainly, he was Julio Parodi's contact in New York, the reason for those visits to Yankee Stadium. Now Frank Parra had produced evidence that the DGI Station Chief was dealing directly with the terrorist who had tried to assassinate Wright Washington. It was the proof—if it could only be used—that there *was* a Monimbó Plan. The question Hockney was now putting to himself was the first that would have occurred to any newsman. How could he get the story out?

"Videotape," he managed to say to Parra. "There must be a videotape of the shooting. I saw a TV camera."

"There is," the FBI man said. "It was a Channel Three camera. There's a hitch. We asked them for a copy of the tape, and they refused to give it to us. I talked to some producer who made it sound like helping the Bureau was the next thing to collaborating with the Gestapo. He said they're putting the videotape out on the national news, and we can get our own copy from that. You know what *that* means. The airports are closed—they're diverting the planes as far away as Bermuda. So we have to wait for one of our people to record the news on a Betamax and drive in from Jersey."

"Wait a minute." Hockney rolled out of bed and staggered over to the closet. He was shaky, but he could stand up. As he pulled his pants off a hanger, he went on, "I know somebody at Channel Three." The station was the local affiliate of Angela's network. He pointed to the phone beside the bed. "You make the call," he said to Parra. "Ask for Angela Seabury."

"I don't know if anyone will be there," Parra said, before he turned to arguing with the hospital operator about why she should give him an outside line. "Channel Three won't be doing much broadcasting tonight. But I think that building does have an emergency generator."

It took more arguing with the man on duty at the TV station's switchboard before Parra got through to Angela's office.

"Miss Seabury?"

"Who is this?" Her pleasant, rather throaty voice sounded strained.

"I'm a friend of Bob Hockney's. He's in the hospital. He got beaten up pretty rough today."

"I know. I saw it on video."

341

"That's why we're calling, Miss Seabury. We'd appreciate it very much if we could take a look at the tape."

"I don't know." Parra was holding the receiver a couple of inches from his ear, so that Hockney could listen to both sides of the conversation. Angela sounded nervous and reluctant.

"Let me," he said to Parra, taking the phone from him. "Angela?"

"Bob? God, I wouldn't have recognized you. You sound terrible."

"Listen, I'm in Lenox Hill Hospital. So is Wright Washington. I'm going in to see him now. We must have that videotape. I can't explain it all, but it's vital that Washington see it tonight."

"I don't know," she repeated. "Simon's imposed an embargo."

"Screw Simon!"

She hesitated, so he threw in something he had been holding in reserve. It was not the kind of card any reporter likes to play, but there was something more important at stake than who got an exclusive.

"Washington hasn't talked to the media yet," he said. "I figure I can get you first bite if you bring me that tape."

There was a short pause before she said, "I'll do it. But how am I going to get up there? The streets are unbelievable. It's like somebody kicked the top off an anthill."

Hockney glanced at Frank Parra. The FBI man said, "We'll arrange something."

"Just wait there ten minutes," Hockney told Angela. "You'll get presidential treatment."

He sloshed the remains of the pink liquid around in his mouth and spat into the washbasin. When he had finished dressing, he said to Parra, "What room is Wright Washington in?"

The FBI man told him, and added, "I'll get you past the cops. You better handle the rest by yourself. Washington has some friends with him who aren't exactly in love with the FBI. I'll field Angela when she arrives."

There were uniformed policemen at both ends of the corridor, but the men in front of the door to Washington's room were blacks in business suits. Hockney recognized one of them from the rally.

"I'm Bob Hockney," he introduced himself. "I'm a friend. I need to talk to him."

"My orders are not to let anyone in. The Mayor's coming. He won't see anybody until then."

"I must see him," Hockney insisted, and his voice cracked.

The man at the door looked as if he had had his share of hard knocks. His face might have been used as a pounding board, but it was a worried, intelligent face.

He inspected Hockney's bandages and said, "You're the one who got beat on by the cops, right?"

"Right."

"Okay. I'll go ask the man."

When he came back and let Hockney into the room, the reporter found Wright Washington half-dressed, his shoulder swathed in bandages and his right arm in a plaster cast. It was the man's mood that disturbed Hockney most. His whole bearing had changed. His shoulders were slumped, and his head lolled between them as if there were nothing to support it.

"I've tried all my life to fight against violence," he said, to nobody in particular. "And my life has been a failure. I belong to the past." He had a rice-paper Bible with a worn leather cover open on the bed. He picked it up and said, "Here it is, in Matthew Ten: Thirty-four. Jesus says, *Think not that I am come to send peace on earth: I came not to send peace, but a sword.*" He closed the Bible, but went on cradling it in his hands.

Washington said, "That's the kind of passage that white Southern fundamentalists, the ones who made out segregation was God's law and that it was right to kill your enemies, loved to quote. I never believed that was the message of the Bible. Maybe I was wrong. You know what's happening out there?"

He turned to Hockney, and the reporter saw that his eyes were moist.

"I know," Hockney said gently. "You have to stop it."

"What do you want me to do?" Washington flared up at him. "You want me to do what I tried to do in Miami? You want me to go around telling black kids they oughtn't to be looting and burning and killing when the power structure is killing *them*? When they all know the police killed several people today just because they were black, or angry, and that a policeman tried to kill *me*? You're asking me to do something I can't do. I don't have the faith to do it anymore."

"There's something you have to understand," Hockney began. He tried, haltingly, to explain about the terrorist in a cop's uniform and the Cubans, and watched Wright Washington's eyelids come down like visors. One of the other blacks in the room came right out and said, "What kind of bull are you trying to feed us?"

"I know it must sound incredible," Hockney responded. "But I think I can prove it to you."

As long as Angela keeps her promise, he thought.

She got there fifteen minutes later, and Hockney had to go out and offer more explanations before the men at the door let her through. He took the Betamax she had lugged down the corridor and rigged it up to the old TV set opposite the bed. Whorls and asterisks like punctuation in an action comic strip flickered across the screen; then they were looking at the scene of the shooting. There was only a brief glimpse of the cop with green eyes moving forward, out of the police line, with his revolver in hand. Hockney rewound the tape and played that part again.

"Can we freeze that frame?" he asked Angela.

She showed him how to do it.

"The Mayor's got a lot of explaining to do," one of Washington's aides muttered. "About why they haven't locked up that murderer cop yet."

"I want you to look at this," Hockney said to the minister as he passed him the snapshot of the terrorist with Teófilo Gómez.

"It's the same man," Washington said instantly.

"Exactly."

Angela went over and leaned across Washington's shoulder to look at the photograph.

Her eyes widened, and she said, "That's Teófilo."

"Right again."

Hockney ran through the whole story, from the time of his first chance encounter with the man with the green eyes on the cruise to San Juan, careful to sift fact from supposition.

"The Cubans wanted you as a martyr figure," he concluded. "They want a race war in this country. They want this city in flames. They want desperation, because they can use desperate people the way they're using the Fedayeen. They don't care what happens to your community. They don't care if Harlem is laid waste."

"It could happen tonight," Washington said softly. "I don't know whether there's any power that can stop it. Not tonight."

"You have to try," Hockney pleaded with him. "People in Harlem will listen to you. They're not going to listen to the Mayor, or the Police Commissioner, or to Robert Hockney or anybody in the media. You have to explain that they're being used."

Angela seized her moment. "I've got a TV crew waiting downstairs," she said. She glanced at her watch. "We could run an interview on the national news at seven. We can send the tape to Newark by helicopter."

"Nobody will see it in New York," Washington observed. He straightened up a bit; swayed his head back on his shoulders, with his eyes shut; then stood up with a new air of decision. "We'll get a truck," he said to his aides. "Maybe a flatbed truck. We'll need some lights, and an amplifier, and as many of our people as we can get. We'll handle our own security. I don't want any cops around tonight."

The aide who had challenged Hockney started to protest, but Washington raised his voice like a roll of drums and said, "I see my way. It's the only way I can go. M.L. used to say there would be no black hooded mobs, no black cross-burnings, no black lynchings. I want that to be true tonight. I'll do it alone if I have to."

345

Angela did not look happy. "You promised an interview," she hissed to Hockney as they filed out of the hospital room in the wake of the black minister. But she was too shaken by what she had just learned about her friend Teófilo Gómez to press her point. She caught Hockney's arm as if to steady herself.

She remembered something the dark, handsome man who had picked her up at the network building had asked her to pass on.

She said to Hockney, "Your friend—Frank—he said to tell you he had to leave. He wants you to call him later."

On the way to Angela's studio, Parra had got a message from Wallace on his walkie-talkie, and pulled over to the curb so he could call the black Agent back from a telephone kiosk. Anybody with a few hundred bucks could buy a Bearcat transceiver that could pick up the FBI frequencies, as well as all the police channels. For a sensitive job, in Parra's book, nothing was as secure as an outdoor pay phone.

"Malone is steaming mad," Wallace told him. "He says we can't spare the men for the stakeout unless we're sure we've got something. He wants us to pull out."

Wallace was out in the Bronx, keeping an eye on a bruised tenement near People's Park, a weedy, overgrown lot where the Puerto Rican *independentistas* and some of the Black Power radicals hung out. It was a place where you never saw patrolmen on foot.

"Have we got something?" Parra asked.

"Maybe. There's a fair amount of action around the building. I saw a couple of heavy dudes go in there fifteen minutes ago. One's in the Fedayeen. I think the other was a P.R."

"What do you think?"

"I guess we could strike it lucky."

"We'll give it another hour. I want to get down to Clinton Street and see what the action is there. But if you see anybody trying to move the merchandise out, you'd better hit them fast. Have you got enough backup?"

"I'll get by."

"One more thing. The guy in the photograph, with the Cuban at the U.N. He's the man we want. We don't have a name yet. He called himself Mitch Lardner in Puerto Rico, but he hasn't showed up in any other files."

"Do we have prints?"

"We got some off his cocktail glass. But they don't match anything in the computers. I'll have somebody trim the photograph and circulate it to the cops. If you run into him, go for broke. But do me a favor, will you? Let's try to take this one alive."

Frank Parra avoided calling Malone at Headquarters. It was always easier to apologize for a lapse in communications than to explain why you refused to obey a direct order, and he was very nervous that Malone would order him to recall his men from the stakeouts so they could while away the rest of the night playing poker in the vaults of a couple of midtown banks.

Times of crisis often bring out the best or the worst in people, but always the unexpected.

As the sun set in a red haze over New Jersey, the clash of electric guitars sounded across Grand Army Plaza, and hundreds of people milling around the Plaza Hotel stopped to listen to the rock band. The ice cream vendors were doing a roaring trade. Tensions were released in a brittle, carnival gaiety. Under the astonished eyes of the motorists trapped along Fifth Avenue, couples of varying sexual composition started dancing to the beat. Inside the Plaza Hotel, the atmosphere was more sedate, but equally removed from the drama that was unfolding in other quarters of the city. The violins kept playing as waiters bearing trays of canapés rustled among the marble-topped tables of the Palm Court.

In German Yorkville, farther uptown, a tiny bookkeeper who lived alone and kept to himself surprised his neighbors when he descended the stairs from his sixth-floor apartment carrying a shotgun, a hunting knife and an antique Colt .45. He proceeded to sandbag the lobby with an old bed frame and some trash cans, lighted a kerosene lantern and swore to Heidi

Schurz, who got around with the aid of a metal walker and spent most of her days sitting by the front door on a folding chair, that their building was one that no looter was going to get into that night.

Down in Chinatown, below Canal Street, some very serious negotiations were going on between leaders of the business community and some young men who sported flak jackets and carried automatic weapons. One of them had just arrived from Hong Kong. He was one of the chiefs of a street gang called the Flying Dragons. He sat across the table from the leader of the Ghost Shadows, his gang's main rival group, in an office above a store that displayed grinning masks and mildly erotic figurines carved from whalebone. At the start of the meeting, the two street warriors looked ready to finish their vendetta over—or under—the table. By the end of it, the businessmen had persuaded them to enter into a compact. For the duration of the troubles, the gangs would forget their blood feuds and assume the role of community defenders, standing guard over the businesses and restaurants that had spilled out of Chinatown proper and were dislodging the Italians from some of the blocks around Mulberry Street. It was a costly arrangement for the sleek men in business suits who sat around the table, sipping brandy or Tsingtao beer, but they had more faith that night in the Flying Dragons and the Ghost Shadows than in the harassed cops at the Fifth Precinct.

In stalled elevators and subway cars all over town, people sweated or swooned, suffered heart attacks and claustrophobic fits, went into labor pains, lost control of their bladders—or tried to wait it all out patiently, trading wisecracks about Con Edison, or the Mayor, and laughing too hard because nothing was very funny.

In the diamond merchants' building on the corner of Forty-seventh Street, a Hasid with a venerable white beard and a black coat that reached to his knees sat in a cramped office with a gun on the desk in front of him and a million dollars in jewels in a satchel between his legs and talked in Yiddish to his son in Williamsburg. The local self-defense group that had been formed there to fight street crime had already sent out cars equipped with CB radios to patrol the perimeters of the Jewish neighborhoods.

In the city's more exclusive male preserves, cavernous and dark even by day without artificial light, members were trying to be very British and stiff-upper-lip, but the calls on bar service were more pressing and more frequent than at the end of a normal business day, even the day of a stock-market crash or a record rally. In leather wing chairs in the smoking room of the Racquet Club on Park Avenue, members went on shaking the dice by candlelight as if there were nothing more urgent to think about. In the Georgian mansion on Sixty-second Street that housed Links, men with dynastic names and homes within walking distance made their farewells and headed back to their families without a semblance of haste, propelled by some hereditary sixth sense that allowed them to intuit when history was going awry.

In the shopping precinct in Crown Heights, a mostly black neighborhood in Brooklyn, Italian storekeepers appeared outside their premises with guns in their hands and just stood there, legs splayed, letting anyone know who was interested that they were ready to shoot to protect their groceries.

In Harlem, squads of the Fedayeen and the Black Berets delivered harangues at street corners, announcing that the fall of America was at hand and that blacks should join in a just war to avenge the attempted assassination of Wright Washington. Some of the militants went around promising that anyone who wanted a gun would have one before the night was through.

"You ask me, how are we gonna kill the pigs when the pigs have all kinds of firepower," a Fedayeen leader in battle fatigues yelled at his audience. "I'm telling you every one of you is gonna get you a gun. We're gonna have more firepower than the Man. In a couple of hours, you gonna believe me."

At 8:30 P.M., the Fedayeen staged an object lesson for the community. Truck 2—part of Captain Fischer's Emergency Services Unit—was tucked away on One Hundred Twenty-sixth Street, opposite a playground where young blacks assem-

349

bled at night to smoke reefers and play their huge box radios and make out. A group of Fedayeen waited quietly in the playground until more than half of the men attached to Truck 2 had dispersed to answer crisis calls. Then their leader calmly blew a hole through the sturdy steel doors of the police garage with a Belgian-made FN mortar. There was only one cop inside the garage, and he was caught totally off guard. The Fedayeen used him as a human shield, prodding him ahead of them with a knife at his throat up the inside stairs from the garage to the station house on the second floor. Two more cops, racing out of the radio room toward the pegs in the hall where their gun belts were hanging, were caught in a burst of M-16 fire. The Fedayeen found the sergeant in the TV room, sheltering behind the clanking old refrigerator. A stolen plaque from the Libyan Mission to the United Nations hung askew on the wall. The sergeant held out for about ten minutes, returning fire from his tenuous position with a pump shotgun. After he shot one of the Fedayeen in the gut, the leader of the group decided to cut things short. He brought up the Belgian mortar, and blew the sergeant and most of the refrigerator out the far wall. Then he swaggered into the radio room and called Fischer's command post.

"We have liberated one of the forts of the colonial occupiers," he shrilled in a high, nasal voice. "This is just retribution for police crimes against our people. We demand the immediate withdrawal of all occupation forces from black and Puerto Rican neighborhoods by midnight. Up yours, honky."

By the time Captain Fischer was able to fight his way through to Truck 2 with reinforcements, the Fedayeen had pulled out. He took one look at the damage and the shape of the shrapnel and said, "Where the fuck are these sons-of-bitches getting *mortars*?"

In both the black and the Puerto Rican neighborhoods, most people stayed at home, trying to keep out of trouble. A few brave men and women—mostly older people who held down jobs—ventured out, trying to reason with the kids on the streets not to listen to the crazies, not to treat a riot like a street party.

They were not getting much of a hearing. The attack on Wright Washington—word of which had spread all over town—on top of the bombings had created a sense of total license, a spirit of Roman holiday. And when news of the Fedayeen's assault on Truck 2 began to circulate, people began to realize that the police were on the defensive, that the thin blue line had been stretched until it snapped like a worn rubber band. It seemed that whatever you did that night, the risk of getting punished for it by anyone wearing a badge was pretty negligible.

But the wildest rumor of all, the one that had the tough kids hyped, stemmed from what the Fedayeen and the Black Berets were saying on the street corners. It was that everybody was going to be given a gun—not just some cheap Saturday Night Special, but a real man's gun, an automatic rifle or a shotgun or even heavy artillery, like a bazooka or a grenade launcher. Some people said the Fedayeen had ripped off a National Guard armory. Others said the Weathermen and the BLA were back, and had hijacked a whole convoy of weapons from the U.S. Sixth Army.

If the people who had set up an impromptu party in an elegant duplex overlooking the Metropolitan Museum had heard any of this talk, chances are they would not have been thrown into any paroxysms of terror. The duplex belonged to the heir to a department-store fortune, and he and most of his guests were deliciously high on cocaine.

"It's beautiful!" kept exclaiming a model who was being assiduously courted by a Senator with a famous name who was making the best of having to stay overnight in the city. "The whole city is dancing inside my head."

They all felt witty and brilliant and sexually aware, secure in a parallel world, the plight of the city a dizzy backdrop to their preferred entertainments.

Someone said something about Nero fiddling while Rome burned, as if he had just invented the analogy.

"That's beautiful!" the model trilled again, and turned to borrow a hundred-dollar bill rolled into a tube from the Senator. "You know what?" she said to him. "We ought to go up to

Harlem so we can show our support. You're a hero with those people."

In a bar on Mulberry Street, near Umberto's Clam House, where the mobster Joey Gallo had been machine-gunned to death by hit men from a rival family in a passing car, Mike Santini was putting in one of a series of personal appearances that he made in Italian neighborhoods that night.

"You don't have to worry about a thing," the Mafia boss assured the owner of the bar, who was the cousin of a *capo* in his own family.

"We're gonna take care of you, like always. We're gonna keep crime off the streets."

Well before midnight, soldiers of the Santini family made their presence felt in the corners of Italy that were still preserved within the island of Manhattan—sharply dressed men who loafed about in the streets or sat up on the rooftops with rifles fitted with night scopes.

Before the turn of the century, a Danish immigrant, Jacob Riis, who had taken up the cudgels in behalf of the city's poor, had observed that a map of New York, colored to designate nationalities and ethnic origins, would show more stripes than the skin of a zebra. That night, the pattern looked more like the spots on a leopard. But it was hard to see the whole pattern from any single vantage point in the city, not even from the eighth floor of Police Headquarters, where the radio and phone operators were engulfed in a churning sea of information. And not from the FBI's emergency command post on Federal Plaza, where Malone used some fine Irish brogue on Frank Parra when he finally reported in by phone.

Frank Parra didn't look much like a Puerto Rican, but he could talk like one, and that was what counted when he went knocking on the door of the house off Clinton Street. He had watched several vehicles—vans and station wagons and a New York Telephone truck that didn't belong on that street at that time of night—pull up nearby. He had a near-photographic

352

memory for faces, and he recognized one or two of the men who went into the building from the mug shots he had pinned to the wall in the bullpen of the antiterrorist unit in San Juan. When one of them came out again, lugging a box, Parra decided that if they were getting ready to move out, it was time for him to move in. He had tried to raise Joe Fischer, without success. He guessed that the police Emergency Services Unit had plenty to think about after the assault on Truck 2 in Harlem. He would have to make do with what he had: four men, one of them a newlywed from Wichita who had been expecting his wife to join him that day. Parra sent two of them to try to work their way up the fire escape at the rear of the house, deployed one across the road with a sniper's rifle equipped with infrared sights and told the boy from Kansas to back him up, but to keep out of the way until he was needed.

The door opened a chink at his knock, and a surly Spanish-accented voice asked what he wanted.

"Soy amigo del Gato," Parra murmured. He had got rid of his suit and pulled on a sloppy pair of work pants he kept in the trunk of his car. The nickname "El Gato" was one of the few leads the Bureau had picked up after grilling scores of suspects in the course of the investigation of Senator Fairchild's death in Puerto Rico. It was as good a nickname as any other. It was worth taking a shot on.

"No está," the man at the door responded, opening it a fraction wider so he could peer up and down the street. Deep pools of darkness behind the blacked-out streetlamp and under the broken steps leading up to the porch covered the other FBI men.

"Me necesita algo," Parra insisted, confident now that he had guessed right, that all the threads were woven together.

The man at the door took another look at him, shrugged and said, *"Espere."* He shut the door in Parra's face and went off to talk to somebody inside.

Parra glanced around to reassure himself that the kid from Wichita was out of sight. He was raw, but they seemed to make them big and brawny in Kansas, and he had a nice steely-blue Remington 12-gauge shotgun. All Parra had was a toy pistol—a .22—in an ankle holster. The door was opened again. The frame was scored and splintered as if that door had been forced open more than once.

"Está bien," the man said.

Parra had not crossed the threshold of the front room when there was a crash at the back of the house, and a couple of gunshots, and yells of *"¡Policía!"* A powerfully built black came running out of the front room with a neat little submachine gun in his hand, and Parra didn't bother to introduce himself before he dropped him with a bullet through the shoulder. The gun clattered to the floor, and the FBI man scooped it up and turned to confront the Puerto Rican who had let him in, a loose-boned youth with nappy hair who was pointing a magnum which at that range might have blown a hole through Parra the size of a man's fist, but didn't because Wichita came smashing through the door as if making a flying tackle, and brought the barrel of his beautiful Remington down across the hollow at the back of the Puerto Rican's neck.

The other Puerto Ricans in the back room died hard, and they took one of Parra's men with them. When Parra stepped over the bodies to take a look inside the room, he understood what sort of perishable commodities had been shipped to Harry Diva's stall all the way from Panama. There were M-16s; Belgian FN rifles; German-made Ambrust 300 automatics, perfect for close-quarters killing; grenades and bazookas and RPG-7 rocket launchers. There were more guns and crates of ammunition and canisters of plastic explosive in the basement, enough to equip an army regiment and to blow up most of lower Manhattan.

"Okay," he said to the black who was nursing the bullet wound in his shoulder. "Now you're going to tell me all about it."

The terrorist they called Plug shook his head and said, "Read me my rights, man. I know my rights."

354

Parra had better luck with the Puerto Rican who had been guarding the door, once he came around. He had him taken upstairs and practiced the old one-two routine. He would send Wichita in to be nice and explain to him about plea bargaining and feed him cigarettes. Then Parra would go in and knee him in the groin.

He ended up telling part of it, the small part that he knew. He was part of a Puerto Rican underground network. He had been training in Cuba. The black guy he called Bujía, or Spark Plug, had contacted him and his friends with a remarkable offer to supply weapons for a full-scale insurrection in New York. He didn't know who the benefactors were, but he had his suspicions.

When Parra was finished, he put a call through to Wallace at his stakeout in the Bronx.

He said only one word: "Go."

He was halfway back to his office when Wallace called back, not wary of using the radio now that the job was done.

"We got two of the Fedayeen who took care of those cops on a Hundred and Twenty-sixth Street," the black FBI Agent reported. "And one hell of a lot of dynamite and gasoline. Looks like they were setting to start a fire storm in Harlem."

"What about guns?"

"We got a few crates of M-Sixteens, and some pistols. I guess the rest of the stuff is already out on the street."

"Shit." But Parra added, "Thanks. You did fine."

Malone, at the FBI command post, was less flattering to him. "You fucked up again, Parra," he told him. "You know what happened while you were incommunicado? The Mayor went over to Lenox Hill to visit that black preacher, with a Senator and some reporters and about half the city pols tagging along. And he found that Washington had just upped and gone off to Harlem. Because you leaked him some classified information. If that preacher gets himself killed up there tonight, I'm gonna bust you down to working the coffee machine."

"I'm glad you're so understanding. I thought you might like

355

to know that we just picked up enough weapons and explosives to start a revolution. Plus a witness who can tell us quite a lot about The Liberators."

"We've got a revolution already. Somebody just bombed the Knickerbocker Club. The Police Commissioner was there."

The Governor called the Mayor, to promise that the National Guardsmen who had been up at Camp Drummond for summer training would be ready for duty in the morning. President Newgate called him, to say that the 82nd Airborne would be available to move in at dawn.

"I don't want those jumping junkies in my city," the Mayor told him, with more bravura than he felt. The Mayor, renowned for his talent as a stand-up comic, had run out of a sense of humor that night.

It was after midnight when Wright Washington arrived at Gracie Mansion, with an oddly assorted contingent in tow.

"I thought we had a date at the hospital," the Mayor said to him.

"No disrespect, but I had something more urgent to attend to." Washington had spent the last couple of hours in Harlem, showing himself under a spotlight on the back of a flatbed truck, trying to explain that people had got it wrong: it wasn't a cop who had tried to kill him. For a change, nobody had tried to shout him down. Some of the steadier folks had drawn strength from his appearance, in his bandages and plaster cast, and had gone out looking for their kids. But his biggest success had come in a series of private meetings, with the kind of men whom Washington usually shunned: a municipal boss who peddled jobs in the antipoverty programs, the leader of the Black Berets and a man by the name of Deuteronomy Jones who liked to call himself the Duke of Harlem. Deuteronomy Jones knew about every racket you had ever heard of. He had done a stint in Attica, but even while inside, he had kept his grip on the highly profitable syndicate of drug pushers and numbers runners who paid their dues to him. He was one of the men Wright Washington brought with him into the Mayor's homey white-painted

356

mansion. Deuteronomy sauntered in in a big panama hat and a white silk suit and enough gold around his neck to pay for the armored Cadillac he had left outside, and the policemen on guard looked at him as if they would like to throw him into the East River. He screwed a long cigarette holder into his mouth and winked at the Mayor.

For the first time that night, Hockney—the only white face in Washington's entourage—was able to smile without looking like cracked ice.

"The President wants to send in the Eighty-second Airborne," the Mayor reported.

"Doesn't he know that enough of this city looks like Dresden in 1945 anyway?" Washington responded. "We've got a better solution."

"I'm all ears."

"The police have been overrun. They're not trusted in Harlem anyway. Right now, we're running the risk of what happened in Miami: different ethnic communities at each other's throats. We know there are outside elements who are doing everything they can to bring that about."

"So what's your answer?"

"We have to rely on the communities themselves to police their own neighborhoods and call a truce before we get into a shooting war."

"Sounds like the Green Line in Beirut before the PLO was thrown out."

"Maybe. But maybe we've reached that point. We need to establish a holding position, and cut the ground from under the people who are out looking for trouble."

"Like *him*?" The Mayor inspected Deuteronomy Jones, from the tips of his alligator shoes to the gold medallions at his throat.

"You don't have to like me, Your Honor," the Duke of Harlem spoke up. "I didn't vote for you, either. But what's going on is bad for business. Your business and my business."

"You could have a point," said the Mayor. Then, to Washington, "What's your proposal?"

"We call a conference," said Washington. "Not a councilors'

357

meeting, not a study group, but a get-together of the people who really call the shots in the parts of town your financial backers don't like to think about. We get them to call a truce. We get them to take care of their own crazies."

"Like the thugs who raped those two Italian girls in Brooklyn tonight?" asked the Mayor, fixing his small, shrewd eyes on Deuteronomy Jones.

"We'll take care of it," said the Duke of Harlem. "You tell the Guineas we're ready to talk."

"What about the Fedayeen?"

"We'll explain it to them." Deuteronomy grinned.

"I don't much like it," the Mayor said carefully.

"If it's any consolation to you," said Washington, "I don't like it either. Would you rather have the Eighty-second Airborne?"

"I see what you're driving at." He suddenly stared at Hockney. "What's *he* doing here? I thought we agreed, no press."

"Without Bob," Washington said, "we wouldn't be having this conversation."

It took all night and all morning to put the meeting together, and the Mayor and the Police Chief had to call in—and offer—a few favors to do it right. When Wright Washington and Hockney showed up, around noon, there were snipers posted on the rooftops along Pleasant Avenue, in the last few blocks of Italy that survived in East Harlem, and there were hard-faced men around the entrance to Rao's, on the corner of One Hundred Fourteenth Street, overlooking the sort of park where you didn't walk your dog. They were both frisked before they were allowed in. The black minister gritted his teeth in pain as one of the Italians poked at his plaster cast.

"Sorry, Reverend," the Italian said. "It's the house rules today."

A couple of dozen cars were angle-parked on both sides of the street—flashy black-and-white limos, a brace of conservative gray Mercedes-Benzes, an armored Cadillac with enough chrome and tinsel on the hood for a Christmas tree.

The first thing Hockney noticed when they entered the restaurant was the kitchen. The floor was clean enough to fry peppers on. A sprightly old boy in an apron and a straw hat and a red-spotted neckerchief was stirring pots on the stove, adding a dash of salt here and there, as if his world had never changed. There was a rich earthy smell of oregano and garlic and basil that reminded Hockney that it was a long while since he had eaten.

The barman was lining up mixed drinks on a tray. Beyond him, the tables in the dark-paneled dining room had been left where you would expect them to be, so each group had staked out its own turf. The Chinese had taken the table farthest away on the left, their backs to the wall as if they thought they were in Umberto's Clam House. A distinguished Oriental in a dark business suit sat between the chiefs of the Flying Dragons and the Ghost Shadows, a human buffer zone. The Puerto Ricans were on the other side, next to the swinging door of the men's room. Deuteronomy Jones and his set were closer to the bar. Deuteronomy was sucking on his long, gold-trimmed cigarette holder. The Italians filled most of the other tables. Hockney recognized one of them. He had had his face in the papers when a grand jury heard evidence that he had made payoffs to the Mayor of New Jersey and the Secretary of Labor.

An Italian with a Julius Caesar hairstyle—thinning strands slicked forward, ending in a line of little curls along the temples—and eyebrows as furry as caterpillars got up to welcome the newcomers.

"I'm Mike Santini," he introduced himself. "We don't get many preachers like you in here," he said to Washington. "But I guess nothing's the same as it was."

There was no love lost between the men in that room. But they were all aware of the business that had been lost the night before, and that—more than the cost in lives and other people's property—was what had brought them together. The fact that the restaurant was in semidarkness—the bulbs inside the translucent beer mugs around the walls were out because Con Edison had not yet managed to restore power to this part of the

359

city—was a reminder of the added expense that all of them would have to bear if the riots were allowed to continue. Now Wright Washington had come among them to testify to what he had already told Deuteronomy Jones the night before: that there was a plan behind the rioting and the bombings. By the time they had heard him out, you could sense a consensus emerging among these hard men who, under different circumstances, would have had no compunction about cutting each other's throats. They weren't going to take it anymore. Any other day of the year, the Chief of Detectives or the head of the FBI's Organized Crime squad would have given an arm to put these characters in the slammer. Today, they almost rated as police auxiliaries; they were about to step into the breach in the thin blue line. After all, from their point of view, crime that they didn't control was very messy. They didn't approve of ripping off grocery stores or mugging old ladies. There was no percentage in it.

"There's one more thing," Hockney said. He was conscious of the muted hostility with which the men in the room assessed him, but plunged ahead with what he had to say.

"This is the guy who tried to off Wright Washington," Hockney continued, as he passed around a set of glossy prints. One was a head shot of the terrorist with green eyes, courtesy of Frank Parra's undercover photographer at the United Nations. Another was an artist's reconstruction of how Beacher had looked when his hair was blond, based on Hockney's description. Copies were being distributed to all police units. "This is the one who was dressed like a cop," Hockney reminded the men in the restaurant.

Deuteronomy Jones said, "If he's still in the city, we'll get him. That's heavy stuff," he added ironically. "Impersonating a police officer."

You can't push a button and stop a big-city riot. But Hockney was persuaded, in retrospect, that the turning point in New York came with that unlikely summit conference in Rao's Restaurant.

Deuteronomy Jones's enforcers swung into action in Harlem

and in sections of Brooklyn. One of the first places they hit was a battered tenement a couple of blocks north of the pumpkin dome of the Malcolm Shabazz Mosque, where the Fedayeen who had assaulted the police station on One Hundred Twenty-sixth Street were holed up, planning their next attack. Commander Ali's lieutenant came out into the darkened street and eyed the men who had gathered in front of the building. They outnumbered the Fedayeen by about two to one. Their leader sported a purple fedora and a matching suit, and lolled in front of his dream car pruning his fingernails with a knife.

The Fedayeen were nervous. "It's the Duke," one of them whispered.

But the man who had led the assault on the station house felt sure of his ground. "What's your problem?" he challenged Deuteronomy Jones.

"I want you out, shitface," the Duke of Harlem responded.

"Ain't you heard? We're making us a revolution."

"Not on my turf, you ain't. You want a revolution, you gotta talk to the Duke."

"What the fuck do you think you are, man? Some kind of cop?"

"You're bad for business, shithead. And you're a helluva slow learner. I'll say it just one more time. I want you *out*, and I want it now."

Ali's lieutenant was aware of the mood of uncertainty among his men. They were primed to withstand a siege by the entire U.S. Army, but they were afraid of this tall black in the flashy suit who stood calmly shearing his nails.

"Go screw yourself," the Fedayeen leader invited the Duke. He then made a serious mistake. He snapped back the safety catch on his automatic.

With a flick of the wrist, Deuteronomy Jones threw the knife. It caught Ali's man at the base of the throat, and he fell backward onto the sidewalk. The Fedayeen inched away from the body, already conceding territory.

The Duke said, "Who's next?"

Nobody answered. One by one, the Fedayeen started drifting

361

up the street, toward their cars. All the fight seemed to have gone out of them.

On the other side of the East River, a no less extraordinary spectacle was being played out in Brooklyn. Armed patrols of blacks and Italians roamed the borders of their neighborhoods, dispersing looters and the formless gangs of youths who were out looking for trouble. When the patrols ran into each other, there were colorful exchanges larded with words like "animals" and "Guineas," but for once, there was no cutting edge to these insults. The men on patrol understood that for the course of that night, at least, they were allies. Similar bands of community defenders appeared in the Bronx and in Lower Manhattan, including many groups that had not been represented at Rao's. The Guardian Angels turned out in force, in their red berets, arguing with looters to go home. Members of citizens' watch committees paired off to cover suburban residential districts in their radio cars. A few self-appointed vigilantes seized the chance to act out fantasies inspired by *Death Wish* or *Taxi Driver*, and the corpses picked up in the morning included those of a few people whose worst crime had been to raid a grocery store.

But the 82nd Airborne never parachuted into New York. And the D.A.'s office mysteriously determined not to prosecute Mike Santini or Deuteronomy Jones on charges that ranged from tax evasion to hijacking and grand larceny. You had to credit New York with one thing, as the Mayor reminded the President: the city bounced back.

Hockney's story about the riots ran on the front page of *The New York World* the following day, together with a news item about the expulsion of Teófilo Gómez, Minister-Counselor at the Cuban Mission to the United Nations. It was illustrated by the pictures of Beacher that Hockney had shown around at Rao's. The story listed some of the terrorist's known associates: a black radical called Plug, currently being held in a maximum-security cell on charges of homicide, gun trafficking and arson;

a Puerto Rican known as El Gato and a sultry Cuban-American girl whose first name was Rosario. The article was picked up on the wire services and ran as far west as San Francisco.

Hockney's piece had several effects. It won him a dinner invitation from Xenophon Parrish Nutting, the *World*'s reclusive publisher. It made him the star guest, together with Wright Washington, on Angela's TV show. And it produced a telephone call from a worried girl in Studio City, Los Angeles, to the local police about a couple shacked up together in the house next door. For once, it wasn't a case of a housewife's imagination run rampant. If he had just kept running, Beacher might well have got clean away. But for reasons best known to himself—nostalgia, perhaps—he had decided, after his escape from New York, to hole up with Rosario at his sister's place in L.A. When the police surrounded the bungalow, he went down shooting. But they took the girl alive, and by the end of the day she had made a full confession. There was one name that dominated her whole story, which encompassed the Fairchild kidnap in Puerto Rico, the riots in Miami and the upheavals in New York. It came as no surprise to Hockney, when Frank Parra told him about it over a celebratory drink at P. J. Clarke's. Everything led back to Julio Parodi.

"What are your plans?" Parra was asking.

"I've got an account to settle." Hockney had taken off the bandages around his neck. He wore an open-necked shirt, with a loose silk scarf to mask the mulberry-colored bruises that remained.

Parra nodded over his beer, but he said, "You can't touch him, you know. Not while he's in Cuba."

Hockney didn't say anything, and that troubled the FBI man. But he too fell silent, giving Hockney room, watching the bubbles in his glass.

Hockney was the first to get up. He dropped a crumpled twenty on the table, like the wrapper from a pack of cigarettes. The last thing he said to Parra was "I'll find a way."

Chapter

11

MIAMI

"I can see you don't believe in the phone," Arnold Whitman said to Hockney when he had got through unlatching his door. It was the second time Hockney had arrived at the unremarkable bungalow in Miami Beach unannounced. He did not waste time apologizing about that.

"My wife's away," the CIA man called over his shoulder, as if to explain the clutter of glasses and rumpled newspapers in the front room, the teetering pile of dirty plates around the kitchen sink that Hockney glimpsed through a serving hatch. He led Hockney into his den. They had to squeeze past a card table whose surface was entirely covered by a huge map board, divided into tiny hexagons. Hockney glanced at it. He saw the names of Russian cities, the winding course of roads and railways, and dozens of little die-cut counters representing military units.

"Don't mind that," Whitman said, rather defensively.

"What is it?"

"It's a simulation of the Battle of Stalingrad. Helps me to unwind."

War games were one of Whitman's secret passions. He could

sit stooped for hours over the board, assuming the role of each of the rival commanders in turn, pitting his wits against himself. It was relaxing to pursue a battle on a field on which the casualties were only cardboard counters, and where it was possible to improve on history.

Whitman brought out an unopened bottle of Chivas Regal— a gift from one of his Mexican counterparts—and poured both of them a serious dose. He took a good long pull on his drink, and said, "I don't mind admitting to you, Bob. You were right from the start. We got taken. It's hard to believe Parodi got away with it for so long. I guess that's what you've come to talk about."

"Where is he?" Hockney had left his drink untouched. He sat on the very edge of his armchair, his whole body tense, his legs shaking a bit. It was only forty-eight hours since President Newgate had gone on national TV to make the formal accusation that the Cubans were behind the troubles in New York and Miami. It was less than four days since he had gone to an Italian restaurant in East Harlem with Wright Washington and watched an unlikely combination of underworld bosses work out a cease-fire agreement that had helped restore peace to the city. The papers were full of wild speculation about the retribution that the Administration was planning to inflict on the men in Havana who had conceived The Monimbó Plan. For Hockney there was only one kind of retribution that mattered. Julio Parodi had to be punished. Not for the sake of all the people whom he and his controllers had made to suffer in New York and Miami; not for the sake of Senator Fairchild; least of all to assuage the wounded *amour-propre* of the Agency and the Administration. For Julia's sake. There were nights when Hockney was afraid even to try to sleep for fear of revisiting the scene inside the Burger King truck where he had been shown her body.

Arnold Whitman was taking his time about answering Hockney's question.

"Goddamn it, he's still in Cuba, isn't he?" Hockney glowered at the CIA man.

365

Whitman nodded.

"What are you proposing to do about it?" Hockney pursued.

Whitman drained his glass, poured himself another shot and said, "Nothing."

"You're lying."

"I don't give a rat's ass whether you believe me or not." Whitman turned prickly. He flushed a blotchy, unnatural color that had nothing to do with the whisky. He was a man who became aggressive when he had something to hide.

"You want Parodi too," Hockney prodded him.

"You bet I want him," the CIA man said. "I'd give my left ball to get him. But you might as well know. We got a directive from the top. The CIA has been ordered to suspend all hostile operations against Cuba until further notice."

"After what happened in New York? It's not possible."

"After New York," Whitman picked up the thread, "our Soviet friends got in on the act. I guess I can tell you, since it's bound to leak out soon enough anyway. The new Soviet Chairman called our illustrious Commander-in-Chief and offered a deal. I guess the Russians thought we might just be mad enough to send the Marines into Cuba this time around. Anyway, the deal was accepted. The Soviets have promised to keep the Cubans chained up, on condition we don't intervene directly. Castro is going to be reduced to a figurehead role, the intelligence services are to be purged and the cigar smokers in Central America are supposed to be pulled out fast. We'll see soon enough if it adds up to shit. I've got my doubts. But for now, the official word is Hands off."

"And you can live with that," Hockney said bitterly.

"What do you want me to do?"

After only a moment's hesitation, Hockney said, "I want you to get me into Cuba."

"I can't do that."

"You can't, or you won't?"

Whitman didn't say anything. He picked up a ruler that was lying on the edge of the map board. His attention seemed to be focused on the Russian defensive positions around Stalingrad.

366

"All I'm asking, for Chrissake, is a boat and a skipper who knows how to get past the Cuban Coast Guard," Hockney went on. "The rest is up to me. I know what I'm doing. I've been inside Parodi's villa already. I know where the guards are posted. Will you stop playing toy soldiers and give me a simple answer?"

Whitman sighed and let his weight sink back into his armchair. It was a pity, he thought, that nothing in life could be resolved as rationally as in the game. He said, "Is that it? Is that your plan?"

"It's a plan."

"It stinks, and you know it. You can't go swanning into a place just outside Havana as if it was the Dinner Key marina. That whole stretch of coast is under constant surveillance—sea patrols, air reconnaissance, radar, soldiers along the beach. If you got through, you'd find Parodi's goon squad waiting for you at the villa. Do you think they're going to run up the white flag at the sight of one crazy American? But suppose—just suppose—that by some miracle you actually got to Parodi. What would you do then? Kill him?"

Hockney met his gaze, and held it. He did not reply.

"You'd never get out of there alive," Whitman said. "And it's no part of my job to help you commit suicide."

"I'll find my own way in if I have to," Hockney said defiantly.

Whitman's eyes drifted back to the cardboard battalions on the map. "If I thought you had a one-in-ten chance of pulling this off, I might help you. Not the Agency. Me personally. But it can't be done your way."

Hockney followed his glance, to a weak spot in the Soviet defenses on the road between Kursk and Stalingrad.

"Well, are you going to come up with a better suggestion?" Hockney challenged the CIA man. "Or are you just going to sit here and make believe you're one of Hitler's generals?"

"The shortest route between two points is rarely a straight line." Whitman's voice was distant and dreamy, as if he were figuring out something on the map board.

"Are you trying to tell me something?"

367

"Be patient. Parodi won't stay in Cuba for good." Whitman looked worried then, as if he had said too much.

"So you do have a plan," Hockney pursued. "You're going to lure him out of Cuba."

Whitman slapped his plastic rule lightly against his left palm.

"How?" Hockney goaded. Before Whitman replied, Hockney had already seen the answer. There was only one thing that might persuade Parodi to risk his neck: money. The Cuban had left Miami in a hurry. Presumably, he had left it up to his henchmen to sort out his business affairs—to sell whatever they could and get the proceeds out of the country before the government moved in and froze all his traceable assets. That meant that a lot of Parodi's loot must be stashed away in bank vaults and safe-deposit boxes in several countries. That would be the bait. However much Parodi trusted his lieutenants, he could never be completely sure of a man who was holding millions—maybe tens of millions—of dollars that belonged to him. Sooner or later, he would want to arrange a pickup, and a full accounting. That would interest his Cuban controllers too, since a cut of Parodi's drug profits belonged to them.

"It's the money, isn't it?" Hockney demanded. "There's going to be a payoff, and Parodi's going to be there. I guessed right, didn't I? Where is it going to be? Switzerland? Panama? Santo Domingo?"

"You're way off base," Whitman told him, with no force of conviction.

"Well, then, for God's sake *tell* me."

"Stay away from this, Bob. Whatever you do can only screw things up."

Hockney brought his fist down on the card table. One of its folding legs buckled, and the meticulously deployed counters showered over the floor like confetti. The CIA man looked as pained as if Hockney had struck *him*.

"Ever since I first heard about Parodi," Hockney said accusingly, "people have been telling me to stay away. *You* wanted me to stay away when he was leading you around by the nose. You were wrong then, and you're wrong now. But it doesn't

368

matter. If you won't tell me what I need to know, I'll find out my own way."

This statement did not impress Arnold Whitman. He knew that Parodi was due to leave Havana to attend a secret meeting in two days' time, and he was highly skeptical as to whether Hockney could find out anything of practical use before then. But after Hockney went storming out of the house, the CIA man put a call through to Mexico City, just to make sure that everything was in hand. He was certain he could rely on Colonel López of Mexican security; the Colonel knew that Whitman was in possession of documentary proof that he had managed, over the years, to smuggle an impressive amount in dollars over the border to certain banks in San Antonio and Miami. Hockney was not the only one who had an account to settle with Parodi. Whitman preferred that the reckoning be made neatly and quietly, without publicity or diplomatic incidents. He was not interested in bringing the Cuban back to the United States for interrogation, let alone trial. What Parodi could reveal might shake the Agency to its foundations. No, it was better that Parodi be silenced for good, by men who knew their business—even if, on this occasion, they happened to be Mexicans.

When he had finished his phone call, Whitman set about gathering up the pieces of the war game that Hockney had scattered over the floor in his rage. It struck him that what he liked best about these games was that they dispensed with the human factor.

The half-hour drive from Whitman's place to the Miami Marina helped to steady Hockney's nerves, and he soon regretted having slammed out the door so hastily. If he had been a little more patient, perhaps he could have prised something more out of Whitman. But he had had nothing to go on; it was like fumbling in the dark with a bunch of keys, hoping that one of them would fit the lock.

At the Dockside Terrace, the girl who looked like Meryl Streep was crooning a couple of torch songs. Hockney settled himself at Jay Maguire's regular table and ordered a drink. By the time Maguire arrived, with his Cuban partner, Wilson Martinez, in tow, Hockney was working on his third, and the torch songs were starting to make him feel maudlin.

Hockney described the talk he had had with the CIA Station Chief, and the hunch he had developed.

"I think you're on to something," Maguire agreed. "You know, a lot of Parodi's associates are under indictment. We picked up that little fag who was running Camagüey Internacional after the arms bust in New York. We got the bodyguard—Mama Benitez—for illegal possession. The SEC came down on Parodi's bank like a ton of bricks. They've got about a dozen inspectors sitting in there going through the records with electron microscopes. Wilson can tell you something interesting about the bank. You've got a cute little friend in there, haven't you, Wilson?" He winked at the Cuban cop, who obliged him by turning bright red. "And you had all of us thinking you were a respectable married man."

"She's a relative of my mother's family," Martinez protested, rubbing the side of his leg where Marín's bullet had chipped the bone.

"The thing is," Maguire continued, serious again, "Wilson got talking to this little secretary at the bank who works for Whatsisname—"

"Señor Costa," Martinez filled in the name.

"Yeah, the stooge Parodi put in as president of the bank to cook the books for him. You tell the rest of it, Wilson."

"Señor Costa has been doing a lot of traveling to Mexico," Martinez explained. He looked very young that night. His shiny mustache might have been stuck on with glue, and he kept stroking it as if to reassure himself that it had not fallen off.

"Mexico City?" Hockney asked.

"Mostly," Martinez replied. "Seems he has banking contacts down there."

"Do you think Costa was trying to smuggle out some of Parodi's cash via Mexico?" Hockney asked.

"Could be." The Cuban cop shrugged.

"It sounds pretty wild," Hockney observed. "Everyone else has been trying to smuggle hard currency *out* of Mexico." During the economic crisis a year or two back, the Mexican Government had decided to freeze dollar deposits, nationalize the banks and ban the export of gold and precious stones. Still, in Mexico you could always be made an exception—if you were rich enough to pay for the privilege. Hockney had heard somewhere that one recent President of Mexico and his family had profited from his term in office to the tune of three billion dollars, the price of a very large number of "exceptions."

"Well, you know Mexico," Martinez said, obviously on the same wavelength. "According to this girl, Parodi's bank has been doing business down there for years. Señor Costa has some very useful connections. As a matter of fact, he's flying down to Acapulco the day after tomorrow. You know about Las Brisas?"

Hockney nodded. Las Brisas was celebrated as one of the finest resort hotels in the world.

"Is Costa taking a vacation?" he inquired.

"That's the bit that will interest you," the Cuban cop said. "Señor Costa has the hots for this girl. She makes it sound like he chases her around the office with his dong hanging out. He's asked her three or four times to go with him on foreign trips. Not this time. Not even though it's Las Brisas, and he's leaving his wife at home. She knows that because he only asked her to make one reservation. It's business. Strictly business."

Martinez had said his piece. He withdrew into silence, sipping his *cafecito*.

Maguire raised an eyebrow at Hockney and said, "Any help?"

"I could be wrong, but I think you've just told me everything I needed to know."

"You figure on meeting Parodi in Acapulco?"

"I'd like that."

"Damn, I'd like to go with you," said Maguire. "You remember that black cop who used to be in my squad? The one we called Magic?"

"Sure. The one who got suspended because they claimed he shot a woman in the middle of the Black Fedayeen rally. The one they framed. What happened to him?"

Maguire bit his lower lip and said, "The Department investi-

371

gation cleared him. They were going to give him back his badge and his gun. But a couple of hoods he had taken the collar for heard he was off the force and went around looking for him. They cut him up real bad." It was one of many things Maguire held against Parodi. It was easier to talk about Magic than about Gloria. "Damn," he repeated. "I'd sure like to catch a little sun in Acapulco."

But Hockney said, "I have to do this alone," and Maguire did not argue with him.

ACAPULCO

The Costera Alemán, Acapulco's bayfront boulevard, was jammed with traffic and tourists. The kings of the road were not the fancy imported sports cars, but the smoky Copala buses. Some of them had a curious inscription on their sides: "YA LLEGÓ LA ESCOBA"—The Broom Has Arrived. Any passerby subjected to the deafening blast of the buses' air horns understood what the phrase meant. The noise swept everything to one side. It drowned out even the machine-gun clatter of the jackhammers and the rumble of new construction work among the resort hotels and discos and showy boutiques that lined the waterfront.

Roving vendors wheeled their little carts along the beach, trumpeting the rival attractions of tamales, corncakes, ice cream, steamed crabs, and *ojo de venado*—a curious seed, resembling an animal's eye, that was held to be a powerful talisman. The old man hawking *ojo de venado* was detailing, in singsong, monotonous formulas, how the seed gave protection against the evil eye and sure relief from hemorrhoids. His claims caused some amusement among the crowd of American tourists who were taking advantage of the collapse of the Mexican currency to gorge themselves on red snapper, squid and marinated raw fish at a seaside restaurant.

A mile and a half outside Acapulco, secluded from the noise and the crush, was a private estate frequented by the kind of people who never need to examine the bill. President Kennedy had honeymooned there. Viewed from afar, the jumble of pink-and-white villas sprawling down the hillside among the exploding colors of hibiscus, bougainvillea and oleanders resembled a canvas by Mondrian.

Some of its regulars insisted that Las Brisas was not merely one of the best hotels in the world, but *the* best. In many of the *casitas,* a private pool extended from inside the living room out into a patio ablaze with tropical flowers. You could swim under the picture window to sip margaritas or munch *almejas colora-dos*—salmon-pink molluscs in shells the size of a silver dollar—outside. Pink-and-white Jeeps ferried the guests from the villas up and down narrow, winding paths to the main hotel building. Down by the water was a private restaurant, La Concha, made famous by early patrons like Errol Flynn and Aly Khan.

For all its self-confidence, Las Brisas made provision for disgruntled guests. At the head of a steep stairway of the kind you would not want to negotiate after a couple of drinks was a sign that read "COMPLAINTS DEPARTMENT." Those who ventured down the steps found a cage containing a pair of full-grown African lions.

The boy at the wheel of the candy-striped Jeep kept up a cheerful patter as he drove Hockney down the twisting path through the palms to a villa halfway down the slope. Hockney had brought only an overnight bag and a briefcase, but the boy handled them like a full set of Louis Vuitton portmanteaux. Hockney wandered out onto the terrace. The sky was a perfect, unflecked blue. When he became conscious of the boy, hovering expectantly by the door, he tipped him a five-dollar bill and said, "Which is Señor Costa's villa?"

The boy pointed out a *casita* closer to the water, a few hundred yards away to the right. Through the trees, Hockney could make out only a flash of turquoise from the swimming pool, and a pair of well-turned legs that did not belong to Parodi or his banker.

As soon as the boy was gone, Hockney slipped into beach clothes, sunglasses and a touristy straw hat and wandered down toward the sea, past Costa's villa. It was obvious that the place was being watched. Two men loitered nearby, in the shade of the palms. They did not look like vacationers, still less like people who could afford Las Brisas. One of them was sporting reflector sunglasses, like official goons Hockney had encountered in low-rent countries like Haiti and Zaïre. There was no easy way to get in around the back of the villa without being observed. He would have to wait until after dark for that.

A Mexican in white shirt and pants greeted him as he came out of a nearby *casita,* bearing a bucket of flowers—yellow, red and pink hibiscus.

"Those are pretty," Hockney said to him. "Do you put them in all the villas?"

"Yes, *señor.* Every swimming pool. Fresh every day."

Hockney remembered the petals he had glimpsed floating in the pool of his own *casita.* It gave him an idea. Maybe he could dress up as one of the hotel servants and take Parodi his bucket of flowers in the morning. A straw hat would help disguise the fact that he was a little pale for a Mexican. But nothing could camouflage his height.

Still, thinking it over, he strolled along the beach as far as the marina, where cabin cruisers and glass-bottomed boats were for hire. He watched some visitors climb into a fiberglass boat. They were going skin-diving out in the bay, between the island and Caleta Beach, where the famous statue of the Virgin of Guadalupe rose from the seabed, a fathom beneath the surface.

Hockney watched the sleek white lines of a yacht, riding at anchor far out in the bay.

An American in a yachtsman's cap, who obviously had him marked as a wealthy tourist, came up and started preaching the charms of chasing marlin.

Hockney said, "Nice boat out there," pointing at the yacht. "Belong to anyone you know?"

"Naw. But I saw some people from the hotel go out there."

"Would one of them be a little fat guy? A Cuban, name of Costa?"

The skipper gave Hockney an odd look. "Could be. What's it to you?"

"It's personal. Something my wife is mixed up in." That was part true, Hockney thought.

"Divorce trouble, huh?" the boat skipper said, not unsympathetically. "I had some of that myself." He scratched at his short salt-and-pepper beard. "I didn't see any women go out there, though. Just the fat man and some kind of Mexican big shot."

"Mexican?"

"Yeah. He had a bunch of thugs with him, and they were treating him like a piece of Meissen. You know what I figure? I figure they're doing a little gambling out on the yacht. One of those no-limit poker games where the heavy hitters fly in from all over. I heard of people renting fancy boats just for that. You want a beer?"

Hockney followed him onto the deck of his cabin cruiser. The skipper disappeared inside and reemerged with two bottles of Dos Equis. Hockney took one of the bottles gratefully and let the full, dark beer trickle down his throat.

It occurred to him that if Parodi was winding up his business in Mexico on board the yacht, he might not return to the mainland, despite that pair of well-turned legs Hockney had spotted by the pool of the Cuban's *casita*. If Hockney wanted to be sure of meeting the man he had come to find, he would have to go out to the yacht. As soon as Parodi's visitors left.

"I guess business is a little slow this time of year," Hockney remarked, poking around the cabin cruiser. He noticed the smell of fresh paint; that suggested its owner had plenty of time on his hands.

The skipper made a noncommittal grunt.

"I wouldn't mind taking a little cruise tonight," Hockney said casually.

"Tonight?" Then the skipper got the point. He peered out at the yacht and said, "I don't know about that. Divorces are messy."

"I'd make it worth your while."

"What time do you want to go?"

"We'll go when the Mexican leaves."

Hockney now had a boat ticket. But he had nothing resembling a plan. He thought of getting hold of a wet suit and trying to swim out to *La Excepción* under cover of dark. Somehow, he could not see himself as an aquatic James Bond. It was better, he decided, to simply brazen it out. There was a chance that Parodi might have him shot on sight. But it was more probable, Hockney reasoned, that here, in neutral waters—and feeling safe enough on board his own boat—the Cuban would hesitate before going that far. Hockney also counted on Parodi's curiosity. The man must certainly want to know how completely his operations were understood by the Americans—and how Hockney had managed to trace him to Acapulco. That combination of curiosity and a false sense of security might just allow Hockney the chance he needed.

On board *La Excepción*, Parodi was toasting the results of a highly satisfactory meeting with Dom Perignon. The Mexican minister who had made himself so unpopular with the Americans because of his florid speeches about economic liberation drank carefully, nursing his liberated Gucci briefcase. It contained nearly four million dollars, his commission for arranging the transfer of an important sum from a blocked account in Mexico City to Switzerland. Costa, Parodi's bookkeeper, was getting happily soused.

It was after 7 P.M. when the Minister rose and made his apologies.

"I have to give a speech to the Chamber of Commerce on the war against corruption," he announced with a soft smile. There was nothing furtive about the manner of his departure. The Minister was not exercised about the risk of being prosecuted under the severe anticorruption law that he himself had introduced. He was merely following custom. The first decree that the new President had signed, in the midst of a financial crisis, had been to award the franchise for a duty-free store at Benito Juárez International Airport to a member of his wife's family. The laws were made *by* the barons of the Institutional Revolutionary Party; they were not *for* them.

Several people on shore watched the Minister's party returning by motor launch from the yacht. On the deck of the cabin cruiser, Hockney studied faces through a pair of borrowed field glasses. The little pear-shaped man, he guessed, must be Costa. He did not recognize the Mexican. He adjusted the binoculars and trained them on the yacht. He saw a large, fleshy man by the railing with a glass and a cigar, and his hand dropped instinctively to the gun he had tucked inside his belt.

"This time I have you, you bastard," Hockney murmured, and overhearing him, the skipper of the cabin cruiser asked himself whether it was worth getting mixed up in this, even for the outrageous tariff to which Hockney had agreed.

Along the beach, at La Concha Restaurant, Colonel López of Mexican security was enjoying a languid cocktail, a tequila sunrise whose color matched the orange smear of the western sky. One of his men weaved his way through to the table and murmured, "The Minister has left, *mi coronel.*"

López nodded and looked at his watch. The divers would have completed their job by now. It was a shame, he reflected, that the Minister was not staying on board. The country would not miss him.

There was a six-day moon, and the night was clear—too clear for Hockney's comfort. From two hundred yards away, he could make out distinctly the shapes of two men on the deck of *La Excepción.*

"I guess she's not expecting you, huh?" the skipper said.

"What?"

"Your wife."

"No, she's not expecting me."

"You want me to hang around for the fireworks?" The cabin cruiser was slackening speed as it nosed toward Parodi's yacht. One of the men on the deck of *La Excepción* leaned over the railing, inspecting the newcomers.

"Come back for me in an hour or so," Hockney told the skipper. "If you don't see me, we'll say it was a one-way trip. Here." He started to unroll a wad of twenty-dollar bills.

"Save it," the skipper said. "I'll be waiting."

There was a hollow thud as the cabin cruiser bumped against the hull of the yacht, and the raised voice of a man yelling at them in Spanish to keep away.

Hockney ignored the voice, grabbed hold of the steel ladder that extended halfway down the side of the yacht and started hauling himself up.

Julio Parodi, comfortably settled in a deck chair, watched the cabin cruiser bobbing away, toward the lights of Acapulco. He wished he could follow it. He knew a whorehouse in the town where the girls were very international, very innovative. He was not looking forward to the return voyage to Cuba. In Cuba, he would be a prisoner. They had treated him well enough so far, but he suspected that his treatment would change dramatically now that his usefulness to the DGI had been exhausted. Since he had arrived at Las Brisas, he had toyed with the idea of jumping ship and trying to make a new deal with the Americans. But he had been obliged to reject this as idle fantasy. He had nothing much left to trade with. And even if the Americans agreed to take him back, he was doubtful whether they could protect him from the Cubans, if the DGI determined to call him to account. He spat out a loose flake of tobacco from his cigar. It was bitter to the tongue, more bitter than coffee dregs.

One of Parodi's crew was leaning over the deck railing—a handsome boy who had been with him on the last drug run from Colombia.

He had a pistol in his hand.

"What is it?" Parodi called to him.

"An American. He says he knows you."

Now Parodi could see the head and shoulders of a man, poised on the ladder. There was something very familiar about his fair, shaggy hair, his strong, sharp-cut features. Curiosity overcame Parodi's caution. Besides, surrounded by armed men on his own boat, he felt secure enough to deal with an American reporter.

378

"Robert Hockney," he called as he struggled out of his deck chair.

"Am I allowed on board?"

"Of course, of course." Parodi nodded to the crewman, who backed away, permitting Hockney to climb on deck. "How clever of you to find me."

"I've been looking for you for quite a while."

"You must tell me all about it." Parodi motioned for Hockney to accompany him to the main deck, where drinks were laid out on a table. He did not think to have Hockney searched—who expects a reporter to be armed with anything more lethal than a felt-tipped pen? But the crewman with the gun hovered within easy range.

"I really am interested," Parodi went on urbanely as he busied himself pouring rum into a couple of glasses. "How did you find out I was here?"

"Your banker left footprints all the way back to Miami."

"Oh, yes. Poor Costa. But he's very imaginative with figures." He raised his glass. "*Salud.*"

Hockney watched without drinking.

"So," Parodi said. "Have you come to make another interview for your newspaper?"

"I've come to ask you about how you had my wife murdered," Hockney said quietly.

Parodi drained his rum, ignoring the question. "You have a lot of courage, coming here all by yourself," he remarked.

Hockney became aware that several men had grouped themselves behind him, beside the crewman who had greeted him with a pistol.

Parodi inspected the reporter's full glass and said, "You don't like rum?"

Hockney reached for a bottle of Scotch, moving between the Cuban and the table. "May I?"

"Of course." Parodi took a half-step backward, making room for him.

In the next instant, Hockney had his gun out, jabbing it into the Cuban's belly, maneuvering so that he had placed Parodi's bulk between himself and the armed men on deck.

"You're out of your mind," Parodi said, still smiling.

"Tell your men to move back," Hockney commanded, trying to keep his voice low and steady. "Tell them to go below decks."

Parodi did not stir.

Hockney jabbed the gun barrel into the rise of his belly. "Do it, or I'll kill you."

"Do that, and you're a dead man."

"It's all the same to me," Hockney said, thinking of the scene at the Miami morgue. At that instant, he was capable of killing Parodi, and his finger tightened against the trigger.

The Cuban must have sensed his tension, because he shrugged and called out to the crewmen in Spanish. Reluctantly, they started inching back.

"You're making quite a scene," Parodi said, seemingly calm. "What do you propose to do next?"

Hockney relaxed a fraction as he saw the crewmen backing off. He had come here with the fixed intention of killing Julio Parodi. But at this point, he became conscious of the gulf between the abstract design and the reality of murder in cold blood. He stood there, wavering—the moment when he could have gone through with it had passed.

He said, "I'm taking you back to Miami."

Parodi started to laugh—a fluting, high-pitched laugh which stopped only when Hockney rammed the snout of the pistol into his belly again.

"You're insane," the Cuban said once he had got his breath back. "This is Mexico. There's no way you can get me back to the States."

"Tell your men to lower one of those dinghies," Hockney said as calmly as he could manage.

"Do you think you're a sheriff in some horse opera?" Parodi mocked him, confident now that he realized Hockney was not bent on killing him straightaway. He could risk calling the reporter's bluff.

"Tell them to do it," Hockney repeated.

"Go fuck yourself."

They stood there facing each other, and Hockney could see at least four rifles behind Parodi. Then something happened that neither man had counted on. A lithe, dark-skinned Latin had climbed warily on top of the superstructure and hung there, drawing a bead on Hockney with his submachine gun, a Czech-made Skorpion. Parodi had his back turned to the man on the roof, and Hockney's attention was focused elsewhere. Hockney would not have recognized the sniper anyway. Calixto Valdés, the head of Bureau 13 of the Cuban secret service, had decided to accompany Parodi on his trip because he believed in taking every precaution to protect an investment, and did not rule out the possibility that left to his own devices, Parodi would grab his money and run, without paying his dues to Havana. Even from his vantage point on the roof, Valdés found it hard to get a clear line of fire at Hockney. The American kept bobbing back and forth behind Parodi, who was also shifting in his place. But Calixto Valdés was not overly concerned about the danger of hitting his own agent. Parodi's job for the DGI was finished. Nobody in Havana would go into mourning if he vanished at sea off the coast of Acapulco.

But Valdés aimed carefully before he squeezed off his first burst. Two bullets caught Hockney in the left shoulder. He reeled back, and Parodi seized his chance. Before Hockney could recover his balance, Parodi was tugging at his gun hand, clawing at his wounded shoulder until he screamed with pain. The gun clattered onto the deck, and both men went after it. They landed in a heap of arms and legs, like a wriggling insect on its back, so hopelessly entangled that Valdés and the crewmen held their fire. Then Parodi lunged after the pistol, and Hockney barely managed to kick it out of reach with his foot.

Suddenly, Parodi's grip loosened, and the big Cuban tried to haul himself to his feet. Hockney realized the trap. He grabbed at the longer hair at the back of Parodi's head, pulling him down, giving himself cover. They had rolled almost to the edge of the deck before Parodi prised himself loose again. He went crawling sidewise, like a crab, away from Hockney.

"Shoot him, you idiots!" Parodi yelled.

Hockney shut his eyes and remembered what it had been like to go tumbling down the grassy hill behind his parents' house when he was a child. He felt a stab of pain below his knee; then another, higher up; then a bump against his ribs; and he was falling. When he hit the water, the chill numbed all sensation below the waist. He sank like a lead weight, straight down. He was dimly aware of the shoals of fish that parted for him, silvery shadows at first, then only a pulse in the darkness. His head was dizzy, and his lungs were bursting. He tried to propel himself up to the surface with his legs, but they seemed to be lifeless, useless appendages. He moved his arms like a man climbing a rope ladder, hand over hand, and slowly, he began to rise. He heard the whine in his throat as he snatched a great gulp of air, then the crack of machine-gun bullets before he ducked under again. He went down twenty feet, and came up right against the hull of the yacht, above the propeller.

Parodi and Valdés were peering over the railing.

"Can't see a fucking thing down there," Parodi complained.

"It doesn't matter," Valdés said. "He was hit at least four times. If he doesn't drown, the blood will draw the sharks. Start the engines," he ordered the skipper of the yacht, abandoning any polite fiction about who was in charge.

Hockney could barely manage to keep his head abovewater. He felt overcome by a tremendous weariness. He was ready to give up the struggle, to let everything slide. But when the yacht began to sail out into the Pacific, he used all his remaining energy to try to hurl himself out of the water and catch hold of the iron ladder that reached halfway down the hull. He missed it completely and slipped back, scraping his wounded shoulder as he fell.

What a pathetic ending, he thought. He had botched the one chance he was likely to get to settle the score with Parodi. He would have done better to listen to Arnold Whitman. *Forgive me, Julia.* Fatigue came over him again in a great tide, and the ocean depths seemed as inviting as a featherbed. He let himself float, face downward, like a drowned man. *I'm closer to you now,* he thought.

Then there was a rough pressure against his back, repeated, harder, like a blow.

"Take it, goddamn you!" a man was calling out.

Hockney turned his head to the side and saw the skipper of the cabin cruiser, leaning over the railing, holding a long pole out to him. Somehow, he got his hands around it.

"I should've left you for bait," the bearded skipper was complaining as he hauled Hockney on board and got a thick towel around his shoulders. "That must be some wife you've got." He started swearing when he saw the bullet wounds in Hockney's legs and shoulder. Hockney was beyond pain. He looked down at his useless legs the way he had looked down at his own body in dreams—as if they belonged to somebody else. One of the bullets, he saw, had made a hole that seemed unnaturally round, laying open skin and flesh all the way to the bone, like a diagram in a book of anatomy.

I lost him, Julia. Forgive me.

"Sweet Jesus," the skipper breathed, and there was awe in his voice. He might have been lighting a candle in church.

Hockney had hardly heard the explosion. His ears were full of water; everything sounded a long way off. But he propped himself up to look in the direction in which the skipper was pointing.

Where the yacht *La Excepción* had been, a great fireball rose out of the water. To Hockney, it was wildly beautiful—the flames dipped and waved like the petals of an exotic flower.

"That must be some wife you had," the skipper said, taking off his cap.

"She was."

The explosion of the limpet mines that had been fastened to the underbelly of Parodi's yacht rattled the glasses and the cutlery in La Concha Restaurant, and brought the guests flocking to the picture windows to gape at the spectacle.

383

Arnold Whitman's friend Colonel López finished his coffee, mopped his full lower lip with a napkin and nodded to the maître d' as he made a leisurely exit. He was mentally deliberating the message he would relay to his CIA friend, and the favors he would be able to exact in return for the service he had rendered. It was a curious thing, he reflected, that the Americans had lost the resolution to finish their own dirty work for themselves.

Two days later, hobbling along on crutches, Hockney took one of the glass-bottomed boats and went out into the bay to inspect what was left of *La Excepción*. There had been no breath of scandal, no diplomatic embarrassment. The newspapers solemnly reported a tragic accident at sea, the result of a faulty boiler. Hockney found that the wreckage of the yacht had already become a tourist attraction, like the huge metal image of the Virgin of Guadalupe planted in the seabed nearby. Through the glass floor of the boat, he peered down at skin divers pirouetting around the burned-out hull.

Back at the hotel, Hockney bought a few postcards.

To Jay Maguire, he scribbled, *"The boating is terrific. Wish you were here."*

To Arnold Whitman, he was terse. *"You prick,"* he scrawled. He did not bother to sign it.

The third postcard showed the Virgin of Guadalupe, like a mermaid at the bottom of the ocean. Thoughtfully, he leafed through the Bible the Gideons had left in his room. He had hardly opened a Bible since he had been in Sunday school. But he had gone to a church, earlier in the day, to light a candle for Julia.

When he found words that seemed right, he addressed the last card to Wright Washington. He carefully noted the reference: *"II Timothy 4:7."*

Then he wrote, *"I have finished my course, I have kept the faith."*

He walked up, through the palms and oleanders, to the hotel bar, and asked for a daiquiri.